D1559789

# THE SOUND OF THE KISS

**Translations from the Asian Classics**

*Editorial Board*

Wm. Theodore de Bary, Chair
Paul Anderer
Irene Bloom
Donald Keene
George A. Saliba
Haruo Shirane
David D. W. Wang
Burton Watson

# THE SOUND OF THE KISS

*or The Story That Must Never Be Told*

Piṅgaḷi Sūranna's *Kaḷāpūrṇodayamu*

*Translated from Telugu by Velcheru Narayana Rao and David Shulman*

COLUMBIA UNIVERSITY PRESS NEW YORK

Columbia University Press
*Publishers Since 1893*
New York    Chichester, West Sussex

Copyright © 2002 Columbia University Press
All rights reserved

Library of Congress Cataloging-in-Publication Data
Pingali Surana.
[Kalapurnodayamu English]
The Sound of the kiss, or the story that must never be told ; translated from Telugu by Velcheru Narayana Rao and David Shulman.
p. cm.
ISBN 0–231–12596–8 (cloth : alk. paper) —
ISBN 0–231–12597-6 (pbk. : alk. paper)
I. Title: Sound of the kiss. II. Title: Story that must never be told. III. Narayanaravu, Velceru, 1932– IV. Shulman, David Dean, 1949– V. Title.

PL4780.9.P49 K313 2002
894.8'27371—dc21
2002025746

Columbia University Press books are printed on permanent and durable acid-free paper.
Printed in the United States of America
c 10 9 8 7 6 5 4 3 2 1
p 10 9 8 7 6 5 4 3 2 1

For Sanjay Subrahmanyam

*aharahar-itihāsa-vastu-*
*bahu-vidha-sambhāra-dhī-vibhāṣita-kṛtikin*
*mahimânvita-vāṇī-kara-*
*nihita-lalita-kīra-vāg-viniṣṭhita-matikin*

*abhyudaya-paramparâbhivṛddhigā . . .*

*bhavyatan ĕlla deśamula prastutik' ĕkkucu mīriy*
*im-mahā-*
*kāvyamu suprasiddham' agu gāvuta nityamu*
*sarvaloka-sam-*
*stavya-nija-smṛtin vĕlayu tāṇḍava-kṛṣṇu kṛpan*
*pavitra-śā*
*stra-vyasanâti-dhanyam' agu saj-jana-koṭiy*
*anugrahambunan*

This story will become famous in all countries.
God, the dancing Krishna, has blessed it,
and so have all learned people who are addicted
to reading books.
—*Kaḷāpūrṇodayamu* 8.265

# contents

# ACKNOWLEDGMENTS

Many friends and scholars in India, Germany, and North America helped us in our efforts to translate Pingali Suranna. As usual with Telugu studies, our first difficulty was in locating surviving copies of earlier printed editions of the text. Chekuri Rama Rao and Vasireddi Naveen provided us with Malladi Suryanarayana Sastri's edition, the only one to document variant readings from manuscripts. Vishnubhotla Ramana sent us the two volumes of the Emesco edition with a preface and notes by Bommakanti Singaracarya and Balantrapu Nalinikanta Ravu. Vakulabharanam Rajagopal gave us speedy access to the rare Vavilla edition with annotation by Cadaluvada Jayaramasastri.

We are profoundly grateful to the early editors for their scholarly introductions and notes. Nonetheless, many questions about readings and interpretations remained. We had fruitful discussions with Prof. Kolavennu Malayavasini at Andhra University; with K. V. S. Rama Rao of Austin, Texas; and with Paruchuri Sreenivas in Grefrath, Germany, a source of unfailing bibliographic guidance and wisdom. To all of them, we offer thanks.

We are grateful for the many thoughtful suggestions about polishing the translation offered by Nita Shechet and the two anonymous readers for Columbia University Press. Students in a seminar on the Sanskrit novella at the Hebrew University in the spring semester of 2001 gave us, with their meticulous reading and enthusiasm as well as their insightful interpretations, our first assurance that the text can grip the attention of a contemporary audience.

We began work on the translation in the summer of 2000 in Jerusalem, in a flat thoughtfully provided by the Institute for Advanced Studies at the Hebrew University. That summer's work was made possible by the resources put at our disposal by the University of Wisconsin in Madison. We brought the work to completion in the congenial milieu and open spaces of the Wissenschaftskolleg zu Berlin, where we had uninterrupted days to read and reread. We hope that all three institutions will find satisfaction in the fact that this unusual book is now accessible to a wider readership.

No less critical to this enterprise was the constant supply of superb sambar prepared daily by Sanjay Subrahmanyam, to whom we dedicate the translation.

# Note on Pronunciation

No diacritical marks are used in the body of the text. Citations from Telugu and Sanskrit in the notes, the introduction, and "Invitation to a Second Reading" are marked in the usual scholarly style. For those who want to pronounce the names correctly, we give a list of characters, with full diacritic marks as well as brief linguistic guidance, as an appendix. All proper names and technical terms also appear in the index with full diacritical marking.

# Introduction

[ 1 ]

Great artists occasionally emerge together, all at once, like a goddess embodying herself in multiple forms. They may belong to a single extended moment, which they shape through their harmonic resonances in the direction of cultural innovation or breakthrough. This happened in Sophoclean Athens, for example; in Russia in the second half of the nineteenth century; in sixteenth-century Spain. It also happened in sixteenth- and early seventeenth-century South India, in the area now known as Andhra Pradesh, where Telugu is spoken. In the early decades of the sixteenth century, under the patronage of a famous king, Krishna-deva-raya of Vijayanagara, Telugu poets produced masterpieces of narrative poetry, *kāvya*, often playing with one another and echoing themes, styles, and a certain intensity of observation and description. The oustanding names are Krishna-deva-raya himself, his court-poets Peddanna and Mukku Timmanna, and, somewhat later, Tenali Ramakrishnadu and Bhattu-murtti. Together, they created a corpus of unique richness, quite distinct from any other literary production in premodern South Asia.

Toward the end of this period of volatile creativity, and still firmly rooted in the idiom of the time, a fertile poetic genius named Pingali Suranna took the impulse of literary invention in a wholly new direction. His master work, the *Kaḷāpūrṇodayamu*, is translated here. We see this book as, in a certain sense, the first Indian novel—that is, as embodying the invention of a hitherto unknown genre, perhaps comparable in its sensibility and adventurous imagination to its roughly contemporaneous work in Europe, Cervantes' *Quixote*, which is also often seen as the first modern European novel. In the "Invitation to a Second Reading," we discuss the analytic features that we regard as essential to such a definition.

The *Kaḷāpūrṇodayamu* is a thoroughly "modern" work—a playful exploration of the limits of linguistic expressivity and of the ecology of available literary genres or forms; a complex psychologizing of the human mind; the elaborate working through of a plot that constantly twists and surprises the reader with its multiple perspectives and unconventional sensibility. At the same time, it is a long poem cast in the accepted modes of courtly poetry that were perfected by Suranna's predecessors. Despite what we are so often told, modernity, in several specific senses, begins in South India in the sixteenth century, and this novel is one of its harbingers. It explodes nearly all the received wisdom about medieval Indian literature—for example, the hackneyed and misleading insistence that character in premodern texts has no interiority or subjectivity and hardly undergoes change; the notion that all major texts in classical Telugu are simply translations or reworkings of Sanskrit models; the strange belief that language in these texts has no transparency and tends to the "baroque" or the "verbose" or the "formulaic"; the nineteenth-century accusation that classical poetic works were replete with nearly obscene sexual representations; and so on. Suranna's book clearly reveals how wrong such views really are.

Suranna actually tells his readers, at the outset, what he intends to do. After describing how his patron, King Krishna of Nandyala, commissioned the work, he reports:

> I began work on the book, to the best of my ability. I wanted it to have the structure of a complex narrative no one had ever known, with rich evocations of erotic love, and also descriptions of gods and temples that would be a joy to listen to. I called it *Kaḷāpūrṇodayamu*. (1.16)

So his express aims were three. He wants to tell a good story that is full of surprises and structured in an entirely unprecedented manner (*atyapūrva-kathā-saṃvidhāna-vaicitrī-mahanīyambu*). He is eager to give a taste or experience of an aestheticized eroticism, habitually known as *śṛṅgāra-rasa*. And he is also interested in singing to or about the gods. The three directions are more or less incompatible in one text, so their very combination here says something about the challenges the poet has undertaken.

But there are deeper, even more compelling impulses driving Suranna that he does not talk about explicitly as goals. His intricate novel is one of the most penetrating statements in the whole of South Asian literature on the inner mechanisms of language in relation to something we could call "reality." This poet is also fascinated by the enormous range of human sexual and erotic experience, and he explores this range with verve and imaginative courage. Moreover, he makes a powerful comment on the literary genres of his time and how they can be renewed and reimagined. In this context, he also offers an implicit, sustained meditation on properly ontological questions, such as the boundary between perceptions of reality and the "hard" facts of a life lived in the world.

Suranna also innovated in the matter of style and texture. Technically, this is a book written predominantly in metrical verse, along with occasional prose passages in the usual elevated, *campū* style.[1] In fact, however, most of his metrical verse reads like direct, straightforward prose. In itself, this new style of fast-paced narrative reporting is no small achievement for a poet who still opted to write in metrical form. At the same time, much of Suranna's prose reads like complex lyrical poetry, with a high level of musicality, alliteration, and powerful rhythms—almost a kind of free verse. Occasionally, of course, there are verses that are entirely within the lyrical tradition of pure, metrical poetry; and there is prose that reads like prose. In effect, Suranna has invented a new style, well suited to writing a novel—a genre that includes many other genres. He is terse, pointed, precise, scrupulous about transitions and connections, tough in phrasing, and extremely economical. He can also be expansive, symphonic, and extravagant in description. His meticulous attention to wording in reported conversation or in narrative events comes through often as one reads through the text and discovers the unsuspected meanings implicit in what looked, at first reading, like simple statements. We have tried, in our translation, to reproduce these carefully layered formulations with the same precision that Suranna shows. We have chosen to translate most of the text into a somewhat compacted prose, close, in our view, to the texture and tone of the Telugu. At times, when Suranna breaks into poetry for poetry's sake, we have tried to follow him in this respect.[2]

There is something more specific to be said about Suranna's tone in the dialogue passages that comprise much of the book. This is a text in which people are continually speaking to one another, often in highly colloquial and idiomatic ways. A wife who is being kissed too hard by her husband may playfully push him away with the direct command, *cāliñcĕdaro*: "Cut it out!"[3] Insults, in particular, are, not surprisingly, far from elegant: thus a sexual rival is taunted with being a "freeloader," *teragāḍu*[4]—a word still current in this meaning in modern Telugu. Men and women banter freely, with sexual innuendo expressed in naturally colloquial language, mostly slang. Two women—as it happens, both of them highly sophisticated and refined—quarrelling over a lover sound like two Andhra women as one might hear them bickering today in villages or towns.[5] In fact, Suranna's ability to reproduce such living speech is a sign of his realistic attention to detail and something of an innovation in Telugu *kāvya*. Note that in Suranna's hands Telugu meter accomodates such colloquial syntax just as readily as it absorbs elaborate Sanskrit compounds. Throughout the novel, distinct speech registers alternate freely and fluidly. One moves rapidly from dense lyrical description to street slang to high courtly language, as context demands.

Such flexibility in syntax and diction, in combination with a relatively elevated narrative and descriptive style, produces a texture that, at first sight, might look incongruous in translation. We have tried to reproduce the variation in level faithfully; hence, certain dialogue passages may appear close to contemporary English idiom. We have resisted the temptation to colloquialize radically by resorting to English slang, but we have, at the same time, avoided an artificially antiquated style. If a disparity in tone sometimes remains, the reader should know that it reflects a real and intentional mixture of registers in the Telugu original.

## [ 2 ]

Literary historians argue about Suranna's dates. We know he lived in Nandyala, a small town in the eastern Deccan, where a local king named Narasimha Krishna was ruling. One cluster of opinions, pioneered by the influential nineteenth-century literary historian Veeresalingam, favors a date circa 1560. Another group suggests 1620.[6] There is no decisive evidence in favor of either position. The earlier date would place Suranna in temporal conjunction with Bhattu-murti, perhaps the most linguistically complex of the Telugu *kāvya* poets, with a fondness for *śleṣa*, that is, double entendre or "bitextuality" of a highly sustained and intricate nature.[7] Suranna himself, in addition to the *Kaḷāpūrṇodayamu* and another *kāvya*, *Prabhāvatī-pradyumnamu*, composed a bitextual tour de force, the *Rāghava-pāṇḍavīyamu*, that simultaneously tells the stories of the *Rāmāyaṇa* and the *Mahābhārata*. It is at least possible that the two bitextual poets, who were also each deeply concerned with music, knew of and responded to one another's work. On the other hand, the later date would situate Suranna closer to the period of intense grammatical and metalinguistic speculation in seventeenth-century Andhra—a period that could be said to contextualize or frame his narrative.

Suranna's paternal grandfather, who shared the same name as his grandson, was also a poet. We know a little about the family background. In his *Prabhāvatī-pradyumnamu*, which Suranna dedicates to his father Amaranarya, he gives an extensive description of his uncles, brothers, and other members of the extended family. He expresses regret that in his earlier works (including some now lost)[8] he had not offered a full account of his own family (*mat-pitrādi-vaṃsābhivarṇana*).[9] The line of descent is said to go back to the Vedic sage Gautama. Did the poet take a certain characteristic pride in this filiation? He tells us that Gautama, the author of the foundational text on logic, entered into a contest with the god Siva himself; when Siva, losing the debate, tried to pull rank by opening the third eye in his forehead, Gautama trumped this by revealing a third eye on the sole of his foot—and won.[10] We can assume that Suranna grew up in a family environment rich with classical erudition and literary interests. But there is another element in this environment that popular narratives bring to the fore. The family genealogy in *Prabhāvatī-pradyumnamu* mentions, immediately after Gautama, an ancestor named Goka, a poet who composed a text in praise of Vishnu's sword; but this same Goka also managed to bring under his control, by Yogic means (*yogitāgurv-anubhavuḍai*, 1.14), a *gandharvi* servant-concubine named Peki—a beautiful woman from the class of singers and musicians to the gods. So this family saw itself as having inherited both the highly intellectual, classical tradition of Gautama and the musical, Yogic, and magical skills of this Goka.

It is, to say the least, an unusual tale of family origins. In popular oral accounts of the genealogy, Peki is a spirit (*dayyamu*) who came to work for the family when one of the ancestors picked up a glass bead he found lying by the path in a forest. He took it home and hid it in a small shelf on the wall. Immediately thereafter, Peki appeared and began to perform various difficult tasks for the family. One night an elder observed her straightening the wick of an oil lamp with her tongue. Immediately realizing that Peki was no ordinary human being, the family tried to get rid of her in every possible way. Spells, chants, and rituals had no effect. They even shifted their house to a new location—but Peki followed after them, carrying even the heavy mortar they had deliberately left behind. Finally, they asked her what would make her leave. "Just give me my glass bead," she said. When they retrieved it for her, she took it and disappeared.[11]

Such stories reflect a perceived reality. A well-known theme—the troublesome spirit that attaches itself, often through some seemingly innocuous object, to a house—has been grafted onto the poet's own genealogical memory of the superhuman servant-concubine Peki. In any case, one senses the presence of a powerful "magical" milieu, with its highly charged verbal and ritual devices, just below the surface of the *Kaḷāpūrṇodayamu* text. The eastern Deccan world of the late sixteenth and early seventeenth centuries was one where sounds, especially those used correctly by poets, could work change on reality; also one where these potentialities hidden within speech generated theoretical grammars that structured the practical application of metrical composition.[12] Grammar has, in addition to its inherited analytic properties, drawn from centuries of linguistic speculation and study in Sanskrit, a deep relation to sorcery. All of this wider range of magical and musical associations is present in Suranna's novel in surprising ways.

Suranna has even more to report along these lines in the continuation of the genealogy. This same ancestor Goka had no children from his wife; so the wife worshiped the Sun God, who appeared in her dream as a Brahmin and gave her a *donda* vine to plant in the yard. The vine grew into a luxuriant state, and as it did so, the wife became fertile; the family exfoliated like the vine.[13] Did the descendants of this family, generations later, imagine themselves as carrying on the line of the Sun God or of the musical *gandharvi* Peki and her Yogic lover—or of both?

## [ 3 ]

To see how close all this is to the explicit concerns of Suranna's novel, and also how such concerns have been reformulated and transformed in the direction of classical images, we need only look to one of the opening, invocation verses of the *Kaḷāpūrṇodayamu*:

Brahma creates the world
by words that come forth
from his four mouths in the form
of the ancient texts.
And these words are the goddess herself,
living on his tongue.
That's why he never disobeys her, while she,
in a way, kisses all his four mouths
at the same moment.
May this god of four tongues
bless King Krishna, Narasimha's son.

Brahma creates the world. So far so good. But in fact this creator is entirely caught up in, or driven by, a process that is identified with his wife Sarasvati, the godess who *is* language. Brahma has four heads, hence also four tongues, and Sarasvati lives on those tongues as Vedic speech—a kind of ultimate, musical utterance that is true. Through this Vedic music-cum-language, Brahma creates the world. He can never disobey it—never, that is, disobey his mellifluous wife. Whenever he speaks, it is she speaking through him; and whenever this happens, he is creating. There is desire latent within this process: the goddess inhabiting Brahma's four tongues wants to kiss all his mouths at the same moment. That is why she is there, and how she comes into play. Simultaneity is critical. To string the order out in some linear sequence would be to distort, or ruin, the creation. Time itself—the gap in sequence between one micromoment and another—has two inseparable sides to it, "he" and "she." When one acts, the other is also acting, and this near-simultaneity is immensely consequential. Reality itself emerges from it, rich with linguistic determination. The four Vedas, which is to say, the four linguistic templates of the world, are like an urge to kiss, and without sequential gaps—without time, the field of creation. In this verse, the urge is located initially in the goddess, whose generative speech is this kiss, though it seems as if *he* is actually speaking. But in the story that lies at the core of the novel, the roles are superficially reversed: there it is Brahma who wants to kiss Sarasvati with all four of his mouths simultaneously. The result is the narrative that Suranna relates.

Because Brahma speaks in this special moment, and in this manner, the story becomes real.

What is this story? We would prefer you to read it as it unfolds, in somewhat circuitous fashion, in the novel itself. For purposes of orientation, before entering into a deeper discussion, we give only a highly condensed summary. Suffice it to say that this is the story of a young courtesan named Kalabhashini from the god Krishna's city of Dvaraka:

*This beautiful young woman falls in love one day with Nalakubara, the most handsome man in the universe, whom she sees in the company of his lover, Rambha, a courtesan of the gods. Kalabhashini also overhears this pair of lovers speaking about a mysterious person named Kalapurna, whose story must never be told. Burning with curiosity and desire, she follows Narada, great sage and musician, along with his disciple, Manikandhara, to Krishna's palace. There she is taught the supreme knowledge of music by Krishna's wife Jambavati; Manikandhara, who is not allowed into the inner part of the palace, still manages to acquire the same musical mastery by listening from outside. Upon completion of these studies, Manikandhara goes on a pilgrimage to various shrines, eventually settling down to a discipline of Yoga and meditation in a grove in Kerala, near the shrine of a local goddess known as Mrigendra-vahana, the Lion-Rider.*

*As a meditating Yogin, Manikandhara is a threat to Indra, king of the gods; so the latter sends the alluring Rambha to seduce him. Meanwhile, Kalabhashini arrives at the same area in Kerala in the company of a Siddha magician named Manistambha, who has his own designs on her. An inscription on the temple wall promises that whoever sacrifices a courtesan of perfect beauty, proficient in music, to the goddess there will become a great king. But before Manistambha can carry out his plan, strange entanglements ensue: Nalakubara, Rambha's usual lover, appears beside his precise double, Manikandhara; while Rambha confronts her own exact image in the form of a magically transformed Kalabhashini. Who is who, and who loves whom? Who will succeed in sacrificing the young courtesan and becoming king?*

*At the very height of these confusions, a Malayali Brahmin named Alaghuvrata arrives at the shrine. In his hand he holds, unknown to him, a necklace that originates with the god Krishna, and that gives omniscience to whoever lets its central jewel touch his heart. He watches as Kalabhashini is sacrificed, rather reluctantly, by Manikandhara—Manistambha has, for important reasons, withdrawn. Fortunately, in Kalabhashini's case, beheading is not quite fatal; Manikandhara, on the other hand, dies in battle with a porcupine demon at the wilderness shrine of Srisailam.*

*After two years of meditation, Alaghuvrata is blown by a great wind into the court of an unknown king, to whom he offers the necklace. In the audience is a baby girl; the king wraps the necklace around her neck, the jewel touching her heart—and at once she begins to recount a mysterious tale of the conversation she once overheard, as a parrot, in another life, in the heaven where Brahma, the Creator, plays love-games and word-games with his wife, Speech. But this story—which must not be told—is not quite unknown to its courtly audience. In the course of its telling, Alaghuvrata discovers his four lost sons, wise Brahmin scholars who specialize in learned, bilingual double entendres. Other parts of the story, however, remain opaque for years, for the baby girl rolls over and the magical jewel is displaced from her heart.*

*Like all good stories, especially secret ones, this one must tell of a great love and its occasional impediments. There are two great loves, in fact—both, in some ways, rather routine. Perhaps the most serious problem, in this case, is the lack of a musical instrument equal to the voice and talent of one beloved, the king's wife, Abhinavakaumudi. To retrieve such an instrument, another visit to the shrine of the Lion-Rider is unavoidable. This is also the perfect opportunity for our king to conquer the entire world.*

It is, of course, a very complicated tale. To make things even harder, its point of departure, the true linear beginning of the events, is buried in the very middle of the novel. We can reach it only by following the precisely planned twists and spins that comprise the story as experienced by its various protagonists. Along the way, the points of view we are offered change constantly, with subtle sensitivity to the psychological reality of each of the participants. Like them, no less confused than they are, we begin to find ourselves in this maze of interlocking cycles and events. There are surprises at nearly every step. Perhaps the most often repeated word in this book is "amazed."

We have appended a list of characters, with brief explanatory notes, to help you find your way. We have, however, refrained from recasting the story in a purely lineal mode. We recommend reading the text slowly, paying careful attention to repetitions and the way the key statements are formulated. Nothing here is accidental or incidental; the author has crafted an intricate, deeply logical design that, like everyday life, unravels in minute segments unintelligible without the largely invisible whole.

This is a book which you should read more than once. Each new development of the story reveals another, unsuspected layer in the earlier episodes, and each reading produces a new perspective. When you have read through the text for the first time, you may find it useful to turn to our "Invitation to a Second Reading," which we have placed at the end. As you already know, this is a story not meant to be told; it is under a powerful interdiction, with sanctions prescribed against anyone who tells or hears it. We feel, however, that if you choose to read it once, with attention, you will want to read it again.

## [ Note on the Text ]

The *editio princeps*, by Baruru Tyagarayasastri in 1888/1889, underlies the first Vavilla Ramasvami Sastrulu and Sons edition (Madras, 1910, reprinted many times). We have used as our basic text the Vavilla 1968 printing, with the *laghu-ṭika* of Cadaluvada Jayaramasastri, the only available, though brief, gloss on the *Kaḷāpūrṇodayamu*. Note that another edition published by Vavilla in the same year lacks this commentary. We have also consulted the edition by Malladi Suryanarayana Sastri, published by the editor in Pithapuram, Sri Vidvad-jana-mano-ranjani Mudra-sala, in 1938. This is the only printed edition that is based on the collation of available manuscripts (the editor cites fourteen of these, including one prepared for C. P. Brown in the early nineteenth century that lacks the eighth chapter). When we prefer a reading by Suryanarayana Sastri, we point this out in the notes.

We have had no access to the 1909 Kakinada edition by P. V. Ramanayya and Company (of Guntur), at the Sarasvati Mudranalayamu. A modern edition by Bommakanti Venkata Singaracarya and Ballantrapu Nalinikantaravu was published in two volumes by Emesco, Madras, and reissued in Vijayawada in 1997.

### NOTES

1. From the very beginning of Telugu literature, in the works of the eleventh-century poet Nannaya and his courtly successors, the *campū* format mixes metrical verse and prose in telling a narrative.
2. We have omitted the following verses from the translation:
   *Pīṭhika* 22–69, 75–95, 97–103.
   1. 4–7, 10–12, 17, 21–22, 27–32, 35, 37.
   3. 30.
   4. 79–80, 133–135, 202.

5. 111,150–55, 157, 162–68, 171, 175–80, 187–88.
6. 196–99, 201–202, 205, 209–212, 216, 224, 230–33.
7. 21, 38–40, 68–73, 77–94, 99–100, 103, 110–115, 124–44, 147, 149–50, 170–71, 173, 175, 178–84, 187–88.
8. 10, 14, 17–18, 24–25, 27, 37, 40–42, 59–69, 97, 99, 103–104, 112, 120–21, 138, 140, 144, 199, 202, 211–221, 223–37.

Most of these passages are either structured around untranslatable *śleṣa* or heavily textured to produce primarily phonoaesthetic effects, for example in the *vacana* prose passages, which we have sometimes abridged.

3. 5.18
4. 3.268
5. The two Rambhas: 3.207.
6. Thus Malladi Suryanarayana Sastri and Kasi Bhatta Brahmayya Sastri, inter alia: see Vedamu Laksminarayana Sastri's introduction to the 1957 Vavilla edition of the text, 64.
7. We borrow the term "bitextuality" from Yigal Bronner's recent study of *śleṣa*, "Poetry at Its Extreme: The Theory and Practice of Bitextual Poetry (*śleṣa*) in South Asia," Ph.D. dissertation, University of Chicago, 1999.
8. Suranna composed a *Garuḍa-purāṇamu*, which is not extant.
9. *Prabhāvatī-pradyumnamu* 1.6.
10. Ibid. 1.12.
11. Marupuru Kodandarama Reddi, introduction to Andhra Pradesh Sahitya Akademi edition of *Kaḷapūrṇodayamu* (Hyderabad, 1980), 2–3.
12. See D. Shulman, "Notes on *Camatkāra*," Israel Academy of Sciences and Humanities, in press.
13. *Prabhāvatī-pradyumnamu* 1.15.

# THE SOUND OF THE KISS

[ *The Beginning* ]

There is a reality
that dawns for perceptive minds
when they are touched by the jewel
over Vishnu's heart that shines
like the morning sun, doubly red
from the saffron on the breasts
of the goddess Sri.
It will brighten your heart, too,
Narasimha Krishna, King in Nandyala.

May Krishna, son of Narasingaya,
see his children multiply
like lotus flowers in a pond,
blessed by his family god,
youthful Krishna who dances
with the cowherd girls.

The right hand moves to the left, toward
her breast. The left hand shyly
blocks it. Now he's afraid
she might be angry, so he caresses
her cheek
and her delicate foot, to appease her.

This god, half female half male,[1]
cares for King Krishna, Narasimha's son.

Brahma creates the world
by words that come forth
from his four mouths in the form
of the ancient texts.
And these words are the goddess herself,
living on his tongue.
That's why he never disobeys her, while she,
in a way, kisses all his four mouths
at the same moment.
May this god of four tongues
bless King Krishna, Narasima's son.

I pay respect to Valmiki,[2] the poet born from an anthill,
and Vyasa,[3] son of Satyavati,
who made a home for poetry
just as Siva's long hair
and the Himalayan slopes
became home to the river of the sky
as it flowed down to earth.

The *Mahābhārata* and *Rāmāyaṇa*
were far away, in a distant tongue,
hard even to think about.
Three poets gave them to all of us,
like a peeled banana,
in beautiful Telugu, the Andhra language.
I praise Nannaya, Tikkana, and Errana.[4]

Now as to bad poets—
we might as well forget them.

1. Ardhanārīśvara-Śiva is divided down the middle into a female half, on the left, and a male half, on the right.
2. Author of the *Rāmāyaṇa*.
3. Author of the *Mahābhārata*.
4. The three poets of the Telugu *Mahābhārata*.

If they praise, it's no honor,
and if they criticize, it's no loss.
They're like a goatee on a goat,
not even worthy of ridicule.

Writing poetry is like milking a cow.
You have to pause at the right moment.
You have to feel your way, gently, with a good heart,
without breaking the rules.
You need a certain soft way of speaking.
You can't use harsh words or cause a disturbance.
Your feet should be firm, your rhythm precise.
It requires a clear focus.
If it all works right, a poet becomes popular,
and a cowherd gets his milk.
If not, they get kicked.

So now I've said my prayers to the gods. I've praised the good poets and observed that the best punishment for bad poets is to ignore them. Fully aware that a major composition that is graced by all good features brings fame, while a poor composition gets you kicked out of the court, I was all set to write a great poem on one theme or another.

One day King Krishna of Nandyala was holding court. His jewels cast an iridescent glow in the space around him, thickly perfumed by the oil of sandalwood and musk covering his body. Around him were his ministers, wise in the wily ways of politics; priests learned in the Vedas and able to ward off evil with their mantras and tantras; logicians and philosophers, expert in the texts of Kanada, Kapila, Gautama, Jaimini, Vyasa, and Patanjali that form the basis of the six major schools, and perfectly capable of smashing the perverse arguments of their opponents; storytellers versed in the Purāṇas, such as *Brahma*, *Padma*, *Varāha*, *Vishṇu*, *Matsya*, *Mārkaṇḍeya*, *Bhāgavata*, *Brahma-vaivarta*, *Kūrma*, *Garuḍa*, and *Skanda*; poets just as good as Bana, Bhavabhuti, and Kalidasa in composing all four kinds of poetry—improvised, lyrical, concrete, and narrative; sharp-witted astrologers who know time in all its parts and who can split a moment into its tiny, tinier, and tiniest fragments; physicians versed in Ayurveda and as skilled at healing as Dasra, Caraka, and the doctor of the gods themselves, Dhanvantari;

musicians no less able than Visvavasu, Tumburu, Narada, Anjaneya, Bharata, Matanga, Kohala, and Dattila; courtesans who could charm the heart of any man; soldiers whose breasts were so calloused by wounds that they had hardened into a kind of armor. Each of these groups stood, attentive, in its proper place. The king was receiving, with a smile, a look, or a word, the subordinate kings who came to pay respect, as their announcers called out their names. At the same time, he was watching his dancers dance to the music and the drums, and he was also attending to the reports his officers were submitting about the various tasks and departments to which they were appointed. He also lent an ear to the elegant ways his bards were stringing out his praises in new combinations of words and phrases.

At that moment he saw me—Surana, the grandson of the famous poet Pingali Surana and, on the maternal side, of Annama; son of Amara and Ambama, brother to Amarana and Erranarya. He knew I was a poet capable of producing complex compositions, so he called me over, heaped gifts of fine clothes and ornaments upon me, and spoke to me in a sweet, respectful tone: "I have in my heart the wish to have you compose a book for me, one that is inventive enough that it won't bore me. You have the power of using words to make beauty come alive. Do this for me, and men of taste will celebrate you. I have heard that you have written many books, including the *Garuḍa-Saṃhitā*. There is no need for me to praise them. But your *Rāghava-pāṇḍavīyamu*, which tells two stories in the same words, is incomparable; no one else could have produced such a book in Telugu."

That is how he commissioned me, and I accepted, without giving a second thought to my competence, trusting in the strength of his wish. I began work on the book, to the best of my ability. I wanted it to have the structure of a complex narrative no one had ever known, with rich evocations of erotic love, and also descriptions of gods and temples that would be a joy to listen to. I called it *Kaḷāpūrṇodayamu*.

Would you like to know something of the family history of Nandyala Krishna, the master of this book?[5] First came the Moon, the original king who

5. The master of a book—*kṛtik' adhīśvaruṇḍu*—is, first, the patron who sponsors the work and its first and chief listener, the internal audience of the work. On another level, the poem or book is always seen as a virgin married to its master (*kṛti-nāyaka*).

rules over the entire world, husband of all the stars, born from the eye of the ancient sage Atri. In his line, Bukka of the Aravidu dynasty was born. His fame spread to the ends of the cosmos and touched the Cakravala mountains at the edge. Poets say he was as sharp in mind as the Creator, as handsome as the god of love, as astute in politics as Brhaspati, the gods' own minister, and as generous as Karna, the epic hero. We tolerate such similes only because poets can do whatever they like;[6] in fact, however, Bukka was beyond compare.

King Naraya Narasimha[7] was in the direct line of descent from Bukka—a man who gave away so much wealth that he made the Wishing Tree, the all-giving cow, and the wish-fulfilling gem look small. He put to shame the most handsome males in the universe—Nalakubara[8] and Manmatha, the god of love. He could fight better than the *Mahābhārata* warriors; he bore the entire burden of the earth, so that the Snake, the Boar, and the great mountains, Earth's usual supports, could have some rest. He married two women, Senior Kondamamba and Junior Kondamamba. The elder wife had two sons, Murtiraju and Timmaraju; the younger Kondamamba gave birth to Krishnamaraju, our hero, splendid as the sun, a new Bhoja in patronizing the arts,[9] wholeheartedly devoted to god Vishnu, guardian of the Vedic ways. He is a true connoisseur of literature and music, a man of impeccable taste. His gifts are never small. A judicious king, he has never been false, not even in a dream. Not even the Snake Adishesa, with his thousand tongues, could exhaust his praises.

It is for him—whose great passion is for poetry, and who is blessed by his guru, Srinivasa, the son of Sudarsanacarya in the line of Tirumala Tatacharya—that I am writing this book, wishing him an endless chain of good fortune, long life, and perfect health. Would you like to know how the story begins? Just listen.

6. *Niraṅkuśāḥ kavayaḥ*, a Sanskrit saying.
7. We omit the detailed genealogy of verses 22–69, which take the Aravidu line from its founder Bukka down to the father of Nandyala Krishna. For a discussion of Aravidu family history, see Daniel D'Attilio, "The Last Vijayanagara Kings: Overlordship and Underlordship in South India, 1550–1650," M.A. dissertation, University of Wisconsin, 1995.
8. Son of Kubera, god of wealth.
9. Bhoja, by (anachronistic) literary legend, was the patron of the great Sanskrit poets Kalidasa, Dandin, and Bhavabhuti.

# CHAPTER 1

*[ Dvaraka City, Where the Story Begins ]*

Treasure trove of fortune
where knowledge grows to fullness,
where Krishna plays at pleasure,
Dvaraka, the city that has everything,

sits like a fully grown daughter
on the lap of the Ocean, caressed
by his waves. When a father touches
his daughter, no matter how old she may be,
no one takes it amiss.

Rays of light reflected from the golden palaces
reached into the sky like hands pulling at
the great
city of the gods, and the vast bustle in
the streets
was a challenge hurled at this heavenly rival
to come down and acknowledge
that brilliant Dvaraka was best.

In a riot of color, the walls of its fortresses
were smeared with dark musk;
its gardens were always in full bloom; gleaming
doves nested

on the cornices of tall palaces fashioned from sapphire and gold,
their porches raised from emerald bordered by red coral.

Students joke about their teachers, who don't practise
what they preach. For example, they tell you never to make love
at sunset. But every day at this hour, when the sun burns
on the waves, you can see the goddess of the city
reflected in the water, her arms wound tight
around the god who lies upon the ocean[1]
and who won't let her go.

Here there were Brahmins, gods on earth, who had taken in
all four Vedas and reached the end of all six schools of thought,
who lightly walked the paths of rituals for home and the world
as they focused on the first light
that is God, that only the inner eye can see.

And there were soldiers, expert in all the arts of war,
whose highest pleasure was the feeling that the goddess of victory
was scratching their breasts with her fingernails every time
they were hit by an enemy weapon. They were famed
for their generosity, more lavish than wishing trees; deep and proud,
they were masters of the land.

Merchants in this city put Kubera, the gods' banker,
to shame. Besides all the wealth that their fathers
had set aside, they earned vast riches
on their own account and saved it all
in secret caches underground, marked by
a cobra's hood above.

Sudras lived happily in their homes
with every form of wealth

1. Vishnu sleeps upon the ocean, with his serpent Adisesha for his bed; the goddess of the city is compared to his wife, Lakshmi (*pura-lakshmi*).

and served the Brahmins, as the books prescribe.
They were all honest people.

Women of pleasure happily plundered their customers.
You could hold their waist between your fingers, but their breasts
and buttocks were heavy and full, their hair long and voluptuous.
Eyes radiant, they walked with an elephant's measured grace,
their faces beckoning with a smile.

Men walking in the street by the courtesans' tall palaces
would stop to listen, thrilled, for the doves nesting in the eaves
had learned to imitate the soft moans of the women making love
with customers who came to them each night
from heaven.

Why say more? Krishna himself lived here with his 16,108 wives,
all madly in love with him. Imagine how happy he must have been.
Did he have anything as good in heaven?

## [ Kalabhashini on the Swing and Rambha in the Sky ]

In that city lived a girl, in the full bloom of youthful grace. Her father was a famous actor. Her name was Kalabhashini, which means "sweet spoken," but that doesn't quite express just how charming and subtle were her words. She was totally irresistible. With her refined musical talent, her gift for dancing, and her consummate skill in making love in inventive ways, she quickly began to steal both the hearts and the hard cash of her young lovers.

One day this splendid woman went out with her girlfriends and servants to play in a garden at the edge of the city. She was wearing her finest, and it was springtime, a riot of blossoming flowers. The girls were bantering and teasing one another as they reached the garden that was exploding into lush color. At first they busied themselves picking flowers. "Look at that young *ponna* tree," said one, when her girlfriend's sari was caught by a branch. "That's how a lover should be—direct, hands on."

"The breeze has broken apart the branches of the *kuravaka* tree, and now it looks like a lover spreading his arms to embrace you. He's really trying hard. It's not fair to turn away."

"That mango tree is like a man who won't give up," said another. "He's pulling at your sari with his branches. And what you think are bees hovering around are actually his dark eyes, staring at your breasts. What are you waiting for? You can say yes to him by accepting the fruit and flowers he's offering."

The sweet fragrance of their breath mixed with the fresh fragrance of the flowers hanging from their hair, already coming loose. They walked languorously, a little tired, and the heaviness of their breasts and buttocks slowed them down still more. Their belts, tied just below the soft folds of their waists, glistened with beads of sweat in the sunlight. Bracelets and anklets jingled in harmony as they walked, adjusting the saris that were slipping from their shoulders. They were giggling and aroused. When they had finished with the flowers, they moved on to play on the swings.

At that time a gandharva named Manikandhara, who had devoted himself to Narada out of his love for music, came walking through the sky along with this great sage, on his way to serve Krishna in Dvaraka. Amazed by the exuberant freedom of the women, Manikandhara said to Narada:

"Look at these startling young women.
Their legs stretch straight up to the sky.
They're so sure of their looks, they're making bets
to see who can swing highest.
It looks like they're itching to fight[2]
the famous beauties of heaven."

Narada answered:

"Yes. You speak like a true poet. I've never seen
such beauty. Your thoughtful description
is just right. Pumping and stretching their legs
on the swing, they might just kick the heads
of women in the sky."

As he was speaking, Rambha heard him clearly as she was passing through the clouds with her handsome lover, Nalakubara, in a flying chariot. She

2. *kāl sācu*, literally "to stretch the foot" = to spoil for a fight. The literal and the idiomatic coincide.

listened; she began to burn a bit inside; her mood changed. She knew it was Narada, but she didn't want to show her feelings. So, as if unperturbed, she turned to her lover and said, "Did you hear that? Judging by his words, he must be Narada, the sage who lives on quarrels. I'd like to greet him properly before we pass."

Narada looked in the direction of this voice. "Seems somebody's coming," he said. At that moment their vehicle emerged out of the clouds, like the morning sun rising over the eastern mountain. Rambha and Nalakubara navigated their chariot right under the sage's feet. Very gently, they touched their heads, redolent of *parijata* blossoms, to his feet. They stood still for a little while. He blessed them: "Love one another, with a love that never goes away."

Rambha smiled. "Thanks for your blessing. Maybe now his love will last. But don't you think he might just fall for the wiles of these, um, *human* women?" She couldn't help showing she was miffed.

Narada didn't quite fathom her sarcasm. "What do you mean?" he asked, standing there in the air.

"If you would step into our vehicle, we can talk as we go," she said. "You needn't interrupt your journey. How often do we get the chance to attend upon such great people?"

They brought both Narada and his disciple into the chariot. Standing on either side, Rambha and Nalakubara gently fanned them. Then she said, "What was it you said a moment ago to your disciple about those women on the swings? Would you please say it again?"

So Narada gave a little smile and said,

"Yes. You speak like a true poet. I've never seen
such beauty. Your thoughtful description
is just right. Pumping and stretching their legs
on the swing, they might just kick the heads
of women in the sky.

"That's what I said. Anything wrong with that? Don't hide whatever is weighing on your mind."

She answered, "You're a great man, worshiped in all three worlds. You can say whatever you like. Who can say no to you? I asked, wondering what you knew when you said what you said. Poets imagine things, and they are allowed a certain leeway in hyperbole. That's probably why you said it.

After all, no other woman in the universe is my equal, and I have proof right here—because the most handsome man in the world, who happens to be the beloved son of the richest man in the world, is in love with me."

He smiled again. "You can say what you like when your lover is so full of love for you. Just don't think that all days will be like this. You might have a rival someday. Can you read the future? You might meet a woman just like yourself, and he could encounter a man like him. It could be very disturbing. I wouldn't bet too heavily on what you have."

"You may be joking, but those words might just come true. I can't stand to hear them. Stop. Be kind to me." She bowed to him.

At Narada's request, they set him down in the garden where Kalabhashini was playing. Respectfully, they took their leave. Bowing to the palace of Krishna directly in front of them, they set off to wherever they pleased. But as it happened, Kalabhashini had overheard something of their conversation, since they were so near. She saw the chariot flying close by, brilliantly illuminating all space. Amazed, she caught sight of Nalakubara standing in it and was overcome by his perfect beauty; she couldn't stop staring at him. Hidden by the bushes and branches, she followed after them for a ways, still straining to hear, until the vehicle was out of sight. Then she turned back, wondering who that lucky woman was who had somehow managed to attract a man of such striking looks. "That's how I would like to be," she thought. "I heard her say that her lover is the beloved son of the richest man in the world. They say that Kubera's son has a spellbinding woman called Rambha as his mistress. So that must be her. To make sure, I should ask this great sage, who must be Narada; from time to time he comes to see Krishna."

Alone, she approached the sage. Certain that he was, indeed, Narada, she bowed to him and asked, "Weren't those two people in the flying vehicle Rambha and Nalakubara?"

"Indeed they were," he said. "How did you guess?"

"I overheard as you were talking, and that's how it seemed."

"So you heard what we said in the sky?"

"I heard. That woman was bragging that because of her great beauty, she had her lover eating out of her hand. I could see by what you said that you weren't too pleased."

"Nobody likes words spoken out of blind arrogance. It's not right to be so proud of what you are. I sense some real rivalry about to happen. And we don't have to scour the earth to find this rival. With a little luck, it could be you."

"Luck like that might come to a woman of remarkable power and beauty—never to people like me, however hard I try."

"That's what you say. But in truth you are no less lovely than Rambha or any woman of her class. In fact, you're even better. But let that be. Haven't I seen you somewhere before? Do you ever come to Krishna's court?"

"I go there often, and I've seen you there."

"Yes, now I remember. Aren't you the girl who heard my disciple, Manikandhara, praise Krishna in a long poem, a *daṇḍaka*,[3] and who then recited it back after that single hearing? Your name is Kalabhashini, isn't it? You have a great talent. It was amazing! Do you still remember it? Can you recite it?"

"Of course I can," said Kalabhashini, and began to sing in sweet, sonorous tones:

"Your beauty beloved of the goddess,
compassion flowing into form,
mirror filled with many colors and rays of red,
brilliant as spring buds,
uniquely praised through the world—
all this and more
is you. Not even the great gods Siva and Brahma
can know you to the end. We, unmindful
of our limits, still hope to know you, so we make poems
about you, showing off our futile skills.
Forgive our faults. We can't comprehend
how you can be both in and beyond language.
Masters of the Veda spend whole lives
trying to reach you through harsh discipline,
renouncing their desire, but we found your compassion
without any effort on our part. Is it not strange?
When every hair on your body holds a billion
solar systems, how foolish it seems to talk about
the avatars you have taken—how you lifted the Mountain[4]
as Krishna, how you raised up the earth as the Boar,

3. A genre of unlimited length made up of repeated feet of one long and two short syllables; usually used in prayer.

4. Govardhana.

how you balanced Mount Mandara on your back as a Tortoise,
how you covered the cosmos in three steps.[5]
That's why some people say that all rituals, all forms
of knowledge, all kinds of Yoga, all silences and gifts
are not worth a billionth of the joy one gets
by touching the feet of your servants' servants.
We cannot elude the net you cast
except by saying your name, over and over,
Lover of Lakshmi, God of Gods.
*Namas te, namas te, namas te.*

"And isn't that necklace your disciple is wearing the one Krishna gave him in return for this *daṇḍaka* poem? Besides,

"Putting words together like strings of pearls in a necklace,
knowing the meaning—whether literal, figurative, or suggestive—
and precisely how it should be used,
weaving textures to evoke the inner movement,
implanting life through syllable and style,
structuring the poem with figures of sound and sense:
this is what a good poet does.
Then he gets everything he wants.

"If cool moonlight could have fragrance,
and crystals of camphor, which are cool and fragrant,
could have tenderness, and the southern breeze
which is fragrant, cool, and tender could have sweetness—
then you could compare them all
to this poet's living words.

"Just being in the presence of people like you is enough to fulfill all desires. For so long I have been wanting to carry this *vina* of yours, and to be

5. Vishnu came as a Dwarf to ask Bali, king of the demons, for as much ground as he could cover in three steps. When Bali agreed, the god grew into his immense form: with one step, he reached the end of the earth; with the second, the end of the sky. For his third step, he placed his foot on Bali's head and crushed him into the Nether World.

with you. Many times in the past, I watched you go into the women's quarters of Krishna's palace, after leaving Manikandhara at the door; you always carried your own *vina*. I used to think I could carry it for you, but I hesitated to ask, since I didn't know your mind. Could you possibly allow me this service?"

She folded her hands as she begged him, and he said, "As you wish."

Kalabhashini was pleased, for now she could reach the end she desired. She was pondering the last sentence she had overheard from the conversation of Rambha and Nalakubara. Still, she was hesitating out of politeness, until opportunity opened up—Manikandhara went aside when he felt she needed to speak privately—and she could ask the sage: "While you were standing here on the ground, that couple, probably out of respect for you, did not take off too quickly into the sky; they kept their vehicle flying at ground level for a little ways. Out of sheer fancy, I followed along after it and heard a snatch of conversation. Let me repeat it for you. Nalakubara was saying, 'Before Narada's words interrupted us, we were talking about Kalapurna. What happened next?' Rambha replied, 'Didn't I tell you already that I can't tell more of that story, even though I know you're dying to hear it?' Now I'm curious. Who is that Kalapurna? What part of his story did she tell? And what's the part she couldn't tell?"

Narada was amazed. "All this is utterly strange. Let me find out what's going on." For a moment he sat in stillness, scanning the universe with his mind, studying all past, future, and present events. When he had found what he was looking for, he turned to Kalabhashini. "That story that Rambha could not tell her lover is a very unusual one. I cannot tell it either."

"If that is so, then leave that part out. Just tell me what led to her mentioning the story."

Narada spoke. "Rambha and this man are totally engrossed in making love to one another. Every laugh, every look, every word or movement inflames their desire. There is a certain kind of love like that in this world. Today, just before they saw me, Rambha noticed the bright rim edging a mass of clouds as the new sun was about to emerge from behind; she compared this line to Sarasvati, goddess of language, in the presence of Brahma, the Creator. Nalakubara was so aroused by this that he hungrily bit her lips. As he did so, a marvellous and delicate mode of speech[6]

6. *vāg-vṛtti*.

moved in her throat and, shattering, emerged as a sound never heard before. It provoked such delight in Nalakubara, and such intense wonder, that he cried, 'Again! Do it again! Just one more time. This is utterly new.' But as he begged her, she said, 'I cannot repeat it, my love.' He said, 'I won't let you go until you do.' And they went on bantering like this for a while. Finally, in order to please him, she gave him another slight taste of it.

"'I've never heard anything like this,' he said. 'How did you learn to do it?' He was pressing her, and she said, 'It's not from today. I knew it long ago. But for a particular reason I could not let it be known. Then today I forgot when I saw that white cloud coupled with the young sun, and though I held it in my heart, your stupid kiss excited me, and I let it out.'

"'But why have you hidden this so long?'

"'Because I was afraid that once this came out, it would lead to the stories of Kalapurna.'

"'Proud, aren't you? So what if the stories come out?'

"'Just listen. Whoever tells those stories or hears them will have to have children, grandchildren, and great-grandchildren and live with vast wealth and happiness on earth for a very long time. That's the condition, from the beginning. If I tell you the story, I'll have to be born on earth. That, my love, is why I was afraid. Do you think I want those things, when I have the joy of touching your body? And if you say to me that I've already heard the story anyway, let me tell you that this condition was attached by a certain person, whose words never fail to come true, *after* I had heard it. That's why I can't tell it, and you can't hear it.'

"That's what she said," Narada finished. "And since I have the exact same fear that Rambha has, I can't tell you the story, either. Still, this story will be known to the world. There are ways it can happen. Just let it be. After Rambha and Nalakubara had had this conversation, their vehicle came close to me, and we talked about *you* and your swinging." Then he called Manikandhara, who had gone away to admire the beauties of that garden. "It's time to go to Krishna. He's holding court." And they set off. Kalabhashini left for home with her friends. She dressed and headed for the palace.

*There's more to come, King of Nandyala. Your eloquence is equal to the thousand tongues of Adisesha, the snake who serves as Vishnu's bed. You speak the truth, like Hariscandra. Great scholars debate in your court. With a blink of your eyes, you conquer all your inner enemies.*

This is the first chapter in the long poem called *Kalapurnodayamu* made by soft-spoken Suraya, son of Pingali Amaranarya, whose poetry all connoisseurs enjoy throughout the world.

# CHAPTER 2

*Listen, Nandyala Krishna, son of Narasimha: Your victories are written by the hoofprints of your horses on the great mountains of Malaya in the south and Himalaya in the north. Now for the rest of the story . . .*

## [ Narada Studies Music ]

"My heart is a little lighter," thought Narada after concluding his conversation with Kalabhashini. "I have sowed the seed of conflict between Rambha, who is so puffed up with her sense of youth and beauty, and a future rival. It's a beginning. In fact, it's as good as certain. This young woman will do it—and listening to her words, I can sense that she is jealous. It was a bit of a detour for me, but never mind. It was necessary to achieve my goal. I can't get through a minute without making someone or other quarrel."

Lost in these thoughts, Narada and his disciple, Manikandhara, entered the city of Dvaraka. As they were moving through the streets, people around them began to wonder.

"Today he landed on earth at some distance from the palace, and now he's walking there. I wonder why."

"Maybe he's hunting for some pretext to create a quarrel."

"Or else it's his way of blessing people by sprinkling them with dust off his feet, carried by the wind."

"This land is lucky. The time is ripe and will bear fruit."

People who knew him stood on either side, their hands folded in salutation. Those closer to him stretched out on the street before him to show him honor. The road was packed with important people who were being carried in palankeens or sedans or riding horses or elephants, but who immediately got down, in all humility, a bit flustered, to pay their respects.

Narada looked at some of them out of the corners
of his eyes, but others he looked straight
in the face. He smiled at some,
said hello to others, held out his hand
to help others up; sometimes he linked his arm
to theirs. He received each one
like someone special.

They proceeded into the city via the moat where the raucous cries of waterbirds fused with the moaning and splashing of the waves, sputtering with white foam, as if to mock the very ocean just beyond. Through the spray cast up by the breakers, you could see rainbow-like flashes snaking through the sky.

Before them stood the tall, gilded palace of Krishna, its emerald walls crowned by carved cornices inlaid with precious gems so luminous that the edges of space itself seemed to quiver with brilliant flowers, while the sky, reflecting the white gleam of the walls and the polished pearls on the spires, looked like a parasol held aloft on a golden rod to shelter the goddess of that city.

Immense red-and-black beads and rubies covered the walls like vines enlivened with leaves of emerald and sapphire and with flowers skillfully crafted from flawless pearls, with sapphire-blue bees hovering over them: Krishna's palace, with its golden cupolas, towered high enough to prop up the wishing trees in heaven and to ensure their fruitfulness. Narada looked at it and said to Manikandhara, "I see it all the time, but every time it's like the first time. It's like seeing into Vishnu's city in the sky. And the brilliance of the audience hall, in particular, floods my heart with joy. This is Dvaraka—the best place in the world."

As they drew near, the women at the gate saw Narada and rushed to inform Krishna. He was lying on a swinging cot made of ivory, with golden chains, finely chiseled coral legs, and newly fashioned knobs. It was inlaid with geese and parrots made from gems; golden flowers were painted all over it, along with various other designs. The frame was woven from fine, crisscrossing ribbons of silk; several little pillows of different shapes rested on the mattress colored in a red saffron-flower motif. When Krishna heard what the women told him, he jumped up: "What? The Creator's own son has arrived! Really? He walked through the main entrance? He always comes flying right into this chamber. This is something new. I wonder why."

And he walked quickly to the main entrance without straightening his hair, which had been slightly disturbed by the swinging. He was still holding the betel leaf that the betel-lady had folded and handed him. He had hastily put on his gem-studded slippers, but they kept falling off his feet. The women from the queen's palace who were fanning him followed him for a short distance before turning back. He forgot to release the woman who had hooked her arm through his as soon as he got up, so she walked along with him. Everyone who saw him withdrew a little ways, leaving room.

He received the sage with a bow. Taking his hand in affection, Krishna led him to a hall near the women's quarters, where the women were waiting, as instructed. There the Lord of the World honored this sage with great attention, as if he had arrived for the first time that day. When worthy people visit again and again, good minds become ever more attuned.

There were, as usual, many waiting outside for an audience with Krishna; they sent word. Krishna, however, hesitated to say to them, "I'll be with you as soon as I send off this guest of mine," so he paid no heed to the messages and kept on talking with the sage. Narada observed this and said, "If you make such a fuss over me and suspend all your business for my sake, the best thing you can do is to send me away right now. If, however, you treat me as one of your people, please ask the others in."

Friends, relatives, generals, scholars, poets, advisers, leading citizens of the town—Krishna graciously invited all of them to enter. As they came in, each was announced by the ushers, holding staffs, in a clear, loud voice. The god quickly concluded the day's business, left the court, and took the sage with him into his inner quarters. As usual, Narada asked his disciple, Manikandhara, to remain outside, as he reached for his own vina.

But Kalabhashini stepped forward to carry the vina for him. Krishna observed this and said, "What's this? Do you want to become his disciple?"

"No, nothing like that" she said, humbly, withdrawing slightly.

"Don't be afraid, young lady. It's a very good idea. Such great people only rarely consent to be served. I don't have to elaborate. You'll do well. Serve this worthy man always. Every time I've seen you, I've noticed your intelligence, your skill at singing, your sweet, melodious voice. I used to say to myself, 'This woman would reach the heights if she only had the chance of being trained by Narada.' "

With these words, Krishna took her together with the sage to his wife Jambavati's house. "I've brought you a student. Take her and train her," he said with a smile.

"Is this the Kalabhashini you told me about?" she asked pleasantly while giving a proper welcome to Narada.

"This sage has been coming here for years to train with you. What have you taught him? Of course he was already a master of music, but because he was jealous of Tumburu, he was determined to acquire what *we* know of this discipline. Nobody else has ever learned it. That's why I brought him to you—so you would teach him all you know. That's why I placed him in your care."

Jambavati said, "I always do what you tell me. But now it's time for you to tell me if I'm on the right track. Listen for a little." Playing the vina, she began to sing in tones clear and sustained as filaments of gold pulled through a goldsmith's plate[1] and as sweet as a fine rain of honey straight from flowers. She knew the precise gradations of tones and semitones, the niceties of the *raga*s (and which notes or phrases should be avoided), the pure forms of various rhythms; she distinguished the scales from one another with absolute clarity and showed mastery of the three pitches. When she sang the text, words and melody were perfectly blended. The love came

1. The goldsmith works with a thick iron plate with holes of various sizes, somewhat larger at the point of entry and thinner at the point of egress; gold filaments are inserted and pulled through these holes with pliars to shape them to the correct thickness. By repeating this operation through progressively thinner holes, the filament becomes delicate and uniformly shaped. See Srinatha, *Bhīma-khaṇḍamu* 4.130; V. Narayana Rao and D. Shulman, *Telugu Classical Poetry: An Anthology* (New Delhi: Oxford University Press, 2002), 178.

through—she was singing about him, and Krishna listened, losing himself in the music.

"It's perfect. Keep teaching him." And he left. For a full year after that, she skillfully went on training Narada. Following this, Satyabhama and Rukmini each taught him for one year. Then Krishna himself brought him to perfection in the course of another year.

Meanwhile, Manikandhara, who was asked to remain outside the gate and thus did not have the benefit of being taught by Krishna's wives, as Kalabhashini did, managed to learn all the secret arts of music through a certain special kindness of the gods' and became no less proficient than Narada and Kalabhashini.

Finally, the moment came when Krishna said to the three of them: "There's no one who excels you in music any more." And afterward, whenever Narada entered the inner chamber, the women remembered these events and said to the sage, "There's no one comparable to you when it comes to music."

One day later, Narada, along with Manikandhara and Kalabhashini, took leave of Krishna and went to roam the world. As they were going, conversation turned to the topic of how the women in Krishna's palace had admired Narada's powerful mastery of music. Narada said, "It's true. All three women—Jambavati, Satyabhama, and Rukmini—have said many times that my skill in music was of a novel order, and that no one else could approach me. But I couldn't tell if they really meant it or were just saying it to please me. Polite people are anxious to make others happy one way or another; you can't take their compliments at face value. Only what they say to their own friends in private is true. Until there's a chance to find that out, doubt will lurk in my heart."

Kalabhashini said, "I can find that out. I know them. I went there with you many times. They know me. I can listen to what they say in private to one another. But then, since they know I'm in your circle, they may hesitate to criticize you in my presence when the talk turns to your music. If only I could take the shape of whatever woman I wanted to, I could assume the form of one of those women's friends and go there at the right moment in order to find out what they're *really* thinking."

Narada thought to himself, "Some excuse! What she really wants is to become Rambha and make love to Nalakubara. But this fits my plan, too." So he looked at her and said, "Fine. I give you that capability. Take the form of whatever woman you want and go find out what Krishna's wives are *really* thinking." And he went away.

Kalabhashini went to see Krishna's wives in the form of one of their maids, making sure, of course, that this maid was not present. She brought the conversation round to Narada's competence in music and, by listening to them, satisfied herself that they sincerely believed him to be incomparable. She then went back to the sage and made him very happy by her report. He looked at her: "You've also cunningly acquired all those skills that I have, and from the same teachers—Jambavati, Satyabhama, Rukmini, and Krishna. You're lucky. Now you will happily make love to the man you wanted, a man so beautiful that he could win Rambha's heart. Trust me. Go home."

After sending her off, Narada went on chatting with Manikandhara for a while and then went his way. Manikandhara, at Narada's instruction, set off on pilgrimage. Meanwhile, Kalabhashini, pleased with what she had got out of Narada, went home. Since there was no longer any occasion for her to go to the palace, now that the music lessons had ended, she had plenty of time to daydream about Nalakubara. She couldn't think of any way to approach him.

## [ Enter Manistambha ]

Time passed slowly and became oppressive. One day she took her vina and went outside to the garden. Suddenly, a Siddha, a man of powers, came flying through the air on a lion. A thin powder of ash covered his body; he had a hooked staff and a mendicant's bag and reddish hair, short and tangled. He carried a book of potions, a cane shaped like a snake, a rather lovely lute, and a horn. His perfume was intoxicating. All in all, a pleasant sight.

Miraculously, he landed in the garden right in front of her. Recovering from her amazement, she welcomed him appropriately. He addressed her: "Hey Kalabhashini! So you're not going for lessons from Krishna anymore. You've apparently completed the course. And that great sage has also stopped coming here. So you have nothing on your mind except for that Nalakubara. . . . When Narada left you, he gave you a blessing—that you'll have your desire—and his word never fails. But you're growing restless, and you're worn out. Your friends can't bear to watch it.

"Moreover, Manikandhara has stopped playing music ever since he's taken to the discipline of self-control.[2] My ears are starved for good music. It hurts. Please, play something for me on the vina. Help me put an end to my hunger for good music. In all these worlds, only the two of you can make me happy by your music."

Every word of his astonished her. She listened, folding her delicate hands. Reverently, she said, "Who are you? A god? One of those Yogis like Kapila?[3] Your presence amazes me. Could you tell me your name?"

"My name is Manistambha. I'm not anybody you thought I was. I'm a Siddha."

"What an honor! The more I hear you, the more astonished I feel. How do you know all this, and so precisely? It looks like you can see everything with your special power. I don't need you to tell me what I already know. But you just said Manikandhara has taken to the discipline. Tell me from there on."

He looked at her. "I have the ability to see and to hear at a great distance, so I have seen everything from here. Whatever I said has verified what you already know. Now let me tell you what transpired from the moment Narada and Manikandhara left you, what they said to one another, and what Manikandhara did before taking up the discipline."

"After Narada had completed his musical training and sent you home, he said to Manikandhara, 'Sing to Vishnu at all times, and your musical training will bear fruit. God will be pleased, and you will become free. I do the same, with my vina, all the time. Visvavasu[4] has Brihati for his vina. Tumburu's[5] vina is Kalavati. My vina is Mahati. The goddess of arts has Kacchapi. All of us sing without pause. Music is the best of all kinds of learning, and if it is offered to God, what could be better than that? You're the luckiest of all. No one can reach Krishna by any form of discipline, but Krishna became your teacher. Think about it. Practise what you have learned. That will bring you whatever you desire, and you will live in beauty.

2. We translate in this way the common Sanskrit word *tapas*, literally the "heat" generated by meditation, self-denial, and other forms of concentrated physical and spiritual praxis.
3. A famous sage mentioned in the classical texts.
4. One of the great *gandharva* singers, a class of demigods.
5. Narada's most serious rival among the *gandharvas*.

"'As for me, I have to go quickly, to defeat Tumburu, wherever he is—in heaven, in Brahma's court, in Indra's world, or at Vishnu's. I have to perform at my best to put down that puffed-up idiot.'

"Manikandhara listened, cupped his hands, and asked, 'I understand from what you say that you are eager to defeat Tumburu in music. But how did this rivalry come about? What have you gone through in order to overcome him? Won't you tell me that?'

"Narada began. 'This was some time ago. Vishnu was holding court in great splendor in Vaikuntha, his heavenly world. Brahma and other gods were in attendance. Great Yogis were chanting. God was protecting the world. Everyone was there—Kaundinya, Marica, Daksa, Kapila, Agastya, Aksapada, Angirasa, Sandilya, Kratu, Kanva, Kutsa, Bhrigu, Vishvamitra, Maitreya, Markandeya, Asuri, Vamadeva, Kapi, Durvasa, Baka, Vyaghrapada, Mandavya, and so on. We went there, too—me, Tumburu, Visvavasu, and others—with our vinas. We wanted to serve, too. Vishvaksena, the gatekeeper, was brandishing his cane, trying to make room as people thronged around. God was watching the dancing women.

"'Like lightning flashing from a chain of clouds, the goddess Lakshmi entered, surrounded by her retinue of maids, straight from the garden outside the palace. As soon as she appeared, a contingent of guards armed with canes began to beat the gathering crowd, which scattered in confusion. Do I have to tell you what was the fate of people like me? Even Brahma ran off in fear when the guards approached, lashing out all around them. After clearing the space, they called out, "Aho! Tumburu!" with a loud voice and briskly took him in. The people outside began to wonder, "Why did they call him, in particular? There must be some special business relating to music. But why him? Don't other experts exist?" I myself was wondering why they called him, of all people. Then I came to know from what people were saying that God himself was listening to his singing, together with his wife. I was burning with rage. They drive all of us away, and they invite this one person to sing to God and his wife? And they happily listen to him?

"'I waited in a corner to see what would happen. When Tumburu came out, his body glistening, with a medal and a shawl embroidered with flowers so bright they flooded space with gold, gods and sages gathered around:

"'"So he sent you off. What did he give you?"

"'"God and the goddess listened to his music. What else would he need?"

"' "The incomparable gifts he received show how pleased God must have been."

"' "Were you there alone, singing to them? Was anybody else around?"

"'The flashing medal and the shawl and the gleaming body set my heart on fire. I was furious that when they called Tumburu, he went straight in without consulting me. All right, he went in; but why didn't he get them to invite me in, too? So he played the maestro, fine: but why did he blithely accept all those presents? Okay, he took them, but did he have to parade them before us instead of slipping away quietly, like a thief bitten by a scorpion? There's no one who can judge fairly anymore. That's how people are. They find their way in through the back door and then make a grand exit from the front. "I'll get you, Tumburu. Watch out!" I said to myself, gnashing my teeth. "Is he any better than me? I will show them what he is. Until then, let him do what he wants. I won't let him get away with it. I'll pick a quarrel with him and humiliate him and make sure that word of my supreme skill in music reaches as far as God's ears." Still, I decided to contain this jealousy in my mind without showing it; meanwhile, I would continue to visit his house as a friend, in order to detect any defects in his musical learning. I thought this was the wise course—how else could I defeat him?

"'So one day I went to his house. He had just tuned his vina and left it on the porch when he went inside. "Is Tumburu home?"I called.

"' "He left his vina here and went in," said the people there.

"'I was curious, so I picked up the vina and plucked it. A perfect purity of sound, such as I had never heard before, overwhelmed me.[6] I put it back, embarrassed, and quickly walked away.

"' "He's really a master. Until today, I never thought this Tumburu could outdo me, the most famous musician in the universe."

"'I was really disturbed. If you're tall enough to kick the head of a palm tree, there's always someone taller who can kick *your* head. The two of us used to perform together in the presence of Brahma and others, but he never exhibited this remarkable skill—until Vishnu himself asked him to

6. In the early sixteenth century, vinas were tuned separately for each rāga—hence the vital importance of tuning in performance. There is a tradition that Ramarajabhusana, the great Vijayanagara court-poet in the mid-sixteenth century, invented the frets that allow for a single stable tuning (Marupuru Kodandarama Reddi, *Kaḷāpūrṇodayamu* [Hyderabad: Andhra Pradesh Sahitya Akademi, 1980], 63, note).

sing for him. That's how it is with experts—they give of their skill only to the extent that the listener can receive it. There's only as much of a lotus as there is water in the lake. Singing for people who can't understand is a waste, like blowing a conch in front of a deaf person.

"'Ever since then, I've been going from place to place in search of truly gifted musicians. I sought them out and studied with them. Still, I couldn't find anyone equal to Tumburu. Finally, after a long time, I concluded that I could achieve my goal only with the help of omniscient God. I prayed to him, at length. And he came—

his body luminous yet darker
than the Dark Mountain,[7] wide eyes
whiter than lotus petals, his earrings
brighter than the rising sun. Lakshmi,
on his chest, was playing with the shadow
of the jewel he wore. He was dressed as a king
with conch and discus, and all the gods
were in attendance as he appeared,
riding his eagle.

"'"What do you want?" he asked. I bowed and praised him as best I could and said, "I want to defeat Tumburu in a music match." He looked at me with kindness. "In the third eon from now, I am going to be born as the son of someone called Vasudeva, in order to protect the good, punish the wicked, and save the earth. At that time I will fulfill your wish in a city known as Dvaraka. Come see me then."

"'He disappeared, and I waited—a very long time. Finally, I did receive musical training from Krishna.[8] I had to go to all this trouble to get my music, but you and Kalabhashini learnt it all without a drop of sweat, just by Vishnu's kindness.'

"'It's a small reward for serving you. People say one becomes great by reaching a great person. Haven't you heard? Anyway, you've made such a big event out of one invitation to Tumburu to sing before Vishnu. I wonder how one could have the good fortune to live in God's presence and serve him continuously.'

7. The mythical Ancanacala.
8. Vishnu's avatar as the son of Vasudeva and Devaki.

"'That's a wonderful thought, rarely contemplated before. In fact, people are so caught up in judging good and bad, do's and don'ts, merits and demerits, that they hardly ever think of their own future life. After making a name for themselves as wise by tireless pursuit of Vedas and Shastras, various practices, and debates, they choose to serve a king. Driven by their karma, they're like the crazy man who says, "Thank God I'm cured—just wind that rock around my head." Listen, young man. Among the elements, living beings are best. Among living beings, intelligent creatures are best. Among intelligent creatures, human beings are best. Among human beings, Brahmins are superior. The best Brahmins are scholars. Those who know the meaning of what they do are the finest of the scholars. Among these, those who act are best. Among those who act, the best are those who know truth. There's no one higher than they. That's what Manu said in his book of law.[9]

"'You yourself have gone almost to the end of this road that I've just laid out. As soon as you came to know about the power that comes from being in God's presence, you asked for the highest step. So let me tell you what I've heard from the elders about how to stay close to God always. It's wrong not to teach a person who deserves to know—just as wrong as it is to teach someone who doesn't deserve it.

Doing good deeds with no interest in results,
just for the sake of God,
avoiding what is forbidden,
standing firm in Vishnu,
living in the company of God's people,
staying off the path of the wrong people,
making pilgrimage to famous places where Vishnu is present,
celibacy, discipline, nonpossession—

anyone who wants a place in Vaikuntha
has to keep to all these.

"'Even if you find yourself doing only a few of them, they won't be wasted. You'll still come to God. Just do your best. Use the incomparable gift of

9. The *Mānava-dharma-śāstra*, central textbook of the dharma specialists.

music that God gave you. Sing to him in the temples at Puri and Srirangam. That will bring you all that is good.'

"As Narada was speaking, he lost himself in Krishna. He was spilling over, jumping for joy, bowing down in praise; his hairs stood on end, his eyes were half closed, and he sang and danced with a sense of wonder. Immersed in this flood of feeling, imagining God's many ways, Narada went off, feeling his way.

"Manikandhara found all of this rather astonishing. 'What a great man he is!' he thought, watching Narada until he disappeared from view. Finally, he turned his eyes away. And with Narada gone, he followed his instructions until thoughts of God gradually took over his heart. Then he left on pilgrimage."

## [ Manikandhara's Pilgrimage ]

"First he went to the Yamuna, the river of rushing black waves and brilliant white lotuses, of myriads of buzzing bees and honking geese that drown out evil, of certain promise. As Brahmins sitting on the riverbank sang the Secret Teachings,[10] the river seemed to follow the rise and fall of their chants, the high tones and low tones, with its waves rising and falling like eyebrows shifting in harmony with the singer's voice. The river, daughter of the Sun, looked like Vishnu himself: the foam on both banks was white as the snake-bed he lies on, and the thick pollen wafted from the flowers could have been the yellow clothes he wears.

"Manikandhara performed all the rituals of pilgrimage and sang at the height of his skill about the qualities of God. From there he went to Mathura, Haridvara, Salagrama Mountain, Badarikasrama, the Naimisha Forest, Kuruksetra, Prayaga, Kasi, Ayodhya, the confluence of the Ganges and the sea; everywhere he bathed, gave gifts to Brahmins, and carried out the rituals. Afterward he reached the Blue Mountain[11] on the shore of the sea.

"'Vishnu's world is right here, where sages find their goal. This is the highest place. This is my protection. Here all beauty is born.' He bathed in the Rohini spring, in the Indradyumna Lake, and sang to Jagannatha, Lord of the World. After serving Jagannatha, the Perfect Being,[12] he moved on to

10. Aranyaka, the "Forest Books."
11. Puri in Orissa.
12. Purushottama.

Srikurmam,[13] a feast for his eyes; then to Simhacalam,[14] another high point of his life; from there to Ahobalam,[15] where he pressed his forehead to the feet of the god. He went on to crown himself with Venkatesvara's feet, dark with bees drawn to the lotus-like fragrance.[16]

"He was at peace. He rushed to the Svami-Pushkarini Tank, which reached out to embrace him with its welcoming waves. The tank is always full of the god, and so was Manikandhara, so they perfected one another. Nearby, he paid his respects to the Boar,[17] beloved of the goddess Sri, his mind gently blending into the nuanced sensations of excitement, surrender, wonder, joy.

"Now he could enter the temple of Venkatesa, whose domes and pavilions shone with a splendor that made fire burn brighter; whose dancing girls waving yak-tail fans imparted strength to the wind; where dust from the feet of pilgrims, coming and going, gave added depth to the earth, while space itself was enhanced by the rich sounds of many musical instruments, and water was enriched with the offerings of aloe and incense. First he worshipped the outer deities; then, his body thrilling with emotion, he went deeper in, toward the god.

"He saw him—golden anklets on his feet, golden cloth around his waist, a golden sword in his belt of gems; a ruby in his navel; the long garland of victory hanging from his neck; the goddess Sri on his breast. One hand was lifted in a gesture of protection, another rested on his waist;[18] two others held the conch and wheel. Strings of pearls fell from his gleaming neck, and a gentle smile played on his cheeks. His earrings were shaped like crocodiles; his eyes were wide as the open lotus; his perfect nose and well-shaped eyebrows, the brilliant white mark on his forehead, his crown of jewels—all these made for an arresting presence. Manikandhara contemplated each part, every limb, taking him in slowly until he had seen him entirely. His wonder intensified minute by

13. Near Srikakulam in northern Andhra.
14. The shrine of Varaha-Narasimha, or Appanna, near Visakhapatnam.
15. The Narasimha temple in Kurnool District, southern Andhra.
16. Venkatesvara is the god of the major pilgrimage temple at Tirupati, north of Chennai.
17. Varahasvami on the banks of the great tank at Tirupati.
18. Note that the present icon of Venkatesvara has no hand resting on the waist, as is described here. See the note by Marupuru Kodandarama Reddi, *ibid.*, 72.

minute. For a long time he didn't know what he was doing. Then he found his voice.

"'My eyes are fixed on his feet. How can I lift them to his golden dress? Now they're fastened on the dress. How can I move them to his waist? Or from his waist to the mark on his breast? And once entangled in the mark, how can I shift them to his hands? Hands, neck, lips, earrings, cheeks, nose, eyes, eyebrows, hair—wherever my sight comes to rest, it won't let go.' He completely forgot the world outside. For a long time he simply stared. Then he bowed many times. Then he sang, his voice and the notes of the vina becoming one in a wave of such surpassing sweetness that people who listened were transfixed. For three days and three nights he sang. Then he came down from the hill.

"He walked until he reached Kancipuram—one of the seven great cities that bring liberation. Siva there is the Lord of the One Mango,[19] with the river Ganges on his head. Kamakshi[20] brought her discipline to fruition here. Brahmins live on the bank of its river, which is the goddess of speech in fluid form. Brahma sacrificed there and became visibly present, so the site is rich in fortune. Manikandhara was overjoyed to see the Lord of the One Mango and Kamakshi. He also worshiped the other deities of Kanci, including, above all, the Lord of Elephant Hill.[21]

"The white clarity of God's conch matched the clarity of his heart. God's inner fire equaled the fiery wheel he carries. The compassionate goddess on his chest embodied the love inside him. The *kaustubha* jewel around God's neck reflected the limpid awareness in his mind. This Varadaraja, giver of gifts, was very much present to Manikandhara, who sang for him, his hair standing on end.

"Manikandhara left Kancipuram and walked south through the great villages of the Chola country, where bees wander in the winds blowing pollen off areca, mango, banana, and many other flowering trees. Sugarcane, paddy fields, areca-nut groves, thick flower gardens, lotus ponds, river canals, row upon row of coconut trees, mango groves—all this made him feel happy. Then he saw the Kaveri River flowing under a vast sky, its waves towering in joy and pride at having outdone in splendor and fame

19. Ekamranatha.
20. The goddess of Kancipuram, "with eyes of desire," who worshiped Siva here as a *linga* of earth or sand.
21. Karigirindra, Vishnu in Kancipuram.

the river of the gods that flows in heaven. He filled himself with the spacious expanse of this incomparable river. No one, he thought, could bring himself to praise another river after seeing this one. 'The two streams flow together as if embracing the island of Srirangam. Its water washes away stain from all who come to worship. No such limpid purity exists in any other water. It is auspicious. It is good. It makes you free.'

"He could hear people saying, 'This river[22] wants to worship the goddess of Srirangam with her watery jewels. For this she needs a thousand eyes and a thousand arms—for this she bears a thousand lotus blossoms on her thousand waves. The lotus is no lotus, and waves are not mere waves.

"'Flowing close to the god, for our sake the river reflects his image, remakes the god in its water—golden dress, lotus eyes, four arms, conch, wheel, bow, club, and dark-blue body.'

"From afar, breezes saturated with the incense of many flowers welcomed all pilgrims. Geese, herons, curlews, and cranes called out greetings. The rising waves reached out in extended embrace. White foam deposited on the banks became silvery seats. Pilgrims received in this manner felt like family, and praised the river. Manikandhara performed his rituals in the Kaveri. Nearby young Tamil women were filling golden pots, full and round like their uncovered breasts, and passersby were asking them for directions though they knew the way well enough, just to strike up a conversation. He followed them onto the island of Srirangam. Passing through Brahmin neighborhoods where the sounds of Vedic chanting and philosophical exposition pleased the ear, he saw before him, on the outer walls, millions of rubies burning like eternal lamps, shattering darkness inside and out. He looked up at the entrance tower with its massive dovecots in many stories and listened to the cooing of the doves mingling in with the jingle of anklets and bracelets from the dancing girls coming and going. He passed through the first enclosure of the temple after worshiping Garuda and other gods. Next he went deeper into the Srirangam shrine.

"Ranga-nayaka Vishnu lay before him in his golden dhoti, the *kaustubha* gem on his breast. His eyes were wider than any lotus. Fragrant musk marked his forehead. The first sounds in the world were sandals on his feet. He lay on a cool, fragrant bed. He was darker than sapphire. The goddess was carried away by his beauty. He wore earrings in the shape of crocodiles and a

22. All Indian rivers, with the exception of the Brahmaputra, are perceived as feminine.

jeweled crown. Manikandhara gazed at the god and threw himself to the ground. 'Each separate part of him steals my eyes and claims them for itself—his crown, camphor mark, the smiling face, necklaces, garland, the gem on his chest, conch, wheel, his deep navel, his anklets and armlets.

He is my family deity. I rest my thoughts
on his feet.
He's my friend, close to me as my breath.
I set my mind on the center of his breathing.
I focus on his hands, that broke the necks
of many demons.
I raise my thoughts to his chest, that enhances
the beauty of Lakshmi's breasts.
I give myself to his face, that lightens the load
of my heart.'

"He composed verses like this one on the spot and sang them to the god.

"Afterward, he headed east. He came to Kumbhakonam, a place that churns the ego out of mind. In its moonlight pavilions, the eyes of tipsy courtesans roll like fish in the bend of the godly river that flows beside great white palaces. The entrance towers to its temples are so radiant that they wash away the turbid darkness of empty space. In a shrine made of rubies, on a mattress of cool air, his feet stretched out on Lakshmi's breasts—firm and silky like little pillows—his head resting on one arm, another arm resting on his waist covered with gold, and the other pair of hands holding the conch and wheel, Sarngapani-Vishnu delights everyone by his presence.

"Manikandhara moved on to the temple of the Lord of the Pot,[23] and from there to Darbhasayana, where he worshiped Lord Rama and sang for him, the vina following his voice:

You're the fruit of King Dasaratha's prayers.
You killed Tataka with a well-aimed arrow.
You killed that mischievous Subahu and saved Visvamitra's sacrifice.
With the dust of your feet, you washed away the lapse of Gautama's wife.[24]

23. Kumbhesvara, Siva in Kumbhakonam.
24. Ahalya.

You broke Siva's bow like breaking a piece of sugarcane.
You were happy inside when you married the Earth's daughter.
Your arms, thick as snakes, sucked out the pride of Parasurama.
Obedient to your father's word, you shook off the kingdom.
You blessed Guha, who worshiped your feet all his life.
You left Bharata the kind gift of your sandals.
You did away with the disasters that came from Viradha's arrogance.
You stayed with the sages in their tranquil space.
You made a demoness[25] ugly to please your wife.
You made the sages happy by destroying Khara and other demons.
You took away the life-breath of the tricky demon in the form of a deer.[26]
You pounded Kabandha with his fierce arms into a ball of flesh.
You savored the taste of the fruits that Sabari offered.
You killed angry Valin[27] and made friends with his brother, Sugriva.
You gave refuge to the enemy's brother[28] when he sought you out.
With your fiery eyes, you humbled the ocean.
Easily, you built a bridge out of mountains across the ocean.
You chopped off all of Ravana's heads in one great blow.
Brahmins praise you, and you cut the bonds that bind them to this world.
Your eyes flow with compassion. Your body thrills Sita.
Your name is fit to be chanted by Yogis. Those who serve you fulfill their wishes.
Your fame is ever white. You are home to all worlds.
You are a terror to your enemies but care tirelessly for the distressed.
Take care of me, too, Ramabhadra.

'When all the texts tell us that your name is the truth that gives freedom, can I add anything at all by my praise, Rama, son of Dasaratha?'

"From there he went south to Ramesvaram, the bridge Rama built to Lanka.

25. Surpanakha, who fell in love with Rama and was disfigured by Lakshmana. The compound *tata-niśācarī-virūpatā-kṛta-priyā-vinoda* is somewhat ambiguous; it could also mean that Rama plays with the woman he loves by making her (here: the demoness) ugly.
26. Marica, Ravana's uncle.
27. King of the monkeys.
28. Vibhisana.

After worshiping, he went on to Ananta-sayana[29] to serve Padma-nabha, the god with the lotus growing from his navel. He sang to him for some days.

"As for me," Manisthambha continued, "I was listening to his music wherever he was singing and watching him from afar. That's how I know his whole story. From Ananta Padma-nabha's place, he went to a small forest just to the west, whose brilliant fruits and flowers rivaled the ornaments worn by the god nearby. He began a harsh discipline, concentrating on Vishnu. Because of that, I can no longer enjoy the pure sweetness of his music."

And Manistambha turned in that direction, stared, and said, "Look! He's sitting there riveted in the lotus posture, in fierce concentration."

Kalabhashini was amazed. "Can you really see him from here? Can you see what he's doing?"

"If you doubt it, just send your friends far away. I'll tell you everything they are doing."

"Mahatma, who am I to test you? Did I ever doubt your words?"

"There's nothing wrong with testing. Don't worry. It's even fun."

And he forced her to send two of her friends some distance away. After he had reported to her everything they did and said, thus proving his point, he said, "Dear girl, in exactly the same way, I described to you Manikandhara's entire pilgrimage and his discipline. Your mind should now be at ease. But if you still have some question about the comparative distances, since Manikandhara is so far away and your friends didn't go too far, there's no way I can resolve it for you."

At that moment, a parrot who happened to be perched on a nearby tree began to speak. "Sir! No one should doubt your words. In fact, I'm here to verify independently everything you have said."

Kalabhashini looked at the parrot in amazement. "How can you verify that? Who are you? Where do you come from? You seem to be a very intelligent bird."

The bird spoke. "I used to live in the Nandana Forest.[30] At the time that Krishna stole the Parijata Tree,[31] the birds who were living in it all flew

29. Trivandrum in Kerala.
30. In Indra's heaven.
31. Krishna had offended his wife Satyabhama by giving her rival, Rukmini, a single flower from the Parijata tree in the Nandana Forest of heaven. To prove his love for Satyabhama, he promised her that he would bring her the whole tree, which he had to steal from Indra, king of the gods.

away. But my wife was about to give birth and couldn't leave. 'Whatever happens, I'm staying here,' she announced, lying low in a hollow of that tree. Afterward, I couldn't budge her until the children had grown their wings. Every time I tried to persuade her to go with me, she would say, 'This garden[32] is much nicer than Nandana Forest. I can't understand why you can't get rid of your attachment to that place.'

"I would say, 'What you say is true, but all our relatives are there. I can't cut my ties completely.' So I started commuting between here and heaven. A little while ago, I was flying on this route when I heard someone mention Manikandhara's name. I wondered who was talking about Manikandhara here, so I waited to overhear your conversation. Now I can confirm the whole story that this Siddha has told you about the pilgrimage and discipline, and I can add the rest, too.

"Recently, Saci and Indra came to Nandana Forest, while I was watching. A spy arrived and informed Indra, 'Lord! Some time ago a certain man came to the forest where I've been living and began a series of austere practices. I waited a while to see how serious he was. The more I watch him, the greater the intensity that I see. That's why I came here to tell you. He's been to all the great sites of power—Kasi, Gaya, Prayaga, Puri, Ahobalam. He himself told me when I asked. Now his red matted hair is on fire from the inner heat that he has generated by immersing himself day after day in freezing water. In eight months this discipline will bear fruit. You posted me to this wilderness to inform you if anyone comes there for such practices.'[33]

"Indra remembered. 'Yes. I did station you there for this purpose.' He sent off the spy and ordered Rambha, the accomplished courtesan, to come to him. When she appeared, he described to her everything that he had heard from his spy about this new man and his practices.

"'My beautiful girl! If this fellow is up to such severely demanding acts, generating so much heat, it must be because he wants to take over my throne in heaven. We have to think of some countermeasure and carry it out, leaving nothing to chance. If we delay now or ignore him, you can't tell

32. In Dvaraka, where Krishna transplanted the Parijata tree, and where Kalabhashini is now speaking with Manistambha.
33. Ascetics who perform such charged acts of self-discipline become Indras—kings of the gods—themselves. For this reason, Indra is always seeking intelligence about such potential threats in order to adopt countermeasures.

what will happen. A fingernail's worth of delay causes a mountain's worth of loss. We know that. You courtesans are very helpful in such matters. I suspect that you're the most effective weapon of all.

"'Weave a net around him with your intriguing glances. Snare him with your smiles. Hook him with your tapering eyebrows. Muzzle his mouth with the mantra of your honeyed words. Go there, siphon off the power he's been building. He's like a tiger now. Turn him into a pet for the Love-God.'

"Rambha listened carefully. 'I wonder if you know who this man is. I hear that he's Manikandhara, Narada's disciple. I've observed him before. He never took a second look at people like me. Now he's deep into his discipline. I can't promise you that I can carry out this mission.'

"Indra looked at her. 'I'm issuing you more youthful beauty and charms than ever before. Don't doubt yourself. You can do it.'

With these reassuring words he sent her off. Truth to tell, she was excited by the challenge. Her body glowing with jewels, she went down to earth along with her companions, brightening the pathway from heaven in their splendor.

"So now," the parrot continued, "you can see that what Manistambha told you is entirely correct. At that point, I left Nandana Forest and came here. By my calculation, Rambha and her friends should be reaching Manikandhara's place any minute."

Kalabhashini was fascinated by this parrot. "I don't want to let you go," she said, "but of course you have to visit your wife. I can see why the great sage Parrot—known as Suka, Vyasa's son—took your name. He's present everywhere. He's the one who knows all the Vedas. With your yellow-green wings, you remind us of Lord Hari, whose name means 'yellow-green.' You can naturally fly up to his world. So it's no surprise that your words are so charming."

*Keep on listening to my story, King Krishna. You delight in meditation on Sri Krishna. Like the Snake, the Boar, the Tortoise, and the Elephants, your arms hold the earth. Women adore you. Brahmins rely on you. You thirst for knowledge and wisdom. You are strong as the great Bhima. May all good things be yours.*

This is the second chapter in the long poem called *Kalapurnodayamu* made by soft-spoken Suraya, son of Pingali Amaranarya, whose poetry all connoisseurs enjoy throughout the world.

# CHAPTER 3

*Listen, son of Narasimha, new god of love. The goddess of wealth looks at you out of the corners of her eyes. You are the source of all right living, and ever attentive.*

The Siddha, Manistambha, said to Kalabhashini, "Woman of intoxicating gaze, I came here to listen to your music, to feast my ears on a new kind of beauty. Please, pick up your vina and sing a little." So she did. She passed the day singing for him.

## [ Rambha Entices Manikandhara ]

While Kalabhashini was entertaining Manistambha, Rambha and her friends landed in the wooded area where Manikandhara was sitting. They looked like streaks of lightning that had quarreled with the rainclouds and come down to earth, while their hair could have been those same dark clouds that, unable to bear this separation, followed after the lightning. Their light-red hands and feet seemed like a sunset out of time, and their fingernails glistened like stars. Their faces created the illusion of multiple moons. Anybody who saw them was dumbfounded.

Their eyes blue as lilies, they came down to the forest, which rose like a goddess to welcome them. The pollen of its flowers was Rambha's yellow sari, dark bees were her long, tremulous hair, and the bird-cries were the jingling of her ornaments. Or, to put it differently, these women blended into the grove, their dark hair merging with the bees, their bodies with the vines, their breasts with burgeoning flowers, their delicate fingers with tender buds, their smiles with everything that blossomed. As they moved among the trees, these women became part of the forest, like water flowing into milk.

All was in harmony. Tigresses lay with eyes half-closed, like cows, while deer suckled at their breasts. Lions watched the deer playing while they went on scratching the elephants' backs. Snakes were swaying to the song of bees that hovered over elephants' temples, while mongooses were entertaining them. Rats clung to the side of snakes, and cats took care of the rats. Parrots were conversing with the sages who were at home in this forest, contemplating God. The women from heaven were amazed.

They saw Manikandhara, like purity personified, like all goodness in one place, like serenity made visible or seriousness made solid or truth poured into a grain bin, like a heap of dispassion, like Yoga with hands and feet, wisdom congealed in a ball. The women cupped their hands to their foreheads, bending toward his feet, and as they did so their black curls were caught between their fingers like dark bees trapped in a lotus that was folding its petals at the touch of the moonbeams coming from his crescent-like toenails. When they saw his fierce, unwavering stare—for he was deep in meditation—they retreated a little, out of fear.

Rambha, too, was afraid. "Just looking at this fierce man scares me. My whole body is trembling. How can I do this job for Indra? I took on the mission without thinking it through." The fluttering of her eyelids seemed to have shifted to her mind.

She composed herself, remembering the gravity of Indra's command. Coming a little closer, she began playing garden games with her friends. Free of fear, they chased one another around the trees and bushes, sprinkled by the honey dripping from the flowers. They swung on branches, clustered around whoever was picking a bunch, humming and singing like the Love-God's lyre. They were singing Vasanta and Hindola *ragas* as their jewels and bracelets jingled seductively. They played at words: "You tender girl, attend to this branch. Why run away? He won't bite." "Why fight over this single flower? If you want to play, there are plenty of others."

And so on. Meanwhile, Rambha closed in on Manikandhara. She was all curves and smiles. She walked, her hips swaying, her hair flying loose, the bodice slipping off her breastline, necklaces dangling. They were very beautiful breasts.

As fate would have it, just at that moment Manikandhara was coming out of his meditation. He opened his eyes just wide enough to catch a glimpse of her, but that glimpse was enough to disturb him. He closed his eyes tightly again and tried to think of God. But those eyes that had seen what they had seen wouldn't stay shut. He couldn't help it. He opened them a crack. Called out to Krishna. Closed them again. Opened them again. Closed them. Desire and control were fighting it out in his mind.

God solved it in accordance with the way things had to unfold. Desire won. The Love-God propelled Manikandhara's mind toward the woman. He cut through the thick iron chains of this Yogi's determination with the sharp edge of a flower.

Manikandhara's heart was burning in the Love-God's flames, so he tried to cool himself in Rambha's fluid beauty, like jumping into a lake. Once inside, he swam in delight and had no wish to get out.

He couldn't take his eyes off her. "Is this Rambha? I never thought she was so beautiful. I've never seen anything like it." He was driven by an urge to speak to her, touch her, embrace. He started fantasizing in his mind. "The *campaka* tree must have studied her nose in order to create its flowers.[1] The *kuruvaka* tree first blossoms in her embrace.[2] I wish I were that lucky. She kicked this tree with her ankleted foot, and now it's flowering—so it must be an *asoka*. Her touch brought the mango to life. What good fortune. The *prenkana* bush blossoms when she sings to it, as the *vavili* does when she sniffs it. You trees respond to every move of hers. It's not for nothing that poets compare you to men.

"It's very clear that sweetness flows from her words, and here's the proof: the *gogu* flowers that unfold their petals as she speaks are dripping honey.

"Rather than going to heaven alone, without this woman, it would be better to become a tree in the forest where she plays.

1. The *campaka* flower is traditionally compared to a woman's nose.
2. The *kuruvaka* tree is said to blossom when a beautiful woman embraces it, as the *aśoka* does when kicked by a woman, and so on. See D. Shulman, *The Wisdom of Poets* (Delhi: Oxford University Press, 2001), 163.

"People may laugh at me for abandoning my life of meditation—let them laugh! If all the power I've acquired by my harsh discipline is wasted—let it go! Let all the clarity of understanding that I've achieved become clouded. I *have* to make love to her."

He cast off all his doubts. With a certain boldness, he went over to where she was playing. He asked, "Where are you from, and what are you doing here with your friends? Can I have the pleasure of hearing your voice?"

"I just came here to play."

"That's not true. You came here because I meditated on you."

She smiled slightly and bent her head. He could see that she agreed, so the earnest sage at once pulled at her sari.

"Some gentleman you are," she said. "There are other people around." She struggled a little. She pulled her sari and his hand close to her breasts.

The women nearby, who were pretending to be busy plucking flowers, moved away, winking at one another. "We got him. What man could possibly resist Rambha's allure?"

He was quivering with desire as he embraced her, pressing cheek to cheek. Twining his feet with hers, he gently maneuvered her into a secluded clearing hidden by thick flowering bushes. A thick carpet of petals—fallen to the ground because of the male bees fighting one another over the flowers—provided a soft bed, never before touched. He flung himself on her, weaving and twining himself into her without control, eager to get everything he could, squeezing her breasts and clawing at her everywhere, biting her lips in his vast hunger that had now been released. Seeing this masterful sage so suddenly engulfed by passion, she smiled and responded. "They say, and today it seems to be true, that when a gentle animal gets excited, you can't keep it within bounds."

## [ Kalabhashini Flies off with the Siddha ]

At this moment, in Dvaraka, the Siddha who was listening to Kalabhashini singing brought up Manikandhara again. She asked him, "Tell me how Manikandhara's self-control is holding up, now that Rambha has gone there under orders from Indra. Please have a look."

He used his telescopic vision and said with a smile, "What self-control? He's busy in her arms, right there in the forest."

She was again stunned by Manistambha's ability to see so far. She praised him over and over and invited him to stay in her house for a few days as her guest. He said, "I came here because I was in love with your music. I'm no garden-variety Siddha, the sort that goes around showing his powers. I will accept your offer if you can keep my presence here secret."

"Fine," she said, and kept him hidden in her garden for two or three days, wining and dining him. She wouldn't let anyone else come in. She made him very happy. But her true wish was to find a way to make love to Nalakubara, so after a while she turned the conversation back to Manikandhara, in the hope of finding out more about Rambha.

"I'm surprised that Manikandhara allowed his discipline to be disturbed. Tell me, though—has he resumed his self-control? Or is he still with that woman? I need to know."

He had another look in the direction of the sage. "No question of self-control any more. Now our great ascetic is living in her embrace."

"Are they going to stay in that place for some time, or are they thinking of going somewhere else? Please look again. I hope I'm not embarrassing you with these repeated requests, but I really must know."

"I'm not embarrassed. I'll take a look as many times as you want me to. A rock is not ticklish. I'm in full control."

Again he turned his gaze in the direction of Manikandhara and cupped his ear, listening intently, signaling with the other hand to Kalabhashini to keep quiet. After a while he said, "This is what you get out of a whore." He laughed.

"Tell me what you saw," she said.

"What can I say? I can't stop laughing. She already ruined his discipline. Now listen to what she did to his happiness. She got him totally infatuated with her and then, at the height of his lovemaking, she called out, 'Hey Nalakubara! Enough. I'm exhausted.' So naturally, Manikandhara's heart sank."

The Siddha was laughing.

"Why are you laughing?" said Kalabhashini. "What else can she do? Nalakubara probably is a superb lover. He drives her crazy. I wonder where he is now? Somewhere far away? Turn your gaze toward him."

The Siddha laughed again. "This is what you really want, isn't it?" He turned his eyes this way and that, zeroing in on Nalakubara. "If he follows her everywhere, she'll be distracted by his presence and won't be able to do her work, which is to seduce sages. Indra won't stand for it; it makes him angry. So Nalakubara doesn't go with her on business trips. On the other hand, he can't not go. He can't stand the separation. So at the moment he's near that forest. He's waiting in a mango grove under a flowering tree.

"Well, I think I'll be off. Your mind is on him, and you can't sing for me at the moment. Anyway, there's nothing else for me to do here. So I'll take my leave."

Kalabhashini was alarmed. "Mahatma! You are my good-luck god. I relied on you. If you leave me, what will happen to my life?"

"What are you saying? I'll come from time to time."

"Sure. Definitely. No doubt you'll be back. Just listen to what I want you to do. Bring me to him this very minute, somehow or other. There's no other way, if you want to help me. Women are notoriously impatient. What's more, no one but you can do this. Only you have the power, and you seem to care for me."

"Listen, woman. If I had the power to take you to him, would I hide it from you? I shouldn't even mention it in so many words, but you don't know how hungry I am for your singing. I know that if I bring you to the man you love, you'll sing again. But just think: Nalakubara is in Kerala, near the temple of the god Padmanabha, resting on his snake. How can someone here in Dvaraka get there in one day?

But then, come to think of it, my teachers trained the lion I ride on. It can go there in a couple of hours. We don't even have to concern ourselves with the cost. But if I seat you on the back, what will other Siddhas think of me? Besides, it's completely inappropriate for people like me even to touch someone like you. Still, there's no other solution. My telescopic sight and hearing won't help us here. Tell me what you want me to do."

"Great Siddha! What difference does it make how you take me there? Who cares if idiots who don't know your power talk about you? Those who know you won't think badly of you. You say it's inappropriate for you to touch someone like me, but is it acceptable for you to watch me die? Enough said. Soon my friends will turn up, and everything will be ruined. So just seat me on that lion behind you and take me quickly to the man I'm in love with."

The Siddha saddled his lion with a tiger skin, tied with a snake-skin girth; he attached stirrups of gold (that he had converted from base metal), strings of conch, a bridle made from the magic vine that gives control to a rider. With a sword hanging in a bear-skin sheath on his side, he mounted this elephant-eating vehicle. "Can you get on behind me, and stay on, without touching me?" he asked. "Grab hold of that handle."

"With your kindness, I can do it."

He made the lion crouch a bit so she could climb on.

"I trust you're taking me via a route where nobody can see us," she said.

"Don't worry. If the bullocks and the cart work together, you can climb any hill."

He spurred the lion, crying "Dhe!" As the lion picked up speed, he looked back a few times at Kalabhashini and called to her, "Hold on tight!" For liftoff, he chose a route hidden by the trees growing on the walls around the houses and the thick shrubs filled with burning incense meant to make them blossom in time. Using them as cover, he managed to fly away unseen. Soon, to his surprise, he saw a line of very beautiful women emerging from behind a massive cloud. They were singing with great skill and sweetness. Their song was like a gentle fragrant shower sprinkling their silk shawls. It was a joy to see them. They were also chattering with one another, and listening to them, Manistambha realized that they were Rambha's friends. He said to them, "What are you doing here? Where is Rambha? Did she decide to stay with Manikandhara for a few more days in the forest? Is she so in love with him that she can't leave?"

They laughed. "What Manikandhara? We don't even know where he is. Rambha is happily lying in Nalakubara's arms, playing new love-games. We saw that she was overjoyed to be reunited with her true lover and that she is totally absorbed in making love to him, so we didn't have the heart to ask her to come with us. We're going home."

They went their way, giggling to one another, "This gentleman can ride a play lion through the sky, but look at what he's wearing—those ugly vines and rags and skins and matted hair. Where did this crazy Yogi find such a beautiful girl? If she were to go to heaven for even a minute, she'd immediately enslave all the young gods."

## [ The Temple of the Lion-Riding Goddess ]

The news that Nalakubara and Rambha were back together had a depressing effect on Kalabhashini, as Manistambha saw at once. He smiled at her. "Don't be sad. Compose yourself. All your worries will end in a few minutes. Believe me." She brightened a little.

"How can you say this so confidently?"

"You'll see shortly. Why ask how the curry tastes when you're about to start eating?"

Suddenly, the lion stopped, stretching its neck upward, as if its way was blocked. Until now it had been flying smoothly.

The Siddha struck it again and again with his whip and yelled "Hum!" He dug his heels into its sides to spur it forward. He held the bridle firmly in his hand so that the lion wouldn't move its head right or left and hit its head with his snake-shaped cane so that it wouldn't move upward. He made a huge effort, but no matter what he did, the lion wouldn't budge an inch. Instead, it gave a terrible roar and, twisting its tail, stepped backward.

Kalabhashini almost slipped off. "What's going on?" she screamed, breaking out in a sweat. Her hair came undone, and the sash of her sari covering her breasts fell off. She lost her seat, but held on to the wooden handle with both hands.

The Siddha realized why they were stuck. "Don't panic," he said to her. "Hold on tight to that handle. It's my mistake. I was lost in conversation, so I forgot." He turned the lion around and brought it down for a landing. Dismounting, he asked Kalabhashini to follow him. Sending the lion off to graze, he said, "Near here there is a temple of the goddess known as Mrigendra-vahana, Lion-Rider. There's a lion standing in front of the shrine. No other lion, no matter how powerful, can cross this area, up, down, left or right, without paying its respects. I completely forgot. That's why our lion was heading straight here, though I tried to urge it forward. We should also worship the goddess, and then we'll succeed. Come with me."

Taking his sword in the bear-skin sheath, he set down the lion's saddle in a safe place and guided the girl to the temple, where he asked her to wait on the front porch. "I'll be right back," he said, "with flowers for our worship."

As she waited, Kalabhashini caught sight of an old lady. White hair, like a bundle of dried-out hay. Wrinkled eyebrows like cobwebs intertwined. Folds of skin like a cracked veneer of gold paint. Arms and sagging breasts like broken-off branches still hanging by a thread to the tree. She was wheezing and hooting like an owl as she struggled forward, like a deserted palace once home to desire.

She came close to Kalabhashini. "Where have you come from, my girl? How were you trapped by this man, like a parrot by a wildcat? Did you think he was a Siddha? I saw you from a distance. How beautiful you are! Your loveliness lights up the forest. I'm worried that you—the whole purpose of creation—have fallen into the hands of this merciless man. Run away quickly, before this treacherous fellow comes back. I can't bear to watch your splendid body fall victim to the sword.

"If I had even a little time, I'd love to ask you your name, your story, and all that. But I'd much prefer that you get away before he comes. You might wonder why I'm being so harsh right away, without even asking if he happens to be your benefactor, your father, a beloved brother, or if he's taking you somewhere you want to go. But I know this man. I've seen his ways. He makes me crazy."

Kalabhashini listened and took it in. "If I think it over, this old woman's words ring true. This Siddha is a con man. Now I understand what he meant when he said, just now, that all my worries would end in a few minutes. He's going to sacrifice me to the goddess. There's no doubt. If you think about it, there's no escaping what Brahma wrote on your forehead at birth. I was born in the city of Krishna, who is known to save us from misfortune. I'm a courtesan. But cultured people still invite me to their company. Narada himself, the greatest sage in all three worlds, treats me no differently than any other disciple. I studied music from God's wife and Indra's wife. And here I am about to be the sacrificial animal in a rite performed by that pseudo-Siddha."

In her unhappiness, she began to regret having escaped from her friends. "You can't cut yourself lose from what you are fated to suffer through—except by suffering through it." Still, she steadied herself and, controlling the shakiness in her voice, asked the old woman, "Mother, what you say appears to be true. I had no idea who this con man really was. I thought he would help me to achieve a certain thing I wanted, so rather desperately I came with him. Now there's no way out. Where can I run to? He's too fast for me. And he has telescopic vision. He'll see me wherever I hide."

"Oh, so you know he can see into the distance?"

"That's how he fooled me and brought me here." She told the old woman her entire story, beginning with his turning up in her garden, right up to the end. In the course of it she also told her name, her family, her training, and her overriding passion. "I had no other thought except to fulfill this desire. You go out to graze and fall into a lethal trap."

"It's all true. He tricked you into coming here, for his own purposes. He can't accomplish what he wants, even after attaining the gift of distant sight and hearing, unless he has a human being. Many times I've heard him say, 'After all the trouble I took to acquire these skills, it would be nice to have a kingdom to rule.' For this purpose he's been searching all over for a woman from the courtesan class of surpassing beauty and superb musical talent. He's always plucking the strings of his lute, and with his ability to hear what is far away and his connoisseur's knowledge, he looks for music from all over the world."

"Was it here that he acquired the ability to see and hear from a distance? How many people did he behead to get those powers? Do you know? Tell me that story, to pass the time. Nobody can avert what's going to happen, good or evil. Why should I worry about what he'll do to me when he comes, or about how I am to die? The goddess will take care of it."

"You're a very intelligent and courageous woman. I'll tell you. Even though the methods of acquiring those powers are terrible, they don't involve killing others. They only require a certain fearlessness. He had to tear out his eyes with a sharp pincer and pierce his ears with a needle. Both these tools are hanging from a pillar near the lion in front of the temple, on which some letters are carved. You may also notice a knife covered with flowers and sandalpaste and a head-chopper, which people use on themselves." The old lady took her by the hand and pointed them out. "They wrote on this pillar what you need to do for each particular wish. Read it, if you know that script."

Kalabhashini read off the text.

*Control your senses and chant the mantra of the goddess Bhuvanesvari for two full years: she will fulfill all your wishes. For instant results, to see far, pull out your eyes with this pincer. To hear from far, pierce your ears with this needle. To become a poet, cut off your tongue with this knife. The great Sakti will be pleased and will give results. If you are tough enough to cut off your head with this chopper, it will again stick to your neck and you will live to kill whoever tries to kill you. You will be king, free from enemies, ruling a vast country, if you sacrifice a courtesan of perfect beauty who can sing to perfection.*

She read it and knew without doubt that she would be killed. She began to shake but gained control over herself and read on.

*Old people who cannot bring themselves to perform these acts will become young again if they die fearlessly before this goddess, in any other way, and their dying wish will be fulfilled from that moment on.*

When the old woman heard her read out the last part of the inscription, she smiled and said, "That's why I'm here. They call me Sumukhasatti. I'm the daughter of the Brahmin priest who serves the goddess of learning in the famous center in Kashmir."

At this point the Siddha returned with incense and garlands for the goddess. When he saw the old woman, he said to her, "How are you, granny? You've been here for a long time in this lonely shrine of the goddess. How do you spend the days?" Then, turning to Kalabhashini: "We have a long ways to go, my dear. It's getting late. Let's worship the goddess and move on. Take leave of this woman."

Kalabhashini was scared. She turned to the old woman. "I'm afraid of going in alone. Won't you come with me?"

The Siddha said, "I'm here. Why do you need anybody else?"

Then he realized the reason for her fear: the old hag must have told her something. But any delay might ruin it all. In haste he said, "Don't be a fool. This woman can't help you." And with that he grabbed hold of her hair and started to drag her into the temple.

She was scared to death. "Help!" she cried, trying to hide behind the old woman. "I'm your daughter. Save me!"

Overcome by pity, the old lady tried to shield Kalabhashini while holding on to the Siddha's hands, begging him not to hurt her.

"So what if you keep her out of the temple?" he said. "Even this spot is good enough. It's directly in front of the goddess." He twisted the old woman's hands and pushed her away. Holding Kalabhashini's long braid in one hand and unsheathing his sword with the other, he cried to the goddess, "Here's your offering." Raising the hand with the sword, he bowed to the Sakti and was about to cut off Kalabhashini's head when the old woman yelled, "In the name of the goddess, I tell you: Don't kill her!" and stretched out her neck in the path of the sword.

She held fast to Kalabhashini with both arms, protecting her from the blow. She wouldn't budge. "You won't get away with this," she cried to the Siddha. "I've sworn an oath on the goddess." And to the goddess she pleaded, "Great Sakti! Make my words come true."

He was so angry that he cut off the old woman's head. In a frenzy he lifted the sword to strike again at Kalabhashini's head, once again grabbing at her hair, when the goddess froze his hand and angrily hurled him a long ways away. That's what happens when you act against an oath sworn before a goddess.

Meanwhile, at the touch of the sword, Sumukhasatti's aged body fell away. Suddenly,

> her face had the brilliance of the moon, and her hair
> was dark as dark can be. Long eyes,
> cheeks soft and shining, breasts taut and full,
> delicate arms, a tremulous waist, all new
> pubic hair, a ravishing behind like golden sands
> emerging from her sari: the enchantment
> was complete.

She was young again. She raised her eyes—now luminous as open lotus petals—and saw the Siddha flying through the sky under the impact of the blow from the goddess, one hand still clutching Kalabhashini's hair and the other holding his sword. At first she didn't waste time thinking about her restored youth, which she had wanted for so long; she was worried about Kalabhashini. Gradually, however, she stopped grieving, as she contemplated the impermanence of life. She voluntarily gave up all sensual desire. Not wanting to waste her newly acquired youthful energy, she decided to spend her time in the discipline of Yoga. She began to practise the self-control that Yoga demands along with various bodily postures and exercises. Her texts were what she'd picked up orally before, and for a guru she had the goddess herself.

## [ Kalabhashini Returns ]

One day Kalabhashini returned and, seeing this young woman, asked, "Who are you? Where are you from?" The woman said, "I'm the same Sumukhasatti, the old woman who stuck her neck out for you and was killed by the Siddha. The goddess gave me this young body and a new life. But tell me, Kalabhashini: When the goddess hurled you and the Siddha far away, where did you land? It's amazing you weren't hurt."

"What's more surprising is how you became young. What's so shocking in my return, when I had your kindness to support me? I'll tell you my story."

As Kalabhashini was about to begin, Manikandhara turned up. He had the vina on his shoulder and gems in his long hair that imparted dignity to his presence. Astonished, Kalabhashini bowed to him, but he was no less astonished. "When I see you, my dear friend, I feel as if all my relatives had gathered here," he said. "Do you ever think of me? How did you come here? You never even wanted to leave Dvaraka. You never went anywhere. Is everything safe at home—your friends, your house, and all the precious things around you? Have you seen Lord Krishna recently? Does he still hold court in the diamond hall like in those days? Does he ask you to sing for him? Did they ever finish building the diamond entranceway that Indra wanted to present to Krishna? Do you ever go to those deep blue porches where our vinas seemed to be swallowed up in the darkness? What about that golden gymnasium they were getting ready for Krishna's sons, since the old one was too small? Is it still there?

"Remember that time you took me to see that new gambling house. We thought none of Krishna's women would be there, so I went in and came right out, because I heard people talking—"Doubles! Twelve! Jackpot!"—but as it turned out, it was only the parrots chattering.

"And that time I happened upon a wall made of crystal. I had no idea that the court was in session. I saw Krishna's image clearly in front of me, so I thought it was Krishna and bowed, when a hundred voices behind me called out in amusement, 'Turn around. He's over here!' Is that wall still there?"

She answered, "Everything is just as beautiful as it used to be. Even Indra's entranceway has been completed."

"Do you ever think of me when you're discussing music? Did you ever sing for anyone the *daṇḍaka* song I composed for Krishna? Has Narada been coming to visit Krishna as he used to? Whatever happened to that vina that Krishna's wives chose for you? You don't have it here, do you? I heard that you had a certain desire in your mind.[3] I hope you haven't given up vina because you were so engrossed in that thought."

She was a little embarrassed and bent her head. "What can I say? It's because of that that I left all my friends behind and came to this godforsaken land."

She told him everything that had happened from the time she completed her musical education: how Manistambha came to her garden, how he used his distant vision and hearing to impress her, how he took her to the temple of the Lion-Rider, how he attempted to sacrifice her there and how Sumukhasatti saved her. "This is that very woman," she said. "Now tell me

3. Manikandhara may know this from the initial encounter between Kalabhashini and Narada in the garden, when Manikandhara was also present.

about you. I've already told you what Manistambha told me—about your affair with Rambha, and how your discipline was ruined. What did you do after that?"

At this point Manistambha himself turned up. "This is the Siddha who tried to kill me!" she said, pointing at him.

"Him?" asked Manikandhara, smiling, welcoming him respectfully.

Manistambha was quite amazed to find Manikandhara there. "How did *you* get here?" he asked politely. Then he looked at Kalabhashini. "I've been looking for you everywhere," he said. "I was surprised that I couldn't find you. Where have you been, and how did you come here?" He turned to Sumukhasatti. "Who are you? Where are you from?"

He heard her story from her. Astonished, he bowed to her. She was also shocked at his presence. "Siddha—where did you land when the goddess cast you away with Kalabhashini? How did you both come back without being hurt? Tell me all."

Manistambha replied to Sumukhasatti, "I'll tell you—that and even more remarkable things. I've been dying to tell the story to someone, and I might as well tell you, since you clearly deserve to know. After I had chopped off your head, still blind with conceit and heedless of the oath you had sworn on the goddess, I lifted my sword to strike at Kalabhashini, whom I was holding by the hair. The goddess caught my hand and threw me far into the air. I was still holding fast to Kalabhashini."

Sumukhasatti said, "You don't have to tell me that. I saw up to that point in this new body of mine. I saw you flying through the air, still holding her hair with a tight fist and your sword in the other hand. Tell me what happened after that."

"It was like being hurled from a sling.[4] We came down in the forest where Manikandhara was working on self-control. This woman and I fell on a soft bed of leaves. Through the kindness of the goddess, we did not die.

"Kalabhashini was still trembling from fear. She could see that I was still holding on to the sword and to her hair. I looked at her and was aroused by her beauty—her face pale as the moon dipped in honey, her long eyes wide with terror, a few strands of hair sticking to her cheeks that were wet with sweat, her breasts heaving, shaking off her bodice. Terror

4. Reading *dañcanamuna*, following Bommakanti Singaracarya and Balantrapu Nalinikanta Ravu, *Kaḷāpūrṇodayamu* (Madras: Emesco, 1997] and the v.l. listed in the Vavilla edition.

had intensified her allure. She was irresistible. In shock. And I had won her as my prize.

"I threw myself on her. I confess. She screamed. 'Help! Help! This hooligan is attacking me. Isn't there anybody around?'

"Her yelling was unbearable.

"A voice was heard. 'Don't be afraid. I'm coming now. Help is here. Who is attacking a woman? Whoever you are, I'll get you. You won't escape. I'll pluck your head off your shoulders.' It was Nalakubara, very angry, emerging from the bushes. I was so scared that I left her there and ran away. He, however, chased me and caught me.

" 'Who are you? Who is that woman you're attacking? You can't get away with such things in my presence. Show her to me. Afterward I'll see to your punishment.' He was already dragging me back to that place.

"Meanwhile, Rambha appeared, tracing the same path. With one hand she was fixing her hair that had come undone. With the other she was wrapping the end of her sari around her breasts and shoulders and trying to knot it at her waist. Some hairs had fallen over her forehead; she was tucking them back into the parting. She kept raising a shoulder to hold back the flowers slipping off her ears. A little worried, she was also feeling for the blades of grass that stuck to her body; someone might think they were nailmarks.

"She said, 'Some hero you are. You come with empty hands, no weapon, no nothing. I had to wear myself out looking for you. I just love your style, my dear.'

"Then she looked at me," Manistambha went on to say. " 'So this is the great man who tried to molest that woman, whoever she is? Desire can reduce a man to anything. There's no controlling it. But where did that girl disappear to?'

" 'That's exactly why I dragged this fellow here, to show us,' said Nalakubara, still twisting my hand. She took pity on me.

" 'Where can he run away to now? Why don't you release your grip on him?'

"She got her lover to release me, and I led them in search of Kalabhashini to the bed of leaves that we'd landed on. This woman, however, wasn't there.

"Nalakubara said dryly, 'But this is where you and I were sleeping, isn't it? This supercharged Siddha deserves a high-voltage bed.'

"Then Nalakubara saw my sword lying there and picked it up with a sardonic smile. 'This man is no Yogi. He's a soldier if I ever saw one.'

" 'Some soldier!' said Rambha. 'He leaves his sword behind and runs away.'

"Nalakubara turned to me, sternly. 'What did you do to that woman? Where is she?' he asked, insistent. He was pressing me, very angrily, but Rambha said, 'Why waste time on him? Let him go. When he ran away from her, she must have found some place to hide. How can he show her to us? We'll search for her ourselves.'

"She led him far down the path that I had run before. One of her breasts was brushing against his arm, and her arm was wound around his shoulder. Step by step, she became more excited. I followed them, hoping that in their absorption with each other, Nalakubara would inadvertently set down my sword somewhere or other. My guru had, after all, given it to me with the blessing that it would never fail.

"Not only that. I was carefully searching for Kalabhashini all over the forest, but even with my telescopic eyes I couldn't find her anywhere. This was very surprising. 'There's some mystery here,' I thought. 'I wonder if they'll find her.' I kept on following them from a distance. Soon they were melting into one another's body and playing all the games of love. I stood there, a little way off."

## [ Rambha Meets Rambha ]

"At the end, while they were busy fixing one another's clothes and make-up, entirely immersed in one another, another Rambha appeared, carefully tracing their footsteps.

"She was struck dumb. So was Nalakubara. Seeing two Rambhas," Manistambha continued, "I was also a bit surprised.

"Nalakubara looked at this new woman and at his woman, over and over. This went on for a little while. He was studying every detail, and he could find no difference between them. It was astonishing.

" 'Why do you keep looking at her and at me? What are you thinking?' asked his woman.

" 'Are you her double or is she your double?' he asked. 'I can't tell you apart. That's why I keep staring. If you move away even a little, I won't be able to tell without error which one of you is you.'

"Now she was really agitated. 'In that case, I'll keep holding your hand. *She* probably came here in this shape to break us apart. They say that a demoness[5] once came in Sita's form to separate Sita from Rama. So don't let her stay around here. Don't be polite.' She started yelling at the woman. 'Get out of here!' Meanwhile, she was holding tight to Nalakubara.

"The new Rambha saw all this. With a disapproving finger on her nose, shaking her head, she let out a long sigh. Nalakubara addressed her, 'Where did you come from? Why this sigh? Why are you so surprised? How could you take the shape of my woman? Are you a demoness, a spirit, or something else?'

" 'How can I explain?' she replied. 'Whatever you say will stand—until I find a way of showing what is true and what is false. If you say I'm a demoness—yes, I am. A spirit? Right again, until the moment everyone finds out that this charming lady, who has so skillfully assumed *my* shape, is herself a demoness. Listen. The distinction between us will become clear. It will happen by itself. Truth exists, and god exists. If they didn't, how could the world go on? As for me, you are my god. Only you. And only you can distinguish between us, if you want to.

" 'A little while ago, you and I were walking through the forest when you spotted a lovely *suraponna* tree and wanted to make love to me under it. In the middle, you heard a woman crying for help somewhere to the west, and you got up and left me. I started to follow you when a deer passed me to the right; at this bad omen I stopped and waited. This woman must have seen me then, and seen her opportunity. That's when somehow or other she managed to duplicate me. Anyway, think it all over without rushing. Gradually you will see truth separate itself from falsehood.'

"But *his* woman, the first Rambha, was still hanging on to his neck. She looked him straight in the face and said with a smile, 'She's telling our story, just as it happened. She must have been watching us from the beginning. What a nice story she tells. Everything fits. She makes it seem that she was the woman who slept with you under the tree, and she was the one who followed when you left. But she's no woman. She's a witch. She took my shape in order to separate you from me and get you. This scheming bitch will tell a lot of fancy lies without a slip. She can steal the pupil right

5. Surpanakha—but in the *Rāmāyaṇa* literature, this demoness comes either in her own form or in the form of some beautiful woman, never in Sita's form. Suranna's innovation merits attention.

out of your eye without touching the eyeball. She's crafty and sly. Let's get out of here. If anything happens, we can take care of it later.'

She was trying her best to get Nalakubara out of that place. The other Rambha was getting angry and said acidly, 'Arrogant, aren't you? Cut it out. You can't declare a holiday just because you've decorated the house. You behave as if you are your husband's true love, and I'm a stranger to be driven away. Let my husband cut off my head with the sword he's holding—I still won't donate my man to you. He's all the love I have. I can't stand to see you falling all over him. Let go of him. Your tricks won't work here. A thief like you won't stop stealing things just because they belong to a god. How did I get mixed up with a demoness like you?'

"'Don't be an idiot.'

"'Don't *you* be an idiot."

"'I'll break your neck.'

"'I'll break yours.'

"'Stop screaming at me.'

"'*You* stop screaming at me.'

"'Watch it, lady!'

"'*You* watch it.'

"'You can't steal another woman's husband.'

"'*You* can't steal another woman's husband.'

"By now Rambha One and Rambha Two were becoming rowdy, even though the man was trying to cool them down.

"Narada, the sage who feeds on quarrels and provokes them for his own amusement, arrived on cue, plucking his vina and waving his fan. He was delighted at the fight. All three of them bowed at his feet in respect.

"He was smiling.

"'Nalakubara,' he said, 'which of these women is yours? I can't bless you with a long, loving life unless I know who is who. Did you create the other one to teach Rambha a lesson, because she was so full of herself, so certain she would never have a rival? Or maybe she doubled herself because one body was not enough to have all of you? In any case, tell me if you love both of them the same. You've certainly made them fight for quite a while. I was watching it all from the sky.'

"'Me? I made them fight?' said Nalakubara. 'I'm confused myself by their identical appearance and their quarrel.' Then he narrated the story of how he was having a good time with one Rambha when he heard a woman's cry; how, moved by compassion, he went to save her and caught me, Manistambha, as I was fleeing the scene; how, as he was pulling me back there, his woman came and persuaded him to let me go; how they then made love for a while until the second Rambha showed up and said what she said, so that they quarreled.

"Nalakubara pointed to one of the two Rambhas. 'This is the woman that I was with before *that one* came. (He pointed to the second.) She, number one, had a fresh musk mark on her forehead. Fresh *ketaki* flowers were sewn onto her braids. She had a trace of golden pollen at the part of her hair. Strings of black and red *kuravinda* beads, tightly strung, rested on her breasts.'

"Rambha Two folded her hands toward the sage. 'With all due respect, Sir, what you said the other day on the outskirts of Dvaraka has caused all of this.' And Rambha One immediately echoed this: 'That's true!' The sage looked at both of the women and said with a smile, 'Both of you are right. My words did come true, didn't they? I was even able to see it all myself. Now, young ladies, I'll take my leave.'

"Nalakubara turned to him. 'You say both of them are speaking the truth. How is it possible? Please clarify things.'

" 'That was the day I couldn't bear to hear Rambha bragging about how beautiful she was and how much her lover loved her, and only her. So I said to her, "You might have a rival someday. Can you read the future?" One of these two ladies was citing those words just now. The other one was remembering how she had wanted to make love to her man by assuming Rambha's form and had made me give her this ability in a different context.[6] That's why she also said that what *I* said had caused all this. Both are right.'

" 'But which woman is remembering which words? I want you to tell me clearly who is true and who is false.'

" 'What *is* true and what *is* false? Is the form you now have the real one? Come to think of it, what is real in this world? Anyway, you're in a win-win situation. You can use one woman to control the other when she gets out of hand. You can enjoy things however you like. You've doubled your luck.'

" 'Sir: if I keep chatting with you here, who knows what will come out? Please go. I'm afraid to keep you here.'

"So Narada smiled and left, saying, 'You're quite right. All the best. Goodbye.'

6. See 2.48, pp. 22–23.

"Nalakubara took the hand of the woman he had been with all along. 'Who is that woman after all?' He pointed to the other. 'Why should we pay attention to such obstacles and miss our pleasures? Come.'

"He turned to Rambha Two and dismissed her. 'Whatever you may say, it all looks to us like lies. Go look for somebody who could prove your identity.' Actually, he was consumed by an irresistible desire to make love at that moment and needed privacy.

"Rambha One was jealous and scornful of the interloper. 'Don't you have even a little shame? How can you intrude upon a husband and wife when they're alone together? What can I say to you if you have such a scheming mind?'

"Rambha Two was furious. Her eyes turned red. 'All this is your fault. And it's his fault too, being so infatuated with you. But this isn't the end. There's Kubera, my father-in-law.[7] And Indra, our king. And Brahma, the Creator. There's dharma. They're all here to save the truth. I wouldn't party yet.'

"Rambha One still had all the poise a woman gets when her man supports her. She didn't even listen to what the other woman was saying. 'Stop blabbering. Go away. When your hands grow teeth, you can come and bite us. Go complain to whoever listens. God knows who that will be.'

"Rambha Two replied, 'Just wait. Don't rush. Do you think the day dawns only for you? Some god will listen to me. I'll prove my case and get you punished.' She went off in a huff, but after a few paces the agony she felt because she was separated from her lover and her burning desire to be with him got the upper hand over her anger. She couldn't bear to be away from him. Her body grew thin; her bracelets fell from her wrists. She turned back, with a plan.

" 'You put on a good show, you bitch. You know how to yell. So you think you can scare me off? Why should I go around whining to others? Come with me to the world of the gods. *They'll* decide.' She pulled at the other woman's sari.

"Rambha One called to her lover in alarm. 'Look at her. She pays no attention to your presence, and nothing deters her. You can't even call her a woman. More like a prowling demoness. We were too soft with her to begin with. Look what has happened.'

7. Nalakubara is the son of Kubera, the gods' banker.

"'What's there to lose?' he asked. 'Let's go up to heaven and tell them about her aggressive ways. Let's get her punished. Why waste time being angry now?'

"Rambha One looked at Rambha Two.[8] "If you're so sure of yourself, let's find out who you really are. I won't let you off, no matter how angry you are. Let's go to the assembly." And she walked with her a few paces, then thought a bit and said to Nalakubara, 'Wait. I am the most famous of all the gods' courtesans. Urvasi, Menaka, and other such beauties treat me with high respect. No one has ever pointed a finger at me. People say that you are lucky because of me. After all this, how can I go to the gods' court and stoop so low as to fight with her? Think about it. Anger and sin go together. When women fight in public, you never know what curses will be hurled. You're a man. Is this any way to live? And you know what else? All the male gods will have a field day. "Rambha met with a rival who dragged her into court." I'll never hear the end of it. They'll turn it into a circus. Even the quarrel that has happened here is beneath my dignity. Whatever happens, I'm not going to leave this earth and go to heaven. I swear it. How can I look the gods in the eye once they hear about this dispute? If you want to go, fine. I'm willing to risk the separation.'

"Rambha Two listened to this speech. 'My *dear* husband! Did you hear what she said? She's afraid that if she goes to heaven her disguise will be exposed, so she's made up this excuse about not being able to look the gods in the eye. She's sworn she'll never leave this earth. It makes you wonder if she's even able to fly, doesn't it? How did you fall for her in the first place?'

"'What you say sounds right,' said Nalakubara, drawing his own conclusion.

"'You imposter!' he said, pushing away Rambha One, who had no answer to these words. Rambha Two saw her opportunity. She was getting angrier by the minute. 'You drove my husband away from me. Because of you I almost died, struck down by the sharp blade of love.' Then she looked at her rival one more time and pronounced this curse: 'You, too, will die, struck by the blade of a sword.'

8. We read *anta bratirambha jūci* in 238, taking *pratirambha* as accusative. Surviving manuscripts generally lack the nasal *arasunna* which could determine the issue. Our reading has the merit of suggesting that Rambha One is attempting to bluff her way through.

"Nalakubara, under the spell of the moment, unable to distinguish right from wrong, said, 'She deserves this curse.' And he pressed her further. "Who are you? What's your real name?"

"Rambha Two, however, said, impatiently, 'Isn't it bad enough that she's kept us apart for so long? Why do you keep talking to that bitch? You don't seem to see how badly I want you. *Now*.' And she drove the other woman far away."

## [ Nalakubara Meets Nalakubara ]

Watching Sumukhasatti, the Siddha continued: "While Rambha was driving off pseudo-Rambha, Nalakubara, approving of this in his heart, made no objection to her harshness. Actually, he wanted Rambha Two. That's how men are. They're always looking for a new woman."

Sumukhasatti asked the Siddha, "What about you? Who did *you* think was the real Rambha? It looks to me like the one who was humiliated and went away without saying a word must, for that very reason, be the pretender. When her bluff was called, she shut up. But look how aggressively she talked before! That's why Nalakubara let her go. Anyway, tell me what happened next. This story is full of surprises. I've never heard anything like it."

So Manistambha went on. "There's one more major surprise. Rambha, having got rid of her rival, now turned to Nalakubara. 'You men. So much for your love. How can I trust you? I left you alone for a second, and already you picked up this gypsy. But what's the point of blaming you? It's my fault for hanging on to you without shame. That's why I suffer like this.' Big tears rolled down her cheeks.

"Nalakubara gently wiped away the tears with his fingers. 'What did I do? I thought she was you. When it became clear that she wasn't you, I threw her out. You shouldn't hold it against me.'

"He hugged her and consoled her and took her to the clearing, and there he started to make love to her—when suddenly another Nalakubara turned up, screaming, 'Who is this guy who has stolen my shape and my Rambha?'

"I was amazed," continued Manistambha. "One illusion after another. Maybe it's something in the soil.

" 'This looks like an entirely magical world,' Rambha said to her lover. 'This man looks exactly like you. I can't see any difference. On top of this, he claims it's *you* who took *his* shape. Tell me how how we can resolve this problem. Just a few minutes ago we thought we had gotten over the problem of that woman in my shape. Now there's this man who's your double and doesn't seem to want to go away. Apparently, there's some demon somewhere who's jealous of us and doesn't want us to be together, so he keeps planning trick after trick.'

"Nalakubara Two came closer. 'Lady, you don't know what you're talking about. I'm your real husband. Take me. This man has very cleverly taken my shape. You're deluded by his magic. If you don't believe me, back off a little and watch us fight it out. I'll cut his head off with my sword, and then you'll know what's real.'

"Now she was scared. She coiled herself around her man's neck to protect him, crying, 'Gods! Save my husband! Some tricky demon is trying to kill my innocent, unarmed husband.'

"Nalakubara Two smiled. 'That's smart of you, making me the demon. Don't worry. I'm not the sort of man who would kill an unarmed, helpless person. I only said I'd kill him because I thought he'd attack me. And if he does want to stand up to me, let him go get his sword. But if you're thinking to yourself that he's the real Nalakubara, and that fights are unpredictable, and you're worried about what might happen to you if something should happen to him—if this is what's in your mind, I'll stand back until it's clear who he is. You figure it out. Listen to the way each of us speaks. Ask us about some intimate things that only you know. Use whatever means you have to find out who is real and who is false. It makes me very angry to see my woman hanging on to another man right before my eyes. I can't promise I won't go berserk even before you settle the truth. For your own safety, take your hands off him. Listen to me.'

"She understood that this was the smart thing to do if she wanted to save her lover. She moved away.

" 'Dear,' Nalakubara One said, "you don't have to go away. I'm not worried by his sword. I'm telling you you don't have to be scared, but I guess it's your nature.'

"But she was already a little distant. She kept looking at her lover and his double with alternating love and a terrible possessiveness. External forms, no matter how beautiful, are ultimately useless. Real love is born out of claiming one's own.

Nalakubara Two looked at Rambha. 'Think it over. You came here on a mission from Indra—to destroy Manikandhara's discipline. What tree did you tie him to? Where did this fellow hook up with you while I was sitting around waiting impatiently for you, tossing and turning in the pain of separation? I didn't come looking for you because I was afraid of interfering with your mission. That's what led to all this trouble. So now I'm reduced to proving that I'm your husband while this freeloader has put you under his spell.

" 'Normally, if I come along with you, you get distracted by love and won't attend to the job, so Indra becomes angry. If I don't come, the god of love takes it out on me. That was my dilemma. I suffered like this for some time. Finally, I couldn't take the torment of love any more, so I said to myself, "Whatever will be will be. I'll face Indra's anger." I took my heart in my hands and came to this forest. But once I got here I kept on thinking of Indra, so I hesitated to come too close. I hid nearby, waiting for you, expecting you at any minute, once your task was accomplished. I couldn't wait to embrace you. The heart-wrenching call of the cuckoo was almost too much for me. Meanwhile, this man, whoever he is, was having fun with you under false pretenses. I was stuck with the futile obsessions of the lonely sentry.

" 'I'd still be there if Narada hadn't come by and said. "You fool, what are you doing here? Some stranger has assumed your shape and is making love to Rambha in quite inventive ways."

" 'Then I rushed here. Tell me how this man got hold of you. When did it happen?'

" 'What can I say?' thought Rambha, looking at her lover. He—Nalakubara One—said to her, 'Why are you looking at me? I'm going through the same things you did. I have to, if you remember what Narada said that day: " '*You might meet a woman just like yourself, and he could encounter a man like him. It could be very disturbing. I wouldn't bet too heavily on what you have.*' " Don't you remember? Can his words fail to come true? But don't worry. I'll cut his head off in a minute. I just have to go get my sword, which I've left under our tree. I'll be back in a minute.'

"Nalakubara Two said, 'If you're such a hero, why run away from a fight? You're unarmed, so I'll put down my sword.' He placed the sword on the ground and stood across from him. A truly ferocious wrestling match began.

"First, they slapped themselves on the shoulders, and the noise echoed through the hollow caves on the nearby mountains, doubling in intensity like thunder from the clouds that gather when the world comes to an end. Their shouts and yells cracked open the corners of space. They threw hard punches at one another, maneuvering and paring and jabbing and pummeling with fists and elbows. As they fought, they grew angrier and tougher with one another. One of them, finding an opening, balanced his wrist on his opponent's chin and, twisting his arm behind his back, pushed him to the ground and dragged him some distance before pinning him down. The other wriggled free of this grip and pounded his enemy with his elbows, until his arms were trapped and held in the enemy's thighs; but he extricated himself by reaching for the other's loincloth, pulling him upward and, in the space that opened up, pushing hard against his chest with his knees until he flipped and fell on his back. But not for long: in a split second the fallen wrestler was up again and reaching for his opponent's neck, strangling the life out of him so that his eyes were popping out. But then the other one, gasping, gripped the back of the other's loincloth and, grabbing his thigh, flipped him over. 'Get up, come back to fight,' he roared, and the other did. So it went on as they collided with one another, pulled apart, came back together, fought again.

"Rambha, watching, could only tell them apart by the color of their loincloths—one, her lover's, was of green silk, and the other man's was a bright, deep orange. They were perfectly matched; neither had even the slightest edge. After a while they became tired and stood apart. When she observed that they were equal in everything—in form, in strength—a certain doubt began to emerge in her mind. She couldn't resolve it in favor of one or the other, so she said to them, 'Wait a minute. Stop fighting. I'm going to ask you about something that happened in the past, an intimate moment. Each of you must answer. I'll decide who is true and who is false. That will be final. You'll have to accept it. The real Nalakubara will stay and the imposter will have to go.'

"They agreed. She spoke to them separately, each out of earshot of the other. 'When did the topic of someone called Kalapurna come up?' she asked. 'What did you hear about him?' Nalakubara Two answered correctly. Nalakubara One turned pale and remained silent. So she knew. 'How awful,' she said. 'Up to this minute I thought you were the real Nalakubara. But you're an imposter.' You could see on her face how amazed, disgusted, and scared she was. She left him and went to embrace the other.

"Nalakubara Two looked straight at the Trickster and cursed him to die soon. Rambha also looked at him and asked, 'Who are you anyway? How did you manage to assume this shape and deceive me?'

"The real Nalakubara cut her short. 'Isn't it bad enough that he prevented me from coming to you and gave me all this trouble? You still want to spend more time talking with him? Who cares who he is? It's like trying to find out if the crow has teeth. You might pay some attention to my need for you for a change. Enough is enough.' He pulled her away—up into the sky. He was smiling.

"The other one stayed there for a little while, depressed, mulling it over. Finally, with a long face, he dragged himself in the direction of Manikandhara's hut.

"As for me," said Manistambha, "I immediately grabbed my sword, which he had left behind in the clearing where they made love, and came here, very happy. My guru had told me when he gave it to me that it would eventually kill whatever person it was aimed at. I tried to use it against Kalabhashini, and even though I missed once, sooner or later it will succeed."

But then he suddenly noticed Kalabhashini standing there and swallowed his words. She, however, addressed him: "Why hesitate? What has to happen will happen."

He appreciated what she said. "You're a wise woman. That's why you talk like this. A tragedy that has to happen can't be averted. Truth is harsh. But tell me what happened to you after I grabbed you and you yelled, and I was scared and ran away. When I came back, you weren't there. Begin from that point and tell me."

*There's much more to report, great king, more generous than the monsoon or the Wishing Cow or the Wishing Trees or the All-Giving Gem in heaven. When you smile, your face lights up the world like the moon. In particular, it is scholars and poets whom you delight.*

This is the third chapter in the long poem called *Kalapurnodayamu* made by soft-spoken Suraya, son of Pingali Amaranarya, whose poetry all connoisseurs enjoy throughout the world.

# CHAPTER 4

*Listen, Krishna Raja: your grace and fame perfume all space.*

Kalabhashini smiled and said to Manistambha, "You yourself have narrated all that I did. What is left for me to say? That Rambha was me—the one you saw when Nalakubara forced you to come back to search for me. I'm the one who made him let you go, and then he and I made love just as I wanted to. Then the real Rambha came. I was the one who kept her from her husband, fought with her, and at the end was cursed by her."

Everyone was astonished and wanted to hear more. "How did you do that? How did you finagle your way into Rambha's shape and Nalakubara's arms? We know you've wanted this for a long time."

She looked at Manistambha and said, "When Nalakubara was chasing after you, Rambha followed him—until a deer came across her path, and she hesitated to go on. I saw my moment. I took her shape and appeared as if she had come there. Everything worked just fine, because he didn't know that his woman had been delayed, and because I looked and sounded exactly like her. Long ago, Narada had given me that ability.

This you've already heard form Narada himself, at the time of our quarrel. Of course, Narada knew at that moment exactly who I was, but out of consideration for me he didn't give me away. But that's all ancient history. In disgust I put off that shape, which led to this unavoidable curse. I've come here to suffer it in front of the goddess. Maybe somebody at least will benefit. What your guru said is true. Your sword is infallible. It's well known. God has brought both of us together here. I'm fulfilled. Do as you like.

"Still, I was under the comforting impression that I had got my Nalakubara, after all the trouble I'd gone through. Now you tell me that the real Nalakubara showed up later and cursed the first one. So who could that imposter be?"

"It was me," said Manikandhara, smiling. "Don't say another word."

"How did you manage that?" she asked. "Rambha's girlfriends told us—Manistambha and me—that right after ruining your self-discipline, she and Nalakubara went off together."

"No, it was me. I'm the one she made love to. I'll tell you the whole story. First she ruined my self-control. But while she was making love to me, she revealed how much she loved Nalakubara by calling out his name. I hated it. I wanted to get rid of her. At the same time, I still wanted her—even more. I wanted to satisfy her the way she wanted. So I expended some of the power I'd acquired by my discipline and took her husband's form. I went back to her, said the right words, and made love to her in a total, mutual way. But as it happened, in the course of our lovemaking, *you* appeared, and then I enjoyed loving *you*. I got this curse as an immediate consequence of my disguise. Then I came to my senses, went back to my hut, took off the mask, picked up my vina and the necklace, and came here—because I know the special power of this place. Maybe something good will happen." He smiled. "When I wanted more of Rambha and made love to her at the height, she turned out to be you. And when you made a huge effort to find Nalakubara and joyfully made love to him, he turned out to be me. In the end, I got what I wanted.

"Let me confess. I was afraid of Narada, so I never let anybody know. My mind was on you all the time, all those years, during our music lessons. At last, my dream came true. I was lucky."

Kalabhashini answered him. "My mind is at rest. I was getting worried, wondering who that ugly-minded man could be who made love to me by tricking me. Now I have nothing to regret. Don't think your love was something I didn't want. I thought I wasn't worthy of you, and I didn't know *your* mind. So I turned my heart away whenever I saw you. You'll never know how much I was captivated by your arresting beauty, your superb music, your perfection in every way. You made me happy all the time. Only my heart knows. There's no point in talking about it all at this point.

"You know what else? Once when I saw you, the name Manigriva came to my mind. It's very much like *your* name. There's that story about how Narada cursed him and his older brother to become huge trees.[1] I kept thinking about that. As a result of that scare, my desire to enjoy your body completely disappeared, as if I'd sworn an oath. From that time on, my mind turned toward Nalakubara. He resembles you to some extent. It was some terribly inauspicious moment that I set my eyes on him. I was focused only on the external form. I thought I was making love to Nalakubara, but actually it was you. I was incredibly lucky. It was like being pushed off the roof and landing on a bed of flowers.

"What a fool I was. I held a precious jewel in my hand and threw it away for a glass bead that had some of its color. Then I got the jewel back, but now I won't live long enough to enjoy it. But no one will believe me anyway. They think a courtesan speaks only to flatter. Moreover, it's very clear that I wanted the other man, isn't it?" She bent her head, suddenly shy.

Manikandhara could see that she was overcome by love and grief. "My dear," he said, "I don't think of you as being like those other courtesans, who tell lies. Do you think I'm that simple minded? In fact, I have a sign that you wanted me even before. Think of what Narada said to you when he sent you home. '*Now you will happily make love to the man you wanted, a man so beautiful that he could win Rambha's heart. Trust me. Go home.*'[2] Those were his words. Narada didn't say you'd make love to Nalakubara. His words came true. I'm the one you wanted, the one you were in love with before. It's not so unusual for a wish like that to fade under the pressure of a deep fear of being cursed by a powerful sage. Such things happen in the world.

1. Manigriva and his elder brother Nalakubara (!) were cursed by Narada to become trees because they failed to cover their nakedness when Narada happened upon them, while they were playing with *apsaras* women in the river. The baby Krishna pulled a heavy stone mortar between these two trees and thus liberated them from their curse. See *Bhāgavatapurāṇa* 10.9.22–23, 10.10.1–43, and discussion in the "Invitation to a Second reading."
2. See 2.48, p. 23.

"It's also no surprise that Nalakubara made such an impression on your mind that you showed no interest in anybody else. He glows with Rambha's presence and is enlivened by her attention. It even happens to men sometimes. I'll tell you a story to prove that. It's a good story—that also washes away your sins. Listen carefully. I'll begin at the beginning."

## [ The Story of Salina and Sugatri ]

"Not long ago, I went to see the god Padmanabha, here in Kerala, to bring my vow to conclusion. I saw some excellent poets singing great poetry to the god. I wondered how I could achieve that skill. They told me the stories of this Lion-Rider Goddess, and I also learned that she wasn't far away. So I came here and followed the instructions inscribed on the pillar. I had the courage to do that deed, and I reaped the results.[3] Then I went back to Padmanabha's temple. An assembly of Vishnu devotees was gathered there. Some were chanting the eight-syllable mantra.[4] Some were meditating on Narayana.[5] They had turned away from all other gods. They were free from passion and anger, lucid in mind, masters of the ancient wisdom in the Vedic books and scientific texts. They knew the stable relationship between god and themselves—between essence and extras.[6] They saw themselves as his slaves.

"I bowed to them over and over. At their request, I gave them my name and told them I was a gandharva. I told them I wanted to sing for the god. 'Receive my song,' I said to them, 'as if *you* were my god.' They looked at me and made me sing for *him*, for they said to me, 'He is complete inside and out, unchanging, without beginning, middle, or end. He has no equal or superior. He knows everything. He has all power and controls all. He is in everything. All phenomena are his excesses, and he exists in excess. He and the goddess are inseparable, like sun and sunlight, moon and moonlight. Sing for him.' They wanted me to sing of the conversation between God and

3. Apparently, Manikandhara cut off his tongue at the shrine and received the gift of poetry.
4. *Om namo nārāyaṇāya*.
5. Vishnu.
6. *śeṣa-śeṣitvamulu*. In South Indian Srivaishnavism, the god is conceived of as the ultimate residue of fullness, while living creatures are the excesses left over from this essential core.

the goddess, for the good of the world. And they blessed me that I would have deep feeling for the god, if not in this life, then in some other one.

"But I wasn't satisfied. I wanted my poetry to be approved by the Sarada Academy in Kashmir, where the goddess presides. So I went there. Now the real story begins. Listen carefully.

"The Academy was in session. I heard people performing all the chants of the Rig, Yajur, Sama, and Atharvana Vedas. Some were discussing household rituals; others were deep in grammar, or arguing over astrology, or studying Dharma. There were seminars on the two Mimamsas, Logic, and Yoga. And there was poetry.

"There, in one of the halls, I saw a Brahmin master engrossed in teaching Veda: first he would give the proper tone, to ensure precision in word and syllable; then he would guide the pupils in the tonal accents by dramatic movements of his eyebrows; he also gave them mnemonic devices to help them to distinguish one section from another. If one of them was not concentrating and uttered a wrong note, the teacher would pinch his cheeks in punishment. When I approached him, he said: 'Come. Who are you? You shine with an internal brightness.' And he asked me about my family and my name. Then he dismissed his class—since the arrival of a guest was reason for a holiday—and offered me hospitality.

"Soon a student arrived, wearing a belt of *munja* grass and a garment yellow with turmeric draped around his delicate body. His face was alive with intelligence and inner fire. He had an antelope skin, a sacred thread, a brilliant forehead-dot and the marks of a servant of Vishnu, a ring, a staff, and a thin tuft of hair. He was carrying a book and seemed rather agitated. The teacher looked at him and said, 'Why are you so late?' He answered: 'There's a good reason. You must not have heard. I'll tell you. I went at your command to the flower garden where Salina was sitting in a pergola while his wife, Sugatri, was rubbing his feet, resting in her lap. They were conversing happily. He saw me and smiled: "Has your teacher sent you for the book? I have kept it here for you." He pointed to a branch above his head. "You can take it; just sit with us for a while." And he showed me a seat in the shade of a young mango tree. Then he put his hands on his wife's shoulders and said to her, "Have you been drinking the juice of lasting life, my dear, or have you found some magical potions? You become more beautiful and youthful day by day. They say women age faster than men, so what is it that constantly enhances your vitality?" She smiled a little and said, "I don't really know. Probably it's because you are so much in love that you always see in me such youth and beauty." Salina replied, "No, I'm not imagining things. If you don't know, I'll tell you. *I* am the reason." He bent her head close to his mouth and whispered something, with a smile, in her ear. She made a face, surprised. Looking into his eyes, she said, "When I asked that goddess earlier for something, she said yes. How is she going to keep her word? Listen, I'll tell you what I asked for." And she brought her lips close to his ear and whispered something. Suddenly, Salina was furious. He rushed off in a huff, with his wife racing after him, and jumped into the lake deep as a hundred palm trees. She cried, "What is there for me to do except to follow his footsteps? I won't leave him even if he has left me!" And she took a running jump into the lake, at the very same spot. You probably didn't hear of this because the place is far from here. All the villagers have been dredging the lake with nets, with no success. They've only now given up. I went back to get the book from the place Salina had shown me.'

"The teacher was overcome with grief and amazement. 'Alas,' he said, 'that happy couple has suffered an undeserved fate. That lake is famous for its depth. No one who falls into it can survive. Who can escape their karma?' I then asked him, in his sadness, 'Who are these two people, Sugatri and Salina? You have praised them as noble; tell me their story.' He replied, 'This book tells their story. It's good luck to hear it—especially now that we no longer have the good fortune to be able to see them.' He picked up the book that his student had brought, touched it to his head and to his eyes, then gave it back to the boy and asked him to read it. Here is what he read:

*Once there was a Brahmin girl called Sugatri, daughter of a priest who served the goddess of learning, who is established on her throne in the middle of the land of Kashmir. Her husband, Salina,*[7] *lived with his in-laws. Sugatri's girlfriends decorated her sumptuously on her nuptial night and sent her to her husband, while they waited outside. But he was so startled by all her jewels that he hesitated to touch her. She waited for some time and left.*

*Her girlfriends told her mother. They were thinking: "This is unheard of on this earth. What could be the reason? What a fine young fellow you've got!*

7. The names of this couple are significant. Sugātri = "Pretty Body," Śālīna = "Shy."

*Anyway, tonight is lost; tomorrow he'll show us his wild ways." They laughed, and the mother said: "Quiet, you silly girls! He'll hear you. Shy people sometimes give up everything if they suspect they are being ridiculed."*

*So she sent her daughter to the son-in-law for two or three more days. But he treated her in exactly the same way as the first night. The young bride went and came for nothing. Her girlfriends, with the mother's permission, said to her: "It doesn't look like you're acting as husband and wife. Both of you are clearly experts. What can we say?*

If the man knows what to do, it's right for the woman
to be shy. If, however, the man is a moron,
and the woman is also timid, what's the point
of being married?

*"Listen. You're no longer a little girl. You can't just sit around waiting, just because he doesn't talk to you. Men are lucky, but a woman cannot keep her pride too long. You should serve him on your own initiative; eventually, his heart will melt. You shouldn't have come back just because he hasn't called you lovingly right away. Offer him betel nut with camphor and a folded leaf.*[8] *You must be a fool. It just isn't right that you waste your youth, so ripe for pleasure, on an empty bed. Women need the joys of a husband when they're young; what good are they when youth is gone?"*

*She listened and said, a bit coy, "You're killing me with all these words. I can't bear to hear them." But that night she tried out their advice—with no results. She thought: "If I do anything more, he'll probably leave me for good. It's no use. At least I have a living husband and a marriage thread." She went on decorating herself fully, each day, to bring good luck to her husband,*[9] *and she begged her mother not to humiliate him. The mother held her tongue for many days, waiting patiently. One day she said, "I've never seen such a good-for-nothing. If I say anything against him, you defend him. Are you about to give birth to a male child who could take care of my property? We've seen his ways. It's like giving a loan with a barren cow for collateral. But if I throw him out, you will be distressed. At least we could use him in the flower garden." So she called him respectfully and put*

8. The offering of betel is a frequent euphemism for sexual contact.
9. A wife adorns herself as an auspicious guarantee of her husband's longevity.

*him to work, taking care to instruct him and to discipline him in the necessary skills.*

*Salina was happy because this work was a service to the goddess Sarada, so he performed it with concentration. He tended the lovely flowers, heavy with honey, pollen, and masses of drunken bees. He watered at the proper times, making channels for every plant; he turned over the earth, carried baskets of manure in his own hands, without any hesitation; grafted plants together, gently bending their tender branches; prepared seedbeds and planted grafts—all with mounting excitement. He would get up early each morning and say his prayers, meditate on the line of his gurus, and carry out the chants as they had prescribed. Then he would skillfully cut the flowers and weave them into garlands and bouquets in many inventive ways to be offered to the goddess of arts.*

*Now Sugatri, out of a sense of duty as a wedded wife and unable to watch from afar the hard work her husband was doing at her mother's behest, wanted to go there and help him—but she was too shy to do so. One day when Salina had gone off to the garden, lightning streaked through the skies, striking everywhere; there was thunder, and a terrifying downpour of rain. From the moment the clouds appeared and the first drops smashed down to earth, Sugatri was afraid her husband would be soaked. She addressed him in her mind: "How will you survive this torrential rain, beloved husband? How did you get stuck with this miserable work in the garden?" She scanned the skies over and over and prayed to her family goddess, Sarasvati: "O Sarada, our compassionate mother, please watch over my husband. I have no support except for you. If I have done anything good in this body, or in some previous bodies—some vow, or act of meditation, or donation—may its merit save my husband from the calamity of this rain. Let me bear the effects of whatever evil he has done that has brought this upon him."*

*Not content with that, and indifferent to the heavy rain, she left the house in desperation, without her mother's knowledge. Because of her loyalty to her husband, the rain did not affect her; the flooding water gave way before her, opening a dry path. She reached the garden where her husband was and watched him from a distance. She saw that he was safe, untroubled by the winds or rain, protected by the goddess in response to her prayer. "Mother Sarasvati,*[10] *you have shown your concern for us," she thought,*

10. Another name for the goddess Sarada.

*overjoyed. She returned home, and no one knew that she had gone there. In her shyness, she went on just as before. People were amazed that the flower garden was undamaged by the storm.*

*Shy Sugatri patiently suffered as her husband toiled. Finally, she conquered her bashfulness, and, her heart full of love for her husband and paying no more heed to her mother's words, she went, dressed as usual, to the garden. At first he would not let her work with him, but she was insistent: she put her jewels away in a corner and tied her sari around her waist. She started digging with a shovel, her breasts swaying up and down, her full buttocks shaking as she walked briskly back and forth. She fed water to the plants through muddy channels, and mud splashed onto her smooth cheeks. She carried bundles that burdened her tiny waist and made it tremble. Sweating a little, her hair dancing, graceful, she performed each task before he could. And as she worked, the god of desire, noticing her quivering buttocks and breasts and hair, let loose his arrows at her husband, as if in target practice.*

*Salina could not fend off those arrows. "You crazy woman," he said, "you just won't stop, even if I ask you. You're so far removed from gardening." With the edge of his upper cloth, he wiped the beads of sweat from her cheeks. But the sweat kept pouring out, through Desire's tricky power. Looking at her glistening cheeks, he said, "You couldn't bear to watch me toil, and now you've exhausted yourself with this work." Hungrily he embraced her neck and hugged her. Then he carried her to a soft bed of flowers and made love to her with joyful passion.*

*Afterward, he held her even tighter, his desire still growing. She said, "All this is quite new. Shouldn't we go home?" Gently she made him let go. Putting on the jewels she had hidden, she walked toward home, her heart full of her husband's ways. After that lovemaking, she was pleasantly tired, like a fresh flower exposed to the springtime sun. Loved by her husband, Sugatri reached home. Her girlfriends could tell at a glance that her wish had been fulfilled; they teased her, and her mother was also pleased. That night her girlfriends eagerly adorned her even more than normally and sent her to her husband in the bedroom.*

*Her tremulous waist, wearied by effort; her slightly soiled, thin sari slipping over her buttocks; the necklace rippling over her swinging breasts, tightly tied in the top of her sari; the dot of turmeric and musk on her forehead, smudged by sweat; her huge bun of hair, trembling at every move—all these combined in a single image as she ran ahead of him to perform the various tasks in the garden, and that image stuck in his mind. So now, at night, he did not even look at her splendid ointments, ornaments, and dress. As usual, he sat distracted. His wife waited for quite some time, wondering sadly what she had done wrong. She thought of leaving, but then she thought: "If I go, who is there for me? I'll wait here. What will be will be." She stayed by the door. After a long time, she gathered herself up and approached him. "You must be very tired after all that work. Shall I go? Would you like to sleep?" she whispered, wafting fragrance, in his ear.*

*Still distracted, he asked: "What do you want from me?" She answered with a languorous lilt in her voice, "What do women usually want from a husband?" Then, patiently: "My lord, forget all the rest. I'm happy that you took enough interest to ask. How can I blame you? It's dawn already, and you haven't even asked me to rub your feet or to come near you. You didn't even open your eyes enough to look at me with a little love. Today in the garden, my good fortune must have ripened fully. It's only after finding your love in that way that I have spoken to you so openly. I know this is not the way a good wife should talk."*

*In her heart she was feeling the pain of increasing desire. She thought a little and said, "Even a rock is better than your heart. You'll never do anything by yourself." She gently touched his foot. Pressing it, she sat on the edge of the bed and placed it on her thighs, soft as golden silk. Then she pressed it against her breasts, brought it near her eyes, and touched it tightly to her cheek in evidence of her love. He remained lost in thought. She wondered what was going on. A little agitated, she said: "Perhaps you're in love with some other woman and can't take your mind off her. So bring her here. Or, if she'll listen to me, send me and I will bring her. I will serve her just as I serve you, as a slave. Believe me. Why all these knots? It's enough if you are fulfilled. You can sell me off if you want. Tell me what's worrying you."*

*All the while she was massaging his foot. He had no idea at all what was happening. He was obsessed with that first vision of her beauty, the disheveled form, the quick movements as she was working, the gentleness and comfort of her affection, her ways of making love. So the night passed, as she tirelessly pressed his feet in true devotion, without another word.*

*The next day she went, like the day before, to work in the garden. Once again she found her husband's love, and she realized: "He cares only for this sort of beauty, but not for ornaments." From then on she went there every day, worked in the garden, and made her husband happy with love-making as he pleased.*

*Eventually her mother came to know about all this. She spoke in private to her daughter: "My dear, your were born with the blessings of the goddess of arts. The goddess came to me in a dream and promised that our whole family would become pure through your acts—as if she knew you very well. My husband, your father, has gone away to another land. I am counting on your children to take care of me in my old age; that's why I keep waiting for you to have sons. But one thing is bothering me. Listen to me. People say that making love at the wrong time produces sons without good qualities. At the beginning, for some strange reason, he didn't want you, and I spoke to him in anger. But we have our old servants to work in the garden, don't we? Why should your husband work there? Why should you, for that matter? You are young in age but old in wisdom. You know what's right and what's wrong."*

*Sugatri broke into a gentle smile. "Whatever my husband likes is right, and what he doesn't like is wrong. That's my natural way of thinking. I won't change it. To me, my husband is God, text, and teacher. I will follow his commands, without considering any other rights or wrongs. I'm not giving anything up just because it is forbidden, nor doing anything just because it is prescribed. I will do what he wants, without any hesitation, and reject whatever he rejects."*

*When she said this, the goddess of arts herself appeared, full of praise for her loyalty to her husband. She held her with a motherly embrace, looked at the mother, and said: "Don't try to fix this fine woman's ways. With her strong love, she has washed away not only her own sins but also those of both families. From now on, her story will be my very favorite. I myself will publicize it in the world."*

"The Brahmin boy finished reading and tied up the book.[11] The teacher looked at me and said, 'It's a good story. The goddess of arts must have immeasurable love for Sugatri and Salina. She came to me in my dream and told me to read this book every morning before sunrise. That same night she also gave this book to all the literate people in the town. Everyone has been talking about this in amazement. Just yesterday I myself went to that garden to see the happy couple. They received me with honor—but I forgot the book there. Today, early in the morning, I wanted to read it and re-

11. Obviously in the form of a palm-leaf book, with covers on either end bound with string.

membered. I sent this boy to bring it, and now this bad news has come.' I left him there, grieving for this couple in many ways."

"I took leave of the teacher," continued Manikandhara. "Since I could see that everyone in the town was preoccupied with these events, I realized that this was not the time to put my poetry to the test. So I went to the world of the snakes. After some time, a desire emerged in me to learn music in full, so I began to serve Narada and to wander the worlds with him.

"Now listen, Kalabhashini. Your mind worked just like in Salina's story. He was obsessed by rustic beauty and repelled by anything that smacked of ornament or fancy clothes. He rejected his finely decorated wife but was impressed by her plain loveliness when she was working in the garden—so impressed, in fact, that he forgot everything else. His story is a variation on yours."

He looked at Sumukhasatti. "You're from Kashmir, aren't you. Don't you know the story of Sugatri?"

"Who says I don't know it? I am that Sugatri."

Everyone was amazed. "If you are that woman, how did you survive? Why did you change your name?"

"When I fell into the lake deep as a hundred palm trees, I was thinking only of my husband's feet. No other man was in my mind. Midway to the bottom, drowning, I was swallowed by a crocodile; but it couldn't digest me and the next day, rolling on the sands of the shore, it vomited me up. That's what the people who were there told me afterward. Everyone was amazed at my survival. I went home and prayed to the goddess: "Bring back my husband. I depend on you." My hair grew white, and I was still praying. I said to myself, "How can I serve my husband at this age? Let the goddess decide what's good for me." I turned away from the world and spent my time in the company of philosophers who knew what was real and with experts in Yoga, who let you *experience* the real. I only regretted that I was no longer young enough to practise the postures that are an integral part of Yoga. That's how I got the name Sumukhasatti: *Sumukha* means "scholars," and *asatti* means "closeness." So I'm the one who is always close to scholars.

"Everyone knew me by this name. I left my mother's place and went wandering over the earth, from shrine to shrine. When I heard about the powers of this goddess, I came here. The rest you know. Though I was respected for my commitment to my husband, I ended up in this sad state. And although I survived, I haven't the foggiest idea what happened to my husband in the depths of that lake."

Manistambha said, "A crocodile swallowed you and then, a day later, you came back unharmed. Don't you think your faithfulness would have saved your husband, too? Believe me, he survived." He pointed at himself. "I am he.

"I'll tell you my story," he said. "You know how I jumped into that lake in my anger at what you said. A little while after that I reached a man, a Siddha who lived underwater as if in his own house. He had the skill of arresting water, and he was so bright that the darkness of the depths was dispelled. Because I had fallen so deep into the water, I was gasping for breath. For a single second, I looked at him. He was in *samadhi*, a fathomless state. He opened his eyes and saw me. I bowed to him. When he asked, I told him my story. 'So you're a very angry man,' he said to me, smiling. 'This is a very lonely place. That's why I'm here. I can't let you stay more than a minute.' But he looked at me with compassion and kept me with him for a whole day. Seeing I was so devoted to him, he gave me a jewel that keeps me young, the lion he rode, knowledge of the herbs that control it, skill in playing music, and this sword. Then he sent me off, saying, 'This sword will eventually kill the person it is aimed at.'

"I bowed and mounted the lion he had summoned for me. No sooner did I spur him with my heel than he rose from the lake high up into the sky. I was happy. I wanted to see all the fascinating things that exist in the world. And because of the jewel that keeps me young, I got the name Manistambha, Frozen Young by a Jewel.

"From that day on, I've been traveling, dressed as a Siddha, with my guru's consent. Lost in the fun I was having, I didn't think of you. You know the rest of the story, since I came here."

Sumukhasatti laughed. "Are you really Salina? If so, tell me what I whispered in your ear that made you so angry, and what you whispered to me after praising my youthful beauty. Tell me all that." She turned to Kalabhashini. "Come here," she said. "I will first tell you the secret. You can verify if he repeats it."

She was bending over to tell her when she stopped. "No, that won't work. He can hear from a long distance. He'll hear it immediately. I'll write it down for you. No—he'll be able to read it from afar." She looked at

Manikandhara. "Listen," she said. "You go get him to say those things first to you. Then I'll tell you my version."

So Manikandhara took Manistambha aside and had him report the early conversation and the reason for his getting angry. Then Manikandhara asked Sumukhasatti to report her version. She said, "Before Salina jumped into the lake, we were alone together. As we were talking, he said, 'Have you been drinking the juice of lasting life, my dear, or have you found some magical potions? You become more beautiful and youthful day by day. They say women age faster than men, so what is it that constantly enhances your vitality?' I answered, 'I don't really know.' He said, 'I know.' And he bent over to whisper into my ear. 'I want you to stay young and attractive. I can't get enough of you. So I've asked the goddess Sarada that you never become pregnant. She was kind enough to give me that wish. That's why you always look so youthful and your body is bursting with beauty.' I was shocked. 'But she—that same Sarada—gave *me* a wish sometime earlier, that you will have a son by me.[12] How could both come true?' He was furious. 'You asked her for a wish that is completely contrary to mine?' Overcome by anger, he jumped straight into the lake."

"Doubt no more," said Manikandhara. "This man is your husband. The versions coincide precisely."

At once, Sumukuhasatti became a little shy. She looked at her husband with joy, respect, love, and humility. She was holding back the tears. "I may have said things about you unknowingly," she said. "I noticed something familiar about the way you walk, talk, and smile, but I said to myself, 'People resemble people.' That was how it had to be at that point, so I didn't think much about it. My luck has flowered today—because of this Manikandhara, who's like a brother to me. The company of good people helps you in this world and in the next."

She looked at Manikandhara. "You know, I heard good things about you and your music, many times, from my husband, here. He heard you playing from afar. You're a gandharva by birth. So handsome the moon is put to shame. In music, second to none. You're a Yogi, devoted to Vishnu. Yet in the end you are bound by this curse, and that makes me sad."

12. The Telugu is deliberately ambiguous and, as always in this book, carefully worded: *nādu saṅgambunana nīku nandanuṇḍu galuku varamu*, literally "a wish that a son will be born by my uniting with you / your making love to me."

Kalabhashini was also sad. She asked Manikandhara, "But why did you have to be cursed by Nalakubara? Didn't you know the answer to Rambha's question?[13] You heard Kalapurna's story before, didn't you?"

He said, "No. I never heard that story. You may have heard it, but I don't know where and when."

She thought for a moment. "Yes, yes, I remember. You had gone away when that conversation occurred between Narada and me." And she told the whole story and its context—how when she first saw Narada, there was occasion for her to ask about Kalapurna; how Narada, surprised at the question, looked through the entire universe, past, present, and future, with his Yogic vision and then said that he could not tell that story, because it would force him to be born and to enjoy the riches of life on earth. She told it all, like stringing every single bead into a necklace.

## [ Enter Alaghuvrata. Kalabhashini Is Sacrificed ]

At that point a Malayali Brahmin named Alaghuvrata appeared. He was eager to be rich and intended to perform the appropriate rituals. He overheard Kalabhashini's narrative.

"Who is that Kalapurna?" he asked. "When can I hear the whole story? Even if you carry out all the rituals that bring wealth, you won't have the good fortune of listening to this unprecedented story. You say that story is so powerful that merely by listening to it, one gets to live a long life in luxury and have a large family of children and grandchildren. Sounds good. I'll pray to the goddess here to let me hear the whole story." He sat right down and began to chant the mantra of the World Goddess.

Meanwhile, Kalabhashini was thinking about *her* curse. She was afraid it might take effect in some meaningless way—a random blow, somewhere or other—if she delayed. So she looked with some determination at the Siddha and his sword.

"Why waste time? Use your sword and make Rambha's words come true. You'll win your kingdom."

Manistambha looked at her. "Remember, this woman Sumukhasatti invoked the goddess and stopped me from killing you. I'm afraid to lift my sword against you again. Once was enough." He turned to Manikandhara

13. See end of chapter 3. Rambha had posed a clinching test of identity: "When did the topic of someone called Kalapurna come up?"

and said, "You take my sword and do what the girl wants. You take the vast kingdom, with all its riches, you'll get as a reward."

"Good idea," said Sumukhasatti. "Do it. I know you have to die soon, because of Nalakubara's curse. You're probably wondering why you should acquire more bad karma by killing this woman and what good a kingdom won by these means will be to you. But it's no bad karma to offer this woman to the goddess, especially when she wants to convert her curse, which she anyway can't avoid, into some benefit to others. She is herself asking to be killed. So do it."

She convinced him by this and many other arguments. A kind man at heart, he finally agreed and prepared himself to perform the sacrifice. Kalabhashini, with tears in her eyes, bowed to Manistambha and his wife and said, "These tears are not because I'm afraid to die, but because I am losing the chance to serve you as my elders."

Sumukhasatti replied, "My dear child. Our mutual affection is not about to end. Even in the future your husband and you will treat us with the love and respect due to elders, just as you desire."

Kalabhashini bowed over and over, her hands folded on her head.

"My ears have been rendered pure by your story of ultimate faithfulness to a husband. Even the most wayward of women will attain that virtue, if you bless her. Please bless me."

Sumukhasatti said, "You will be the most faithful of wives. Live happily with your husband in a wealthy kingdom, and take care of people like us.[14] I hardly need to tell you not to be afraid, to stay calm, and so on—you look like a bride going to her wedding. You're all aglow and full of joy. You're more a goddess than an ordinary woman."

Kalabhashini took leave of Sumukhasatti and looked at the Siddha. "You've already said goodbye. Now give me the sword." She took the sword from him and handed it to Manikandhara. Then she decorated herself with garlands of flowers and sandalpaste, as is fit for such an occasion. She sat in the lotus posture, facing the goddess. Her face was bright, her heart strong.

She was ready. To Manikandhara she said, "Have no qualms. Don't be afraid. Sacrifice me to the goddess. Swing the sword without doubt. Let me see if that right hand of yours, that knows how to behead aggressive foes, is

14. The Vavilla edition, alone among the printed texts, indicates that some text has been lost here.

still as strong as it used to be. It is in your nature to slay enemies that dare to oppose you in battle. You need no less courage now. Don't be confused."

Amazed at her lucidity, he took a moment to steady his mind and then somehow did as she asked.

The Lion-Rider Goddess spoke. "Manikandhara! You delayed a fraction of a second out of compassion. Therefore, you'll enjoy the kingdom you've won only in your next birth. Then you'll be born as a fully-grown man. As for Kalabhashini, since she was totally focused on pleasing me and showed absolutely no fear of death, by my order she will have her head reattached and will go home to her friends and relatives."

At that very moment, Kalabhashini opened her eyes. She looked around her and saw that she was in Dvaraka, in the courtesans' quarter, in the garden of her own house. She knew this was the blessing of the goddess. She praised her and entertained her friends with the story of how she had left and come back and all that happened in between.

## [ Manistambha Tours the World with His Wife ]

Manikandhara and the others were surprised that the pieces of Kalabhashini's body had completely disappeared. They praised the power of the Lion-Rider's words. Manikandhara bowed to the goddess many times and took leave of Sumukhasatti and Manistambha. Anticipating his early death because of the curse, he handed over his jeweled necklace to Alaghuvrata, who was performing his chants and prayers, and hid his vina in a secret alcove in the temple, where no one could find it. Driven by Nalakubara's curse, he went to Srisailam, where he intended to throw himself off the mountain.

Manistambha went into the temple and gave himself over to Yogic exercises, controlling his senses, with Sumukhasatti nearby to serve him. With his permission, she also continued her own practices, as before. Finding no space in their busy schedule, Desire went away.

Still, Manistambha had an inner urge to see new things around the world. He summoned his lion and, mounting it with his wife, took off into the sky. From high up he looked down at the ocean—

> its waters restless, sleepless,
> moaning, as fearsome
> crocodiles and whales moved
> in the depths.

He pointed it out to his wife:

"Its water foaming and glistening
like a liquid sun, the ocean displays
on the surface its inner nature,
a secret cache of gems.

"The ocean is spraying Ganga,
his wife in the sky, from his arsenal
of water cannon. Whales spout
columns from the opening
in their head.

"Or these geysers spouted by whales
could be the coiled snake that is the ocean
hissing as it lifts its hood.

The tall waves are the ocean's long arms
stretched to the limit
to embrace the godly river flowing
from the sky, for he can bear no longer
the fiery heat of separation
which we call the Mare burning
in his heart.[15]

"Don't the black clouds above, stooping to drink the water,
look like the hair of the goddess falling loose
as she makes love on top of Vishnu?
Aren't the streaks of lightning
like the glistening of her body, enveloped by her hair?
And the dark blue ocean lying beneath
is God himself.

Sumukhasatti smiled shyly at these suggestions and bent her head. He found this even more arousing. Desire possessed him.

15. A mare's head breathing fire is hidden in the depths of the ocean.

He let her know. She said, "I'm always ready to do whatever pleases you. I don't want the freedom to do anything else." He was delighted and began to make love to her with great passion in forests and groves filled with vines and flowers all over the world. As for Alaghuvrata, the Malayali Brahmin, he sat in the temple counting his beads for two full years.

*O king of cooling words, terror to your enemies, wiser than the teachers of the gods and the antigods, constant support of scholars and poets, son of Narasimha!*

This is the fourth chapter in the long poem called *Kalapurnodayamu* made by soft-spoken Suraya, son of Pingali Amaranarya, whose poetry all connoisseurs enjoy throughout the world.

# CHAPTER 5

*Listen, King Krishna, of unbroken glory. Your wealth, which nourishes all scholars, outshines the richest in the world. Your greatest joy is in comforting those who come to you in need.*

## [ The Baby Who Talks ]

For two full years Alaghuvrata chanted the mantra of the World Goddess. The Lion-Rider spoke to him: "Brahmin! Your desire will be fulfilled elsewhere." Instantly he was hurled by a great wind into a royal court in the middle of a city in a faraway country. Because of the violent disturbance, he sat there for a short time with his eyes closed. When he opened them, he looked around and saw a group of courtiers, rather surprised at the way he had dropped in. Right in front of him was an impressive king, radiant as the king of the gods. Before the king a sweet baby girl lay in her baby clothes, in a golden cradle. The Brahmin was still for a moment, overcome by surprise. Then he quickly got up, blessed the king, and presented him with the jeweled necklace that he had received from Manikandhara. The king received the gift with respect and asked the Brahmin to sit near him. He asked him only his name and that of his family. "Your arrival here is quite unusual," he said, "but you can tell us about it later. For now, just rest yourself quietly. Any gifts I receive today go to this girl." So he had the necklace put on the baby's neck.

The baby moved her head to get a look at the necklace, with her chin pressing down against her neck. With light playing on her soft cheeks, she smiled, as if there were something she knew. Suddenly, she began to speak. "After two long years, I now see this necklace again. My luck has come to fruition."

What can I, a mere poet, say? Everybody there was stunned and stood like pictures painted on a wall.

The king thought to himself, "These words are amazing. The child must be a goddess, born for some special reason. Let's get her to talk some more." He asked her, "Wonder girl—you were born only two months ago, and you're already talking. Where did you see this necklace two years ago?"

"In my previous life. I remember it very well. That's why I said this."

The king looked at the baby. "You're no ordinary human child. My heart is eager to learn all about you. What were your previous lives? Why were you born now?"

She thought through her previous life and the one before that and all the memories related to them. They were all fresh in her mind. She spoke, as they listened in total silence.

"In two lives before this one, I was a pet parrot of the goddess of speech. Because of a curse, I had to be reborn. I'll tell you all about it. The story is a new one, utterly unlike anything told before, and compelling in its beauty; if you listen to it, you will live long in health and wealth. At last I can tell it.

"One day while I was living in the palace of the goddess, her husband, Brahma, took her out to the lakeshore garden. Both dressed in gold, their bodies oiled and perfumed, radiating a new kind of brilliance, they sat to the east of the lake, with its golden steps leading down to the water. In the middle of the lake stood a crystal pillar inlaid with sculpted geese. Brahma lay down facing the lake on a bed of flowers in the shadow of the wishing trees. The goddess took his feet onto her lap to massage them. Desire flooded him, and he pulled her to the bed, each of his four faces trying at once to pull her face to itself, trying to kiss her.

"Smiling at his games, she said, 'Enough of your pranks. It isn't fair. If all four of your faces want me at the same time, what am I supposed to do?

I'm a one-faced woman. Cut it out. It's too much.' She stiffened her neck and pulled her face back. Guarding her lips with her hand, she curved her eyebrows and gave him a sharp look, in a pose of charming anger. This excited him even more.

"Brahma bent her face forcibly to his, pushed her hand away from her lips, and bit her slightly. As pleasure awoke inside her, a soft moan of enchantment slipped from her throat.

"The goddess of speech tried to cover up the moment of ecstasy that had overpowered her deep inside. She was a little embarrassed. Looking for a way to get through it quietly, she pretended her lower lip was hurting, and she turned around, as if angry, to prevent him from provoking her further. I, watching from my cage, understood her feelings from her body language. She was pressing her thighs tightly together and closing her eyes. It was a textbook case.

"Brahma, thwarted, having lost the initiative, put on a show of anger. Not wanting to reveal his real feelings, he turned to me in my golden cage hanging from a nearby tree. 'My little parrot,' he said, 'I'm bored. Won't you tell me a story?'

" 'How can I tell you a story? You're God. I'll listen if *you* tell one.'

" 'In that case, listen,' he said. 'Once upon a time, there was a city called Kasarapura. A rich place, ruled by a king called Kalapurna. He conquered all other kings by virtue of his incomparable brilliance. When he had come of age, a certain Siddha called Svabhava gave him a unique gem, a splendid bow, and gleaming arrows. The gem was of a deep red color, the arrows inexhaustible, and the bow could win over the god of love himself. Because the giver was so noble, the king carried these gifts constantly. A certain king, called Madasaya, happened to enter the kingdom with his wife, Rupanubhuti, and his minister, Dhirabhava, to show off his strength. Skillfully using his bow, Kalapurna drove out Dhirabhava. Madasaya and his wife surrendered, and the king made them his slaves. They followed his command and performed menial tasks.'

"Sarada, the goddess of art, was listening to the story with finely attuned ears, her eyebrows dancing over her darting eyes. She said to me, 'Ask him what happened to this Kalapurna. Who were his father and mother?' She taught me to say all this, and I asked these questions.

"God said, 'A woman called Abhinavakaumudi fell in love with him and married him. His father was a lady called Sumukhasatti and his mother was a gentleman called Manistambha.'

"The goddess laughed and hugged him. 'Relax. Your story is all upside down.' She patted him on the back. 'A male mother and a female father? That's what their names imply.'[1] She couldn't stop laughing. 'Tell me more, my dear husband.'

"Brahma, overjoyed and encouraged, hugged her back. With his four faces, one by one, he kissed her, drinking at her lips, twisting his neck into position over and over and stroking her cheeks and neck. One of his faces bit her a little hard, and she showed anger. 'You never know when to stop,' she said. 'Enough of this. Tell me what happened to the hero of your story.' She wriggled out of his embrace and, raising her arms, took hold of all his faces in her two hands.

"He could see her breasts clearly now, and also the curves of her waist. Getting excited, he kissed her again. 'I know you're good at this,' she said, 'but go on with your story. What happened to the king?'

"So he continued. 'What could have happened? He had a minister named Satvadatma, who crowned him ruler of the city Kramukakanthottara in Angadesa. He reigned happily there, rich in splendor. Madasaya built a golden wall around that city, and the king was pleased. While Madasaya and his wife, Rupanubhuti, were serving him without pause, they had a daughter named Madhuralalasa, born because they kept staring at the king's special jewel. Four wise Brahmin advisors[2] to Madasaya—Agama One, Agama Two, Agama Three, Agama Four—came there and, each in turn, held the jewel. Touching it brought them immense joy. The king allowed all this to happen, because they were all under his control and because he made the rules.

"But one of the advisors mischievously pressed too hard on the jewel, and this made Kalapurna angry. He threw out all four of them, and because of their fault, he also had the golden wall built by their lord, Madasaya, dismantled. Madasaya said to himself, 'What difference does it make? I'm still his man. I'll live somewhere else in his country.' He took his family and traveled south from Kramukakanthottara City. Immediately he came upon two golden pots of surpassing beauty; admiring them, he went to the Middle Country, where he stayed for some time. He hardly noticed that his young daughter, Madhuralalasa, had grown thin from the stress of the

1. The Telugu names have masculine and feminine endings, clear indications of gender.
2. *Purohita*.

journey. People who are intent upon higher comforts they will attain in the future often don't even notice the pain that others in their family may be feeling in the present.

"Still, something in him made him go back to the city. Maybe it was the girl's good fortune. As soon as she caught sight of Kalapurna, she recovered her vigor, her weakness gone. Her body glowed. Madasaya brought her to Kalapurna and told him the secret of her recovery. 'Only you have this kind of power,' he said to the king. They lived happily, praising him. The four advisors also returned, and this time the king favored them.

"From then on, my dear, Madhuralalasa grew into a fine young girl and enjoyed the full fruits of her youth in the company of the king."

## [ Sarasvati Decodes Brahma's Story ]

"The goddess listened. She knit her brows in feigned displeasure that barely concealed the gentle smile arising from her endless love. 'Wait a minute,' she said. 'You're really something, aren't you? I know you can put together entire worlds, but do you have to practise the craft of words on me?'

"Brahma smiled. 'What did I say? What do you mean by craft?'

"'I've known you for a long time. You think I can't see through your story? After all, *I* taught you to speak with hidden meanings and moods. This story you told is about us. I listened quietly because I wondered how you would end it. I'll tell you what it means. Just listen. Kasarapura is the lake. *Kāsāra* means "lake." Because my face reflected in the water looks like a full moon, you spoke of King Kalapurna, whose name means "full moon." When you said he conquered all other kings by virtue of his incomparable brilliance, what you meant is that the reflection of my face outshines every other face. As usual, you were exaggerating. It's what they call "hyperbole." That's all very clear. Then there is that Siddha, Svabhava, who gave him a bow and arrows and a red jewel. Since *svabhāva* means "one's own nature," anybody can see that you were referring to my eyebrows, my sharp looks, and my naturally red lips. Then you mentioned a Madasaya, his wife, Rupanubhuti, and his minister, Dhirabhava—that is, My Heart, Love of Beauty, and Sense of Pride. And you said that Kalapurna, the Full Moon, defeated Dhirabhava, your Sense of Pride, with his bow and made Madasaya, My Heart, that is, *your* heart, and Rupanubhuti, your

Love of Beauty, into slaves. In other words, when you looked at the reflection of my face in the lake, you lost your sense of pride, and your heart and your love of beauty were totally drawn to me.

"'That was when I smiled. My smile was reflected in the water, and to you it looked like a thin layer of moonlight. So you made the identification explicit and named it Abhinavakaumudi, New Moonlight. Since this is a noun in the feminine gender, you gave it to a woman for her name and married her off to Kalapurna. And when you said that Kalapurna's mother was a gentleman called Manistambha and his father was a lady named Sumukhasatti, what you meant was that the reflection off the crystal pillar, *maṇistambha* (a masculine noun), was caused by the proximity, *āsatti* (a feminine noun), of my lovely face, *sumukha*, to that pillar. For some reason you slipped and inverted the genders of the father and the mother, and this made me laugh so hard that I turned back to face you. I was also curious to hear more. So the reflection disappeared from the lake, and my face was in front of you. My face happens to be on top of my neck, so you had to say that Kalapurna, the Full Moon, was crowned in Kramukakanthottara City, that is, Beyond-the-Smooth-Neck Town, in Angadesa, Body Land. Since I'm the owner of that country, you had Kalapurna crowned there by a minister named Satvadatma, Close to Yourself, that is, Myself. The name means someone closely connected to "you," that is, me.

"'At that point you hugged me. Because your heart drove you to it, and because your arms glow like gold, you described this event as Madasaya, My Heart, building a golden wall around Beyond-the-Smooth-Neck Town. Now that your heart and your eyes were locked on to my face, an incessant desire for my lower lip was born in you. What you said was that My Heart and his wife, Love of Beauty, gave birth to a daughter, Madhuralalasa, Craving for Sweetness, through the power of that red jewel. When you said that the four advisors of Madasaya became happy when they touched the jewel, that was a way of saying that your four faces kissed my lips as soon as that craving was born. And since your four faces are the sources of the four Vedas—Rig, Yajus, Sama, and Atharvana—and since they are under your control, you called them Agamas, that is Vedas, One to Four, the Brahmin advisors of Madasaya.

"'Just then, as you may recall, I was mad because one of your faces was biting my lips too hard, and I released myself from your embrace. In your narration this turns up as the Brahmin who pressed so hard against the jewel that Kalapurna got angry, drove all of them away, and had the golden wall dismantled. Your eyes and your heart now shifted away from my face toward the parts of my body that were exposed once I pried myself away from the hug. That is, Madasaya and his wife left Kalapurna's service and went down to Body Land. You also said that on their way down they saw the good omen of two golden pots, and that they were so entranced that they stayed a while in the Middle Country. Isn't this a way of saying that you were excited by seeing my breasts and lingered a while over the curves of my waist? Now that your desire to kiss me waned a little, you said that Craving for Sweetness lost weight. But soon you turned your eyes and your heart back to my face, and your desire to kiss me intensified and was fulfilled when you did kiss me. These three events were described, respectively, as the return of Madasaya with his wife and child to Kalapurna's service, the consequent recovery of Craving for Sweetness, and her marriage to Kalapurna when she came of age.

" 'You have a very artful way of telling the tale of a man's desire. Tell me if I'm right.'

" 'Absolutely,' he said, and smiled.

"She admired his truthfulness. 'You never lie even when you're joking,' she said, and blessed him: 'May the lotus growing from Vishnu's navel, that gave birth to you, stay cool forever.'[3]

"Delighted at her words, he embraced her again, wanting more and more."

The girl concluded the story that Brahma had privately told Sarasvati, in the words of the parrot. The audience was riveted.

"Maybe because the god and the goddess were so absorbed in themselves, or maybe because they thought I was only an animal and therefore ignored me, I"—the parrot[4] continued—"was able to overhear all this. I was afraid to leave in the middle.

But then I hopped
out of my cage, and

3. Brahma was born out of a lotus growing from the god Vishnu's navel. The blessing playfully reformulates the conventional one, "May your mother's womb be cool" (*mī amma kaḍupu callagā*), that is, "May you live long."
4. In fact, the parrot reborn as the young baby, now narrating the story.

inch by inch
I moved away.
'My God!' she said,
'the parrot's here.
We didn't see.'
A little upset.
'So what?' God said,
laughing it off.
'So what if she heard?'

Some days passed. One day Rambha came along with Indra, who was paying a visit to Brahma. She went into the inner palace to see Sarasvati. Passing through several doors, she came upon me in my cage. I was practicing for my own pleasure (as I had been for some time) that special moan of love that came out of the goddess of words.

" 'That's very interesting,' said Rambha, coming close to me. 'Is this what the goddess does when she's with God?'

"I told her everything, holding nothing back—how that sound emerged, and the story that came after it. She wouldn't let me stop. She kept coaxing more out of me. You can teach a lot to a parrot, but it never becomes wise.

"I finished telling the story, and then she asked me to repeat the special sound. I did it, two or three times. That's when the goddess saw us.

"She knit her brows as she looked at me. 'So you're telling stories, you idiot bird. We didn't notice. You're a blabbermouth, gabbing away. Are you crazy? Get out of here. Go live on earth as a whore.' She was very angry, so it was a heavy curse.

"As soon as Rambha heard the furious voice of the goddess, she hid herself behind a big jeweled pillar. She was terrified.

"Brahma came. Gently he asked, 'I've never heard you speak so angrily. What happened?'

"She smiled a smile that added to the charm of her anger. 'Have you heard what this parrot has been saying? It's telling Rambha everything that we said to each other in the lakeside garden, from beginning to end. I heard it myself from behind the door.'

" 'What does it know? It's a parrot. How can you curse it so mercilessly?' He looked at me kindly. I was feeling devastated by that curse, I can tell you. 'Nobody can say no to a mother's curse,' said Brahma. 'But don't feel sad. You'll go through it and then, in one life after that one, you will be born as Madhuralalasa, the daughter of a king named Madasaya. You'll marry a king called Kalapurna and live a life of incomparable wealth and joy with natural, inborn faithfulness to your husband. You'll do whatever is right, and you'll be fulfilled.'

"'What is this?' intervened the goddess. 'Those same names—Madasaya, Madhuralalasa, Kalapurna—you're still talking about them. Or dreaming about them. Wake up.' She laughed.

"'I'm always dreaming about everything connected to your lovely face,' said God. 'But this is no dream. There *is* going to be a king called Kalapurna—on earth. And this bird will be his wife.'

"'That's a story I'd like to hear,' said the goddess.

"'Dear—it's not a new story. It's the same old story you already heard. All the names, nouns, verbs, words, sentences, and meanings that are lexically present in that story also exist in this one. All you have to do is to convert all the past-tense verbs into future tense: for example, "was" becomes "will be," "did" becomes "will do," and so on. That's the only difference. By the way, I like your smile.

"'Incidentally, the story will expand a little into branch-stories, depending on the listeners and the context. But the main story is what you already know.'

"Sarasvati was astonished and thought a little. 'But you said that this king will have a man for his mother and a woman for his father?'

"'Definitely. In fact, *you* will make this happen.'

"This astonished her even more. 'You're the Creator. You can do whatever you like, and you *do* do what you like. But don't make me a party to your lies. And don't even think of linking what you're doing with the story that came out of our kiss, not even in your wildest dreams. Down there, if you just scratch the surface, a flood bursts out. This was a story we told each other very privately. It was born right here. You couldn't leave it at that. Now you've made it happen on earth. People will say, "This all came from Brahma to begin with." They'll wonder what the reason was and someone will say, "It was the reflection of Sarasvati's face in the lake." Then they'll say, "This particular incident caused all the rest." I'll be a laughingstock all over the world, and all because of you. I beg you: Don't mention this to anyone. If *you* don't talk, we can still keep it quiet.'

"'You're just saying that,' Brahma replied. 'Is there anyone who doesn't want to be known as a good lover? If you really mean what you say, touch your nose with your tongue, and I'll believe you.' She burst into laughter.

"With an effort she held it in. 'No matter what you say, I don't like it. It isn't funny. Stop laughing.' She hit him with the bunch of flowers she was holding, big as her breasts.

"As you can see," the parrot continued, "Brahma was insistent, while she was begging him to stop even as she clung to his neck, cheek to cheek, with his chin in her hand and her breasts rubbing against his chest.

"He said, 'Why are you so persistent? Whatever you say, I know you really want this story to become known. Tell me, don't you want people everywhere to know this wonderful tale? How else will you become famous?

" 'Come to think of it, everything is known only through language. And all language is you. This being the case, nothing you disapprove of can ever see the light of day. That story of Kalapurna that came out of your love-game and that was born from my lips is going to be famous all over the world. You can't tell me you don't want this. Of course, I can understand what you say. That's how women are. They like everybody to know how their husbands love them, but they don't want to tell it all themselves.'

"The goddess looked at him. 'If you're so intent on having your way, why should I object? Anyway, that king is certainly going to be born on earth. He will rule the kingdom. His story will anyway become famous. This much is given. But why should my story become known along with his?'

" 'That story will happen first, and your story will be known later.'

" 'In that case, I have to see to the channels through which it will be known. But don't you talk about it anywhere.'

" 'I won't,' said Brahma. 'Not me.'

"Then the goddess looked at me. 'This parrot is going to be born as a whore. There's no question of her remembering any of this. But where is that woman Rambha? We have to teach her a lesson.'

"Rambha emerged, trembling, from behind the pillar and fell at the goddess's feet.

" 'Get up,' said Sarasvati. 'If you tell this story anywhere, you know what will happen. You know what I can do.'

"Brahma chuckled. '*I* know—better than anyone. This is how it will be. From now on, whoever tells this story or hears it will have children, grand-children, and great-grandchildren and live with vast wealth and happiness on earth for a very long time. All this is my blessing.'

"His wife said, 'Fine. If that's how you like it, let it be like that on earth. Nothing need stop it.' She broke into a big smile. And I, the erstwhile parrot, at her command left that place and began my life as a courtesan in Dvaraka."

The baby, who seemed to know everything, narrated all that she had done in her courtesan existence. Then she said to the king, "I lived through the curse of the goddess as someone called Kalabhashini. Afterward, by Brahma's blessing, I began this life in this body. It was in my previous life, at the temple of the goddess, that I saw this necklace. You heard me tell you about it. That's why I said, 'After two long years, I now see this necklace again.' "

At this point Alaghuvrata, the Malayali Brahmin, stood up politely, bowed down at the feet of the girl, and rose to speak. "I can verify one thing you did in your previous life as Kalabhashini."

"What is it you can attest to?" asked the king. So he reported how he had first heard the name Kalapurna from Kalabhashini, how he had prayed so long to hear the whole story, and how he had fallen into this court. Then he folded his hands and said to the girl, "Your words cannot fail. The proof is that you've now become Madhuralalasa. When can I see your husband, that great man and king, Kalapurna?"

"Good Brahmin," said the child, "it's not proper for me to answer your question.[5] These people here know the answer. Ask them."

So he looked to the king. "Did you hear what this girl has said, O king? Please tell me your names, what you do, and who all these people are. What world am I in? What city? Who are you? Who is this girl? I'm in a daze. I have no idea about any of these things, and there was no time to ask because of the arresting way the girl was telling her story."

"True," said the king, "there was no time to ask. I also had no time to ask you about yourself. It was one story after another until now. We heard only a little about you. Anyway, let me tell you about us. My name is Kalapurna. Here are the jewel, bow and arrows that Svabhava gave me. These four are Agamas One through Four. That man over there is Satvadatma. Next to him is Madasaya and his wife, Rupanubhuti. This amazing girl is her daughter.

"Her father, Madasaya, used to serve me, but he went away. Now's he come back, saying that his daughter, who had become weak, has revived

5. Madhuralalasa has good reason to be shy at this point, as soon becomes clear.

upon seeing me. He and his wife placed the child before me in this golden cradle. Her name is Madhuralalasa.

"This country is called Angadesha. We are in Kramukakanthottara City, but I was born in Kasarapura. It's not far from here. But the point is the following.

"All the names and events in the story that Brahma told Sarasvati are, without exception, exactly the same as our names and our lives. But Brahma was only making up a story with names invented to explain the reflection of Sarasvati's face and the games they were playing. How does all this fit so perfectly with our lives? There's no disparity whatsoever. We were wondering about it all the time, but we didn't want to interrupt the narration. Only when she came to the end of the story were our questions resolved."

Alaghuvrata asked the king, "Then tell me, king, is your father really a woman and your mother a man, like in the story Brahma told? I'm curious."

"I'm curious, too," he answered. "This little girl seems to know everything. Let's ask her. There are two things that remain unclear from her story. One is this matter. The other is the question of what will happen when this child comes of age. That one lies in the future and can be imagined. The other one is past and must be told."

So Alaghuvrata begged the girl. "You know everything. Would you please tell us how this king was born? You first mentioned the power of his story to me, and you told the whole story here, just as I had hoped. Furthermore, I got to see the hero of the story. Now tell me the events of his birth."

## [ Manistambha and Sumukhasatti Exchange Genders ]

"You know," she began, "that when you arrived at the temple of the Lion-Rider, two people were talking to me—the Siddha called Manistambha and a woman called Sumukhasatti. You also know that they spent a long time in the temple, disciplining their senses through Yoga. Then they left the temple and made love in a grove. Suddenly the Siddha, wanting the upside-down position, said to his wife, 'I want you to be a man, and I'll be the woman.' She obediently replied, 'You become the woman, and I'll become the man.' Instantly their genders were transposed.

"Somehow, at once the Siddha became a woman. A thin waist, full breasts and buttocks, languid eyes, a certain gracefulness, a pretty face framed by thick black hair—all these made up his now delicate body. His wife, in turn, took on his form, losing nothing—including his sparse mustache and reddish matted hair. Sometimes in couples, one becomes more attractive than the other—or less so—but a total exchange of genders is totally unheard of.

"Since at the moment they were changing they were deeply engrossed in one another, taking one another in through the eyes, each acquired the other's exact form. What you have in your mind is what really counts.

"It was surprising even to them—seeing their appearances precisely transposed. They couldn't quite understand why it happened.

"Sumukhasatti thought back and found the reason (she was staring at her husband's face). 'This is the power of the words I just uttered. It can't be any other reason. Some time ago, when I was surrendering my old body in the presence of the Lion-Rider Goddess, I asked her to make my words come true.[6] And if you remember what the inscription on the temple pillar said, you know that my last wish *had* to come true.'

"'Don't say more,' Manistambha cried. 'You never know what might happen.' He was under the sway of the future. 'Remember, Sarasvati has blessed us both. She promised me that you will never become pregnant, and you that you will have a son by me. We don't know how this will unfold. We shouldn't say anything too hastily.

"'And one more thing. They say that women have more fun than men in sex and in what precedes and follows it. I want to find out for myself. So I want us to stay as we are for some time. You can enjoy being the man.'

"Sumukhasatti agreed. 'You can ask me to take whatever form you like, and I'll treat your words as God's command. I'll do as you say.' She stayed a man. Manistambha kept on making love as a woman. They also began calling one another by the other's name, to conform to the change in gender.

"After a while, the artificial woman wanted to take his new husband for a ride on the lion, to visit faraway fields and forests. He called the lion over, and they mounted it and flew away, enjoying the speed. As they were looking down from the sky, they noticed a city, and he said to his dear hus-

6. At the moment that Manistambha was trying to behead Kalabhashini, Sumukhasatti interposed herself, taking an oath on the goddess, warning Manistambha that his effort would not succeed, and praying, "Great Sakti! Make my words come true." Since according to the inscription, her dying wish *must* come true, she retains this ability into her life as the young Sumukhasatti. Everything she says does come true.

band: 'Look at this fine city with its high towers, a treasury of delights. The wall that circles it could be an anklet on the foot of a beautiful woman.

"'Geese, cranes, and herons
are calling out from the lilies and lotuses in the moat
that holy Manasa, Lake of the Gods
far to the north, is nothing remotely
like this paradise.

"'Even the wall inside the moat has the shape of a lotus. They call this place on the lakeshore Kasarapura, Lake Town. Dear husband—you can smell the delicious betel mixed with camphor that women chew as they play on the roofs of their jeweled palaces.

"'I came here once before, and I know this city. I'm still amazed at its beauty. I'd like to live here, my dear husband. We have to get off this lion.' 'She' brought the lion down to the ground and dismounted with the husband.

"The king of that country was named Satvadatma. He was out riding when he caught sight of this woman. He couldn't take his eyes off her. 'I've taken as tribute from enemy kings the finest women they had in their harems. They're in my house. Now I've seen a woman who takes my breath away, like no one before. Even heaven does not have a woman as lovely as this one. Why bother even mentioning my palace or those of all the other kings in this world? How can someone so beautiful have a husband like that? But let's not jump to conclusions. Let's find out from them who they are.'

"At that moment she happened to look at him. He spurred his horse to a gallop, as if he were jumping over a whole line of soldiers. Then he suddenly reined it in, playing with it to attract attention. The light from his jeweled crown glittered and danced as the horse moved. He made it paw the ground, he made it prance, back up, come to a halt, his gem-studded bracelets jingling all the while as he stroked its mane. To show off his brilliant armlets, he stretched out his arm and clapped his companion on the back. He twisted the lotus he playfully held in his fingers, so that the sunlight glittered off the jewels on his rings. Simply to show off his good teeth, he pretended to consult with his aide-de-camp, who was riding alongside him. At the same time, he was joking with his confidant, laughing so his pearl earrings would shake and be noticed. He lifted his crown from his head and replaced it. He twisted the ends of his mustache with his gleaming fingernails. Observing that she was noticing him, he flirted brazenly, full of himself.

"As he became more and more excited, he could barely hold back. Someone handed him a bunch of flowers, which he pressed to his chest with both arms, stealing a glance at her. As for her, she let her sari slip slightly from her breasts and bent her face.

"He got off his horse and walked toward them alone. 'Where are you from, Mahatma?" he asked the Siddha. "Where are you headed to? What are your names? And what is this woman to you?'

"The Siddha told him how they had come there and said, 'I call myself Manistambha, and this woman goes by the name of Sumukhasatti. She is my wife.'

"The king was thinking, 'Just let me keep this woman somewhere around me. If I'm lucky, things could happen.' With a veneer of politeness, he folded his hands and said, 'We have a deep desire to host you in our house for a few days and to serve you to the best of our not inconsiderable abilities. We would be honored if you would accept our invitation, great Siddha.'

"Manistambha looked at the wife. 'Let's accept. We have to stay somewhere or other,' she said to the husband. She was smiling.

"So the king led the two of them to a palankeen that took them to his home. He set them up nicely in a big palace with golden beds and rich perfumes and a huge retinue of maids. He would visit them often under the pretext of looking after their needs. He was always extremely courteous. Then he sent an appropriate messenger to ask her to come to him.

"She sent a message back, suggesting a postponement. 'I suspect I may be a little pregnant. Until I give the Siddha his child, I won't take another man.'

"Soon there were signs of morning sickness. Her body became tired, and she had a craving for the taste of earth. Now her pregnancy was certain. Formerly, in the contest between breasts and waists, the breasts always had the upper hand—her waist being so thin. Now the waist was thickening, and the breasts became so worried that her nipples became dark. They got darker and darker, like the night sky in winter, and her face took on the pallor of a winter moon. As her waist expanded, her desire for her husband contracted. The folds of flesh on her belly disappeared. Her navel opened up. Easily exhausted, she walked more slowly. As her due date approached, she felt drowsy and dull.

"At last this king," said the child, pointing to Kalapurna, "was born at a moment when five planets were exalted, under the best stars. Cool breezes blew, flowers rained down under clear skies, the gods played their drums and cried 'Hurrah!,' the three fires blazed up, good people felt joy, bad people sank low. Moreover," the girl explained, "when Brahma said that Manistambha, the man, would be Kalapurna's mother, and that Sumukhasatti, the woman, would be his father, he was deliberately ignoring the temporary change in their names at that period and citing their real names given at birth. Brahma's words don't ever go wrong, do they? Immediately after the birth, Manistambha, the new mother, made his wife again speak her words of power, so that they would revert to their original genders—he reacquiring his masculinity, and she her feminine identity. They also re-exchanged their names and resumed their Yoga practices. They're still in Kasarapura, not far from here. You can check with them if you want confirmation.

"The moment Kalapurna was born, he was already a young man; and at that very moment the Siddha called Svabhava came and gave him a jewel, some arrows, and a bow. No one can tell which came first, his birth, his youthful manhood, or these gifts. It was the Siddha who named him Kalapurna. The king of the town, Satvadatma, heard about this and thought, 'He must be a man of godly powers and superhuman greatness. I thought his mother was just an ordinary woman, like anybody else, and was infatuated with her. This was wrong. Somehow or other, I should make amends.' He went to her and said, 'Mother, I didn't realize who you were. If I offended you in any way, please forgive me. I am surrendering all my kingdom to your son. I'll serve him as his minister.'"

Alaghuvrata wanted to know who that Svabhava was and why he gave the jewel, arrows, and bow to Kalapurna.[7] Madhuralalasa explained:

"The Siddha named Svabhava is none other than Sumukhasatti's father. When she was born, he left his wife and wandered around the world until he came to Mahuripura. There he met Dattatreya, who knew all the secrets of Yoga. He served him and learned from him all the arts of Yoga. Since in the course of his Yogic practice he focused his thoughts entirely on his inner nature, he got the name Svabhava, "one's own nature."

7. Note that the story now jumps backward again, to a point before Kalapurna's birth.

## [ A Lecture on Yoga ]

Alaghuvrata wanted to hear more. "You're a treasure of wisdom. There's nothing you don't know. Tell me what you mean by Yoga."

The girl embarked upon a discourse on this subject.[8] "Yoga means connection—that is, the connectedness of the individual self with the ultimate Self. It has eight parts. Let me explain. They are known as discipline (*yama*), control (*niyama*), postures (*asana*), breathing (*pranayama*), and four advanced meditative states—*pratyahara*, *dharana*, *dhyana*, and *samadhi*. They are further subdivided into many elements. For example, discipline means the following ten rules: truthfulness, compassion, tolerance, courage, moderation in eating, sincerity, celibacy, no stealing, nonviolence, cleanliness. 'Truthfulness' means not telling lies in the sense of not causing hurt to others. 'Compassion' is being sensitive to another person's distress. 'Tolerance' is not getting angry at other people's shortcomings. 'Courage' is not taking to heart a loss of property or separation from loved ones. 'Moderation in eating' means that an ascetic should eat only eight mouthfuls a day; twice that number are acceptable for a person retired to the wilderness; a householder can have twice that amount; other people should take light meals. 'Sincerity' is being truthful in thought, word, and deed while performing prescribed actions and avoiding prohibited ones. 'Celibacy,' for a renouncer, a person retired to the wilderness, and a bachelor student, is total avoidance of sexual relations with a woman in thought, word, or deed; for a married man, sex is permitted with his wife during her fertile periods, but he must have nothing to do with other women. 'No stealing' is not taking others' property. 'Nonviolence' is avoiding harm to any living being. According to the texts, 'cleanliness' is of two kinds, external and internal; the external kind means washing your body with water and with earth; the internal kind means purifying your mind by meditation on the truth.

"The ten forms of control are: *tapas*,[9] contentment, faith, charity, piety, study, sense of shame, attention, chanting, and ritual. Only a person who has held to these rules of discipline and control is eligible for the further practices of postures and breathing.

8. We have omitted several verses from this rather self-contained discourse on Yoga.
9. "Heat," that is, discipline in praxis and meditation.

"There are many bodily postures and exercises. Chief among them are, for example, the following: in the *Svastika* posture, you sit with a straight spine while putting the sole of each foot in the space between thigh and calf of the other foot. In *Gomukhasana*, the cow's face, you rest the left buttock on the left ankle and the right on the right and maintain stable posture. In *Padmasana*, the lotus, you put the right foot on the left thigh and the left foot on the right thigh, stretching your hands to catch hold of your two toes. Then bring your chin down to touch your chest. Focus your eyes on the tip of your nose. But some people say there is no need to bring your chin to your chest. And there is another variation of this posture where you place the soles of your feet flat against your thighs and your hands between your thighs while staring at the tip of your nose. In this posture, bring your chin down to your chest and suck in your breath while pressing your tongue against the root of one of the two front teeth. Similarly, there are the Hero's posture, the Lion, the Secure, the Released, the Hidden, the Peacock, the Western. All of them produce agility of body and make you healthy as well as purifying you of evil.

"As for working with the breath, it has three stages, *puraka*, *kumbhaka*, and *recaka*. This is called *pranayama*; if one practices it over and over, he will control the winds in his body, and all the energy channels will open. In the body, there are 72,000 such channels. Among them, 101 are really important. Among these, 14 are special. Three of these merit further mention. One of them is the most important of all—the *sushumna*, also called the *brahma* channel that leads to the opening to ultimate space at the top of the head. The best form of Yoga involves directing the breath into that channel.

"First, turn the senses away from their objects. Then, think of whatever they dwell upon as your own self. Perform your daily activities only in your mind. Fix your breath on the eighteen secret spaces in your body. This is what experts in Yoga have called *pratyahara*, 'total reabsorption.'

"If you stabilize your entire mental activity in Vishnu, without letting it wander, that is *samadhi*, 'totality.'

"Together with control of breath, all these make up the total Yoga."

## [ Svabhava and Madasaya at Srisailam ]

"By practising these Yogic methods assiduously and concentrating his thoughts on his inner nature, that Siddha became Svabhava. He was searching all over the world for a suitably secluded space for his *samadhi* when by chance he came to the land of his birth, where he found a lake as deep as a hundred palm trees. This, he decided, was the ideal place for Yoga.

"He dived into it and stayed there, holding his breath. But then his son-in-law suddenly appeared down there. He had jumped into the lake because he was angry at his wife. Svabhava gave his son-in-law a jewel that kept him forever young, and other things. But he didn't tell him how they were related. Why reconnect to the entanglements that you've already let go?

"Eventually, after a long time, he completed his Yoga, according to destiny. He left the lake and went to Srisailam,[10] where all wise people go. Its slopes were studded with sapphires and rubies; a sculpted wall circled the temple, carved with images of new, benevolent gods. It was a place where you could become free. You could see huge boulders reflected in the water of the Ganges of the Nether World, which, like an anklet circling the foot of that towering mountain, seemed to contain these images of rival mountains it had subdued. This densely wooded mountain was like an arm thrust into the sky to keep it from collapsing on to the earth.

"With reverence, Svabhava climbed the great mountain, so rich in a special kind of power, and paid his respects to Mallikarjuna-Siva, the lord white as jasmine. Afterward, as he was strolling along the slopes, he suddenly caught sight of Manikandhara, who was about to throw himself off the mountain. 'Who are you?' he asked, 'and why are you so eager to kill yourself?'

"Manikandhara told him his name and his family and also his entire story up to the point of his impending suicide. Svabhava was excited to hear in this story the names of his daughter and son-in-law, Sumukhasatti and Manistambha, or Sugatri and Salina.[11] He asked for more details, as much as Manikandhara could provide, and introduced himself as Sugatri's father. He told him about his own life, meanwhile wondering how the contradictory blessings given to Sugatri and Salina by the goddess Sarada were going to come to fruition. Of course, he assured himself, somehow or other it would surely come to pass.

10. The wilderness shrine of Śiva-Mallikârjunasvāmi, the Lord White as Jasmine, in western Andhra.

11. Note that Manikandhara had met both of these people in their later lives as Sumukhasatti and Manistambha, and he had also heard and reported the story of Sugatri and Salina as a result of his visit to the Sarada-pitha in Kashmir.

"Svabhava said to Manikandhara, 'You're definitely scheduled for a great future. As the disciple of Narada, you were trained in music by Krishna himself. At the sage's advice, you went on pilgrimage to all the great Vishnu shrines. You've transformed an accidental curse into the promise of ruling a kingdom. Anyway, you're a gandharva, which is in itself a great gift. If you consider all of this, it's clear that your next life will be one of immeasurable success. Your previous karma won't come to nothing. Everything will bear fruit. In fact, all that you've done so far is more than adequate for a great rebirth. What additional benefit are you expecting to derive from jumping off this mountain?'

"'I'm hoping to be born as the son of very honorable and righteous people,' said Manikandhara.

"'If that's the case, you can't find better people than my daughter and my son-in-law to choose as your parents,' said Svabhava. 'I would be happy if you would do so. What's more, I can do you a big favor. Long ago, I asked my guru for a sword, for self-protection. Something inside me made me ask. He created a sword and gave it to me, saying, "This will never fail. Your family will be, from now on, a line of royal warriors." If you think about it, to be born as my son-in-law's son would therefore be very fitting for you. You will rule the world. Put an end to all your doubts and take my advice.'

"Manikandhara said, 'Listen. There is already a guarantee that I'll be reborn as a king. But that's not enough. I'm jumping off this cliff in order to be reborn in a virtuous family.[12] And I still have a few worries in my mind. You can be a king, you can be born in a good family, but still it is hard to overcome one's enemies, inside and out. This disturbs me. Moreover, if the demon of political power possesses him, even the wisest person will become a little blind, a little mute, and a little deaf. One could perhaps hope to rid oneself of the drawbacks of political power by associating with learned Brahmins who know the ancient texts. But why should such people want to come to you? They don't want what you can give them—in fact, they're beyond desire—and they avoid kings, who can only give them *things*. You have to search them out actively, and it's rare for a king to have the good fortune of finding them and enticing them to his court. That's how life is. You need a lot of wisdom to be able to please them and bring them to you. Think how long it will take for me to acquire such wisdom.

12. To die at Srisailam on Sivaratri Day brings blessings such as this.

These questions and others like them pierce my heart like a sharp arrow. You seem be to capable of making things happen. Show me a way to resolve these worries.'

"He persisted in this vein for a while, until Svabhava said, to free him from his problems, 'I can give you a bow that bestows certain victory and a new set of arrows. They're the right weapons for you. This I can create through the help of my guru, Dattatreya. There's nothing that his blessing can't achieve. I'll also make you a magical jewel[13] that will attract great scholars of all texts and knowledge to your patronage. Merely by looking at it, those who come to you will find health, protection, and long life.'

"And right in front of him he produced these items—a bow; sharp, glistening arrows; and a red jewel. 'I'll be there at the moment you are born, even a little before, with these in my hands. You don't have to worry about when you'll get them and how long it will take.'

"While he was saying this, Madasaya approached him with his wife and advisors. They were visiting Srisailam on pilgrimage for the Night of Shiva.[14] As they were passing by, they heard Svabhava speaking and, after asking who he was, fell at his feet. 'Today our pilgrimage to the God White as Jasmine has been fulfilled,' said Madasaya. 'I've been looking for you everywhere. Now I'm in luck. I am King Madasaya of the Hehaya lineage. This woman is my wife. These men are my advisors, great minds all of them. They bear the tradition of all the Vedas, Rig, Yajus, Sama, and the Fourth. My wife and I served the great Dattatreya, who lives in Mahuri City, with their help. The great hero Kartaviryarjuna rose to be an emperor and became famous everywhere because of Dattatreya's blessing. I myself come from Kartavirya's royal line, and that is why I went to serve the sage myself. He came to me in a dream and told me to look for you, a Siddha named Svabhava, his student. He promised that you would you make my wishes come true. Since I never saw you before and had no idea where you live, I was going everywhere, asking everyone. When I heard you mention Dattatreya, I had to find out who you were. Now I've found you at last. It's almost as good as having my wishes come true.'

"Svabhava was very pleased. He realized that this was his guru's strategy, a way to make him famous. 'My guru really loves me,' he thought to himself, making a mental bow to him. Then he looked at the king. 'Who am

13. *maṇi*.

14. Śiva's festival in the month of Magha (February–March).

I to give you what you wish? But you claim my guru said I would, so let whatever he planned for you come to pass.'

"Madasaya said, 'What I want is two things: victory and children.'

"Svabhava showed him the bow and arrows he had just created, and he also pointed out Manikandhara. 'This is Manikandhara. I have just now made a bow and arrows for him that will bring him victory in his next life. You will conquer all the kings of the earth except him. That is certain.'

"'That's fine,' said the king, a little sarcastically. 'Your kindness is enough for me. In the end I will take care of things myself. After all, he can't conquer except with the help of this bow and these arrows.'

"He was bragging, and Svabhava didn't like it. 'There's no doubt about his defeating you in that next life, but what's more, he'll make both you and your wife his slaves.'

"The wise advisors intervened with great politeness, bowing. 'Noble mind! What does this man know? If he says three words he makes six mistakes. Can we make amends to you? Won't you take into account our humble words? He searched you out and came to you because you are in his guru's line. Take that into consideration and give him what he wants, somehow or other.'

"'My words will not fail," said Svabhava. 'They are just like what God writes on your forehead when you are born. Your king will conquer all others except the one I mentioned. That one he will also serve, along with his wife, in a very humble way. Your king will also have a child when he and his queen see a certain jewel that the king possesses.'

"The advisors thought a little. 'We've been with this king for a long time, and he has been treating us well. He took our word as his word, our happiness as his. Now whom should we serve when our king himself becomes a slave to another?'

"'Your king's king will be your king. A certain jewel he wears will bring you happiness. You'll even forget—all four of you and Madasaya—your past preeminence, and still you'll be happy. Until Manikandhara is reborn, your king can go on enjoying the pleasures of conquest. After that, he will become a servant, as I have said. As for you, you will touch the jewel and find great joy.'

"With this, Svabhava, the great Siddha, sent them off. He also took leave of Manikandhara and went away, wherever he wanted to go.[15] Just

15. This is the last we hear of Svabhava.

as he had predicted, Madasaya conquered king after king," concluded Madhuralalasa.

Alaghuvrata had another question for the girl. "What did Manikandhara do after taking leave of the Siddha?"

*That's what he said, O king, delighting in great poetry. With a gleam from the corner of your eye, you cast away the gloom of your enemies' dark pride.*

This is the fifth chapter in the long poem called *Kalapurnodayamu* made by soft-spoken Suraya, son of Pingali Amaranarya, whose poetry all connoisseurs enjoy throughout the world.

# CHAPTER 6

*Listen, powerful, radiant King Krishna, son of Narasimha.*

Madhuralalasa said to Alaghuvrata, the Malayali Brahmin: "I'll tell you the rest of Manikandhara's story. Listen."

## [ Manikandhara Fights the Porcupine Demon ]

"He had made all his preparations for jumping off the cliff. He took a purifying bath, as the wise suggest for such an occasion. Then, very determined, he took up his position at the edge of the abyss. As he was about to leap off, a sudden uproar erupted, like the fury of a tidal wave. The terrified pilgrims to Srisailam scattered in all directions; mothers had no time even to grab their children. Manikandhara's mind was deeply disturbed. Then a very striking woman appeared, her sari tightly wound around her bursting breasts. She was holding a dazzling sword, which she handed to him. 'Gandharva,' she said, 'save these pilgrims. You will still get the fruit of your great leap.'

"Immediately there was a huge shower of porcupine quills. They shot right through the thick trunks of nearby trees, smashed boulders into pieces, pulverized elephants, tigers, lions, and other animals. They fell so thick it looked like someone had stretched out a canopy in the sky; you couldn't tell if they were iron bars with silver bands or silver bars with iron bands. Manikandhara was amazed at this unprecedented barrage, so he asked the woman, 'What is this shower of quills? What do you want me to do with this huge sword? And who are you?'

"'There's no time for you to hear anything now,' she said. 'Show what you're made of. The demon is getting closer, the quills are falling thicker. Face him now, cut him down with the sword. You can see him over there, coming at you in the shape of a porcupine. Don't let him get past this spot. Strike at once.'

"'Don't worry,' he said. 'I'll kill him. You go and calm the pilgrims. Trust me.' And he headed toward the enemy, brandishing his new sword, tossing it high into the hair and catching it by the handle. Moving ahead with great panache, he cut his way through the hail of quills with swift and dexterous strokes of the sword. He saw the porcupine, bristling with quills, and the littered slope of the mountain. 'You fool of a demon,' he cried, 'what do you gain by this ugly form and this ugly violence? Your evil acts will certainly rebound against you. You must know what happened to the Elephant Demon,[1] who was more powerful than the elephants who hold up the world. What happened to Indrajit,[2] who was shooting arrows from behind the clouds? And what about Vritra,[3] who took over all space in the universe? Or Hiranyaksha,[4] who rolled up the earth like a mat? And there were many others, like Sambara the magician. What good is this unsightly shape? I'm going to kill you.'

"The demon laughed. 'Who is this man? Has he lost his senses? Did he go insane? Or is he too arrogant to know who he is? Or was he born crazy? How strong does he think he is? Does he think he can take me on, after I've crushed the elephants who hold up the world? God must want him to die.' He addressed Manikandhara. 'If you don't care any more about living, come fight. I've had enough lectures. Do you think there are sticks that can't take on a pile of pots? I'll show you who I am.'

1. Gajasura, whom Siva killed and flayed.
2. Ravana's son, slain in the *Rāmāyaṇa* battle.
3. The enemy of Indra, king of the gods.
4. Hiranyaksha stole the earth and was killed by Vishnu.

He shook himself a little and drowned Manikandhara in a flood of quills. Manikandhara cut through them with flashy swordwork and cut off the demon's head in the little space he had to move."

Madhuralalasa stopped speaking, but Alaghuvrata was still curious. "Who was that demon? And who was the woman who got him killed? I have to know."

"I'll tell you both their stories," said Madhuralalasa. "Listen. The demon was the Buffalo Demon's cousin.[5] Because the goddess Durga killed his cousin, he wanted to take revenge against her. They called him Salyasura, the Porcupine Demon. Since his quills were as big as crowbars, they also called him Crowbar. He couldn't forgive Durga; hate filled his mind. 'What shall I do?' he thought to himself. 'Should I kill every single worshiper of the goddess, searching them out everywhere in the world? Shall I knock down all her temples, wherever they might be? How else can I handle this rage that is burning me up inside? Indra may not like it, but what can he do to me? A poor man's anger can only hurt his own lips. Great Sukra[6] has blessed me; the gods are powerless against my strength. I'm not afraid of the goddess. I'm stronger than she is. My one fear is that Vishnu is tricky; somehow or other he'll find a way to overcome the demons and protect the gods. I must do something to outfox him. Until I think of a way, I'll clothe myself in a garb of peace. People will say that even though I may be a demon, I'm a good person.'

"Thinking like this, he was wandering in the wilderness when, as fate would have it, a certain *apsaras* woman named Abhinavakaumudi, born from a ray of moonlight, came there. He was taken by her beauty and forgot everything he'd been thinking. He was overtaken by desire.

" 'Lady,' he said, 'this whole world is in the palm of my hand, like kneaded dough. I can bring you anything you want from anywhere. I can also assume the form of any male worthy of your beauty. Take me. I'm yours.'

"She walked away with a withering look, saying nothing.

This made him mad. 'Lady, do you think any man will touch you after this? No one would have the courage to approach a woman I love.'

"He was trying to scare her, but she was stubborn. 'Listen, you beast. I will marry only the man who kills you,' she said. 'This is my vow.'

5. Mahishasura, the buffalo demon, was killed by the goddess Durga.
6. The Minister and adviser (*guru*) of the demons.

"He was very hurt by such cruel words but let her go without doing her any harm. His dogged hope that someday, somehow or other, she would let him sleep wtih her was stronger than his anger.

"From that moment she was searching for a man who could kill this demon. He himself was looking for a way to acquire the power to kill anyone trying to kill him. Eventually, fate brought him to the temple of the Lion-Riding goddess, where he read the inscription on the stone pillar: *If you are tough enough to cut off your head with this chopper, it will again stick to your neck and you will live to kill whoever tries to kill you.* He understood at once that this was the answer he'd been seeking, so he followed the directions precisely.

"Finding his head back on his neck, he was convinced that there was no one stronger than he, so, full of himself, he instantly started to demolish the stone temple of the goddess. Abhinavakaumudi, for her part, still searching for someone who could kill this demon, heard about the goddess and thought that maybe *she* could show the way. So she came there, too, and found him there—Crowbar himself. 'How did *he* get here?' she thought. 'How can I get away from him?'

" 'Still beautiful, aren't you?' he said to her. 'Remember what you said to me in the forest the other day, when I begged you to take me?'

"He was very puffed up with the power he'd recently acquired. She replied—now bear in mind," said Madhuralalasa, "this isn't addressed to you, I'm going to turn my head away when I say the words[7]—'Of course I remember. I said I would marry only the man who kills you. Do you have any problem with that?'

" 'What do you mean, do I have a problem with it?!' said the demon. 'Haven't you read the inscription on the stone pillar? Just read it and have a look at me. I've cut off my head and got it back. Need I say more?'

"She read the inscription. She looked at his head. She saw the slight scar on his neck. She saw blood on the ground. It all added up.

"Very depressed, she ran into the temple and fell at the feet of the

7. The internal narrator, Madhuralalasa, doesn't want her listeners, especially Kalapurna, to go on nodding their heads or to take the harsh words as meant for them. This aside gives us a glimpse into the nature of oral storytelling, where the audience tends to nod and say "hum" in response to the narrator, who assumes the personae of all the characters in turn. Suranna's sensitivity to the performative context of the narrative is evident here.

goddess. 'Only she can save me now,' she thought. The demon waited for her outside.

"Lying at the feet of the goddess, she told her the whole story—the vow she had taken, Crowbar's amorous proposal, and the reason for his over-confidence. 'Great goddess,' she cried, 'I don't know what to do. I'm in big trouble. It's up to you to save me and to keep me from breaking my oath.' The Lion-Rider was happy that she had come, since this meant a temporary reprieve from the imminent destruction of her temple. So she immediately responded to this prayer, appearing before Abhinavakaumudi.

" 'This man will indeed kill whoever comes to kill him,' she said. 'That's inevitable. Can anyone stop him from getting the fruits of his act of self-beheading, as the inscription prescribes? Let's think of another way to save your vow.'

"She thought for a minute. 'Young lady,' she said, 'if you read the text carefully, it says that he'll kill anyone who comes to kill him. But there's nothing that says that he won't be killed himself in the process. So a courageous person could still kill him and then die because of the rule. Your vow was to marry the courageous man who will kill the demon, right? But you could marry him in his next life. That would be just fine. All we have to do now is to find such a man.'

"She thought a bit further. Her face alight, she said, 'There is a certain worthy gandharva called Manikandhara. In special circumstances, he received a sword that never fails and left it in my temple.' She pointed out the sword to Abhinavakaumudi. 'Take it and put it in Manikandhara's fearless hand. Make him kill the demon, who will be following you wherever you go, enslaved to your beauty. Lure him to Manikandhara. No matter how fed up he gets with you, he'll never harm you. You have nothing to fear. Originally this sword was given by Dattatreya to a Siddha called Svabhava. He gave it to his son-in-law, Manistambha, who gave it to Manikandhara for a special reason. So Manikandhara came by it legitimately, and it will work for him. It won't work for anyone else. So hand it over only to him. At the moment, he is at Srisailam, about to jump off the mountain. You'd better hurry. Tell him he'll get the same result he wants by using this sword. Stop him from jumping and get him to kill the demon. This same gandharva, Manikandhara, will be reborn as someone called Kalapurna, in a city called Kasarapura. You can marry him and fulfill your vow.'

"Abhinavakaumudi tightened her sari around her waist, tied up her hair in a bun, grabbed the sword in her hand, and ran out of the temple, like a missile launched by the Love God. The demon saw her and was alarmed—for her sake. 'Maybe she's coming to kill me,' he thought, 'and she'll have to die for that.' Disturbed at that thought, he cried to her, 'I invoke all your own gods: Don't come at me! Not that I'm afraid. I'm worried for you, worried that you'll die if you attack me.'

" 'You don't have to invoke my gods to protect me. I know you. I won't attack you. I'll do as you want.' She walked on. It appeared to him that the way she spoke was encouraging, so he walked after her. She didn't wait for him, but she didn't move too far ahead either. If he fell too far behind, she would find some pretext to linger a little until he caught up. She was leading him on.

"Completely absorbed in his fantasy, staring at her all the way, not even aware of the vast distance, the demon walked behind her all the way to Srisailam. Love is blind.

"But he was tired of her game. He called her. 'You said you would do as I want. What's going on? Are you trying to fool me?'

" 'Have I not done as you wanted? What did I do differently? You were afraid I was about to attack you, so you invoked my gods and warned me not to approach. I said I would do as you want. Even now I'm sticking to my promise.'

"He was angry now. 'Do you think I'm scared of you? You think I'm a nobody just because I didn't want to kill you and followed you this whole long way. Anyway, it's no wonder. I haven't shown you my strength. Just look.' Without touching her, he let loose a shower of quills by shaking his body. Mountains shattered, tree trunks were pierced and sewn together, and living creatures fell dead.

"Revealing his full strength in this way, he declared, 'If you still don't love me, I'll scorch every place you go so it looks like a path struck by lightning. You'll bring bad luck wherever you go. Nobody in your family ever had such a bad name as you will. Think it over. Wouldn't it be better to love me?'

"She realized that if she delayed any longer the opportunity would be lost. Quickly she went up the mountain at Srisailam with the demon following, shooting quills.

"It was Sivaratri time on the mountain, with a huge crowd of pilgrims from different countries gathered there. She yelled that the demon was coming and that people should find shelter wherever they could. She looked for Manikandhara and, identifying him, rushed to give him the unfailing sword. She had him kill the Porcupine Demon. Since

Manikandhara also died as a result, she waited for him to be reborn. When he was born again as Kalapurna, she went to him and told him her story.[8] She didn't go back to heaven but instead married him in the *gandharva* style of love-marriage and agreed to live wherever he asked her to, as long as he lived.

"Meanwhile, Madasaya, just as the Siddha Svabhava had predicted, conquered country after country until he attacked Kasarapura, as fate would have it. He was defeated by this king"—Madhuralalasa pointed at Kalapurna—"and began to serve him, with his wife, as a slave. I was born to them as a result of their seeing the king's jewel. My parents fell out with the king. You already know all that from the story of Sarasvati and Brahma's love-game. My parents went to Beyond-the-Smooth-Neck Town, but I became weak from the journey; so they brought me back. I recovered as a result of seeing that jewel again. They reported all this to the king and praised him. Madasaya's advisors were also attracted by the jewel and are now here."

## [ The Story of Alaghuvrata and His Sons ]

Alaghuvrata folded his hands together and asked the girl, "Who are these advisors? I'd like to know their story."

She answered with a little smile, "What do you want to know? They're your sons. Your good luck brought you to them."

"It's not funny," he protested, amazed. "How could they be my sons?" He looked at the king. "It must be a joke. They can't be my sons. I lost my loving wives just as we were beginning to play the games of love.[9] And their death was no ordinary one. They fell into the ocean and were never seen again. Because I loved them so much, in all their beauty and goodness, I never touched another woman. There's no question of any sons. It's impossible. I can't imagine how this mother of all strange stories can tie a bald head to a kneecap."

8. Note that Kalapurna has thus apparently heard from Abhinavakaumudi about his former life as Manikandhara, at least in its final moments, even before Madhuralalasa enlightens him in the court about the circumstances of his birth.
9. *aṇṭi kuñciy āḍunaṭṭi prāyamu*—an opaque phrase, perhaps relating to a children's game.

The king smiled at him. "I bet she can." And turning to her, he said, "Wise child, resolve his doubt. Tell us about this Brahmin's life and times. Tell us how Vedas One to Four became his sons and the advisors to Madasaya."

"I'll be happy to tell you," she said.[10] "Listen, my king. In the Pandya country, in a city called Snake,[11] there was a Brahmin called Somasarma, learned in the Vedas, disciplined in Yoga, and wealthy. Although he had ultimate knowledge, he hid it in himself and lived the life of an ordinary family man for the sake of the world. Above all, he was committed to feeding Brahmins, the most important duty of a householder. He had a son called Yajnasarma. No knowledge stuck to him, no matter how hard he tried to study Veda and other sciences. To make him forget his grief over this, the father married him to four exemplary and beautiful women. To make his son happy, the father also gave his daughters-in-law all kinds of gifts, like ornaments, saris, and perfumes, so they lacked nothing.

"When it was time for him to die, the father summoned his son and said to him in the presence of the daughters-in-law, 'You must continue our practice of feeding Brahmins without break. If you do this, the four Vedas will be your sons. My word will not fail.' The son agreed without hesitation.

"For many years he kept to his father's command, feeding Brahmins fine rice with ghee, lentils, puddings, cakes, and ripe fruits. To pay for the feeding, he spent all his wealth—his harvest, his gold and cash, his servants and slaves, cows and calves, fields and trees. When it was all gone, he went for his wives' ornaments. He was worried in his mind: Which wife's jewels should he sell off first? But all four of them came of their own accord, with love for him, each pleading, 'Take mine first.' Now he wondered which wife to favor by taking hers first.

"With the exception of their marriage threads, they peeled off everything that adorned them and made them into a heap, competing with one another in this task. Their unadorned loveliness melted his heart even more than before. The best ornament for a loving wife is devotion to her husband.

"People who heard about it were astonished. Co-wives usually quarrel over who gets what, but these women were competing at stripping themselves bare of gold.

10. Note that the king is now the primary listener to Madhuralalasa's story.

11. Uraga—perhaps Alavay/Madurai. However, later in the story there is a link to the Tamraparni River further south.

"Their husband simply took the whole heap and began to spend it. Remembering his father's promise that the Vedas would be born as his sons, he kept close to learned people. Though he so far had seen no results, he went on feeding the Brahmins. 'Who knows how a father's words come true?' he thought.

"That Yajnasarma is this man, Alaghuvrata, O king. People called him Alaghuvrata, a Man of No Small Vow, because he never broke his vow to feed Brahmins. When the money from his wives' ornaments was exhausted, he decided to sell off the wives. God knows what happened to his love for them. He wanted to keep feeding a little longer. He didn't inform them, however, but looked for some way to trick them into being sold. One day he said to them, 'Some boats have docked at the Tamraparni riverbank. I'm going with a friend of mine to do some trading, to earn money for feeding Brahmins.'

"They said, 'We can't stand to be separated from you even for a minute. We'll come along with you.'

" 'Great,' he thought. He struck a bargain with a certain trader and took the money under condition that the deal would be kept secret. Then he took them down to the shore. He put them on the boat at the last minute, when there was no time for him to get on; and the boat set off on time, as he had arranged before.

"When the boat had moved some fifteen arm-lengths away, he broke down, as if lightning had smashed the rock of his determination. 'Alas, my greed for money has brought you to this terrible moment, my lovely wives,' he cried in unbearable grief. 'With all your beauty and nobility, you've fallen into the hands of these shippers. This is what you get for marrying me.'

"They heard him from the boat. They thought the captain must have deceived their husband in taking them away, so all four of them, in despair, jumped into the water. No one was able to stop them. On the boat others raised the alarm. The sailors, shouting and cursing, cast nets into the water and lowered divers, but no matter how they searched, they couldn't find the wives.

"The trader returned to shore and caught hold of their Brahmin husband. The trader complained to him that all this had happened because he had cried, and took the money back. The Brahmin suffered a lot—I can understand," said Madhuralalasa, "why he won't believe me when I tell him he has sons."

"But listen to what happened afterward to the wives. Swept along by the waves, they were carried into the mouth of a whale that was sucking up water. The whale swam a long way and then sprayed them out through his spout in a burst of water that looked like the Sea-God's unfolding banner embroidered with gold. Sent flying through the sky, the women fell onto a passing aerial chariot where a young couple was playing dice. It took the women a moment to recover from their shock. When they opened their eyes, the young couple took pity on them and gave them dry clothes, comforting them. 'Who are you?' the couple asked them. 'How did you happen to fall into our vehicle?' Still shivering, the women answered in melodious tones.

The young woman was astounded as she stared at their lips, red as if they had just been kissed. She was afraid her lover might fall in love with them, since they were so charming; and the coquettish manner of their speaking disturbed her still more. She said to her lover, 'Stop staring. Leave them alone. Concentrate on the game. Stop trying to gain time. You're losing.' She addressed the women, 'Please don't take offense at what I just said. This man is always trying to distract me, then he claims to have won and argues with me. I can't stand to hear it any more.'

"Then, again, to him: 'Did you have your turn?' Picking up the white dice, which looked even whiter in her delicate, pale hand, she shook them with her fingers and cast them to the jingle of her bracelets.

" 'Stop cheating! This is a serious game,' he yelled.

" 'Keep your voice down. The "birds"[12] will get scared.'

" 'I just "ate" one of your pieces.'

" 'You won't get full on that.'

" 'Those two are mine: don't touch them, lady.'

" 'But your mind is always on *those* two.'

" 'If you hit twice, they're good for cooking.'

" 'Sure. I'll have you boiling like rice.'

" 'Where did you learn this doubletalk?

" 'From being your double.'[13]

"They went on bantering like this in the midst of the game.

"Poets praise the *cakravaka* birds for their love-sickness for one an-

12. i.e., the dice [*pakṣulu* < Sanskrit *pakṣin* = *sārikā*].

13. This verse includes jokes apparently used by couples in a situation of play. Some of the terms are obscure, though the erotic suggestion is clear.

other every night, when they are separated.[14] But the 'birds' in the game come together in broad daylight and die as soon as they are separated. Anyone can see who are more in love.

"The couple fought one another like soldiers. When they suffered a hit, they didn't get discouraged but struck back at once, throwing the dice hard against the gameboard as if hurling them against an elephant. Their only goal was to win.

"Finally, the man won. Since they had wagered on drinking wine from the loser's mouth, he pouted his lips, demanding she pay up. But she shook her head and winked, pointing out the presence of other women. That turned him on even more. He threatened her, begged her, and cajoled her with his eyes to get her to do it anyway. The four women turned their heads away, embarrassed. He pulled his wife's face to his. She had wine ready in a jeweled cup, and now she sipped it, filling her mouth, and kissed his mouth, feeding him the wine, though the whole time she kept glancing at those women, to make sure they weren't watching. As if that were not enough, they went on drinking, getting more and more excited and savoring the reflection of each other's faces in the glistening wine in the cup. Cheek to cheek, with an eye to those reflections, tasting the many fragrances, they went on sipping mouthful after mouthful and kissing, biting each other's lips, feeding all five senses. Their sense of shyness disappeared as they got more and more drunk, their words coming out slurred and indistinct. Soon they lost all shame. Their eyes became heavy and red.

"After a while, she saw her own face and her husband's staring back at her from the shiny cup. 'Hey, who is that other woman?' she said, lisping. 'You brought in somebody else to drink with? That was fast.' She was so angry she stopped drinking.

" 'Have a good look, lady,' he replied. 'There's no other woman here. It's your own reflection.'

"She pointed at the four Brahmin wives. 'What about them? Do you want to say that they're all my reflections, too? And if that's the case, are you planning to make love to them like you do with me? No way. Get rid of them.'

14. By poetic convention, the *cakravāka* birds are separated each evening as darkness falls and spend the night moaning in longing for one another. A "bird" piece captured on the game board is metaphorically said to have been killed.

"She was really drunk and had no sense of limits. She was suspicious of those women and wanted to throw them out of the vehicle. Suddenly, en route through the sky, they were almost level with a tall building near Dharmapuri on the banks of the Godavari River. It was a bordello run by the city's chief courtesan. The drunk woman directed the vehicle to the upper terrace, open to the moonlight, and one by one, she helped the four women down from the plane. Her lover wasn't too happy about this. She looked at him and said, 'Get away from them. I swear that any man who approaches them out of lust will suffer the consequences—from me.' And she climbed back onto the plane.

"He said, 'I wasn't thinking about that at all. My only worry is what they're going to eat in this godforsaken place.'

"She coolly pointed out to him the shelves and cabinets visible as they flew past the tall building.

" 'See, they have rice and ghee, saris, ornaments—as if stacked up as free gifts for a king. They won't lack for anything. And if any fool tries to touch anything in this building, he won't survive.' She pronounced these charged words and went away with her lover.

"She was jealous and anxious less her lover's mind wander, and she was also drunk; and the words she spoke in this state of mind actually served to protect the Brahmin women."

"They had been put down on the roof of a building with many stories that belonged to a madam in charge of a bordello. And the madam heard and saw everything without being seen. She was very frightened. 'Whoever they are, these women came from heaven and took over this place. We can't hope to use anything from here from now on.' She slipped out of the building and, from outside, bowed to the women and said to them, 'You who have taken over this building—I hereby offer you everything inside it as a gift." She poured out water and yellow rice as a sign of the offering. 'It's all yours now, the building, the garden, the whole property all around. Please stay away from us and save us. Even a touch of your feet will help us.[15]

"She gathered all the whores from the building and informed them as well as the rest of the town's population. They were all amazed. Meanwhile, the Brahmin women saw it all from the roof. 'God protects those in dis-

15. The madam is afraid the four Brahmin women are deities of some kind, descended from heaven.

tress,' they thought and went down into the building. They lived there in comfort, never opening the front door.

"Reading from omens that they would be reunited with their husband, they kept their spirits up and also took good care of their bodies. The townsfolk would see them through the windows as they came and went on the street, and they would bow to them, but no one ever dared desire their beauty. They remembered the story the madam had told. 'They must be goddesses, spirits, women from heaven. Look how radiant they are. If anyone looks at them with lustful eyes, he'll surely die.' Still, the honest people of the city would wait for an opportunity to catch a glimpse of them. 'These women who came from the sky are living like anyone else, cooking and eating the supplies the madam left them. How lucky she was to have her gift accepted! What is the nature of the vow they have taken? How long will it last? Will they accept food from us as well?' They cleaned the entrance to the house with cowdung and began to leave lentils, rice, ghee, and milk on their doorstep. They would then stand at a distance with folded hands until the women took in the food.

"After some days the women began showing signs of pregnancy. As the pregnancy advanced, the little boys in their wombs would sometimes chant sections of the four Vedas or argue over fine points in the learned texts or, at other times, recite from the epics and enjoy discourses on statecraft. In the course of time, the four women delivered four sons in the proper order, beginning with the eldest wife, at an auspicious moment. It so happened that a certain Yogi was passing by; he performed the birth rituals and gave them names. At the time of the naming ceremony, he looked into the future with his inner eye and knew: these four boys were the four Vedas in person. So one by one he named them: Agama One, Agama Two, Agama Three, and Agama Four.

"The four mothers knew at that moment what their father-in-law had meant when he said the four Vedas would be born to them. They begged the Yogi to come back when it was time to perform the boys' initiation. Although the boys already had within them all there was to learn, still they studied all the texts in a very short time with the Yogi, in order to have a teacher's approval.

"The mothers realized that they were unlikely to find their husband if they stayed in that place; they wanted to move on. When they informed their sons, the boys said, 'If women as beautiful as you move around without a master, we will lose respect. People will talk. Stay here a little longer, maintaining the illusion that you are women from heaven. In the meantime, we will search for a king and win his patronage. Until such a time, it will not be easy for us to go looking for our father.' And they left the house in secret.

"They walked through the town and learned that its ruler was a man called Madasaya. They went as far as the entrance to the palace, where they gathered from people around that the king was a great scholar in his own right, but that no Brahmin could see him without the permission of the royal family priest. And since this priest was an ignoramus and was constantly afraid his ignorance would be exposed, he controlled access to the king through a dense net of gatekeepers and guards. The king, moreover, had wanted to perform a Vedic ritual and had asked the priest about it, but the latter insisted there was no one around capable of singing the chants. The priest feared that the king might come to know about some great scholar or other, in the course of conversation with visitors to the palace; so he instructed the gatekeepers to let no one in from outside, for any purpose, with the exception of inarticulate morons. Moreover, anyone in the latter category who was allowed to enter was coached on how to behave: 'If the king asks you how you are doing, just answer, "So long as you are our king, everything is just fine." If he asks you what's new, say, "We're simple people who stay at home; we don't know anything else."' Unless they swore to keep to such responses, they were not allowed in.

"The boys, hearing all this, developed a strategy. They dressed themselves as low-caste villagers and practised a certain cryptic way of speaking. Like coolies, they came to the gate of the palace carrying baskets full of mangos, and they spoke to the doorkeepers in a suitably low-caste dialect. Allowed to enter, they put down the baskets in front of the king. As they politely backed away, the king looked at them kindly and asked, 'Are you well? Is everything going well for you in life? I hope you have no worries. Tell me honestly; you can be frank.'

"They answered in unison,

*māya mmāna su nīve*
*rāyala vai kāva devarā je je je/*
*māyātuma lāninayadi*
*pāyaka santosa munna palam ilasāmī//*

We swear by our mother
that since you are king, unbroken

happiness fills our hearts. All good things
come from that.

"The king saw that while the surface meaning of the words meant that these boys were happy so long as he was ruling, there was really a hidden meaning that was an appropriate answer to his question and which directed him to perform rituals and to take care of scholars. Observing them with astonishment, he could see they were like burning coals covered with ashes—their glow of wisdom hidden. He stood up and fell at their feet in deep humility."

Kalapurna was listening to all this. "I didn't know until this moment," he said, "that our Madasaya is a great linguist." He looked at him with respect. "Please take a seat," he addressed him, repeating his request three times until Madasaya sat down. The king asked Madhuralalasa to tell what happened next. She continued,

"Madasaya bowed to the four boys and offered them proper seats in the court. He said to his courtiers, 'You're probably wondering what there was in what they said that makes me honor them so much. Let me explain the hidden meaning. It looks like a Telugu sentence, but actually it's in Sanskrit, the gods' language. Those among you who have learned about words can see that the phrases divide in two ways. In Sanskrit it means:

"'Money isn't everything.
Your good character is your capital.
Only such wealth is indestructible.
That is what brings fulfillment.
Wealth comes to a king who performs rituals
for Vishnu; evil can't touch him.
You are our protector.
When learned people approach, don't turn away
in pride. Enjoy their company.
They are your true riches."[16]

16. Madasaya gives a Telugu paraphrase, which we have translated, based on the following, highly arcane reading of the text as Sanskrit:
*sunīve* [Oh one who has auspicious capital]
*āyaṃ mā māna* [don't care for income]
*rāḥ* [cash] *alavā* [undestructible] + *ekā* [alone] *avat eva* [only it protects]
*rāje (a)jeje* [for the king who worships Vishnu]

"Madasaya then turned to Agama One and asked him, with folded hands, 'Who are you? Why did you come here in disguise? Tell me everything about the four of you.' And Agama One related to him the whole story beginning with their father's vow to feed Brahmins and all that they had heard from their mothers, up to the point where they saw the king. The king was ashamed that he had allowed himself to be influenced by the weakness of his priest and had therefore turned away scholars deserving of respect. 'That's probably why people call me Madasaya—Deluded Heart,' he said.[17] 'Just look how I behaved. Swayed by the priest, I couldn't see my own scholars.'

"He removed his priest from office but didn't punish him further, at the request of Agamas One through Four. However, everyone who had been part of the priest's clique was given appropriate, corrective punishment. The king appointed Agamas One through Four as his family priests and advisors. They were reunited with their mothers, and all were married to proper brides.

"Honored by the king, they lived happily, busy performing royal rituals. They sent men off to search for their father in Snake Town, the Pandya, Kerala, Chola, and Dravida lands, but there was no sign of him anywhere. Very worried, they continually reassured their mothers with some vague hopes.

Meanwhile, Alaghuvrata, ashamed that he had tried, in vain, to sell his wives and thereby lost them, could no longer show his face in public in his town. He went off to faraway lands, where he lived by begging. He still fed Brahmins with whatever paltry means he earned; and when he had nothing to feed them, he gave up rice himself, surviving on roots, berries, fruit, and milk. But he was not satisfied with this limited form of feeding Brahmins, which was so often interrupted; he kept looking for a way to make

---

*mā* [Lakshmi] + *āyātu* [comes by herself]
*malāni na* [ there are no sins]
*pāyaka* [king!]
*santaḥ yadi* [if scholars come]
*asamut* [without joy]
*na pala* [don't turn away]
*mila* [meet with them]
*sā* + *amī* [they are Lakshmi].

17. Madasaya here offers a new reading to the name given him by Brahma in his story (< *mada*, delusion).

more money. At some point he heard about the power of the Lion-Riding Goddess. From a certain person he learned a mantra to be used for invoking this goddess. He went to her shrine, where he learned that by hearing *your* story"—Madhuralalasa looked again at Kalapurna—"he could attain all kinds of prosperity, long life, children, and grandchildren. He said to himself, 'Forget about the children and grandchildren. Let me at least get the other benefits.' With this in mind, he continued chanting his mantra and, as a result, finally got to hear your story—today. As you can see, this necessarily produced the full range of benefits, including finding his children. Oh son of Manistambha! You can see the power of your story." Madhuralalasa paused.

Kalapurna asked Alaghuvrata, "Are all your questions answered?" To Agamas One through Four he said, "Go meet your father. It's wrong to hesitate now." So they got up and approached him with a mixture of fear, love, and joy. They bowed at his feet. He was overcome as he embraced them and kissed them, his eyes welling up with tears of joy.

Kalapurna was still thinking about the boys' remarkable skill in punning between Telugu and Sanskrit. "Can you still do that?" he asked, looking at them with an encouraging smile mixed with curiosity. Agama One at once replied,

*tā vinuvāriki saraviga*
*bhāvanaton ānun ativibhāvisutejā*
*devaragauravamahimana*
*māvalasinakavita marigi mākun adhīśā*

"Your gift, wise king,
is to imagine with feeling.
The kind of poetry we like
comes to us of its own
just because *you*
are our listener.

The king said, "What a great poet! The answer you gave to my question immediately became a poem." The poet smiled in response. "Now," said the king, "read it over." The Brahmin was pleased at this wording and complied.

These two men were engrossed in their own conversation, while meanwhile the whole court watched, listened, and understood nothing. They were confused. So the king helped them out. "When I asked him to read it over, I didn't mean for him to read it *again*. Just listen. There's a deep meaning to the Telugu poem if you read it backwards *in Sanskrit*, starting at the end.

*śādhīna kum ā-giri mata vikanasi lavamāna mahima-vara-gaurava-de/*
*jāte suvibhāv iti nānu nato nava-bhā gavi rasakiri vā-nuvitā//*

"Rule the earth as long as the mountains last.
You are loved by all.
You have the dignity of Lava, Rama's son.
So long as a king like you, who loves poets,
is in power, can a man whose power
is renewed by the honor you give him
fail to praise you in poetry
filled with feeling?"[18]

The courtiers, reading the poem backward, were delighted to discover the new meaning. They marvelled at the poet's ability to improvise something so complex so quickly and at the king's ability to understand it on the spot. Kalapurna lavished upon Agama One gifts of jewels and clothes.

## [ Satvadatma's Question ]

The king's minister, Satvadatma, now came forward and bowed to Madhuralalasa. "Great Yogini," he said, "I have forgotten my real name and fam-

18. Reading *śādhi* [rule] + *ina* [king]
*kum* [the earth]
*ā-giri* [as long as the mountains last]
*mata* [loved one]
*vikanasi* [you flourish]
*lavamāna* [like Lava, son of Rāma]
*mahima-vara-gaurava-de jāte suvibhau* [loc. abs., so long as a good king like you is alive]
*iti nanu nā* [a human being] +*ataḥ* [from this (respect)]
*nava-bhāḥ*[has renewed power]
*gavi* [with speech]
*rasakiri* [that expresses beauty]
*vā*+ *a-nuvitā*[won't he praise?]

ily. While I was wandering alone, the people of Kasarapuram brought me there and gave me this name I bear, Satvadatma. Tell me who I am. I can't find anyone old enough who knows."

In the middle of his question, the child, rubbing her eyes and twisting her lips and arching her back, started to cry. Satvadatma said to her, "Why are you playing these games? Why don't you answer my question? This is more than strange." He bowed to her again and again.

The courtiers around her also began to speak. "You know things that even the wisest do not know, but still you get hungry and cry like a child." "You can toy with us, but we won't leave you alone. You have inborn, superhuman powers. Help us." "We've been hoping to learn more and more from you; hoping you would answer all our questions. So why are you pretending to be an ordinary child?"

But no matter what anyone said or how much they begged her, the child showed no sign of knowing anything; she was really crying, and she was hungry. The king said, "Such expert articulation—such wisdom—can't last forever. Some superhuman power must have possessed her for a while. And we, alas, were not intelligent enough to ask her *then* about the source of her extraordinary understanding."

He turned to Rupanubhuti and Madasaya. "You heard all the stories your daughter told. You are very lucky. From now on, you are my mother-in-law and father-in-law. You are freed from my service. Take this girl home and take care of her."

Satvadatma said, "Great king, from the moment you put this necklace around the child's neck, she became your bride, and these people became your in-laws.[19] That is what I thought, and the stories she told have confirmed this. If you study her features, you can see that she will wear anklets made from the gems of all the world's queens."

Pleased with these words, Kalapurna sent them off with even more stunning gifts. But he took care to prevent word of the stories from reaching the inner chambers of his palace and, in particular, the ears of his queen, Abhinavakaumudi. He also gave Alaghuvrata as much money as he needed to go on feeding Brahmins for the rest of his life and sent him off with his sons to meet their mothers.

19. The act of putting the necklace on the girl is here analogous to the tying of the marriage-necklace, the *maṅgala-sūtra*.

## [ Madhuralalasa Comes of Age ]

Delighted with the honor the king had shown them, Madasaya and his wife took their daughter home. The mother raised the girl with constant care, shampooing her hair, rubbing her skin with a cleansing dough,[20] pouring water over her head with cupped hands, nursing her, swinging her in her cradle. Because of the power of Brahma's words, Madhuralalasa, even as a baby, was devoted to her future husband. When her mother would rock her to sleep in a golden cradle, she would sing to her songs about Kalapurna. The baby would always brighten and laugh. But if they sang about anyone else, she would become grumpy and start to cry. "She's already in love with her husband," people would say with a smile.

A little older, she would happily jump into the lap of any visiting relative when they stretched our their hands to her. Giggling and squirming, she would dance with her hands on her waist when they asked her. She was a constant fountain of joy.

As she grew from young childhood into girlhood, she began to avoid the company of men—even of her own father. She began to notice the beauty of her body and to care for it. She never let her sari slip from her shoulder. She learned the art of playful glances and dancing eyebrows. When older women would start to talk about their love life in her presence, she would run away in embarrassment.

She was maturing into a young woman. Her youthful breasts and thighs began to encroach upon her childhood, which, like her waist, grew increasingly thin. Her breasts were little hills; her navel was a deep well, with the hair below flowing like a beckoning stream; her fingers were leaf-buds, her arms were vines, her thighs smooth as the banana tree, her tender lips—red *bimba* fruits. When she smiled, you could see flowers unfolding. When she spoke, parrots and mynas began chirping. Her hair was a dark swarm of bees. All in all, she was a complete, lush garden, made for love.

She studied music and literature and other arts, and she became expert at composing poetry because of residual memories that she carried from her past lives.

Meanwhile, Kalapurna completely forgot about Madhuralalasa, busy as he was in affairs of state and in the pleasures of love with Abhinavakaumudi.

20. *nalugu*.

Madhuralalasa, for her part, was already feeling the budding sensations of desire; she was eager to marry the king. She was lovesick and distracted: intending to call one of her girlfriends, she would turn to another by mistake; or reaching for one ornament, she would put on another; or heading in one direction, she would end up elsewhere. There was only one thing on her mind.

Whatever she saw
she didn't see
without seeing him.
Whatever she heard
she couldn't hear
without hearing him.
Whatever she touched
she couldn't feel
without feeling him.
Whatever she tasted
she couldn't taste
before tasting him.
Day and night she was lost
in thoughts of love-games
with him, her body tingling,
her words all jumbled,
like talking in a dream.

During daytime her eyes were white lotus blossoms, wide open, as the poets would say. By night they were dark water lilies, still wide open, as the poets would say. In short, she was in love. She rarely touched her vina. Even more rarely did she pay any attention to her pet parrots. She hardly ever gossiped with her girlfriends any more. Games became strangers. She was somewhere else.

Her girlfriends said to one another, "For some days now she's been acting strange. Let us see why. She's getting thinner, and her face is turning pale. Her mind is always distracted. This must be love. In recent days we haven't mentioned Kalapurna very often; we haven't been praising the fullness of his virtues and his great looks. That's probably why she's depressed. The merciless Love-God never wastes an opportunity to torture girls of her age. We had better provide some diversion, so she doesn't get any sicker. Let's take her for a walk in the woods."

They managed to get her to come with them. The forest was alive with bees sipping honey, mating in the midst of the sweetness. The girls came upon a pool with steps leading down to the water. Tightly gripping the folds of their saris between their thighs, they went down, their delicate feet turning the water red as brilliant lotus flowers. A light breeze played with the upper ends of their saris, so they drew them closely around their bodies, still gripping the lower folds with their thighs. Holding their hands in front of their faces because the first ones to enter were splashing, they were startled by the fish darting through the waves and by the honking of the waterbirds flying up from the reeds. Bees disturbed when the girls entered the pond flew wildly in circles and then settled back on to the lotus blossoms, like dark seeds cast in the air and caught in the games that water-goddesses play.

When they emerged from the water, they dressed themselves in clean saris and put on their jewels; but Madhuralalasa was still lost in thought, though under the pressure of her girlfriends she had somehow or other played along in the water. At that moment Kalapurna, handsome beyond description, happened upon that place. He was out falconing and had just called back his hawk from pursuing some other bird. Half hiding her face on the shoulder of her girlfriend, she saw him—her husband. He saw her. Their eyes met in the middle space for a split second before shyness took over.

When she looked at him, he averted his eyes. When he looked, she averted hers. Still they kept stealing glances, back and forth, tying a swing for desire to play on. She wanted to rush to him. Though she had fallen in love with him just from hearing about him, this was the first time she really saw him.

For his part, he was so taken by her that it hurt to tear himself away. He kept turning back, on one pretext or another, to get another look. She was burning; she couldn't bear it. She wanted to bring her hands to his tender feet, her breasts to his broad chest, her cheeks to his cheeks. Her friends saw this. "We were so busy with our games that we didn't pay attention to her," they said. "These pleasures are not for her. Our plan didn't work. Her pain, far from diminishing, is intensifying. Just a moment ago Kalapurna was here, stunningly dressed for the hunt. Something happened to her when she saw him. That's when things started to get worse. Everything here—the cries of the cuckoos and myna birds, mad with the joy of spring; the humming of the bees; the fragrant breezes; the opening buds and flower-beds—all joined the enemy camp; all are sapping her strength. We didn't foresee this. We wanted to take her mind off the pangs of love, and we ended up bringing her to Love's own kingdom. It's like the man who took the long way out of town to avoid paying the toll, walked all night, and found himself at dawn at the very same tollbooth."[21]

While they were reviewing their mistake, Madhuralalasa's body became so hot with passion that she nearly fainted. Flustered and alarmed, they rushed to cool her: they built a shaded pavilion out of banana stalks at the edge of the pond where the breeze blew off the lotus flowers; they made a hedge out of cooling roots bound together with a mortar of sandal paste; inside it, they laid out a bed of water lilies on a pedestal covered with camphor, with a pillow of delicate *gojjenga* flowers, heavy with honey. They put her to bed and fanned her with flowers; they covered her breasts and feet and hands with a thick layer of cooling sandalpaste. Very quickly, the flowers dried up and the sandalpaste, burnt by her body, fell away in brittle flakes.

One of her most skillful friends adjusted Madhuralalasa's sari and dabbed her eyes with cool rose water as she spoke to her: "Your body is so hot that if we touch you, we might get scorched. None of our attempts to cool you down has helped. My dear friend, I'm telling you: Desire never dies if you suppress it. Don't be shy. How long can you suffer within yourself? I'm not a stranger to you. You don't have to hide anything from me. I'm as close to you as your breath. There's nothing you can't tell me."

She was speaking very boldly, asking her to reveal her true wish, and Madhuralalasa, still a little shy, was disturbed. But as her friend pressed further, she finally spoke. "How can I keep it back from you? My lover came to me one night in my dream and gave me the ecstasy of love. That happiness is beyond words. How can I describe it?" Remembering, she broke out in a sweat, her eyes half closed. "Before he left, he also promised he would never leave me. Today when he came falconing and I saw his beauty, I lost control. Nothing you do to cool me off is going to help. All I need is him. Why are you wasting your time? When this moonlight burns me from the sky, does my body have any chance? The Moon is as hot as the

21. This is *ghaṭṭa-kuṭī-prabhāta-nyāya*, an illustration drawn from popular Sanskrit.

summer sun; why do people say he's cool? He's like a tiger with the face of a cow. And these parrots are driving me crazy with their chatter; it's no wonder they say that an idiot can only parrot someone smart. These stupid parrots—could they be taught compassion? And those miserable cuckoos who grow up in the crows' nests—I can't stand them either. Even if you beg them, they won't stop cooing. They're all my enemies—moon, parrots, cuckoos—don't ask them to help. I'll hang on to life if you'll just go and bring my husband. Otherwise, you can give up hope."

The girlfriend said, "Take my word for it. I'll bring your husband to you as quickly as possible. I can say this because I know, for a fact, how loving he really is. Trust me."

These words revived her. Madhuralalasa, somewhat relieved, went home with her friends,

*O King of Nandyala, grandson of Narayya, great-grandson of Narasimha, son of Narasimha: you're a warrior in love. You conquer the hearts of women with their darting eyes. You delight in music, horses, elephants. You are famous throughout the world, praised in the royal courts of the Kuru, Karusa, Videha, Kosala, Kuntala, Anga, Kalinga, Barbara, Pulindaka, Matsya, Malava, Pandya, Kerala, Chola, Ghurjara, Saka, and all other countries.*

This is the sixth chapter in the long poem called *Kalapurnodayamu* made by soft-spoken Suraya, son of Pingali Amaranarya, whose poetry all connoisseurs enjoy throughout the world.

# CHAPTER 7

*Listen, son of Kondamamba . . .*

## [ Kalapurna in Love ]

From the moment Kalapurna, that celebrated king whose stories are always music to the ear, caught sight of Madhuralalasa in the forest, he could think of nothing except her amazing beauty, which had robbed him of his strength. He was unable to attend to any business, for his mind was filled only with her. He sat alone in his private palace.

One day he invited his intimate friend, the aged Brahmin astrologer, and said to him after a while, "Dear friend, I've been thinking of asking you something, but every time you came, I hesitated. Now I have to ask.

"You know the jewel-studded palace of Madasaya to the east of our city and, just beyond its golden walls, the luxuriant forest set aside for play, which is always in bloom. I went there the other day, following my falcon. As I was calling to it, I saw a woman. She was playing with her friends. One life is not enough to study her beauty. One tongue is not enough to talk about her loveliness. One pair of eyes is not enough to take in the joy of seeing her. What more can I say? She's breathtaking. A total beauty. You can use all your metaphors, your hyperboles, all your powers of description, but no poetry can match her charm.

"How lucky is the universe,
and in it the Rose-Apple Continent,[1]
and the Bharata Land,
and Anga-desa,
and Beyond-the-Smooth-Neck Town
to have such a garden
where she set her foot.

"She cut right through me with her exquisite braid of hair, which could have been a double-edged sword, slightly curved at the end, with an ivory handle—the white flowers she gracefully ties at the top. I can't stop thinking about that rich, black braid and the black curls; the fine line of her eyebrows; her soft, wide eyes; her smiling cheeks; in fact, her entire face; and then there's the perfect curve of her breasts; there's her tiny waist, to say nothing of the way she pulled me toward her with a shy but somehow inviting look. From the moment I saw her, the Love-God has been working his vengeance on me.

To my eyes, she looked unmarried. Do you know her? Tell me if you do. If you don't, go find out as much as you can."

The Brahmin thought, "This king's in love. Let's tease him a little." He said, "Never mind if she's unmarried or not; God bless her. She deserves to be queen of ten thousand countries. I'm thrilled you're in love and that she's torturing your mind. You want to know why? You're always busy with your pandits and their eternal arguments. With your bards[2] and their meaningless stories. With your poets and their screeching, like a Saturday rain.[3] With your political advisors, who are a pain in the stomach. And

1. *Jambū-dvīpa*, the vast continent within which India, *Bharata-varsha*, is situated in the medieval cosmological map.
2. *Paurāṇikas*, keepers of the ancient stories.
3. Astrologers say that if it starts raining on Saturday, it will go on for some days. Saturday is called *sthira-vāsara*, the day of Saturn, the slow and steady planet (Śanaiścara); so what happens on Saturday can be expected to keep on going.

when you disappear into the women's quarters, finding you is like searching for Mercury at dawn. Do you ever take a moment even to say, 'How are you?' Now you finally found time to talk to me."

"Enough," said Kalapurna. "I know you like to scold me. Just find out what I need to know. Who is she? What's her name? Her family? What does she do?"

"My friend, I hesitate to tell you who she is. What's the idea? You may need some extra income to pay for refrigerants. If that's the case, we can collect it from all the towns and villages. We'll call it a "love tax." These people don't pay enough respect to the king. Actually, I'm only joking. You don't need such extra income. All the kings of the world are sending you whatever you need for free. The king of Kerala has sent a huge supply of sandalwood trees. The Pandya king sent bushels of pearls. The king of Kamarupa sent cartloads of rose water. The lord of Kashmir sent tons of moonstones. The Turk sent bags of camphor. Just listen. You can hear your servants announcing out loud the arrival of all these gifts. You may or may not be joined to your beloved, but those kings are definitely being separated from their riches. In fact, they don't have to spend all this money to keep you cool. Half would be enough—to bribe that girl to marry you."

"You old windbag—you top the list. You can't be trusted. But if you could bring this off, I would bribe you myself."

This made the old Brahmin really mad. "You call me a windbag just because I don't put on airs like those Brahmins who are always bathing and fussing with the *darbha* grass[4] and sitting tight, doing nothing." He marched off in a huff. Kalapurna rushed after him. "You're a real Brahmin, gentle as a cow. No one should call you a windbag. I won't do it again. Please come back."

Turning back, the Brahmin said, "It's true what you said. I can't be trusted. I'm one of your men. As people say, 'Like king, like subject.' I'm true to the proverb. But tell me, what happened to your promise to Rupanubhuti and Madasaya? Did you not say, *'From now on, you are my mother-in-law and father-in-law'*? You're now paying for forgetting this. And because you forgot her, Rupanubhuti's daughter is suffering, and you're suffering, too."

4. Often used in rituals.

"You mean that girl in the forest is Madasaya's daughter? Why didn't you tell me? How quickly she's grown into a young woman! It's amazing."

"Why are you so surprised? Who else could capture your heart? As to how fast she's grown up, it only seems that way because you're so busy all the time in your daily routine, taking care of the kingdom, exercising, riding horses, talking philosophy, eating, bathing, going to the theater, receiving ministers and guests and all your subjects. Meanwhile, the girl is miserable, tormented by love, as her friends keep telling me in the hope that I'll report it to you. And you know what these rotten kings are like. Pride comes before life. Her parents will never come to tell you what's happening with their daughter, even were she on the verge of dying. They think you should notice her yourself. Anyway, I'm only telling you this because you said you'd pay me a bribe.

"This is a good match. There's nothing lacking on either side. Her father comes from the family of the famous Kartaviryarjuna; and he is a world-conqueror in his own right. And you must have heard the expression "as noble as Sugraha"—this has become a byword among people, because Sugraha nobly offered protection to any king who asked.[5] Let me tell you that *he* is the brother of Madasaya's wife, that is, Madhuralalasa's uncle. Because his lineage was so noble, many kings offered him their daughters in marriage, but he disregarded these offers; they became angry with him, and he disappeared without a trace. It's no small matter to offend the family pride of kings.[6] Sugraha got his name, "Good Planets," because he was a born at a moment when many planets came together in an auspicious constellation. I wonder what happened to that prediction.[7] But don't let that bother you. I just mention this by way of telling you that Madhuralalasa comes from a good family.

"If you want to make that girl happy, all you have to do is to marry her—fast."

And with this, he opened the almanac and looked over the weeks and the dates. Counting on his fingers, he figured out the planetary positions. Suddenly, he brightened. "Tomorrow there is a beautiful moment suited to both

5. We thank K. V. S. Rama Rao and Kolavennu Malayavasini for insightful discussions of this difficult verse.
6. Reading *alpamul' ayya kulâbhimānamul*, with Malladi Suryanarayanasastri.
7. See Madhuralalasa's story of Sugraha, narrated toward the end of chapter 8.

your horoscopes. As a king, you don't have to make any special effort to get things ready for a wedding. Your city is always festive in any case. It's not for nothing that your city is named Beyond-the-Smooth-Neck Town, because the areca trees, bearing their golden-red fruit, stretch their smooth necks over the houses like a towering goddess of wealth. Therefore, the doorways always look like there's a wedding going on. Still, we can decorate the city a bit more. All you have to do is get the bride. Dispatch the elders to your father-in-law's house to ask for the hand of his daughter."

## [ The Wedding of Kalapurna and Madhuralalasa ]

Kalapurna was happy. First he summoned Satvadatma and informed him. Then he sent Agamas One through Four to his first wife, Abhinavakaumudi, to win her agreement to the new marriage. She agreed at once, saying, "Don't they call me Abhinavakaumudi, 'New Moonlight'? My family—the *apsaras* caste—is also moonlight.[8] My whole nature is cooling joy. How could I make my husband unhappy? You don't need my permission. I want whatever he wants."

She sent them off, and they reported back to Kalapurna. He then sent them to Madasaya's house to settle the details of the wedding and to seal the agreement with the exchange of betel. An announcement was made in the town.

The city was in a flurry of excitement day and night. Wherever you looked, you could see freshly polished golden pots. People were sprinkling the courtyards with cool water mixed with sandalpaste and smearing the walls with fragrant civet. Gem-studded porches were covered with musk, and threshold designs were drawn in camphor. They hung canopies with garlands of water lilies and built arches out of mango leaves. Old women went from house to house, with musicians beside them, to distribute yellow rice, betel leaves and betel nuts, saffron powder, oil and fruits as an invitation to the women of the household to attend the wedding. On every street in the city, men were mixing camphor, musk, and sandal in golden cauldrons; they heaped up jasmine, *campaka*, and *vakula* flowers and perfumed betelnut in the streets, along with mountains of betel leaves, tender and golden-green. They distributed betelnut and garlands to the entire population.

8. *Apsarases* are said to be born from the moon.

The next day, married women with many children gave Madhuralalasa a wedding bath as music played, at a lucky hour. One woman smeared the ground with musk; another drew designs on it with pearls; another set up the seat of gold; another spread a new cloth on it, making sure its border was turned to the north. Then an older woman and two of the bride's girlfriends made her sit facing the east and soaked her hair in *campaka* oil. Lovingly, they mixed a paste of myrobalan in turmeric and applied it to her head, pouring water from golden pots. They dried her with fine cloths and dressed her in white with yellow borders. After drying her hair, they braided in flowers. They smeared her body with sandalpaste, then wiped it off, leaving behind the fragrance. They painted vermilion designs on her breasts and fixed the forehead mark out of musk. Delicately they outlined the edges of her eyes with kohl and drew patterns of red lac on her feet. They covered her in ornaments from head to foot,[9] but she herself was the real ornament to everything that adorned her.

When she was ready, the women called her mother. "Take a good look at your daughter," they said. "Our idea of beauty may be different from yours. Your very name, Rupanubhuti, means Love of Beauty, and it also means Experience of Beauty; so nobody knows better than you what beauty is." The mother smiled and took a step backward, regarding her daughter up and down from the corners of her eyes. "It's perfect," she said.

At the auspicious moment, with the elders of both families sitting on either side, Agama One sang the chants for the bride and groom—Madasaya's daughter and Manistambha's son. The King of Anga tied the marriage thread around his bride's neck, while women sang wedding songs and barbers played their sweet instruments.

Afterward the bride and groom poured rice on each other's head. Her girlfriends cheered her on, standing on either side, as she lifted her head for the first time, shedding a little of her shyness with a smile. She raised her hands high toward the groom's head, so her full breasts came into view as she stretched, while her tiny waist started to tremble. Married women placed her hands in the rice on a golden plate and filled them again and

9. The ornaments are listed by name: *billāṇḍlu, babblilkāyalu, maṭṭiyalu, vīramuddĕlu, andiyalu, mŏlanūḷḷu, ŏḍḍāṇamulu, nevaḷambu, puṅjāladaṇḍa, pannasaramu, mŏgapu tīga, aṇimuttĕpu perlu, sandidaṇḍalu, sūḍigamulu, gauḍasaramulu, kaḍiyālu, ungaramulu, mungara, kolāṭampu kammajoḍu, cĕvulapūvulu, bavirālu, cerucukka, kŏppuvala*.

again, not letting the groom go any faster. Her graceful movements as she poured the rice offered everyone who was watching a new vision of beauty, never seen before.[10]

It was time for the mother to say goodbye to her daughter. "Some wives make their husbands happy by their beauty; some by their goodness. You have both, like fragrant flowers given by the god. Don't be too proud of your youthful beauty or of your husband's love. Never forget your modest ways. Be kind to your husband, his friends and relatives, and to your co-wife." Her voice was choking, and she held back her tears as she sent off her daughter, hardly able to let go. And the daughter, too, could hardly take her leave. Even great love for a husband doesn't make it easy to separate from a mother.

Kalapurna paid all the usual courtesies to the kings who had come from many countries to honor him at his wedding; then he gave them leave to depart. The bride, meanwhile, heard her girlfriends whispering among themselves that she would be with her husband that night for the first time. It excited her; she started moving back and forth in an absentminded way in the palace. They combed her hair and covered her with decorations, which, out of shyness, she tried to shake off.

When they had got her ready, they held up a mirror so she could see herself; but she was too shy to look. Only when they left did she study herself, adjusting her curls with her fingernails. When her friends came back, she said, "What a mirror—you can see everything," as if she were merely testing its quality. She was hoping her husband would see her before everything got creased.

She sat down, quite alone, on a bed made of flowers, her cheek resting on her hand. Even if the Love-God had his own mirror, it could still not capture all her beauty. She was thinking. She wanted her husband that very minute, in her arms; but he wasn't there.

When will he come? Could anything stop him?
Something Abhinavakaumudi might do?
Surely she accepts that he and I
will make love. If she doesn't, he'll never come.

10. This is the *talabrālu* ritual performed immediately after the tying of the marriage necklace.

But then he's in love with a woman from heaven, so why should he want me?

"When I went to see her and bowed to her, she embraced me as if she really liked me. She even blessed me and said, 'Live long and happily with your husband.' So it seems that she wanted this. But can I really believe her?

"What's more, a woman who has had the unbelievable good fortune of making love to this man, handsome beyond anyone in all three worlds, wouldn't want him to leave her even for a single second. She'd be planning and scheming all the time to find a way to keep him for herself. People constantly compare my man to Kama, the god of love. It's nothing more than a habit, as the Sanskrit proverb goes: *gatânugatiko lokaḥ*, "People follow people." If Kama were really *that* handsome, the whole world would be flooded with happiness. Siva would have had no reason to burn him up."[11]

She was adrift in these thoughts, imagining her husband in all his parts, in her arms, when it suddenly occurred to her that her friends might be looking all over for her. As she was about to get up, they appeared, giggling and excited.

One of them, somewhat more experienced, touched up her hair and fixed the mark on her forehead. "It's time for you to go to your husband," she said. "Come with me." She stood there, waiting for a moment for Madhuralalasa. "Now," she said. "Your husband is waiting. You know what you're supposed to do."

Madhuralalasa stood motionless, her head bent, eyes focused on her breasts. Her friends coaxed her forward. "What's going on? Is this any way for a girl to behave? Come on." Somehow she managed to move just a little, until shyness paralyzed her again. An older and bolder woman appeared and pressed her, "Are you coming or not? I can tell you: even women who have bunches of children still feel a little embarrassed when they have to go to their husbands. You think you're the only one?" She pulled her by the hand.

Kalapurna was waiting, listening to the bustle around him. He couldn't wait to see his bride. He stood up and looked through the window. Amazed, he stared at her from top to toe, lingering at every spot. He lay down on the bed, waiting.

11. Śiva burned the god of love to ashes when Kama disturbed his meditation.

"Go in, you silly girl," said one of the women. "Look—he's watching you." Covering her mouth with her hand, she pointed to the king. Madhuralalasa tried to hide behind her; her feet were shaky, but her skin was tingling as she looked back and caught a glimpse of him from the corner of her eye. Still, she tried to withdraw, but her friends physically caught her and dragged her into the room. One of them picked her up under her arms and forced her to sit on the bed, near Kalapurna's feet. Then this friend left the room, saying, "Someone's calling me. I have to go see. I'll come back." "Nobody has fed the parrot," said another, on her way out. "I forgot the betel leaves," said another. "Have to go get them." "Where's *she* going?" called another; "I'll fetch her."

"Wait for me," cried Madhuralalasa. "Don't leave me alone." She tried to get up from the bed—but Kalapurna placed his foot on her thigh, pressing her down. She struggled to get up, bracelets and anklets clattering. "So much noise, my dear," he whispered in her ear. "No one will believe you are so coy." He held her.

"I can't move without making a huge noise," she said and started removing some of her jewelry, beginning with the anklets, drawing out the pins. "That's a good beginning," he said, touching her cheeks with his.

She didn't turn away. She was listening to his words. He was able to touch her hand. This itself was the height of happiness for the king.

To calm the fear in her heart, he told her tales of love. Under one pretext or another, he managed to touch her breasts, bringing their bodies close. He made her smile by gently teasing her. First once, then again and again, he touched her secret places, so she had to hide her excitement. He prepared her for the highest teaching, the science of loving.

He was restoring the Love-God, who had been hiding inside her fear and shyness, to his full power. Soon the knot of her sari was untied. He kissed her, inflamed her, embraced her; they lost themselves in one another.

Days passed. Day by day her passion grew, and her timidity diminished. She had no time for anything else. At first she wouldn't allow him to touch her breasts. She wouldn't let him put his lips on hers. She wouldn't let him touch her down below. But eventually the constant struggle wore her out, and she gave in, and gave him all of herself. It went on like this for some nights. After a while, though she still put on a show of resisting, she would let him kiss her—as if she lost attention for a moment. Or, pretending to be deep in thought about the bite he left on her lip, she would allow him to scratch her breasts with his fingernail. Or, as if busy examining her breasts, she would let him untie her sari. Then she would bend over to pick it up, meanwhile letting him reach between her thighs. So she managed to be at once both coy and intimate; she made it easy for the Love-God to steal past her defenses; easy for her husband, too.

Pretending to sleep, she would touch her lips to his lips and hug him; this went on for some nights, to her husband's delight. After some time he knew she was pretending but didn't let on—until he could contain it no longer and broke out in laughter. She laughed, too. Before long, she was beyond her self-imposed limits. She started laughing and chattering even while fending off his hands. Finally, she bit his lips and said, "That's what you get for what you've done to *my* lips."

Then he said, "Look what you've done to my lip. I'm going to show this to everyone—unless you do what I want you to. Don't try to wriggle out of it." As if frightened by this grave threat, she made love to him on top. He was lying back and enjoying the sight of her breasts, so, a little embarrassed, she lay close to his chest. He begged her to sit up and tried to prop her up with his hands; she tried to close his eyes with *her* hands. "Don't worry, I won't stare at them anymore," he promised her. "Let me cover them myself." He folded his hands around her nipples and played with them. This trick gave her a chance to be a little angry. Gallantly, he offered to help raise her heavy behind with his hands, and again she held him off. Suddenly, she realized she was completely open; desperately wanting to cover herself, she tried to dismount. All this was new to her. The beginning was slow, but once she began, she couldn't stop.

His desire for her was continually increasing and his love grew deeper as they found ever new ways of making love. Spring turned to summer. They spent the hot days playing at love in ponds perfumed by the lotus and the blue water lily, in cool pavilions flowing with rose water, on terraces paved with moonstones and marble, or porches painted with camphor and draped with red water lilies. They dressed up in delicate cottons with necklaces of pearl and jasmine garlands, their bodies covered with sandal to heighten their passion.

Then the rains came. Madhuralalasa, as if startled by the lightning and thunder, hung on to her husband's embrace; and he happily held her close to him and would not let go. After the monsoons, there was autumn, followed by the cold season. Under thick, hand-woven blankets, on warm beds enfolded by mosquito nets, with the brazier burning with coal and aloe, the king spent the cold months taking refuge in his new wife's burning breasts. Season after season, he made love to her, his passion deepening as they enjoyed the bounty of each new day.

## [ Abhinavakaumudi Becomes Jealous ]

The king, being the perfect lover, showed equal passion for Abhinavakaumudi, his first wife. One day, when Abhinavakaumudi was singing for him and playing her vina, the king sent a messenger to bring Madhuralalasa. She came and listened for a while. Kalapurna then said to her, "My dear, I hear you are an expert at this. Why don't you take the vina and sing for me?"

She was afraid to say either yes or no. She took the vina and started fiddling with the tuning pegs. "Is something wrong?" asked the king repeatedly.

"Actually," she said, "I'm wondering, lord of all the world, if my voice is right for the pitch of this vina."

"Just sing as you normally would," he said. So she showed her proficiency. It soon became clear that the tone of the vina was not up to her mark. Still, the king was amazed at her voice, as was Abhinavakaumudi, who thought Madhuralalsa must be unique in the universe.

The king thought a moment and said, "Bring your own vina. Let's see how good *it* is." Eyes wide as an unfolding lotus, she modestly replied, "Normally, I accept what anyone says, but I can't hide the truth from you. There is no vina in the world that matches my pitch. That's why my singing doesn't sound quite right. I had heard about this vina, before, and I wanted to test it. You have heard the results yourself. Now you know."

Said the king, "At the moment, this is the best available vina. This is the one I know from the beginning, so I never thought of looking for a better one. Only now, listening to your singing, which establishes the true limit to all three pitches—low, middle, and high—have I understood that the tones of this instrument are not the best for you." He turned to Abhinavakaumudi. "Do you think there is a vina suitable for her somewhere?"

She answered, "I already told you, when we were speaking about music, that this vina of mine is the best of them all. That's why Tumburu used to play on it; and he gave it to me, since I was his most gifted disciple. Where can you find one better?" She thought a while and added, "I heard that Tumburu was recently defeated in a music competition by Narada. I wonder what could be the reason."

These words brought back to the king's mind the story that Madhuralalasa had told about Narada's determination to beat Tumburu.[12] This then led him to memories of his previous life as Manikandhara. He also remembered that, as Manikandhara, he had left *his* vina in a secret place in the Lion-Riding Goddess's temple. That, he decided, was the right vina for Madhuralalasa's voice. In his mind, he decided to look for it and bring it to her. He turned to her and said, "There *is* another vina, and I know where it is. That might be the right one for you."

As he was saying this, Abhinavakaumudi's friends made a sign to her and took her away to a private place. "For a woman, you are very naïve. Not only are you supporting your husband in his love for your co-wife's singing, but you are also helping him find a better vina for her. He knew from the beginning that her voice is better than your vina. He invited her here only to insult you. Believe us. For all external purposes, he was listening to your singing in your palace. So his mind wandered to *her*—that's not too bad. But then why should he invite her here? And you want to know more? He's wearing her little toe-ring on his finger. You don't seem to notice. Why not pretend for a little while to turn your face away in pique? You don't seem to be capable of getting angry with him. He takes you for granted and has just demonstrated that he's in control. Have you ever listened to what we say? Just for our sake, somehow or other, take your life in your hands and stop talking to him—at least for a little while. If he really loves Madhuralalasa's singing, he could listen to her in his own place any time. Why did he have to insult you, and why did you put up with it? He'll make amends and restore your pride—if you just stop talking to him for a minute. Trust us. We know what love is all about."

Their words set off a change of heart in her. She thought to herself, "I never really thought about the way my husband treats me. I was too much in love. What my friends say is true, if you think about it. I shouldn't be so friendly to him. People who hear about this will laugh at me if, out of passion, I blind myself to my husband's shortcomings."

She gave some temporary answer to her friends and went on behaving calmly, with her usual confidence. Later that night when the king came to

12. In fact, we know this story from Manistambha, not from Madhuralalasa, who is not said to have spelled it out as the young baby in the court—unless she offered a condensed version of Manikandhara's previous career in the course of narrating his encounter at Srisailam with Svabhava (chapter 5, pp. 101–4).

her house, she showed him all the usual courtesies, but she did not put on her jewelry; she poured the water on his feet without saying a word, as if welcoming an ascetic sage. She didn't smile or joke or flutter her eyelashes or give any hint of desire. She made their bed, smoothing all the wrinkles and spreading a soft comforter; she fluffed up his pillow. He lay down, and she sat nearby rolling betel leaves on a golden seat.

He noticed. "Usually all I need to do is to stand here and her face lights up with a gentle smile of desire; her eyes shoot arrows of love, volley after volley; her voice turns to honey, and her words are full of hidden meaning; her breasts bristle with goosebumps, like a thick bed of rice shoots. Today it didn't work. Nothing is happening. She's just acting the part of the dutiful wife—without feeling. She's up to something." Upon reflection, he concluded, "Today's singing must have set off something. Let's find out."

"Is something wrong?" he asked her. "You seem a little off. I've never seen you like this."

She didn't say a word.

"Listen.
I love you.
A lot. I won't last
if you won't
laugh. Am I an unfeeling
log?"[13]

Wearily, she said, "Go talk to women who are good at singing. Why talk to someone like me? I always lose. Don't try to be nice to me. Your love is elsewhere. I don't want to whine. Anyway, what can I do? You were kind enough to come here, and I'm delighted to see you. This is all that I'm good for. I don't expect anything more. To tell the truth, this would be the right moment to die, while I still have your respect, your love and closeness. Unfortunately, I can't die; I'm stuck with this cursed life.[14] But I can't blame you. You're perfect. There's nothing wrong when a man

13. This verse is a *dvyakshara-kandamu*, using only two consonants—*m* and *n*—as if conjuring up the resonance of *mana*, "we," reassuring her that they are together.

14. Abhinavakaumudi is an immortal *apsaras*.

exchanges one woman for another just because the new girl entices him with her singing."

He listened. "You accuse me of so many things. What did I do to make you feel so hurt? You excite me, arouse me; you're about to overwhelm me with your love—and then some bad luck of mine takes hold of you and plants doubt in your mind. But truly, I never did anything that should cause you hurt. I swear it." He got up from the bed and fell at her feet, holding them with his hands.

"Don't touch me," she said, moving away from him. "Go grab the feet of the woman you really love. Why put the blame on me, great king?" She pried his hands away with hers.

"There's no one I love more than you, my beautiful wife." He stood up, raised her toward him, and embraced her tightly, chest to chest.

With tears in her eyes, her voice choking, she said, "I don't doubt your love, your affection, or your kindness. But for some reason, today my mind is troubled. I feel humiliated, hurt, angry. It doesn't go away."

"I know why you're feeling bad," said the king. "Until today, your vina was incomparable. Suddenly, because of another woman's singing, it has been found to be inferior. That's what troubles you. I know a special vina that is far better than yours. I used to carry it myself in my former life—so I'm told. I am going to find it and bring it to you, whatever it takes. I'll teach you to play it so that you'll be the best in the world, better than anybody you can imagine. Trust me."

Now she knew very well that he had once been Manikandhara,[15] so she easily accepted that he might well have had such a vina. This made her happy. Kalapurna, once he had eased the pain in her heart, happily made love to her.

The next day all this spread, from mouth to mouth, from Abhinavakaumudi's girlfriends in the palace to Madhuralalasa's friends, and from them to Madhuralalasa herself. She started to think. "Some women, like me, have to win their husbands' love by their singing. Other, luckier women don't have to do anything like that. Even if they can't sing very well, the husband takes it upon himself to make *them* happy. *She* made him promise to give her the vina he was going to bring for me. She set a trap for my husband's love. That's what I call a woman."

15. Abhinavakaumudi, as the reader recalls, met and fell in love with Manikandhara, that is, Kalapurna in his previous life.

She went on musing in this vein. That night Kalapurna found her a little different. When it was time to make love, he cheered her up by falling at her feet and promising to bring her, very soon, new anklets made out of the jewels from the crowns of the queens whose husbands rule the eight directions of space.

So now he had promised something to each of them, and he had to plan his moves. Both promises were on his mind. He tried to think things through. "If I tell Abhinavakaumudi where that vina is, she can easily go there and fetch it by herself. After all, she's a woman from heaven. But that would not be right. It would mean that I am not capable of getting it myself. So that won't work. If I send someone who can do the job, I have to be sure they can handle anyone who could cause problems. If instead I ask the king of that country to get it for me, he might fancy it for himself. If instead of all of these, I invade the country myself, I'll get not only the vina but also the riches of all the kings en route. Besides, there doesn't seem to be any way to keep my promise to Madhuralalasa except by conquering the whole world."

He summoned his minister, Satvadatma, for consultations in the secret strategy room, with guards posted outside to keep everyone else away. The king set out his idea in some detail. Satvadatma was pleased. "Didn't I tell you so?" he asked the king. "What I said that day, after studying Madhuralalasa's features, has now come true."[16]

"That's true," said the king, smiling. "What do we do now? Tell me what the strategists say, step by step. Advice by a good minister, given in private to the king, is as effective as Vedic mantras chanted by an expert during the ritual. That's what people say. But to my way of thinking, all these traditional strategies are for cowards and weaklings. What are they really good for? Victory comes out of courage. Whenever a courageous man decides to strike, with whatever weapon, against whatever enemy, he will win. The moment he strikes is the right time; the place he chooses is the right place; the weapon he wields is the right one. When he sees the enemy before him on the battlefield, a certain power energizes the hero. If Fire wants to burn down a forest, does he prepare his flames in advance? Elephants may be as big as a mountain, but they are slow in movement. That's

16. See 6.188 (p. 124), where Satvadatma says to Kalapurna: "If you study her features, you can see that she will wear anklets made from the gems of all the world's queens."

why they get killed. Lions are smaller, but they have the advantage of swift attack. They are the killers. Victory belongs to the brave. People supremely skilled end up serving a powerful king. No talent can equal sheer power. If you're really strong, you won't waste time thinking about whether a task is easy or difficult. Only small-scale operators think like that. Does a blazing fire stop to ask if the wood is wet or dry? Therefore, a brave man should attack when the spirit seizes him. I think this is the right time to move—right now."

Satvadatma replied, very humbly, "Great king, your understanding of politics is far deeper than mine. Nevertheless, I'll tell you what I think, with your permission, and without fear. Good friends don't talk just to please. If you feel my mild advice is appropriate to your fierce mood, take it. It might work like water on a red-hot sword. A king who forsakes the science of strategy, like a swimmer who lets go of a float or a sick person who disobeys his doctor, may still survive; but if they don't, they can't escape the blame. On the other hand, if a king follows the rules of strategy and still fails, people won't blame him; they'll say it's his bad luck. If an immoral man gets rich, people curse the goddess of wealth: How could she choose *him*? Look, elephants are much taller than humans, but we use strategy to climb on to them and ride them. The science of politics tells you how certain tasks can be accomplished. Such wisdom doesn't automatically come with strength. If you want proof, remember how Siva used a whole, strong mountain as his bow in his war on the Triple City.[17] If you shoot an arrow from a bow, it goes quite a distance. But if you just throw it with your bare hand—if even God tries just to throw it—will it go even half as far? The moral is, strategy is better than brute strength.

"Listen. There are six strategies: making peace, making enemies, invasion, staying put, creating dissension among your foes, and taking shelter with a more powerful king. The main thing is to act on them at the right time. If you use them at the wrong moment, it's disaster. There are four means of success: conciliation, division, bribery, and sheer force. Everybody can name these four and define their characteristics, but it's hard to find someone who can tell you when to adopt them and when not to. Some people use an axe when a fingernail would be enough; others try to use their fingernail when they really need an axe. If you can't estimate the size

17. Śiva made Mount Meru into his bow when he attacked the flying three cities of the demons.

of the problem accurately, it won't help you to know about the four means of success. When your enemy is similar to you in status and power, try conciliation. If he's stronger than you are and not easy to defeat, try to divide and conquer. If he has a lot of allies, try to buy them off. If you're absolutely certain that he's so weak that you can beat him, then, and only then, go to war.

"A king can suffer from fourteen weaknesses. He can be indiscrete about secrets. He can be indecisive or waste time fretting. He may be grumpy or unable to recognize intelligence when he sees it. He could act when it is not appropriate. He can be self-indulgent. He might tell lies. He can be lazy. He could be an atheist. He can fail to recognize what is good for him. He can take forever to make up his mind. He can be vindictive. He can procrastinate on routine matters. You should know these weaknesses and avoid them.

"Pay your servants on time. You need their love and support. You should keep people within their limits and rule them fairly. Make sure your country is free from thieves and other nuisances. It's a mistake not to punish those who should be punished, and it's just as bad to punish those who don't deserve it. Both these defects will send a king straight to hell.

"I'm sorry if I've run on. Once I start talking about these things, I find it hard to stop. You know them all anyway, as everyone can see by your noble behavior. We knew when you conquered Madasaya, who had himself conquered the whole world, that your word is law everywhere. But peace, for kings, is unstable.

"So it is quite right for you to take action against any overly shrewd kings who, in recent days, may have become too strong and are planning to attack. Show your power. As you yourself said, the best time is now. If you ask me why, it's for the following reason. You said you made a promise to Madhuralalasa to give her, very quickly, new anklets made out of the jewels from the crowns of the queens whose husbands rule the eight directions of space. She's a lucky woman, and her good luck is what made you make that promise. The same good luck will give you certain victory. Moreover, needless to say, Abhinavakaumudi will also benefit. My advice to you is to proceed with the invasion of the world—bearing in mind all the excellent strategies I have outlined.

"There may be some casualties, and you may loose some money on the army's expenses. Even then, victory is victory, and your wife will still be lucky. But if you follow scientific strategy, such losses will not be that heavy.

Lord, conquering the world should begin in the east and proceed via the south to the west. The powerful king of Magadha is likely to attack you from the rear. It would be a good idea to make peace with him first."

*Listen, grandson of King Narayya, praised by all men. Your ministers are equally expert in the science of military strategy and offer advice in a single voice. That is why all the world's kings worship you.*

This is the seventh chapter in the long poem called *Kalapurnodayamu* made by soft-spoken Suraya, son of Pingali Amaranarya, whose poetry all connoisseurs enjoy throughout the world.

# CHAPTER 8

*Listen, Nandyala Krishna, king of all the earth, loved equally by the goddess Fame and the goddess of empire . . .*

## [ Kalapurna Conquers the World ]

Kalapurna listened with satisfaction to his minister's words about strategy. He agreed that it was right to make an alliance with the king of Magadha. He despatched one of his best emissaries, a man endowed with dignity, self-discipline, loyalty, diplomatic eloquence, courage, and a gift for winning the heart of a foreign people. He knew exactly when to display pomp and when to be humble. He sent an advance party to make friends with the Magadha king's advisors and ministers by conciliatory words and proper gifts. When he arrived at the court, he was admitted with great honor, and, wisely answering the king's questions and in full awareness of his place in space and time, he spoke of Kalapurna's greatness without in any way compromising his host's self-importance. With diplomatic finesse, he worked out a treaty of friendship between the latter and his king.

Meanwhile, Kalapurna, in his foresight, strengthened the fortifications of his capital and of the surrounding fortresses, also stocking them with provisions, cash, troops, and war machines. He made certain they were well protected and that there were no shortages. He gave marching orders to his commanders, and they, in turn, announced them in the areas under their command.

As evening fell, the sun slowly sank into the western sea, turning red like a mass of coral carried by the waves and gradually giving up its heat. In the west, the sky was heavy with reddish gold, as if Time were a peasant who had harvested a golden crop of rice and were carrying it in huge bundles on his shoulders. Or you could say the sun was like solid gold melted in red flames by the goldsmith who is Time, blowing at it with his torch; and when the gold was fully ready, the goldsmith dipped it in the water of the ocean to cool it. As if the whole world had become the Dark God Vishnu in his endless form, or as if Siva had dressed all his eight bodies in the elephant's skin,[1] or as if space itself had been swallowed up by the black demon Vritra,[2] a subtle darkness enveloped the universe.

The sky was still tinged with red, and the first stars became visible like cotton ripening in the field when farmers offer blood sacrifice to the crop. People looked up at the stars in amazement and thought to themselves, "The world above is all light, you can see for yourself, since the ancient ceiling of the sky is clearly riddled with holes. They just look to us like stars."

Imagine a weaver setting up his loom inside his house, weaving brilliant white threads of silk, and from outside you can only see the window, dense with light: night came on, the moon rose, casting its silky rays. Like a white sari spread wide, like a stream of milk or a dusting of white flour, moonlight flooded the world.

As night deepened, flower girls began to sell their wares to young men, who stopped to banter.

"These flowers are just right for you," they would say, and the young men would reply, "Why do we need to buy them? *What's right is the one I'm looking at*."

1. Śiva is *aṣṭa-mūrti*, endowed with eight forms (the five elements plus the sacrificer, the sun, and the moon); he also slays Gajâsura, the elephant demon, and dances in his blood-soaked skin.
2. Vritra is the enemy of Indra, the king of the gods, in classical mythology and, as such, a dark force that blocks movement and swallows up space.

"You think you can get it just by words?"

"We don't want it for free. Here's the money."

"So which one do you want?"

"The bunch you're hiding."

"We won't sell *those* until *these* are sold."

"As if we didn't know."

And still laughing, the young men reach for the flowers hidden under wet cloths, in the back of the shop.

Meanwhile, the commanders of the army were getting ready to march. Kalapurna went to Abhinavakaumudi's palace and said to her, "My dear, in order to fetch the vina I promised you, I have to go conquer the world. I'll be away for a few days. I'm off at dawn." Then he went to Madhuralalasa and said, "Tomorrow is the lucky moment for me to embark on my conquest of the world, in order to fetch the jewels for your anklets." This pleased her.

The soldiers were waiting impatiently for the dawn, eager to set forth—so eager that they showed no interest in embracing their wives. Their attention was riveted on the eastern sky. Night passed.

When an alchemist makes a pill out of mercury, he steeps it in milk to test it—to see if it turns what it touches into gold. Just so did the magical moment of dawn bathe the morning star in fading moonlight, turning the east a radiant red and gold. The city awoke. People rose early, afraid they might miss the hour of the army's departure. The charioteers busied themselves with the horses and flags and all the rest of their equipment; the elephant drivers began covering their elephants with brilliant banners and bells; the cavalry started saddling their horses and fussing with the bridles and reins. Soldiers, relishing their breakfast, were bantering with women hawking buttermilk, curds, and pickles. There were palankeen-bearers fixing up their palankeens and guards of the harem padding these conveyances with pillows, so the ladies could ride comfortably. Officers were maneuvering their own troops into conspicuous positions along the road. Officials of the treasury were getting golden boxes of cash packed onto wagons drawn by camels, mares, and bullocks. The whole scene was alive with commotion and energy, like the ocean at moonrise.

Brahmins sang mantras to bless the expedition, and bards called out the cries of victory. Tributary kings came forward and bowed as their names were announced by the heralds. The royal elephant and golden palankeen and the palace horse were brought forward to the deafening beat of drums.

At this auspicious moment, the king emerged from his palace. He mounted his elephant, and trumpets sounded the victory march. Surrounded by his great chariots, with flags waving, his elephants moving like huge mountains, his horses, swifter than wind, and the infantry, he moved out of the royal city.

Like the vast radiance of the cosmos that would filter through if a crack opened up between earth and sky, the sun rose in the east, bringing joy to the town. As the huge army passed through the city gate, people felt lucky if they escaped the crush unhurt.

The royal force left Beyond-the-Smooth-Neck Town behind them. Always just a little way ahead of them, enterprising merchants set up small tents by the road to sell food and whatever other supplies the army might need. As a result, the wealthier among the army, who were also travelling with their wives in palankeens covered with thick curtains, had everything they could possibly want; for them and their women, the royal campaign was like living at home.

Kings of the surrounding region heard that Kalapurna was coming with this ferocious army; some fled their kingdoms, and others sent gifts as tribute or came in person to attend on him. Satvadatma had sent letters to all the local rulers, informing them as follows:

> His Majesty the King has promised his beloved wife, the magnificent Madhuralalasa who was born with all the marks of good fortune, the wife of the only true warrior in the world, to make her new anklets from the jewels in the crowns borne by queens of all the world's kings. For this purpose he has set out with a large army to conquer the world. Take heed. Save your wealth and your lives by presenting him with what he wants. Signed, His Majesty's Chief Minister.

Many obeyed. Kalapurna accepted their gifts and went on. The stubborn Gauda king tried to contest him. Engaged by the fierce Gauda army, Kalapurna's soldiers at first fled the field in fear, right up to the king's tent. He rallied them: "Don't give way!" He was surprised by the attack, for he had assumed the Gauda king was coming to bring him gifts; but perceiving his true intention, Kalapurna called to his attendants to saddle his horse and unsheathed his sword. "Does he think he can get away with his life? Does he have any idea of my strength?" He left his tent and moved directly toward the foe. His horseman brought the mighty horse, fully equipped for battle and richly caparisoned, neighing so loudly that the enemy army became terrified. The king mounted, and, seeing him there so courageous and determined, his four-fold army took heart. As the king encouraged them, they counterattacked. Wielding swords, spears, and long knives, they hacked the enemy to pieces—so thoroughly you could no longer identify the bodies. The Gauda rallied his men, who rushed at Kalapurna; the latter pretended for a moment to leave himself open to attack, but as an enemy cavalryman came close and was about to strike, the king, rapidly shifting his sword from right to left, sliced right through the attacker's sword, body, horse, and saddle, leaving eight severed pieces on the ground. This was unheard of: until then, great swordsmen had only managed six pieces. Even the gods watching in the sky were amazed at Kalapurna's tremendous heroic feat. "It's normal for a warrior to defend himself when an enemy lifts his sword against him, but this king is different. He must have perfect confidence in his own skill. He cut right through the sword raised against him and cut the enemy into eight whole pieces."

The Gauda king and his army gave up and rushed back into the town, trampling the bushes in their rout and paying no heed to the thorns. Kalapurna and his soldiers chased after them to the gates of the fort with a roar like a thousand drums. The Gauda guards closed the gates of the fortress and got ready to defend themselves with muskets, cannons, catapults, and other weapons. At this moment, Satvadatma, scorn in his eyes, ordered scaling ladders to be placed against the walls. The people inside panicked, and the Gauda king saw there was no way out. With gifts in his hands, he emerged from his fort and surrendered to Kalapurna, and the latter pardoned him.

Proud of his achievement, Kalapurna moved on against the Utkala king[3] who was next to attempt resistance. A great battle took place: the Utkala king had drawn up his troops for a frontal attack. They fought until blood settled in the dust; then they fought on because they were too proud to stop; and when they began to get tired, they still fought on because they were too angry to give up. Even when their anger was satisfied by killing enough enemies, they kept on fighting for the sake of their reputation. The Anga king, Kalapurna, mounted his elephant, which was like a mobile mountain, and, with his commanders on either side and behind him, fell

3. Also called Oḍḍīḍu, the king of Oḍhra-deśa = Orissa.

upon the enemy. The Utkala ordered his elephants to meet the attack. No one had ever seen such a collision; the spectators were amazed. The elephants circled one another, showing off their strength; then, pacing backward, they rushed to attack each other, breaking their tusks. Hanging on, entangled in one another, they pushed and shoved and wouldn't let go even when their drivers were killed and fell. The air was filled with the shattering of tusks, the ringing of bells, the wild trumpeting. Kalapurna's elephant smashed into the enemy's elephants, and these fell to the earth on their backs, crushing their drivers.

As Kalapurna pushed into the space that was opened up and the Utkala army gave way in despair, the Utkala king leapt on to his own fierce elephant and attacked. The two elephants circled each other, searching for position. Time after time, they crashed into one another, their trunks intertwining as they trumpeted furiously. But the moment came when Kalapurna could see the back of his foe's elephant before him and, quickly jumping on to it from behind, he pounded the Utkala king's back with his fists. He twisted the Utkala's arms and pinned them behind his back, tying them with the ropes hanging from the elephant's middle. Then he jumped back across the open space onto the back of his own elephant. Seated there, he stabbed at the Utkala's still rampaging mount, cutting at its temples. In this way he captured and humiliated his foe. He left him with some good advice: "From now on, don't fight with someone beyond your strength." He took the jewels he was seeking.

The Kalinga, Dravida, Cola, and Pandya kings came of their own accord to submit and offer gifts. Kalapurna, heady with success, proceeded to the shore of the southern ocean, where he attacked the Kerala king. The two armies clashed like the northern and southern seas. Blood flowed like a pure flame newly fed, after the smoke rises to the sky.

One warrior had all his weapons
cut away by the enemy. With nothing but
bare male courage, he rushed at the foe with an arrow
pulled from his own body. He was determined to kill
the man who had wounded him; he targeted him,
not forgetting, and struck at him as he fell
while the women of heaven waiting to receive this hero
began to quarrel among themselves, each wanting him
for her own.

Another grabbed the trunk of an elephant, pulled it down,
and using it as a foothold, clambered up to the top.
With his left hand, he took hold of the elephant's temple,
with his right he stabbed at the warrior
sitting above, who stabbed him back. Dying,
he found his left hand on the breast
of a woman from heaven, rushing
to embrace him. This alarmed him: "Did I hit a woman
by any chance?" he thought, a little ashamed.

The two armies were going at it with great gusto and great loss of life. The Kerala king sent an emissary to Kalapurna with a message: "Why cause the death of so many soldiers for no good reason? Let us fight it out between the two of us, alone." Kalapurna agreed. So they stopped their armies from fighting.

The two tough men faced off, gilded swords in their hands. They glared at one another. They roared, their muscles taut, swords extended. "Take that!" they cried, or "Here! Watch out!" or "Hurrah!" Not for a moment did they let their eyes shift from the target. Then Kalapurna, with a quick flourish of his hand, made his opponent lose his balance and cut him lightly in many spots. The Kerala king was shocked at this show of skill, and also, to be honest, rather grateful to Kalapurna for not killing him, so he threw his sword away and fell humbly at his feet. He folded his hands in worship. "Great king—" he began, "but then you are no ordinary king—you're something godlike. For a long time I practised the science of swordsmanship under the training of a great master from Andhra-desa. I defeated many well-known swordsmen. Proud and confident of my skill, I challenged you to this duel. It amazes me that you defeated me so easily." He took Madhuralalasa's husband together with his retainers into his palace and gave him all the jewels that had graced the heads of his wives. He sent him off with honor and affection.

Kalapurna learned from the Kerala king where to find the Lion-Rider's temple. He went there, worshiped the goddess, and searched through all the temple alcoves until he found the vina he had left there in his previous life. He took it, more than satisfied.

Now he headed north. All the kings en route gave him the jewels he wanted and paid homage. He marched against the king of Ghurjara, about whose pride and power he had heard. The latter came to fight with a huge army that turned the skies to dust. The armies clashed to the beat of the drums, and soon all space was filled with sounds—*thang thing khang khing*. Kalapurna saw that the enemy forces were no less mighty than his. His eyes blazing red with anger, he swiftly drove his chariot into the front, his arrows swirling like a blinding storm. The Ghurjara met his arrows with equal force, but soon he found himself without his charioteer, without his flag, without his strength, without his courage. He had no choice but to give the king the jewels of his queens.

Kalapurna moved on, preceded by news of his great victories. The kings of Kuru and Kasi came to serve him and to say to him, "Ever since Krishna died, who else is there, except you, to care for the world?" Kalapurna had already heard that Krishna's city of Dvaraka had been drowned in the ocean. He asked the people there to tell him more about what happened. He was grieved—for now he could no longer see his old music teacher from his former life. Still, longing for him, he went near the spot where Krishna's palace had been and bowed deep in respect.

He went on to defeat the Malava and Barbara kings in a brilliant military campaign. The Huna warlords, hearing at a great distance of Kalapurna's victories, promptly sent him all their queens' jewels and other fine items with a humble note. Now Kalapurna turned east, toward the Himalayas. The King of Pragjyotisha, who had a very inflated view of his own strength, thought that at last he had found a worthy match; so fearlessly, eagerly, he went to battle against him. Space turned gold from the light reflected off the spears and jeweled banners of his vast army. The two armies smashed into one another; conches blared, drums pounded, trumpets sounded war calls, but all these blasts were drowned out by the twang of Kalapurna's bow. Dense volleys of arrows, flowering like fireworks, sapped the enemy's resistance. It was like breaking a dam.

In the Pragjyotisha army chariots came apart. Flags were torn in tatters. The archers were thrown helter-skelter. The drivers were killed. Elephants were hacked to pieces. The mahouts fell to the ground. Horses died. The cavalry bit the dust. Saddles were pulverized. The infantry were shattered. Shields, swords, and spears were smashed. Jewels were hurled to a distance. Blood flowed freely, with flesh and broken bones floating on it. Everyone watching experienced terror, amazement, and revulsion. Kalapurna's army roared in victory, seeing the enemy destroyed. But the Pragjyotisha king rallied the forces he had left and hurled them into the battle, while he maneuvered his own chariot toward Kalapurna. His close friend, Candabahu, moved ahead of him to engage the king. Arrows followed so fast on one another that they seemed to be one continuous shaft in the hands of the two warriors. As the fight went on, Kalapurna, becoming weary, called to mind his guru for archery, Svabhava the Siddha, who had given him his weapons. "How can I defeat this tireless foe?" he wondered as he addressed his bow and arrows: "Can you tolerate this unending struggle with a rather ordinary bow and arrows? This is the time for you to show your special power." With a loud "*hum*," he shot an arrow, skillfully aimed, at Candabahu, who fell dead to the ground as his army scattered in terror.

Seeing Candabahu fall, the Pragjyotisha king surrendered to Kalapurna and handed over the jewels of his queens. The kings of Kosala and Magadha, terrified by this news, arrived of their own accord to give the son of Manistambha whatever he wanted.

## [ Homecoming ]

So now Kalapurna had conquered the world and all its kings. With jewels from the crowns of all their wives, he returned, happy and triumphant with no rivals left, to his city. Bards and court genealogists sang his heroic feats.

The soldiers became more and more excited as they neared home. "If we walk just a little faster, soon we'll be resting in our own houses. Move it!" cried some.

"Just beyond that hill we'll see the golden palaces of our city."

"See how lovely these woods appear, where the rivers Ganga and Sarayu meet."

"We've wandered over the entire earth, and nowhere did we see anything so beautiful."

"Look! There's the gate and the golden wall of the city."

"Thank God we're back in Beyond-the-Smooth-Neck Town, our hometown."

Meanwhile, their friends and relatives were already coming out to greet them. As they caught sight of everything dear to them, one thing after another, the soldiers forgot the strain of the long march. They passed through the old part of town, where they marvelled at the still bright-as-new mansion that Romapada had built for his son-in-law, Rishyasringa. "It could have been built today!"

"And here's the rivulet that Karna's son, Vrishasena, jumped across on his horse. In those days, that was considered quite a feat. Today, any old horse in this city could do it."[4]

"A couple of miles to the east is that rich place, Kasarapura. Remember how Satvadatma built it himself? Remember how he crowned Kalapurna king of that city and became his minister?"

In their joy at coming home, unmindful of the long road they were walking, they pointed to each familiar landmark and told its story. The townspeople stepped aside to watch them enter. Drums and conches and trumpets were thundering as the resplendent Kalapurna re-entered his palace. The women of the city watched him through the latticed windows of the high, white-plastered buildings, which looked like the tall white waves of the Ganges with its golden lotus flowers.

One woman with a long dark braid
rushed out of the house to get a glimpse
of him. In her haste, she tied her belt
around her neck and was trying to get her necklace
around her waist, but it wouldn't reach.
Holding the two ends in her hands on either side,
close to her navel, she stood there stunned,
as if offering herself
to him.

Another one came, retying the knot of her sari
that had come undone as she was making love.
Her bodice was between her feet, and she was
covering her breasts with her husband's dhoti,
the first thing she could find.

One had just finished her bath. She quickly threw on
a red silk sari and tied up her hair in a red-ochre towel.
From a distance, she looked like a Yogini
with matted hair. In her rush to see the king,

4. Note the shift from the far more usual glorification of the past in relation to the present. Here, as would suit the new sensibility of the period, the present and future are more interesting than the past.

the pearl pendant between her breasts
danced and trembled, like the soft light of truth
pulsing from her heart.

That was how Kalapurna came home to Beyond-the-Smooth-Neck Town. It was the height of royal brilliance, a feast for the eyes of all who lived there. He gave the incomparable vina to Abhinavakaumudi and ordered his minister to have the anklets made for Madhuralalasa.

Happy, Madhuralalasa was dressing herself in the new ornaments when, in the course of conversation, she heard from her companions about the necklace that Kalapurna had given her when she was a baby. She wanted to put it on that day, because it was the very first gift she had received from her husband, so she ordered it to be brought to her. But it no longer fit her neck. She therefore had new gems added to the chain on either side of the central stone, so that the latter would rest upon her heart. Taking her fan, she went to see her husband.

Satvadatma also entered the court with the pair of anklets in his hand. The king gestured to him with his eyes, ordering him to place them before her. "Here," said Satvadatma, "are the anklets made from the gems of all the queens in the world, whose husbands surrendered to you." Turning to her, bowing low to her, he said, "Please place them on your feet."

"Don't bow to me," she said. "Stop. I should bow to you. You are my mother's brother. Until today, we didn't know this." And she bowed to him.

His whole body shaking, he stepped back. "It's the truth," she said, rising to her feet. "Don't back away."

At that moment, Kalapurna smiled and looked at him. "Whatever this woman says must be true," he said. "Ask her what she means. Remember you asked her before, when she was a baby, about your real name and family. Maybe today the answer has come to her. Ask her again. We'll find out." Looking at her gently, the king said, "Did that special knowledge you had as a child come back to you again? How can this man be your mother's brother? And how is that you can tell us today when before you could not answer his question? I've always regretted that I didn't ask you then, when you were a baby, how you had that kind of knowledge. So tell me now."

"I'll tell you all," she said, fanning her husband with her fan.

## [ The Story of the Necklace ]

"This man was once the king of Maharastra. His name was Sugraha. My mother, Rupanubhuti, is his elder sister. Because of the nobility of his family, all kings wanted very much to give him their daughters in marriage and sent him letters to this effect. He, however, couldn't make up his mind which to accept and which to reject, and for a long time he dithered. Eventually, these kings became offended and advanced against him with their armies on one pretext or another. He thought he would do better fighting them from outside the city, so he mounted his famous horse and left. When the kings found that he was no longer in the city, they went home. 'What glory is there in attacking a kingdom that has no king?' they thought.

"But Sugraha didn't know they had left. He was wandering far away in a wilderness, wondering how to conquer his enemies. Guided by the way the future must unfold, he thought to himself, 'I was disturbed by the sudden attack and left the city alone and in haste without even thinking of telling anybody. I wonder what happened to the city? I wonder what happened to my subjects? And what are my enemies up to? I wish I had a way of knowing. I was afraid of being followed, so I kept changing my route, over and over. Now even my own people can't find me. And if I were to try to find my own way back, there's the danger of being captured. It won't work. How lucky it would be if I could only know everything while sitting in one place! Life is worth living only if I have that power. What use are other forms of power? They're all a waste of effort.'

"So, determined to achieve omniscience, he rode north toward Brindavana, on the banks of the Yamuna River, where young Krishna is always present. He focused his thoughts on the god who lies on his back on the banyan leaf.[5] And the god appeared in his infant form, pressing his two little feet to his face with his hands, sucking on his toe: the image Sugraha had in his mind had emerged into external form. 'Ask whatever you want,' said the god, but Sugraha was dumbfounded and could think of nothing. After a while, he pulled himself together, and, folding his hands in respect upon his forehead, he said, 'I could not speak because of this overwhelming happiness. But what I want from you is the gift of omniscience.'

5. Krishna, as a young infant, lies sucking his toe on a banyan leaf floating on the Ocean of Milk.

"The god pulled the tiny necklace from his neck and gave it to him. 'A person who wears this necklace will have omniscience and eloquence as long as the central jewel touches the area of that person's heart. However, this necklace will be lost if the person causes distress to a Brahmin.' With this, the god disappeared.

"Carrying the necklace, Sugraha wandered into a temple in that wilderness. There he saw, near the entrance, a certain sculpture of a woman. Her breasts were full and voluptuous, her waist thin enough to be held between two fingers, her cheeks sleek as a mirror and alight with a smile, her face more beautiful than anything in the known world. He was admiring this image from close up when an ascetic turned up. This man, dressed in ochre, exhausted by his journey, seated himself in the same sculpted pavilion of the temple; he was murmuring to himself, 'Hari, Hari.' Then he saw the stunning image of the woman, sculpted from rock and plaster. '*Oho*. This sculptor did better than God himself could have done.' Shaking his head, he wondered, 'Are there any women in the world as beautiful as this? Hard to believe. But an ascetic like me shouldn't look at her.' He turned his head away.

"And back. He was already overtaken by passion . . . "

Madhuralalasa hesitated a little at this point. Satvadatma, seeing this, withdrew on some pretext or other, out of propriety. But the king looked at his wife's face and said, "What happened next? I'm curious."

Madhuralalasa continued. "What more is there to say? The ascetic, unable to control himself any longer, went and embraced the sculpture rapturously. He hadn't noticed Sugraha, who was watching him nearby. At this point, Sugraha couldn't hold back and giggled.

"The ascetic heard him but pretended he hadn't heard. He wanted to cover up what he had done, as if it were only a certain idiosyncrasy of his, so, thinking quickly, he went and embraced each one of the sculpted images in the pavilion, beginning with those at the entrance. He bowed to them one by one and walked around them. But Sugraha knew this was all pretence. He said, laughing at him, 'You can go on like this, but I know what you did in the beginning, and I'll never forget it.' The ascetic was highly distressed, so he cursed him: 'Whatever you remember, from your birth up to this moment, will be lost to you.'

"Now Sugraha was alarmed. He fell at the ascetic's feet and begged to be released from the curse. The Yogi said, 'When this secret of mine comes out, somewhere or other, your memory will come back to you—for by that time, it won't cause any displeasure.' And he went away. From that moment on, because of the curse, Sugraha totally forgot everything that had been in his mind.

"He also forgot to pick up the necklace that he had put aside, in a clean spot, only a minute before. God had, after all, told him that the necklace would be lost if he caused distress to a Brahmin. But although he had heard this, he still caused pain to that Brahmin—and lost the necklace. No one can escape destiny. To mention another person's failings is itself a failing. Even a good person may have the occasional fault, but it's never right to talk about it.

"Driven by fate, Sugraha left that place and wandered from one lovely land to another. He had forgotten his name, his family, his entire past, like a person who has gone crazy, like a little child. Everything he saw amazed him. He lost the names of things, their qualities, and words for actions; he lacked even the slightest idea of how to use them. Little by little, in a new way, there arose in him, as for a child, the ability to distinguish things, actions, attributes, and abstract categories, through observing older people of different classes in their various activities. In the course of time, he became an expert at handling things. He knew everything except his family of birth and his name. He met with no one who knew of them—until today.

"Wandering around, he happened upon a forest area at the confluence of the Ganga and the Sarayu Rivers. At that time, Kasarapura had lost its king. The ministers, the nobility, and the citizens needed to choose a king, so they decorated an elephant and put a garland on its trunk; the person the elephant garlanded would become king. This was the pact they made before god. They set the elephant loose and followed it until it cast the garland around Sugraha's neck. Even before the elephant's choice, the ministers and others, who were quite helpless without a king, felt a certain strength and knowledge return when they saw Sugraha's face. Reassured by both these signs—the elephant's choice and their own intuition—they mounted him on the elephant and led him into the town, where they crowned him king. Since his mere appearance brought them strength (*satva*), they named him Satvadatma, 'the one whose person (*ātma*) gives (*da*) strength (*satva*).' Since no one knew his real name and family of birth, he became known in the world by this name. He enjoyed the pleasures of being king in Kasarapura, where he met with your parents, Highness, that is Sumukhasatti and Manistambha, and, while serving them, became your minister. I told you all those stories at length while I was a little baby," said Madhuralalasa. "Remember?

"After he became minister, he conquered Angadesa and built this new city of Beyond-the-Smooth-Neck Town, where he crowned you king. You know all that. You asked me why I wasn't able to tell him before about his name and story, and why today I *am* able to, and what the source was for all this knowledge. I'll tell you. The necklace that Sugraha forgot in the temple was picked up by a certain Brahmin from Mathura who happened by. He brought it home and for many years worshiped it as a deity. Then he decided the necklace was the right gift for Krishna, so he took it to Dvaraka and presented it to God. Krishna graciously accepted the gift and offered him whatever he desired. Later, when Manikandhara composed a *daṇḍaka* poem in his honor, Krishna was pleased and gave *him* the necklace. Manikandhara took it as a great honor, but because the necklace belonged to the god in his form as a baby, it clung to Manikandhara's neck and didn't reach down to his chest—so the jewel that had the quality of imparting awareness never touched his heart. In the end, Manikandhara gave it to Alaghuvrata, who gave it to you, Kalapurna. You kindly gave it to me. When the jewel touched *my* heart, when I was but a baby, total knowledge came to me. Great king! In your previous life, you were Manikandhara, who received this necklace from Krishna. In this birth, you received it from the Brahmin Alaghuvrata and gave it to me. When I rolled over, as a child, the jewel shifted away from my heart, so my awareness was lost. That was when this minister of yours asked his question. That's why I wasn't able at that time to tell the name and family of Satvadatma.

"Since no one knew that the source of my knowledge and its loss was this necklace, they treated it as an ordinary ornament; they put it away and forgot all about it. I never wore it again until today. Because I was to receive the new anklet from you today, my girlfriends started talking about my jewelry, and they reminded me of this one and how I got it. I thought today would be the perfect opportunity to wear it again, since it was your first gift to me, given at a memorable moment. So I had it brought to me and put it on with the central jewel touching my heart. As Satvadatma came in carrying the anklet, I thought to myself, 'What a lucky man he is to be allowed such intimate service in the inner palace!' At that moment, everything about his name and past became clear to me.

"Here," she said. "Wear it yourself. You will see anything you want to know in the past, present, or future, in all the world, as clearly as the back of your hand." She pulled the necklace out from under her sari, where it was dancing between her lovely breasts like a dancer who appears from behind a curtain and then disappears.

"Don't take it off," he cried. "It's not right for me to take back what I gave you. There is a better way of letting me feel its power—while you're wearing it."

She laughed. "You're quite the expert." She bent over him where he was sitting, so that the jewel touched his heart, and said: "See whatever you want to see." As if pulled down by the weight of her breasts, she fell onto his lap.

"*That's* what I wanted to see," he said. He embraced Madhuralalasa with both arms.

But that wasn't enough for him. He pressed further, and Madhuralalasa said, "This isn't exactly what you asked for, is it? Still, neither of us can ever wait. God got it right. We're a perfect match."

So at last, now that the jewel hanging between her breasts was touching his own heart, the king saw that the entire world of the story she had told was right from beginning to end.

Satvadatma was released from the curse. By itself memory of all his experiences from childhood on returned to him. Everything he had heard from Madhuralalasa fit exactly. Amazed, he waited for the right moment to see Kalapurna. He told him that he had recovered his memory—and why. "It must be because the little girl, Madhuralalasa, told you all about that ascetic and his lust. That's how I was freed from the curse." He praised both the king and his wife. "I'm much happier now, with you, than I was as king of Maharastra. Let me stay with you forever." The king sent him home with the honor due to a newfound relative.

Meanwhile, Kalapurna enjoyed making love to Madhuralalasa even more than before, because each time he learned something new and realized a new desire. And because the jewel touched each of their hearts at the same moment, each of them knew how much the other loved; so their delight was always strange and new.

Along with a vibrant imagination, Madhuralalasa was gifted with lucidity and elegance, because of the necklace. The king, whose past memories were brought back to life, trained her in music until she became an expert artist on the vina. When they embraced, she would tell the king about the good points and the weaknesses of his subordinates and rivals, for she had the good of all the citizens at heart.

One day, while he was discussing the peculiarities of the necklace with Madhuralalasa in private, he remembered that he had once composed a poem on a conversation between Lakshmi and Vishnu—the supreme goddess and god. This was in his former life, when he had visited the temple of Padmanabha sleeping on his snake, at Ananta-sayana.[6] He wanted to hear Madhuralalasa sing that poem. So he said to her, "I've heard—from you, when you were a baby—that in a former life I composed a poem on Lakshmi and Vishnu in conversation. Have a look with the help of your jewel and sing it for me now. At the moment I embrace you, though I can see everything with total clarity, my love for you takes over."

She said, "I love to do whatever you want me to do. I'll sing the poem." First she folded her hands in respect to the jewel of omniscience; then she called to mind the people through whom it came to her, starting from the end—Kalapurna, Alaghuvrata, Manikandhara, Krishna, the Brahmin, Sugraha, and the baby Krishna who sleeps on the banyan leaf. "May this line of my gurus bless me," she prayed, and then sang the poem exactly as Manikandhara had composed it.[7]

*There's a world called Vaikuntha,*
*beyond the river of death,*
*where suffering stops.*
*In that world, there are no logicians,*
*no ritualists, no grammarians,*
*no arguments about what things mean.*

*All that is there is God,*
*Goddess, and their love.*
*On earth, people still suffer.*
*Even the goddess wonders why.*

*Is it because there are still gaps?*
*He's always overflowing.*
*He's always free.*

6. Trivandrum: see 4.37 (p. 67).
7. We have condensed this "conversation" considerably so that it can work in translation. The question at its center is Lakshmi's thought addressed to Vishnu.

*There are places on earth*
*where God lives: Srirangam,*
*Tirupati, Ahobalam, Purushottama.*
*If you go there, you'll find him.*

"That," said Madhuralalasa, "in short, is the poem you composed in that other life."

Kalapurna was amazed at the power of God's places and at the love that God has for his creatures. From that time on, he spent his life focused on Vishnu, ruling his kingdom in fairness. He had two sons, Suprasada, born to his first wife, and Sarasa, born to Madhuralalasa. He had no enemies capable of standing up to him in battle; or if there was one, he could cause no wound to Kalapurna's soldiers; the worst he could do was to scratch with his fingernails on the breasts of the beautiful women who welcomed him into heaven after the king's elephants had killed him.

Brahma promised that whoever hears or reads this story of Kalapurna, the perfect man, will live in wealth and happiness with his children and grandchildren. Keep this in mind. Read this story, all of you.

This story will become famous in all countries.
God, the dancing Krishna, has blessed it,
and so have all learned people who are addicted
to reading books.

*O King Krishna of Nandyala from the line of Araviti Bukka: You are the grandson of Narayya and the son of Kondambika and Narasinga. You are true as the mountains. You heard it, too.*

This is the eighth and final chapter in the long poem called *Kalapurnodayamu* made by soft-spoken Suraya, son of Pingali Amaranarya, whose poetry all connoisseurs enjoy throughout the world.

# INVITATION TO A SECOND READING

[ 1 ]

We have called Suranna's book a novel—in fact, the first South Asian novel, in the modern sense. We have to explain why we use this term. But first let us quote Suranna himself, who articulates a radically new aesthetic in a verse from the *Prabhāvatī-pradyumnamu* that addresses this question of form. Indra, king of the gods, is talking to a goose who is being sent as a love messenger between the hero and heroine of this lyrical romance:

You prevent even the slightest slippage
from the definitive nature of the word.
You let the richness of meaning arise
from the way you combine words.
What you intend comes through unmarred
and luminous. You avoid any repetition.
You follow through as the anticipation
  inherent
in the sentence requires. You don't jump
from branch to branch. You connect things
in such a way that the primary focus is fully
  grounded.
Whatever logic is in play comes out in all

its force, without conflict between what you say first
and what you say later. All the individual parts
and subplots, each with its own meanings,
fit well with the larger statement.
That's what speaking really means.
You're lucky when it works.[1]

The goose, incidentally, was trained by Sarasvati, goddess of speech, herself. We are thus once again in the metaphysical domain discussed earlier, where God creates by speaking as the goddess on his tongue. But here the eloquent goose is almost an alter ego for the novelist, who gives us his poetic credo. Nothing like it exists before in Telugu. Note in particular the consistent theme of syntactical connection, widely understood. Syntax, for normal, sequential speech, is primary: meaning, even the meanings of individual words, depend entirely on syntactical connections. An extended utterance—*mahāvākya*—has many subparts, which must, however, conform to an integrative pattern. In effect, the whole book is perceived as a single sentence. An inherent syntactic, anticipatory drive, *ākāṅkṣā*, propels the sentence forward. This notion, drawn from classical linguistic discussions in Sanskrit, is here amplified to exclude any kind of loose, disconnected, or redundant parts. A comprehensive, syntactic unity structures speech. Within this well-integrated utterance, there is no room for slippage or confusion. Words, syntactically patterned, are definitive. But within this densely conceptualized connectedness, there exists a space for diversity and highly individualized perspectives or nuances—*tat-tad-avayava-vākya-tātparya-bhedamulu*. Each part works as a limb, *avayava*, of the larger statement, and each limb has its own expressive force.

This is the vision of a novelist. We take as a primary feature of this analytic, cross-cultural form a propensity to allow for the concretization of split pieces of self and reality within a total statement. Consciousness models itself to itself, isolating segments of self for inspection and reflection, framing them in a manner that incorporates internal distance. The novel, as Bakhtin has taught us, is by nature polyphonic.[2] Voices arise within it and speak with one another. Even the author may not predetermine the playing out of these voices in the reality he imagines—even if the author/novelist is the Creator-God himself, as in *Kaḷāpūrṇodayamu*. Real personae, like real persons, have their own, unpredictable autonomy. At the same time, the novel, precisely because of the space it gives for far-reaching splitting and fragmentation, tends to problematize the relation between what is thought or uttered and what is realized. In a sixteenth-century European ontology, such as we find in the *Quixote*, this relation may take the form of an intensely imagined inner reality locked in struggle with an external, harsher one; the latter tends to crush the former, at least superficially. In sixteenth-century South India, this relation is articulated along other lines: the novel inhabits the space between the authorial intention—of God the Creator, who tells the story in outline—and the actual psychic and experienced world of each of the characters separately and of their combined interactions. In this sense, the novel is a field within which these issues of multiple realities can be worked out, played with, liberated into form.

Bakhtin has also argued forcefully that the novel pushes past the limits of any given ecology of genres. Open-ended and unfinished in itself, the novel undermines the givenness of all earlier forms. It destabilizes and illumines the artificial features of existing canons. Parody—including ontological parody, which mocks the crystallized status of "reality"—is never far from the surface. We see this feature strongly present in the *Kaḷāpūrṇodayamu* as well, in a somewhat unexpected mode. Earlier genres are actually incorporated within this novel as parts of its overall statement, even as the author brings to bear a certain irony upon their function.

A new temporality is established—again, a classic feature of the novel. Time is tightly historicized. Each statement by an individual speaker and each reported event has its specific meaning only with reference to the singular moment in which it happens. The passage of time, carefully recorded and quantified, reveals inevitable changes in meaning for each such moment as it is remembered or reimagined. All this takes place with a cast of characters that superficially seems drawn from a preexisting mythology, with elements of the fairly tale, but that turns out to be individualized, humanized, historicized, and remarkably realistic. Each character presents, at each defined moment, a uniquely individual perspective, empathically imagined and brought into relation with competing perspectives.

Are there precedents in classical or medieval Indian literature for this kind of literary creation? On a formal and rather superficial level, one can, of course, detect elements that are present in earlier works. Most compelling in this respect is Bana's seventh-century Sanskrit prose-romance (*gadya-kāvya*), *Kādambarī*, often classified as a novel by modern literary historians.[3] *Kādambarī*, like the *Kaḷāpūrṇodayamu*, situates a parrot in the central storyteller's slot; moreover, it presents the reader with a narrative that weaves unevenly between past, present, and future in a strangely convoluted sequence of previous lives breaking into consciousness. The heroes discover themselves, to their surprise, in a story reported by an external narrator, as they do in the *Kaḷāpūrṇodayamu*. Complex linguistic mechanisms constantly come into play, transforming awareness. Nonetheless, Bana's masterpiece never approaches many of the analytic features that we are claiming for Suranna—interiority, far-reaching psychologizing of character, a radical perspectivism, highly individualized voicing, a realistic imagination in depictng persons who develop and grow over time (as distinct from realistic empirical observation in descriptions, which we do find in Bana as well), complex analyses of motivation, precise context-sensitivity, and a historicized temporality that reshapes the telling of the narrative. To draw in such distinctions in no way detracts from the unique merits of *Kādambarī*, which still awaits a satisfactory interpretive study; but it is crucial to recognize that Suranna's sixteenth-century sensibility marks a significant new departure, an innovation. He has drawn raw materials for the construction of his story from the existing, well-known *kathā* literature—a large and dynamic corpus that emerged from the sophisticated urban culture of North India in the middle of the first millennium.[4] To these materials he has added themes such as the self-recognition motif (*pratyabhijñāna*) prominent in works such as the Kashmiri *Yoga-vāsiṣṭha-mahārāmāyaṇa*, and Tantric and Yogic motifs popular in medieval Deccani culture. Siddha magical praxis and alchemy and the ritual achievement of perennial youth appear as routine aspects of the available physical and metaphysical spectrum. But the mere presence of such elements in the text tells us rather little; far more important is the far-reaching integration and transformation that Suranna works upon them.

If we seek a proximate context within which to situate this poet's vision, we can turn to the great Telugu *kāvya*s of the early sixteenth century by Peddana, Krishna-deva-raya, and Rama-raja-bhusana.[5] All of them reveal intense awareness of language as a subjective force and a gift for rich, lyrical description. Thematically, too, Suranna's text shares certain broad similarities to Peddana's *Manu-caritramu*.[6] In this sense, Suranna was clearly a product of his time and deeply connected to the powerful literary production at the Vijayanagara courtly centers. He certainly knew these earlier works intimately and built upon them. Where he differs from them is in the complexity and sensitivity he expresses in delineating the individual psyches of his characters and their interactions, and in the fast-paced, nuanced tone he brings to bear in telling their stories.

[ 2 ]

At the heart of this novel's design, and also at the structural center of the narration, lies a subtle statement about language and its world-creating potential. It is not a theoretical or philosophical statement per se but, like everything else in this text, an embodied narrative in which metaphysical themes emerge as enveloped in, and sometimes masked by, experience. This central core episode is a story of play and banter between the two creators of language and, through language, of the world—Brahma and his wife Sarasvati, Speech. In the invocation verse cited earlier, we are told that Sarasvati is moved to kiss the four faces of her husband simultaneously, and that this impulse of desire generates the four Vedas—one from each of Brahma's mouths—that give a blueprint for universal creation. When we come, however, to the narrative reworking of this theme, the lines of force seem, at first glance, reversed.

The story is told by the young girl Madhuralalasa, who knows it by virtue of her former existence as a parrot in Brahma and Sarasvati's house:

> *One day while I was living in the palace of the goddess, her husband Brahma took her out to the lakeshore garden. They sat to the east of the lake, with its golden steps leading down to the water. In the middle of the lake stood a crystal pillar, inlaid with sculpted geese. Brahma lay down facing the lake on a bed of flowers in the shadow of the wishing trees. The goddess took his feet onto her lap to massage them. Desire flooded him, and he pulled her to the bed, each of his four faces trying at once to pull her face to itself, trying to kiss her.*
>
> *Smiling at his games, she said, "Enough of your pranks. It isn't fair. If all four of your faces want me at the same time, what am I supposed to do? I'm a one-faced woman. Cut it out. It's too much." She stiffened her neck and pulled her face back. Guarding her lips with her hand, she curved her eyebrows and gave him a sharp look, in a pose of charming anger. This excited him even more.*
>
> *Brahma bent her face forcibly to his, pushed her hand away from her lips, and bit her slightly. As pleasure awoke inside her, a soft moan of enchantment slipped from her throat.*

*The goddess of speech tried to cover up the moment of ecstasy that had overpowered her deep inside. She was a little embarrassed. Looking for a way to get through it quietly, she pretended her lower lip was hurting, and she turned around, as if angry, to prevent him from provoking her further. I, watching from my cage, understood her feelings from her body language. She was pressing her thighs tightly together and closing her eyes. It was a textbook case.*

*Brahma, thwarted, having lost the initiative, put on a show of anger. Not wanting to reveal his real feelings, he turned to me in my golden cage hanging from a nearby tree. "My little parrot," he said, "I'm bored. Won't you tell me a story?"*

*"How can I tell you a story? You're God. I'll listen if you tell one."*

*"In that case, listen," he said. "Once upon a time, there was a city called Kasarapura, Lake Town. A rich place, ruled by a king called Kalapurna. He conquered all other kings by virtue of his incomparable brilliance. When he had come of age, a certain Siddha called Svabhava gave him a unique gem, a splendid bow, and gleaming arrows. The gem was of a deep red color, the arrows inexhaustible, and the bow could win over the god of love himself. Because the giver was so noble, he carried them constantly. A certain king, called Madasaya, happened to enter the kingdom with his wife, Rupanubhuti and his minister, Dhirabhava. Skillfully using his bow, Kalapurna drove out Dhirabhava. Madasaya and his wife surrendered, and the king made them his slaves. They followed his command and performed menial tasks."*

It hardly looks like a thrilling tale at its start—or, for that matter, in what comes later—yet this is the story that must never be told. It has its own rather unsettling riddles built in from the beginning. Sarasvati asks for clarification:

*"Ask him what happened to this Kalapurna. Who were his father and mother?" She taught me [the parrot] to say all this, and I asked these questions.*

*God said, "A woman called Abhinavakaumudi fell in love with him and married him. His father was a lady called Sumukhasatti and his mother was a fellow called Manistambha."*

*The goddess laughed and hugged him. "Relax. Your story is all upside down." She patted him on the back. "A male mother and a female father? That's what their names imply." She couldn't stop laughing. "Tell me more."*

*Brahma, overjoyed and encouraged, hugged her back. With his four faces, one by one, he kissed her, drinking at her lips, twisting his neck into position over and over and stroking her cheeks and neck. One of his faces bit her a little hard, and she showed anger. "You never know when to stop," she said. "Enough of this. Tell me what happened to the hero of your story."*

So Brahma continues, gently teasing out a conventional, rather pallid story about the ups and downs of courtly politics in this King Kalapurna's city. The details are available in chapter 5. And since the goddess Speech is, as we might expect, very well versed in what she calls "the craft of words" (*vaco-racana-kauśalamu*, 5.44) and thus perfectly able to see through her husband's intention, she has no difficulty in instantly decoding the entire story as an allegorical restatement about the lovers' games the two were playing that day on the shores of the heavenly lake. Kalapurna, the hero, whose name means "moon," turns out to be the reflection of Sarasvati's moon-like face in the water. His odd parentage, with a male mother and female father, has a similar poetic and linguistic explanation—and so on through the entire plot of Brahma's narrative. After Sarasvati's lengthy exegesis of her husband's text, she forces him to acknowledge the correctness of her reading.[7]

But this is, after all, only the beginning. When God speaks, his words become reality. When he tells a story, this story must exist in some time and space. Decoding will only take us, like Sarasvati, so far. The mere uttering of the words is a creative act with existential consequences. It is also a form of playing. Formally, this kind of play is strongly linked to the technique of *śleṣa*, the paronomastic "bitextual" mode of punning and linguistic superimposition we mentioned earlier with reference to Suranna's other work, the *Rāghava-pāṇḍavīyamu*. *Śleṣa*, literally an "embrace," conflates two or more levels of perception, expression, or experience. In the present case, as Sarasvati at once perceives, the *śleṣa* extends systematically throughout the whole of Brahma's text; each element corresponds to a moment or movement in the field of force between her and her husband. In actual fact, there are three levels operative here, all somehow congruent. First, there is the literal level of the story about Kalapurna, King in Kramuka-kanthottarapuram, Beyond-Smooth-Neck Town. Then, we have the encoded narration of what passed between the god and goddess in the palace, perfectly correlated to some external or objective sequence of intentions and events, and even incorporating a hiatus or silence between the opening of the story and its continuation after the successful episode of the quadruple kiss.

Such silence may be a necessary component of any articulated sequence. But the names of nearly all the dramatis personae in Brahma's story have, in themselves, a much wider resonance; thus we find people named "One's Own Nature," "My Heart," "Love of Beauty," "Sense of Pride," and so on. So, either overriding or underlying the correspondence between act and linguistic report is a more properly allegorical level that appears to relate to various epistemic or metalinguistic processes: here Brahma, whose intentionality may, after all, be quite different from Sarasvati's and also entirely opaque to her understanding, may be saying something about the experience of form, about aesthetic perception, about a natural mode of being or becoming, about empathic identification. Suranna's God is a philosopher who uses carefully selected words. Add to this, if you like, the fact that the central "hero" of the story, Kalapurna, is himself a double reflection, from face to crystal pillar to the water of the pond; and remember that he is also, at bottom, so to speak, a pun. But the true poignancy of this multiple conflation arises from the presence of yet another, critical level.

In a world where words have weight and consequence, where words shape or actually create worlds, *śleṣa* is never trivial. It generally presumes a process of congruence among levels of being; more specifically, in the present case, it suggests that the story in Brahma's mind, once clothed in words, is to be lived out in some still more objectified domain, and not only in the immediate setting by the lake in heaven. Suranna's novel is largely about this transition from godly speech into lived human experience and about the awareness that is achieved when this transition is internalized and understood. Its heroes will find their place within the skeletal text of Brahma's playful tale. Indeed, this form of self-revelation recurs regularly, in different intensities, in Suranna's book. Again and again a story is told, and suddenly someone who is listening to it unexpectedly recognizes himself or herself and says: "This is my story. It differs not in the least from what you are telling us. I know it because I have lived it. You are describing me, but until this moment I did not know who I was. It is all condensed into that one, total word."

This experience could almost be seen as defining the condition of being human, or, perhaps, of being aware, of having and knowing a self. It applies no less to us, the readers or listeners "outside" the text, than to the characters fully within it. We are living in a story that God has told—actually, to be precise, we are *repeating* the story, which is an intradivine conversation between parts of God's self or selves—and, although we in some sense already know the main coordinates of this text, we do not know that we know it. Moreover, unless the story is told, always by someone else, we can never discover ourselves. This is true for Sarasvati, as it is true for Kalapurna, and it must be true for us. It is always a matter of recognition. As the Russian poet Mandelstam says, seemingly recapitulating the widespread Indian theme, "Everything existed of old, everything happens again, and only the moment of recognition is sweet."

## [3]

How does all this work out in the novel? Perhaps the central point is the lack of isomorphism between the god-spoken story, which already contains all who unconsciously are living it out, and their subjective experience. No character experiences the story in anything like a schematic manner; his or her perspectives always emerge in the gap between the bare structure and the rich exfoliation of that structure moment by moment. Brahma himself hints at this inevitable transformation as the story becomes manifest in reality: "The story," he tells Sarasvati, "will expand a little into branch-stories, depending on the listeners and the context" (*śrotṛ-janâpekṣânusarambuna*, 5.61). Expansion (*vistāra*), here, actually suggests transformation: as the narrative embodies itself, each name acquires new meaning—sometimes more than one meaning, depending on context—and the events ramify in unexpected ways while retaining the lineaments of the prophesied frame. Words, that is, retain their canonical shape and phonetic structure even as their semantics shift into new spaces. Each time someone hears or repeats these words, they have a new, contextually appropriate meaning. For example, in Brahma's story there is the minor figure of a king called Madasaya, "My Heart"—a meaningful nuance in the complex dialogue between Brahma and his beloved wife. But when this very Madasaya turns out to be an almost autistic king totally ruled by his cunning minister, it takes a moment of poignant revelation to bring out the true meaning, for him, of his own name. After the four young pandits, Vedas One through Four, manage to steal into his presence and explain to him how real scholars were being driven away from the palace,

> The king was ashamed that he had allowed himself to be influenced by the weakness of his priest and had therefore turned away scholars deserving of respect. "That's probably why people call me Madasaya—

> Deluded Heart," he said. "Just look how I behaved. Swayed by the priest, I couldn't see my own scholars." [6.168]

The name, phonetically identical with that given by Brahma but reflecting a different parsing of the Sanskrit compound, suddenly reflects an entirely new reality. This kind of shift in meaning occurs regularly throughout the novel.

So we are living in a divinely framed tale that we, at best, perceive dimly, and that even God himself, the only one who knows it completely, cannot fully predetermine. The details, the meanings, the experience, the relationships and connections—all these unfold in a contingent manner and with an astonishing range of shifting perspectives. The story itself changes as it takes place. This perception, so subtly worked out in precise and believable ways, allows for great psychological depth and penetrating insights.

Take, for example, the relationship between the two primary figures, Kalabhashini and Manikandhara. Incidentally, neither of these two appear, under these names, in Brahma's master-narrative; they embody the prehistory of Madhuralalasa and Kalapurna, respectively. Yet, in effect, the novel is their story. It is not so much Madhuralalasa and Kalapurna's love and marriage that provide a central axis for the story—although the last two and a half chapters of the book do focus on this theme, in a specific manner that we analyze below. This axis is rather formed by the strangely oblique relationship between Kalabhashini and Manikandhara. Their story is one of conflated confusions, projections, and superimpositions that, taken together, describe the adventure of discovering one's love.

Kalabhashini is a courtesan—therefore, knowledgeable about sex and free to fall in love. Ostensibly, from the very opening of the novel, she is infatuated with Nalakubara, the handsome, divine companion of Rambha, the most beautiful courtesan of the gods. With single-minded determination, she schemes to find a way to make love to Nalakubara. Effectively, this requires that she assume Rambha's bodily form—a gift she extracts from her teacher, the sage Narada. Manikandhara, seemingly absorbed in Yoga and meditation on God, is easily diverted from this course by Rambha, sent by a jealous Indra, king of the gods, to seduce him. A shocking story of duplicates and lookalikes unfolds from this point. Manikandhara makes love to Rambha until she, at the height of passion, calls out the name of her "real" beloved, Nalakubara. Deeply hurt in his sexual ego, Manikandhara takes on the form of Nalakubara, by the power he has acquired in Yoga, and returns to Rambha. In the middle of their lovemaking, he hears Kalabhashini's cry and rushes off to save her. She, however, has by now assumed Rambha's shape, and in this form makes love with Manikandhara-as-Nalakubara. Has she then achieved her life's goal?

Yes and no. She thinks she is with her longed-for lover. Only later, as the duplicates confront one another—and later still, when the story is retold at the temple of the Lion-Riding Goddess, when both Kalabhashini and Manikandhara confess to their disguises—does it transpire that she was deluded in the surface identification. But this moment of truth actually produces a much deeper recognition and reveals the latent, mostly unconscious search for the truly desired partner. A twisted path has led to a straight conclusion. At the Lion-Rider's temple, Kalabhashini herself states the conclusion that she has arrived at through such devious ways. She is speaking to Manikandhara, whom she suddenly sees in an entirely new light:

> My mind is at rest. I was worried all along, wondering who that ugly-minded man [that is, the pseudo-Nalakubara] could be who made love to me by tricking me. Now I have nothing to regret. Don't think your love was something I didn't want. I thought I wasn't worthy of you, and I didn't know *your* mind. So I turned my heart away whenever I saw you. You'll never know how much I was captivated by your arresting beauty, your superb music, your perfection in every way. You made me happy all the time. Only my heart knows. There's no point in talking about it all at this point.
>
> You know what else? Once when I saw you, the name Manigriva came to my mind. It's very much like *your* name. There's that story about how Narada cursed him and his older brother to become huge trees. I kept thinking about that. As a result of that scare, my desire to enjoy your body completely disappeared, as if I'd sworn an oath. From that time on, my mind turned toward Nalakubara. He resembles you to some extent. It was some terribly inauspicious moment that I set my eyes on him. I was focused only on the external form. I thought I was making love to Nalakubara, but actually it was you. I was incredibly lucky. It was like being pushed off the roof and landing on a bed of flowers.

So ultimately, and mostly unknown to herself, Kalabhashini was fulfilled in love, though only in the course of making love to her longed-for lover in the guise of the man she *thought* she was in love with. She even has an explanation, certainly worthy of Freud, to offer for the initial suppression of her feelings for Manikandhara. It remains only to add that Manigriva—the interfering association that diverted Kalabhashini's attention from Manikandhara—is the name of another son of Kubera's, like Nalakubara, the ersatz beloved. We will return to this point.

As for Manikandhara, a very similar, complementary conclusion will apply. For an extended, passionate moment, he thought he wanted Rambha—and had attained her. Yet when he heard a woman scream and immediately rushed to the rescue, did he not unconsciously identify the voice as Kalabhashini's—a voice he had heard over many years of musical practice in Dvaraka? His leaving Rambha, for whose sake he had "become" Nalakubara, and his response to Kalabhashini's call reveal the more profound desire. He confirms this surmise himself:

> "Let me confess. I was afraid of Narada, so I never let anybody know. My mind was on you all the time, all those years, during our music lessons. At last, my dream came true. I was lucky." (4.16)

The two lovers have found one another through indirection, a rather long and intricate process of disguise and conflation; and they are, at this point, also about to lose one another again. But the indirection is in no way incidental to the statement about love. In fact, it seems to be at the very core of the psycho-physical experience of loving. The compounded mistakes both lovers make are, in fact, what eventually bring them to one another. Desire fulfills itself, in this perspective, precisely through and because of displacement. A strikingly similar theme turns up in Suranna's great predecessor, Peddana, where human generativity seems to depend upon some such process of impersonation and sexual delusion.[8]

Suranna's implicit theory of human loving requires a sense of a many-layered mind that is often opaque to itself. Look again at the process that leads Manikandhara and Kalabhashini to one another. Initially, both love one another without recognizing this. Both suppress their love out of fear, real or imagined, of being punished or cursed (by Narada). There is something more to this mostly unconscious fear. Narada is famous as a troublemaker who feeds off others' quarrels; but in the present case—as in nearly all cases in the classical mythology—the strife he generates ultimately aims at producing self-knowledge and self-realization in the participants. Suranna offers a deep reading of this mechanism. On the surface, it appears as if Narada wanted to humble Rambha, who offended him by boasting of her beauty and, as its direct result, her lover Nalakubara's undying love for her. To this end, Narada sets up a complex scheme, in which Rambha finds herself faced with severe competition from her own double—as does Nalakubara. But the deeper aim of this entire episode has little to do with Rambha and Nalakubara. It has everything to do with Kalabhashini and Manikandhara, who can discover one another—or, more precisely, their abiding love for one another—only in this way.

Narada's plan is perfectly calculated, as we see from the moment he grants Kalabhashini the ability to assume another woman's form. Listen to the way the boon is formulated: "*Now you will happily make love to the man you wanted, a man so beautiful that he could win Rambha's heart. Trust me. Go home.*" Like every other such pregnant statement throughout the novel, this one is precisely worded, with an internal ambiguity that allows it to mean different things as the context develops and a deeper awareness comes into play. As Manikandhara himself rightly points out at the moment of full recognition, the wording clearly suggests that Kalabhashini would realize her love for someone she already desired, someone *similar* in form and beauty to Nalakubara, Rambha's lover (*munnu nīv'ātmalo gorinaṭṭi kāntu rambhā-manoharâkāru*).

> "Narada didn't say you'd make love to Nalakubara. His words came true. I'm the one you wanted, the one you were in love with before. It's not so unusual to have to repress a wish like that, under the pressure of fear. Such things happen in the world."

Originally, of course, Kalabhashini understood this in terms of her superficial desire for Nalakubara. Only later does the true meaning become clear. Notice also that Kalabhashini was supposedly trying to persuade Narada to give her this boon—of assuming another form—in order to gain access to Krishna's inner palace, where she could overhear Krishna's wives talking among themselves about Narada's musical talents. For his own reasons, Narada agrees:

> Narada thought to himself, "Some excuse! What she really wants is to become Rambha and make love to Nalakubara. But this fits my plan, too [*madīya kāryânukūlama kadā*]." So he looked at her and said, "Fine. I give you that capability. Take the form of whatever woman you want and go find out what Krishna's wives are really thinking." And he went away. [2.46]

The critical word is *kāryânukulama*—the suggestion that this strategem "fits my plan, too." At first reading, it seems to relate to Narada's scheme to humble Rambha. Upon reflection, we can see that the underlying *kārya*—the deeper plan—is to bring Kalabhashini to the realization that the man she really wants is not Nalakubara but Manikandhara. She can achieve this only by actually getting Nalakubara—or, more precisely, his lookalike. She makes love to the Nalakubara she holds in her mind.

It seems that the fullness of loving (*krithârthata*)[9] may emerge out of the conflation of these two levels—the illusion, externally and consciously lived out, and the true, internal, at best half-conscious wish. The recognition comes later, when the two levels merge in the mind. The shortest course to release from illusion is *straight through* the illusion. Experiencing the depth of delusion is necessary but not sufficient. Motivation is usually skewed. Kalabhashini asks the Siddha to take her to the forest where Manikandhara is busy with Rambha—ostensibly, because Nalakubara was there, alone and available. This is what she thinks she wants. But she has also just been told that Manikandhara was unsatisfied, in fact insulted, by Rambha when the latter called out to her usual lover in the midst of their embrace. Kalabhashini's "real" wish centers on this opportunity. Manikandhara is, on the surface, truly infatuated with Rambha and thinks he can reach the fullness of loving with her only if he has the form of Nalakubara. Kalabhashini, perhaps obscurely sensing the true passion within her, follows a necessary and convoluted path of impersonation: she has to become Rambha, become jealous of Rambha, and fall in love with Nalakubara, even make love to Nalakubara—who is actually Manikandhara in disguise—and all this in order to realize the true object of her desire. All of this happens in the mind that is constantly reworking the sensations of body, feeling, fantasy, disappointment, hope.

Manikandhara goes through a very similar course of development with reference to his apparent wish to achieve perfect mastery of music and to sing to God all the time. With considerable pride he says to Narada, quoting a proverb, "People say one becomes great by reaching a great person" (*tann' andinavāru tanantalu*, 2.104). Narada at once gives him a prescription for religious discipline that should allow him to achieve his desire. But at the first opportunity, Manikandhara surrenders everything and falls for Rambha—apparently a more immediate and realistic wish that eventually leads him to the understanding that he is more a lover than a Yogi, and that the woman he truly wants is Kalabhashini. Narada has brought him to this realization by giving him his literal, conscious wish.

This way of reading the complexities of the Manikandhara-Kalabhashini relationship is sustained by the story Suranna tells us, through the words of Manikandhara himself, about Salina and Sugatri. This story is explicitly classified as an illustration of the experience shared by Manikandhara and Kalabhashini. Here is what Manikandhara tells Kalabhashini as a preface to the story he is about to narrate:

> "I'm the one you wanted, the one you were in love with before. It's not so unusual to have to repress a wish like that, under the pressure of a deep fear of being cursed by a powerful sage. Such things happen in the world. It's also no surprise that Nalakubara made such an impression on your mind that you showed no interest in anybody else. He glows with Rambha's presence and is enlivened by her attention. It even happens to men sometimes. I'll tell you a story to prove that. It's a good story—that also washes away your sins. Listen carefully. I'll begin at the beginning."

Manikandhara, we should recall, himself had a similar fear of being cursed; hence his empathic remark. He goes on to tell the charming, complex story of the shy husband, Salina, married to the voluptuous Sugatri whom he refuses to touch so long as she is fully dressed and ornamented, in his bedroom at night; he makes love to her only during the day when she is dressed in her work clothes and toiling beside him in the heat of the garden. After narrating this tale with its intriguing ending, leading directly to the gender inversion that produces Kalapurna, Manikandhara draws the moral:

> "Now listen, Kalabhashini. Your mind worked just like in Salina's story. He was obsessed by rustic beauty and repelled by anything that smacked of ornament or fancy clothes. He rejected his finely deco-

> rated wife but was impressed by her plain loveliness when she was working in the garden—so impressed, in fact, that he forgot everything else. His story is a variation on yours." (4.144)

But how are we to understand the parallel that is being drawn for us? In what ways is Sugatri's story a variation on Kalabhashini's? The problem, not surprisingly, is one of penetrating a surface image fixed in the mind. Salina has a problem with ornaments and is "obsessed by rustic beauty." In effect, this is his curse. He has to find his way to his own wife through seeing her in another form—unadorned, disheveled, covered with sweat in the garden beside him. In this case, the lack of ornament is itself a veil. Eventually, Salina manages to bring the two images of this single woman together in his mind, thereby realizing his love. Kalabhashini's course takes her through her own fear of a curse—the mental association of Manikandhara with Manigriva, who had been cursed by Narada—into an all-too-similar situation, where she finds Manikandhara in a veiled form, as Nalakubara. Penetrating the veil ultimately brings her to the insight that allows her to combine the fantasy lover with the actual person. In both cases, the entire progression uses misperception or delusion, lived out fully, to expose illusion and bring about self-knowledge. The stories, not immediately similar on the surface level, actually constitute a deep thematic repetiton.

And there is one more suggestive level to this parallel. Kalabhashini's experience is compared to Salina's—the woman's to the man's. But Salina, this appropriately named "shy man," will soon become a woman, while his now beloved wife turns into a man. This exchange of gender seems to be foreshadowed by the cross-gendered comparison set up by the two stories. Here, too, lies an implicit statement about the convoluted workings of desire.

## [4]

Pingali Suranna is a penetrating psychologist, deeply aware of the complex forces at work in his characters' minds. He masterfully shows the effects of shifting perspectives and the interlocking energies and fantasies of many individuals. But he is also keenly attuned to the odd displacements that continuously come into play in the interval between the consciously held wish in the mind and the more deeply felt psychic reality. In a certain sense, Narada assumes the author's role and voice in this respect. We have already shown how, while ostensibly teaching Rambha a lesson, he is actually bringing Kalabhashini and Manikandhara to a place of self-understanding. There is, however, a still richer and more intricate level to the process Narada sets in motion.

Let us briefly revisit the moment of Kalabhashini's anagnorisis, when she explains the nature of her choices to Manikandhara during their reunion at the temple of the Lion-Riding Goddess.

> "You know what else? Once when I saw you, the name Manigriva came to my mind. It's very much like *your* name. There's that story about how Narada cursed him and his older brother to become huge trees. I kept thinking about that. As a result of that scare, my desire to enjoy your body completely disappeared, as if I'd sworn an oath. From that time on, my mind turned toward Nalakubara. He resembles you to some extent. It was some terribly inauspicious moment that I set my eyes on him. I was focused only on the external form. I thought I was making love to Nalakubara, but actually it was you. I was incredibly lucky. It was like being pushed off the roof and landing on a bed of flowers."

In this strange account of omissions, anxieties, and displacements, one truly significant slip should be noticed. The story Kalabhashini refers to is about Narada's curse against Manigriva and his unnamed "older brother." What happened is the following: one day Narada came across these two brothers, sons of Kubera, playing water-games with a group of *apsaras* courtesans from heaven; all were naked. When the sage appeared, the courtesans quickly covered themselves in shame, but the two brothers remained defiantly naked—and for that reason were cursed to become two huge trees. (Much later the baby Krishna will crawl between these two trees while dragging a mortar tied to his waist; under pressure of the mortar, the two trees collapse, and the brothers are released from the curse and regain their true form.[10]) But what Kalahabhashini conveniently forgets is that the elder brother in this story is none other than Nalakubara, her fantasy lover. This critical detail has slipped her mind.

What sense can we make of this? Why should Kalabhashini have opted to abandon her love for Manikandhara out of a fear rooted in a curse that was directed against someone whose name recalled his, but then choose for her lover someone who had himself suffered precisely this same curse? Has Suranna made a mistake?

Hardly. There is, perhaps, a contextual explanation of Kalabhashini's behavior. Her love for Manikandhara was born in the period that both she and Manikandhara were studying music from Narada. There was reason to fear that he would not approve of any erotic tie between his students. After all, Narada had shown how hostile he could be to the open expression of erotic love; the Manigriva story provided the prime example. The confusion between the two names—Manigriva and Manikandhara—feeds directly into Kalabhashini's fear of the curse. But her choice of Nalakubara and her attempt to seduce him transpire in Narada's absence. Kalabhashini had no reason to fear the sage's intervention at this point.[11] One displacement is more than enough.

But if we look a little more deeply, there is more here than simple displacement. We could even go so far as to suggest that Kalabhashini *had* to fall in love with Nalakubara, whose name and fate she has somehow suppressed, for her own internal reasons—precisely because he suffered the same curse as Manigriva/Manikandhara. The latter two figures are, we must recall, identified in her mind. In this case, displacement is actually, as so often, a replacement. Nalakubara duplicates more than he displaces. He has a double necessity for Kalabhashini, for he combines Manikandhara's external form with Manigriva's curse. In this sense, it is almost as if Kalabhashini needs the curse in order to achieve the secretive fulfillment of her desire. There is no way she can go straight to the "true" object of her love. That path is blocked; even the telltale name, which reveals the necessary zigzag in consciousness, has been obliterated in her telling of the story. Fear rules her conscious choice, even as the passionate wish fastens unerringly on the one logical surrogate, whose fate reproduces both the original object and the danger attached to it. Forgetting is perhaps the most persuasive form of remembering. Kalabhashini's whole history shows us with shocking lucidity how desire works through the mind that denies it.[12]

Similar insights emerge regularly as Suranna tells his stories. In fact, the *Kaḷāpūrṇodayamu* as a whole is a ramified exploration of the multiple modes of desire, or of sexuality, fantasized and enacted in various, sometimes outlandish forms. Each of the erotic relationships described in the book reveals a particular, inner complexity; each seems to interest Suranna for its own sake and to elicit an individualized portrait. In effect, these stories function like small, self-contained novellas or short stories growing out of the central narrative. Incidentally, many of them are entirely outside the frame of Brahma's master-narrative and thus independent of his intent.

We can list a few of these branch-stories. We have already discussed Sugatri and Salina, who provide a key, or analogue, to Kalabhashini's experience with Manikandhara. Ultimately, this story moves toward the moment of gender exchange that allows the male fantasy of female sexuality, as well as the male envy of the woman's pregnancy and generativity, to be tried out in laboratory conditions. Suranna offers us an extended, searching essay on these matters. Then there is the slightly ludicrous but touching demon Salyasura, hopelessly in love with Abhinavakaumudi, whom he alternately badgers and cajoles. Even when he discovers that she has tricked him and is certain she cannot love him, he still takes care to protect her from destruction. Abhinavakaumudi, however, devoid of any affection for this awkward would-be lover, has no qualms whatsoever about getting him killed. In Salyasura's case, love turns out to be a fatal weakness. Who among the male readers of the *Kaḷāpūrṇodayamu* will fail to identify with this doomed and lovable figure?

Or take Sugraha, alias Satvadatma, who rejects all the inviting brides that are offered to him because he is afraid of giving offense to any of them. Wandering alone, inconceivably alone, he seems to feel the first stirrings of passion at the sight of a carved stone image of a beautiful woman. Almost as if his desire could only be expressed by someone else, a Brahmin Yogi happens along and actually embraces, with utmost passion, the same stone image. Is it any wonder that the upshot is the curse of forgetfulness mingled with the promise of regaining memory when the story comes to be known? This apparently simple story reveals the rather desperate psychology of Sugraha, so deeply inhibited that he is not able even to embrace a stone. Only through a surrogate, or alter ego, can the desire he truly feels come to the surface. Not surprisingly, Satvadatma-Sugraha is the one major character in the novel who seems to have no wife or lover. He falls in love with a woman who is actually a man—Manistambha in Sumukhasastti's form—and even that love cannot find fulfillment. Moreover, the condition for his falling in love, in this case, is that he forget his name and his entire past. In that state, and only in that state, does he rid himself of his shyness and allow himself a fearless, if barren, courtship. Satvadatma must ultimately remain content with serving Kalapurna, the man he has crowned king.

No less intriguing a specimen is the winsome and pivotal character Alaghuvrata, originally Yajnasarma. For once, we begin with a story of a happy marriage. Yajnasarma adores his four loving wives. Alas, this harmonious affection does not prevent him from selling all four into slavery, although the treacherous husband regrets his action almost before the slave ship sets sail. As for the wives, they come to inhabit a bordello in the Godavari Delta after surviving a surrealistic journey with yet another peculiar couple drunk on wine and dice. Chastity and faithfulness are, in this case, ingredients in a dreamlike drama that brings these qualities into the same space as an exuberant, voluptuous eroticism. No wonder the children born from these mothers speak the language of *śleṣa* paronomasia, embracing two meanings in the same words.

And so on. Each example has its own integrity and expressive focus relating to some deeply held human desire. Even what looks like the most conventional and straightforward of relationships, that between Kalapurna and his young bride, Madhuralalasa, has its own twists. Remember that Madhuralalasa is a courtesan reborn. Remember that she was once a parrot. At the time of her first death as Kalabhashini at the temple of the Lion-Rider Goddess, she asks to be blessed with "ultimate faithfulness to a husband" (*pātivratyamu*), a virtue that even "the most wayward of women" can attain (4.183). When she is cursed as a parrot by Sarasvati, Brahma mitigates the severity of the curse by promising that she will live, on earth, "a life of incomparable wealth and joy with natural, inborn faithfulness" (*sahajamb'aina parama pātivratyambu*) to her husband (5.59). As Madhuralalasa, she apparently achieves this state. But the progression she undergoes is itself important. Perhaps only the courtesan, who has lived out a life of uninhibited desire, can become the faithful wife. Yet there is still more to this sequence. Faithfulness is not all. In particular, even intimate loving still leaves open the existential problem of doubt. Is the love fully and symmetrically mutual? Does the person I love, love me equally? This is the eternal shadow of any love experience, which at some level may also reflect doubt about the depths or ambivalence of one's own love. Issues of transparency and symmetry—or, more concretely, the problems inherent in the intricate business of interweaving the fantasy lover with some tangible and present person—arise regularly throughout the novel. Even assuming that Madhuralalasa and Kalapurna are an ideal pair, fully ripe for loving and whole in heart, the doubt about symmetry can still emerge.

And Suranna addresses this doubt. At the very moment of the wedding in chapter 7, the new bride is distraught with doubts as to the fullness of her husband's love for her. Will he even come to be with her that night?

Perhaps he loves Abhinavakaumudi, the *apsaras* woman who is his first wife, more than anyone else? Why should he leave her? And why should Abhinavakaumudi, who has the most handsome man in the world for her husband, let him go to another woman? These thoughts go on and on, as they must in any serious love. Suranna's innovation is in articulating this doubt, understood as normative, and in producing an unconventional means of resolving it—the *maṇihāra* necklace that allows omniscience to its bearer at the moment the central jewel touches his or her heart. With the aid of the *maṇihāra*, the agony of loving is put to rest; the always hidden shadow is removed. Kalapurna and Madhuralalasa make love with the jewel strategically placed between their hearts:

> And because the jewel touched each of their hearts at the same moment, each of them knew how much the other loved; so their delight was somewhat strange and new. (8.198)

It is a matter of revealing the *makkuva-pasalu*—the strength or intensity of love—to one another. Each one knows exactly how the other feels, and this form of loving is *citramu*, something wondrous or new, different from all the other forms of loving described in Suranna's text. The couple are reaching toward a form of ultimate fulfillment. Yet it is striking that they cannot do this by themselves but need the interpretive help of the magical jewel. Human consciousness is incapable of fully realizing the other.

## [5]

What is this *maṇihāra* necklace that brings closure to the story? On one level, it seems emblematic of knowledge in general: Alaghuvrata, the Malayali Brahmin, actually holds this necklace of omniscience in his hands for two whole years without even realizing how close he was to total knowledge. This is our common fate. Even Madhuralalasa, who as a baby holds the necklace on her heart, does so only accidentally; and she, too, loses contact with the gem when she rolls over. Knowledge, inherently available to us, is subject to capricious gaps and discontinuities. A context of fullness is needed to recover it. Or, paradoxically stated, memory has to be activated, that is, remembered, in order to remember.

We see this clearly in the pregnant moment, at the very end of the novel, when Madhuralalasa wishes to recite the forgotten text of the *Lakshmī-*

*nārāyaṇa-saṃvāda*, the dialogue between the goddess and the god that Kalapurna had sung, long ago, in his previous life as Manikandhara. In order to recover this lost text, Madhuralalasa invokes the strange genealogy of the *maṇihāra*, all of the carriers seen now as her gurus. She traces the lineage backward—Kalapurna, Alaghuvrata, Manikandhara, Krishna, the Brahmin, Sugraha, and, again, the baby Krishna who sleeps on the banyan leaf. If we order this sequence in the linear pattern of their occurrence, we get the following progression. The baby Krishna gave the necklace to Sugraha, the wandering king who wanted omniscience. Sugraha, cursed with amnesia, forgot it in the temple. A Brahmin from Mathura found it there, took it home, and worshipped it for many years as a deity. Then he decided that it was the right gift for Krishna, so he brought it to the god at Dvaraka. Krishna, having accepted it, bestowed it on Manikandhara in reward for his composition of the *daṇḍaka* poem. Manikandhara achieved none of the knowledge the necklace could have offered, since it was too small to reach down to his heart. He passed it on to Alaghuvrata at the shrine of the Lion-Rider, just before Manikandhara decided to die. Alaghuvrata used it as a rosary while chanting in the temple for two years, before he was blown by the wind into Kalapurna's court. He offered it to this still unknown king, who placed it around Madhuralalasa's neck. At this point, the infant gnostic recited the prehistory of Kalapurna and his friends and courtiers. Kalapurna unfortunately failed to ask, at that time, the source of the baby girl's knowledge. So when she rolled over, this invaluable source was lost for years, forgotten in a chest until the day Madhuralalasa remembers it—out of love—and decides to wear it again as the first gift of her husband.

Such are the vicissitudes of potential knowledge, including self-knowledge. Perhaps it can only be activated through love. Moreover, to know it one must know that one knows it. To remember the lost text one has to remember to remember. The whole chain has to be recalled, including its connections and blank spaces. Knowledge originates in the god and also temporarily returns to the god. Timing matters: Manikandhara had what he needed but had to go through a whole life before he could use it—and even then, he needed Madhuralalasa and her love in order to know himself. Sugraha had the gift but could not use it. Knowledge requires the right vessel and the true recipient. Such a recipient can still misplace or forget it.

There is another, critical series of links and associations that lead us from the *maṇihāra* necklace to language itself, the source of all knowledge.

The necklace is a chain (*hāra*) of jewels (*maṇi*). This is a text of many *maṇis*. We have the central male figure of Manikandhara; the Siddha Manistambha; the unhappy Manigriva, cursed by Narada; the *maṇi* of perpetual youth given to Manistambha by his underwater guru and father-in-law; and the *maṇi* given by Svabhava, this same guru, to Kalapurna at his birth and that appears repeatedly in Brahma's story about Kalapurna: when the infant Madhuralalasa is distant from this *maṇi*, she becomes weak, and she recovers upon seeing it again. In the *śleṣa* allegory underlying the story, this *maṇi* is Sarasvati's exquisite lower lip.

Most significant of all in this rather loaded series is the sound that comes from Sarasvati's lips—the *maṇita* love-moan that lies at the very heart of the entire story, the sound of the kiss. This *maṇita*, generative of all the story's intertwined realities, is memorized by the parrot in heaven and repeated by this parrot in the presence of Rambha, who repeats it for the benefit of Nalakubara. This is the sound that must never be heard, though it is also the one sound that must and will be heard. Madhuralalasa knows it, too—which is why the *maṇihāra* necklace works for her. Again, traces of memory, the right kind of memory, enable the working of memory.

The *maṇita* leads to the *maṇihāra* as pure sound leads to syntax—the primary aspect of speech as story, as we saw above. Sarasvati's love-moan explodes into language. Such a sequence contains within it the inherent tension within all language between nonutterance and utterance, or silence and speech. A resistance is built into expression along with a driving urge to speak. The root of language is hidden, as Indian texts from the *Ṛgveda* on regularly insist. This unmanifested form of language, which constantly seeks appropriate contexts for expression, inheres in the story of the *maṇita* that *should not* but nonetheless definitely *will* be told. Brahma articulates this two-sided aspect of linguistic knowledge when he says to Sarasvati,

> "That story of Kalapurna that came out of your love-game and that was born from my lips is going to be famous all over the world. You can't tell me you don't want this. Of course, I can understand what you say. That's how women are. They like everybody to know how their husbands love them, but they don't want to tell it all themselves." (5.69)

Desire operates on both sides of this boundary: the speaker both yearns to speak and hopes to be hidden, wishing not to speak. Nonetheless, the world-creating or story-creating moan—this *Om*-like syllable of love—is itself entirely motivated by desire. Here is the central distinction between Suranna's metaphysics of language and the linguistic philosophy of Bhartrihari and the medieval grammarians, who think of language as evolving continuously out of some restless quality within the holistic order of pure, potentially meaningful sound, *sphoṭa*. For Suranna, as for the *Ṛgvedic* poet,[13] desire inheres in the process of linguistic manifestation. The story that unfolds into reality is born out of the erotic playfulness (*śṛṅgāra-līla-nimitta*) between the male and female parts of God. From a place of hiding deep inside, this urge into sound and language breaks out, overpowering the still reluctant goddess, who wants to keep it unknown, *aprakāśa* (5.20). She feels a supreme joy that literally bursts out from her secret spaces of pleasure (*kaḷā-marma-bhedhana-sāṃrājya-sampad-anubhavâvastha*, *ibid.*); but she fears a loss of pride (*māna-lāghava-śaṅka*) and tries to cover it up. Brahma soon informs her that this cover-up is in itself impossible—for language is the source of all knowledge, and Sarasvati *is* language (*vāg-jālam' ĕlla tvan-mayambu*, 5.69)—and, moreover, Sarasvati also, at some level, wants to be known.

Another register implicit in this entire sequence is tied to music. The *maṇita* moan is itself a kind of music, and all the major characters of the story are musicians, playing with ultimate, nonverbal sound. But just as the story itself translates into an empirical, manifest reality, so the deep musicality of nonverbal utterance eventually translates into syntactical speech—the chain of total knowledge and memory that constitutes the *maṇihāra* necklace. Once there is syntax, we also have breaks in the chain, spaces of forgetting, lost knowledge, and the convoluted sequence of transmission and recovery. Reality becomes knowable in oblique and only partial modes, from always incomplete and distorting perspectives. Whatever is real, when present in language, is poorly translated.

In such a world, where syntax dominates and shapes perception or understanding, both knowing and remembering depend upon "marking." Bhartrihari, the great fifth-century philosopher of language, says it very starkly: "Language marks the thing. It cannot by its own power directly touch objects" (*vastûpalakṣaṇaḥ śabdo nopakārasya vācakaḥ/ na svaśaktiḥ padârthānāṃ saṃspraṣṭuṃ tena śakyate*).[14] An entire metaphysics rests in this observation, which focuses on naming in relation to real objects. Elsewhere, Bhartrihari connects this process with what he calls memory, that is born out of sounds and that gives the illusion of "meaning" (*arthâvabhāsarūpā hi śabdebhyo jāyate smṛtiḥ*). This connection is very close to the way language and memory function in the novel. As A. K. Ramanujan has pointed out, in Dravidian memory is usually, literally, "putting a mark" or recognizing a mark: Telugu *gurutu pĕṭṭu kŏnu* [cf. Tam. *kuri*].[15] Interestingly, Madhuralalasa uses this phrase to refer to the *maṇihāra*: she tells Kalapurna that she remembers the necklace from the moment, two years before, that she had seen it and marked it (*gurutugā ganu gŏnnadānan*, 5.9). In effect, the *maṇihāra* is itself the mark that triggers memory and awareness. For Madhuralalasa, this means a process of recognition, when the forgotten past comes flooding back. Her experiences in her two previous births—as Kalabhashini and the parrot—can now find expression on the surface of her awareness. But this mark also has another, deeper function.

For the *maṇihāra* allows its bearer access to knowledge that is not simply remembered—knowledge that the bearer could otherwise never have attained. Madhuralalasa also knows, as long as the jewel touches her heart, all kinds of stories that are in no way part of her own accumulated experience (over several births) and also not included in Brahma's original, master text. For example, Sugraha, the Maharastran king, undergoes a series of adventures before he becomes Satvadatma and, at that point, meshes with Brahma's story; Madhuralalasa is perfectly capable of knowing and recounting this entire biography. This suggests that the *maṇihāra*, like language itself, marks reality not merely by triggering memory but also by revealing what was not known before. Language has within it this capacity to reveal a truth not perceptible on the surface level. In effect, the musical being present in the *maṇita*-moan breaks through to a surface fashioned or moulded by the mark. This surface should never be mistaken for reality in its totality. Moreover, in the course of this emergence, the *maṇita* acquires all the features of the *maṇihāra*—morphology, syntax, semantics, and potential discontinuity. At the same time, all of these surface features just listed in no way exhaust the deeper reality that language always conceals, and that the mark can reveal.

What we are calling a "mark" has two sides, or aspects. It is again a matter of positioning and perspective. For those situated on the expressive side of language, within the syntactical-semantic domain, the mark shows all the standard features of language that the grammarians and poeticians discuss. For those located within the revelatory sphere of language, the mark serves as a window to the total reality that makes normal language possible. Linguistic habit tends to render this window opaque. The same mark that opens up the surface, that even structures the surface in its own shape and form and continually restructures it in relation to the revelatory level, also, by this very token, obscures this deeper relation. To put it in an emblematic, linguistic form: the sound-unit *maṇi*, which recurs with such resonance in the novel in name after name and at different layers of Brahma's story, faces, like the window of language, both inward toward the *maṇita*-moan and outward toward the *maṇihāra* chain of morphology and syntax. The novel is the story of the transitions between these two aspects.

Again, very ancient sources have articulated such a notion; Suranna is situating himself within a powerful strand of the tradition. *Ṛgveda* 10.71, one of the first statements in Indian literature about the deeper potential of language, tells us that

> You look, but you may not see the word.
> You listen, but you may not hear it.
> It shows itself,
> full of desire, fully dressed,
> like a woman to her lover.[16]

Language reveals, but only while fully dressed. It is always fully dressed. This is both the promise and the tantalizing allure of all speech. The word that beckons, embodying the desire to reveal, driven by that desire, is never openly naked. For those who cannot hear it, the surface becomes static—a kind of noise. Habituation always does this: the next verse in this poem speaks of the person who is *sthira-pīta*—someone who repeats a conventional meaning already known.[17] Such repetition then turns language false and barren, like a "milkless cow," as the Vedic poet says. Both possibilities—that is, a certain freshness of perception and understanding as well as habitual, barren repetition—inhere in the same sounds in which language comes to us. As the verse warns us, it is more than likely that we look and listen without truly seeing or hearing. This is the double nature of the window that is the mark, the surface that *is* the depth.

We can attempt a somewhat abstract formulation of this entire process, working inductively from what the *Kaḷāpūrṇodayamu* story suggests. What is the actual nature of the transition from an intralinguistic, aural, godly mode to one of a linguistically driven human consciousness? Or, asked from another vantage point central to this text, just how does language create? We are often tempted to speak of this question in a rather facile manner. It is one thing to say, with the great Kashmiri philosopher Abhinavagupta among others, that the world is mostly a matter of language, that reality is linguistic before all else—and quite another to claim that we come into existence as living selves at the moment when someone utters our name or, perhaps, when we enter into a version of a story, our own story, which we have somehow overheard and even unconsciously repeated, not knowing it was ours. Suranna's text presents us with a rich meditation on these themes, though usually in nonexplicit modes. It is difficult to say how much he owed to sources such as the Tantric Saiva texts on language and creation,[18] or to the classical works of Bhartrhari and later grammarians. Viewed in a certain light, this is a Tantric novel, deeply informed by theories of language that we encounter in both Sanskrit and classical Telugu works on grammar, metrics, and semantics (understood as the study of the process leading from nonreferential sounds to meaning). As already stated, we feel that the *Kaḷāpūrṇodayamu* belongs naturally to the medieval South Indian milieu of both speculative and pragmatic grammatical rethinking that reached its acme in the sixteenth and seventeenth centuries in the Deccan. We should also note that, geographically, the novel moves largely in a triangle, connecting inland Andhra (Srisailam), the goddess shrine in Kerala, and the Sarasvati-pitha in Kashmir—though a detailed discussion of possible channels of transmission must be postponed to another occasion. Nevertheless, it is, in fact, possible to restate in relatively simple terms the basic notions implied by Suranna's complex story about a self-creating, self-fulfilling story. We limit ourselves to three major themes that relate to repetition, to semanticity, and to sequence.

1. Once uttered, God's story emerges outward into the world, complete with sequence and internal structure and direction. It preexists relative to the consciousness of its own actors, even relative to their physical birth, although they may, upon hearing it, recognize themselves and their place within it. Partly, but not only, for this reason, it is experienced mostly as repetition. This story is not simply told but rather retold and repeated *as overheard*—by a parrot, the master-narrator.[19] Literalizing a linguistic token—a word—in a living, interpersonal domain entails this mode of repetition. Breaking out onto an experienced surface, as Kalapurna and his court must do from their original sphere of existence within Brahma's mind, is itself classed as repetition, a reliving, as it were, of the initial narrative impulse; and this entire process has no real integrity, and no

completeness, until the story itself is repeated, indeed retold more than once. New elements keep cropping up in ways that reinforce and complement the first retelling, tying the pieces together until everything is accounted for and most of it makes sense. In a sense, each separate figure has to undergo this process of repetition and orientation within the wider, self-repeating whole.

Stated more abstractly, language—the mere articulation of audible sound—is a form of repetition, at least insofar as these sounds have sequence and, therefore, discursive meaning. The linguistic retrieval or triggering of selfhood is a recursive, necessarily discontinuous act of repetition. What is sequent exists in relation to another, nonsequential level of language, which somehow survives into any normative linguistic usage. Sequence unrolls the latent and potential reality from within language and gives it structure, meaning, direction, and time.

2. Where and what is this nonsequential whole? The novel shows it to us again and again. At the heart and origin of the core story told by Brahma to Sarasvati lies its restless trigger, the atemporal, purely sonar *maṇita* love-moan. In a sense, the entire book is the story of that sound, just as it is, in effect, contained *within* that sound.

The *maṇita* moves toward the *maṇihāra*, as we have seen. What began as a love-moan becomes a story to be remembered, revealed, and perhaps partially understood. This progression is bound up with questions of meaning in relation to musical sound. It is all too easy to trivialize the notion that language creates reality. But there are nontrivial, analytically powerful ways of approaching such a theme. What if we were to reformulate the claim by limiting its application primarily to the nonsemantic aspect of speech, so that semanticity would now become, in effect, the detritus of language, existing mostly as small, scattered pockets of reference, all of them, incidentally, self-referential? What manner of consciousness would emerge as normative? What form of self or selves? Reference would belong, that is, to the surface, surviving wherever real language—poetry or music—cannot reach or has petrified and died. Still, certain parts of language may be closer to the non-semantic and atemporal core. *Śleṣa*, for example, the paronomastic fusion of levels superficially distinct from one another but actually inhering in one another, may reproduce on the surface something of the continuous flux and fusion going on underneath. Hence the enormous transformative potential of a text built, like the *Kaḷā-pūrṇodayamu*, around *śleṣa* and its creative repetitions in the consciousness of its heroes. Suranna's empathic depiction of these figures seems to issue precisely from a sense of their inner relation to the sheer music that evolved into their story.

3. But "sequence," too, is a word we may use too lightly when we take it as a property of articulate sound. We tend to disturb or distort the natural rhythms of emergent being. For one thing, we impose tense-time, a grammatical phenomenon, on a temporal reality that is itself nonlinear. We have used the word "recursive," suggestive of a dense curvature continuously revolving or looping around a central point, just as our text seems to circle round its point of origin in the *maṇita*-moan. For another thing, trapped as we usually are within this linear tense-informed modality, we regularly see the world backward, as if reality were moving from past through present into the future. Only in the most primitive and limited sense can this progression be taken as true. The whole force of Suranna's narrative leads us to consider the possibility that the present, far from evolving out of the past, is actually wrenched from the future—a potential future, already structured fully by the linguistic utterance which holds within it a completed story.[20] The life that Kalapurna is living out together with all the others who intersect with his experience is, as he himself acknowledges, already present in some detail in Brahma's story, although, as we have seen, gaps and unstructured spaces remain.

Brahma himself formulates this process when he describes to Sarasvati how his story, which she has just successfully decoded, will emerge on earth.

> "Dear—it's not a new story. It's the same old story you already heard. All the names, nouns, verbs, words, sentences, and meanings that are lexically present in that story also exist in this one. All you have to do is to convert all the past-tense verbs into future tense: for example, "was" becomes "will be," "did" becomes "will do," and so on. That's the only difference." (5.60)

He has narrated the original story in past tense, but it will be embodied and experienced, according to the contours he has spoken, in the present-future. This everyday fact of experience should not confuse us. Perhaps only the repeated act of recognition within the story can be seen as a true movement forward into present-future from out of the past; but this same act also dissolves temporality in the course of bringing the surface-subject, linguistically moulded and preyed upon by time, toward a fuller identity. "Normal" temporal consciousness, like normally externalized speech, is, as Bhartrhari says so starkly, "infested with sequentiality" (*kramopasṛṣṭa-rūpā vāk*, 1.88).[21] Suranna tells his story in a manner meant to push the listener past these distorting limitations. At the very least we have to allow for a confluence at any given moment between two vectors, one moving foward, as it were, from the past, the other backward from a preexisting latent or potential future.

The structure of the *Kaḷāpūrṇodayamu* narrative itself is beautifully suited to such an understanding. This is a text focused on the single moment of Brahma's story—the *ślesa*-infused translation of his playful desire into words—and this moment, which in a linear narrative would occur at the beginning, is here hidden away in the midst of events, both past and future, that enact it, on the one hand, and converge upon it, on the other. One begins at the edges, so to speak, with Kalabhashini, whose future birth and life as Madhuralalasa have already been described by Brahma to Sarasvati, though nothing of this is known at the start; we work our way in loops and circles backward in time but forward in narrative sequence toward that very description. The experience of reading this book is thus rather like being sucked back again and again, from every possible vantage point, into a hidden vortex at the center, where time has no hold and language exists in its most creative, and least sequential, form.

## [ 6 ]

The Telugu reader who comes to the *Kaḷāpūrṇodayamu* with some familiarity with the great golden-age poems of the sixteenth century inevitably notices a shift in tone, or a disjunction, between the first six and a half chapters and the last two and a half (beginning at 6.191). The highly complex, interlocking narrative structure of the early chapters reaches a point of suspension here, following Madhuralalasa's long explication of events in her and Kalapurna's former lives. From this point on, Suranna launches into a long and intense description of Madhuralalasa's childhood, her coming of age, her falling in love with Kalapurna and his love for her, their agonies of yearning in separation, their elaborate wedding, their lovemaking over many seasons, and the rivalry between Madhuralalasa and Abhinavakaumudi that culminates in Kalapurna's *digvijaya*, the conquest of the whole world. The earlier style of fast-paced, intricate narrative development picks up again only after Kalapurna's return to his capital, when the story of Sugraha/Satvadatma is recounted as the final link in the entire chain (8.149 to the end). The intervening descriptive section (6.191–8.149) follows standard themes and patterns in Telugu *prabandha* texts and has its own, seemingly somewhat conventional texture distinct from the unprecedented novelistic narrative style of the early chapters. This disjunction poses a problem for interpretation and has powerfully influenced prevalent attitudes toward this book in modern Andhra.

For the traditional reader, who is perfectly at home in the *kāvya*-style descriptive section, it is the first, innovative narrative part that constitutes the problem. If we opt for the c. 1560 dating for Suranna's text, then we may find an oblique criticism of his work in a verse by Bhattumurti/Rama-raja-bhusana, placed in the mouth of the latter's patron:

*Kevala-kalpanā-kathalu kṛtrima-ratnamul' ādya-sat-kathal*
*vāviri puṭṭu ratnamul' avārita-sat-kavi-kalpanā-vibhū-*
*ṣâvaha-pūrva-vṛttamulu sānala dīrina jāti-ratnamul*
*gāvunan iṭṭi miśra-katha-gān ŏnarimpumu nerpu pĕmpunan*

Stories totally invented are like artificial diamonds.
The old stories are precious stones
straight from the mine.
But ancient stories reworked by good poets
with their irresistible imagination
are precious gems perfectly cut.
Make a poem like *that*
for me.[22]

Some scholars[23] feel that the first line of this verse was directed at Suranna, who had, for the first time in Telugu literature, invented a story without reference to a classical source. The ideal poem was rather one that reworks in some imaginative way a story known from an old *purāṇa* or epic text. And even if Bhattumurti's verse was not aimed at Suranna specifically, a popular *cāṭu* verse offers a similarly critical perspective, this time entirely explicit:

*Ūhiñci tĕliya rākuṇḍa sūraparāju*
*bhrama kaḷāpūrṇodayamu raciñcĕ.*

Suranna invested vast effort in producing a poem,
the *Kaḷāpūrṇodayamu*,
that nobody can figure out.[24]

This comment seems to be focused primarily on the convoluted narrative, although it may also, like many *cāṭu* verses, contain a touch of ironic praise. In any case, the evidence is enough to suggest that the traditional reader felt some difficulty in accepting the complex narrative sections of this book.

In contrast, modern readers have been perplexed by, even hostile to, the descriptive section—ever since C. R. Reddy, the first vice chancellor of Andhra University and a highly influential literary critic, published a famous essay on the *Kaḷāpūrṇodayamu* in 1913.[25] C. R. Reddy is largely responsible for both the vast popularity and the distorted understanding of this book in modern Andhra. He celebrated Suranna precisely for his supposed originality in inventing a previously unknown narrative, as well as for his technique of realistic narration. The sensibility C. R. Reddy brings to bear upon the text reflects his training in Cambridge and his fascination with English literature; he compares the *Kaḷāpūrṇodayamu* to the *Comedy of Errors* and highlights features of the text such as characterization, surprising twists of plot, wealth of invention, and so on. Where he draws the line, however, is in dealing with Suranna's explicit depictions of love and lovemaking. C. R. Reddy shows a profound distaste for this subject and considers all Telugu literature of the *prabandha* type to be depraved.[26] This Victorian standard is applied fiercely to the descriptive section of the *Kaḷāpūrṇodayamu*, where the love of Madhuralalasa and Kalapurna is elaborately portrayed. Were it up to C. R. Reddy, this entire part of the novel would be eliminated. He sees the eroticism of the hero and heroine as mere animal passion, *paśu-prāya*, unredeemed by any more "elevated" elements; he abhors the realistic descriptions of physical love; at the same time, he mocks the conventions that Suranna uses as silly and artificial: Who in their right mind would waste time trying to cool off a love-stricken girl by applying sandal paste to her body?[27] How many hours, exactly, would this refrigeration require? Where was the girl's mother at the time? And so on. When the young couple are at last left alone with one another after the wedding, C. R. Reddy protests that the poet does not even have the grace to withdraw. He insists on wallowing in the crude details of their lovemaking. All of this adds up to what C. R. Reddy calls, with brutal sarcasm, *tuccha-śṛṅgāra*, "cheap sex." Suranna, in short, has done himself and his readers a vast disservice by adding this part of the book.

A mechanical realism is invoked in support of this reading and extends to other elements of the plot. Verisimilitude becomes a supreme value against which to measure the poet's failures. The *maṇihāra* necklace stretches credibility beyond its limits; couldn't Suranna have found a more rational explanation of events? "It is regrettable that a necklace, that serves as a thread connecting so many parts of the story, should be subjected to so many twists and turns."[28] Kalabhashini is revived by the goddess after being beheaded by Manikandhara and then waits some two years before being reborn as Madhuralalasa; this, C. R. Reddy informs us, is an aesthetic lapse. Would the story not be much finer if left as a tragedy, like any good European text?[29] The unities of time, place, and action are lacking here; so the *Kaḷāpūrṇodayamu* only approximates the ideal type of a European masterpiece.

This judgement was accepted and consistently repeated by nearly all major scholars and critics over the century that has passed since the publication of C. R. Reddy's essay, with one minor exception—a counter-essay published in 1940 by Kaluri Vyasa-murti, a traditional pandit from Vijayanagaram who defended the aesthetic norms implicit in Suranna's work.[30] This dissenting voice was largely ignored, while C. R. Reddy's militant text acquired, in accordance with its pretensions, a status akin to that of Aristotle's *Poetics*.

Today we can see how wrong C. R. Reddy was. Nevertheless, the problem that he articulated with such severity, and with considerable distortion, remains. There is, in fact, a salient change in tone as we move into the description of the love between Kalapurna and Madhuralalasa. This disparity provides a real test to any reading that wishes to preserve the book's integrity as a coherent work. It is easy to offer the usual kind of apologies—which, however, must neglect the beauty, even genius, of many parts of this section. Perhaps the author was being paid by the verse, or page. Perhaps, having more or less concluded his complicated story, he wanted to include in his text the standard subjects prescribed by the authoritative poeticians for a long *kāvya* poem—sunrises and sunsets, the changing seasons, love-in-separation, battle scenes, and so on. Perhaps it was all an afterthought not meant to be taken seriously. Maybe the poet's patron demanded these additions.[31] The poet could not make himself stop and had no sense of what a highly controlled narrative would mean (but everywhere else he shows truly remarkable control and attention to minute details of plot and structure). Perhaps the book just wasn't meant to be coherent.

At one point, troubled by such doubts ourselves, we considered the possibility that this novel, like so many others—from Flaubert to Thomas Mann—developed, out of the inherent teleology of the genre, in the direction of a long stretch of rather tedious, predictable description that more or less intentionally reproduces the boredom of the everyday. The realistic aspect of the novel may demand this flattened-out temporality, a staple of human consciousness. The very contrast between it and the magical inventiveness of the other parts could be thematized in the manner, say, of Cervantes. A novel may pose as its most pressing question, the primary mark of its own identity within the ecology of forms and genres, the question of what is real, or what it means to be or feel real.

The problem with such a reading is twofold. It means turning away from the subtlety and strength of many verses in the *prabandha* segment of the text. More than that, it misses the playful and often ironic tone that the poet adopts in this context. Although Suranna does not go the extent of outright parody of the conventional love sequence, he does seem to stand slightly at a distance, gently, sometimes ironically, reframing the "events" he describes. This tone, which we have attempted to capture in the translation, seems fundamental to any understanding of the total text.

As with Cervantes, the real issue—in fact, the heart of the author's creativity—centers upon the hero's consciousness. The first half of the *Kaḷāpūrṇodayamu* moves toward producing a perfect person, Kalapurna. Prefigured in Brahma's playful story, Kalapurna acquires reality and tangibility. At the same time, he lives in a world in which language is continually unfolding a changing reality from out of its hidden depths. In such a world, the status of objective facts is not one of brute solidity. In such a world, a full-fledged, mature consciousness, embodied in a living person, engages itself with reality in a playful mode. The complete individual, who knows his own history, is one who can play. His experiences are somehow lighter than one who mistakes external objects for rigid truth. Whether he loves or goes to war, whether he is listening to music or falconing, he brings a pliant innerness, an inner freedom, into play. Something of this quality comes through, again and again, in the long *prabandha*-like descriptive passages. Here the similarity between the *Kaḷāpūrṇodayamu* and the somewhat earlier, sixteenth-century Telugu masterpieces such as Pĕddana's *Manucaritramu* is inexact. Peddana's descriptions of love, hunting, and war are rooted in a profound, lyrical realism, "serious" in a somewhat more limited sense of the word. For Suranna realism is itself a matter of playing. He has moved the style of lyrical description onto a new plane, where a slightly ironic perspective colours experience. Once your ear becomes accustomed to this subtle tone, it is unmistakable.

Irony is a blanket term, rather crude. It is perhaps more a matter of how much self is invested in a collectively fixed reality, or mortgaged to the experience of what passes for objects. Kalapurna inhabits an ontology where one can only touch the world by letting go. At times, he seems like a dancer, not entirely bound by the usual gravitational field. Perhaps it is a matter of being able to hear the story, or the music, the goddess's moan, the whispered conversation between voices internal to god that are also internal to the living self. It is the special sorcery of the poet to make this music audible to us as well.

To present us with the consciousness of mature playfulness at its fullest is no small achievement. It makes sense of the disjunction we have pointed out. Without the playful second part, the first, narrative sequence may seem little more than a complicated and sophisticated detective story. It is, in itself, a truly amazing tour de force, but it still lacks the depth and fullness of an awareness capable of lightness. The descriptive segment recreates the actual experience of living within an ontology where there is room to move relatively freely among various surfaces and planes. Kalapurna is, first of all, made of language. He is modeled after Sarasvati's moon-like, radiant face. The creative love-moan is his conception. He is born from a male mother and female father. Gender seems to constitute no impenetrable boundary within him; he is a totality, always in movement. He is a musician, a poet, a lover, and a warrior—like the classical image of the Indian king, only significantly less solid than the traditional image suggests. Kalapurna has been released from such constraints. At every opportunity, he enters into play. Happily married to Abhinavakaumudi and to Madhuralalasa, he creates by his own volition a jealous conflict between them, which he resolves by promising to provide the former with a vina and the latter with anklets made from the crowns of all the world's queens. Neither task is felt as in any way daunting. Joyfully, he rushes out to conquer the entire world. Here again, a prestigious classical model has been transformed. Kalapurna's triumphant campaign through the known universe closely follows Kalidasa's description of the mythic king Raghu's *digvijaya* in *Raghuvaṃśa* 4. The same enemies are engaged in the same order, to the same effect. But whereas Raghu, like any ideal Hindu king, really wanted and needed to conquer the world in Kalidasa's text, Kalapurna is playing at it because of amorous complications back at home. The entire trajectory has been reframed.

Listen, for example, to the minister Satvadatma's proclamation to the various kings of India:

> "His Majesty the King has promised his beloved wife, the magnificent Madhuralalasa who was born with all the marks of good fortune, the wife of the only true warrior in the world, to make her new anklets from the jewels in the crowns borne by queens of all the world's kings. For this purpose he has set out with a large army to conquer the world. Take heed. Save your wealth and your lives by presenting him with what he wants. Signed, His Majesty's Chief Minister."

The tone is what matters: the venture is poised on the brink of parody. Framed in this way, the descriptions of battle and heroism, in all their gory details, lose their horror. One linguistic entity slaughters another. Death in combat has its own charms: the dying hero with his hand on the elephant's blood-soaked temple finds himself, to his own bemused surprise, squeezing the breasts of an *apsaras* courtesan from heaven. The old conflation of eroticism and war is here taken to an ultimate, and ultimately playful, limit; it has become light and devoid of harshness. Kalapurna cuts one of his foes into eight pieces with a single stroke. This establishes a new record; previous warriors had only managed six (8.70). The feat, like all others in this section, has a crowd of happy spectators, like a soccer match.

But within this series of light touches and ludic experiments, there is also a powerful question of self-knowledge in relation to the linguistically fashioned world. Again and again, to moving effect, the hero at play hears his own story, which until that moment he has not fully known. The story situates him in relation to the god's initial, playful invention and provides a sense of who he is. Listening to his own story is what frees Kalapurna and brings him fully to life. He "remembers," first, that he is a part of Brahma's text, in some sense subsumed by this preexisting text. This dreamlike creativity on the part of the god activates a full-blooded aliveness in the individual who hears the story. This doubled quality—of being both a character in a story and a living human being—is the tensile texture of reality and the secret of wholeness. It creates at once a rich complexity of awareness and a certain nonsubstantiality of existence that translates into total play. If you want to know how it feels to have fully internalized the perception of reality as born out of musical sound, translated into syntactical speech, and further spun out into an eventful narrative, where the self knows itself in relation to its origins in god's game, you have only to imagine your way, with the help of the poet, into Kalapurna's mind.[32]

Such an awareness seems to require us to go through a hidden text. Notice that this theme occurs at least four times in the novel. First there is the *daṇḍaka* poem that Manikandhara had sung to Krishna but that was hidden in Kalabhashini's mind. She recites it to Narada in the first chapter, at his request. This poem, resurfacing at this point, had originally produced for Manikandhara the god's gift of the *maṇihāra* necklace, though Manikandhara was unable to use the gift. Moreover, as we shall see in a moment, this text elicits a relatively superficial commentary by Kalabhashini, as befits the relatively superficial location of this first, hidden text. It lies not too far below the surface. Then there is the story of Sugatri and Salina, which exists in the form of a book published by the goddess Sarasvati, and which enters the novel as this written text is read out by a Brahmin student and later repeated by Manikandhara. This is a text made available by the goddess but lacking an author; like other such embedded narratives, it seems to have its own autonomous existence and, in its somewhat distanced and hidden nature, holds a key to the explicit external events of the still unfolding story.

Even more striking are the two embedded conversations between the male and female parts of divinity—in one case, Brahma and Sarasvati, in the other, Vishnu and Lakshmi. The Brahma-Sarasvati conversation is, as we have seen, the original, revelatory blueprint for the entire story. The dialogue between Vishnu and Lakshmi is recited by Madhuralalasa to Kalapurna at the very end of the novel; Kalapurna had composed it as Manikandhara and had sung it at the Ananta-sayana temple in Trivandrum at the request of the sages there. Now transformed into Kalapurna, he has forgotten his own text and has to hear it afresh from Madhuralalasa, who knows it by virtue of the *maṇihāra* necklace. In fact, Kalapurna knows about the very existence of this text only because Madhuralalasa had mentioned it in the course of her narration of his life as Manikandhara. Her recitation is what brings closure to the entire novel. In effect, the text circles back or implodes to its necessary, revelatory conclusion, which is close to its point of origin. At this point, it also becomes difficult to distinguish which text is embedded in which. Ostensibly, the Lakshmi-Vishnu *saṃvāda* is contained within Brahma's originary story, that has mapped out, in outline, the very existence of the poet who will eventually compose this dialogue. But in another perspective, Brahma's playful invention itself belongs to the play of the all-embracing god Vishnu as he converses with *his* female part. The two stories contain one another. In both cases, we have a version of the same subtle conversation. You can hear it both deep inside the text, as it were, or on its periphery—in both cases, of course, with the help of the triggering *maṇi*.

There are further examples of this pattern. Think of the inscription on the wall at the Lion-Rider's shrine, which sets up a field of force within which certain effects must ensue—if you know the script, both in the sense of the technical knowledge of writing, *lipi*, that Sumukhasatti mentions to Kalabhashini, and also in the sense of a programmed linguistic teleology. A similar set-up operates when the goddess gives both Kalabhashini and Abhinavakaumudi their boons, which emerge from what could be called a close reading, or a semantically and syntactically nuanced interpretation, of the language of the inscription. Basically, all real language operates along these lines in the *Kaḷāpūrṇodayamu*, once speech has broken through to the surface. The linguistic text, usually hidden or forgotten, preexists its own embodiment and necessarily fulfills itself through the lives that are unconsciously moving in the direction it has defined. Articulation by itself shapes reality in this way, and the word (*vācaka*) always precedes and determines its referent or meaning (*vācya*). A deeper fulfillment, however, awaits the moment when the speaker, living and acting within language, achieves access to the originary impulse. Only this process allows the playful lightness that Kalapurna exemplifies.

The surface level of language and linguistic existence is rule-bound. The musical origin is not. The key, or trigger, to the connection is, ironically, always available and nearly always neglected, overlooked, or lost—by linguistic habit. One of the most unsettling features of the novel is the almost continuous presence of the *maṇihāra* necklace, that offers access to total knowledge, and the continuous blindness of the various bearers to its existence. The *maṇihāra* runs like a thread through the text, linking its episodes in a syntax that becomes apparent only once the total narrative has been told. Perhaps most poignant is the first time we see this necklace, when Kalabhashini, in chapter 1, recites the first hidden text, Manikandhara's *daṇḍaka* to Krishna. No sooner has she finished this recitation than she says, casually, to Narada: "Isn't that necklace your disciple is wearing the one Krishna gave him in return for this *daṇḍaka* poem?" She sees it right before her eyes and marks it, though she has no true sense of its meaning, just as Manikandhara remains completely unaware of the *maṇihāra*'s power. Language habitually produces this forgetfulness, or blindness, out of habit.

The necklace weaves itself in and out of this story, tantalizing us with its promise, as language does. At least Kalabhashini has marked this mark and will recall it as Madhuralalasa—although even Madhuralalasa only truly recognizes its full potential when she comes of age. It is in the nature of the mark to be forgotten or misperceived, and of the window to be closed.

When the hidden text resurfaces, those who hear it may be liberated into play. But still there are distinct levels of hiding and emergence. Suranna has found a way of articulating or encapsulating these distinctions in three metapoetic verses. One, on what we have called syntax, in a wide sense, was discussed at the beginning of this second Introduction.[33] Here he shows us a fully connected, tightly structured "sentence," or story—the logical prerequisite for a novel. Another such statement emerges from Kalabhashini's recitation of and commentary upon Manikandhara's *daṇḍaka*, the first hidden text to emerge into view.

Putting words together like strings of pearls in a necklace,
knowing the meaning—whether literal, figurative, or suggestive—
and precisely how it should be used,
weaving textures to evoke the inner movement,
implanting life through syllable and style,
structuring the poem with figures of sound and sense:
this is what a good poet does.
Then he gets everything he wants.

If cool moonlight could have fragrance,
and crystals of camphor, which are cool and fragrant,
could have tenderness, and the southern breeze
which is fragrant, cool, and tender could have sweetness—
then you could compare them all
to this poet's living words.

Beautifully phrased and tenderly conceived, this is a more or less standard statement of the classical Sanskrit poeticians' worldview. It tells us about the three normative levels of language—literal, figurative, and suggestive—and the various styles and figures and combinations of sound that a poet should command. Suranna also provides us here with something of the *feeling* of good poetry from a connoisseur's point of view. But he has something far more trenchant to say about language than anything either the *ālaṇkārika* poeticians or the grammarians have formulated, and he uses the whole length of the novel to make this statement, the logic of which we have attempted to tease out in our discussion.

But he also gives us, at the very outset of the book, in the culminating invocation, a strong hint of this deeper view:

> Writing poetry is like milking a cow.
> You have to pause at the right moment.
> You have to feel your way, gently, with a good heart,
> without breaking the rules.
> You need a certain soft way of speaking.
> You can't use harsh words or cause a disturbance.
> Your feet should be firm, your rhythm precise.
> It requires a clear focus.
> If it all works right, a poet becomes popular,
> and a cowherd gets his milk.
> If not, they get kicked.

It looks like little more than a playful exercise in double speech registers. The same words apply to writing poetry and to milking a cow. How profound a statement could this be? But *śleṣa* is rarely innocent, and if we look a little more closely, we see the classic features of Suranna's conceptual understanding. He has perhaps borrowed the cow from very ancient, Rig Vedic notions of speech, *Vāc*, as a cow waiting to be milked. Poetry, that is music, that is speech at its most real, has to be milked out of this potential carrier, a living and generative being. In the process of coming out, the milky stuff of poetry acquires all the features of the surface—rhythm, connectedness, pauses, lucidity, rules. The words, not surprisingly, are nurturing and fluid. Sometimes it doesn't work. For it to work, the milker must love the cow. The whole process is rooted in their mutual affection, just as Brahma's love for Sarasvati, and hers for him, generate the *maṇita* sound that sets the story into motion, and just as the final, compassionate conversation between Vishnu and Lakshmi brings out the hidden poem that offers freedom. Feeling of this sort, pregnant with desire, lives inside language; and language brings us alive. Syntax alone, words alone, cannot achieve this result. As we see in the other two verses, they belong mostly to the surface. The creative level, which sparks understanding, is reached through a certain gentleness or good-heartedness—*saumanasya*, the emotion resonant in musical sound.

## [NOTES]

1. *Prabhāvatī-pradyumnamu* 2.3.
2. M. M. Bakhtin, *The Dialogic Imagination*, edited by Michael Holquist (Austin: University of Texas Press, 1981).
3. Thus A. K. Warder, *Indian Kāvya Literature*, vol. 4. *The Ways of Originality (Bana to Damodaragupta)* (Delhi: Motilal Banarsidass, 1972–). See, opposing this view, Vasudha Dalmia, "Vernacular Histories in Late Nineteenth-Century Banaras: Folklore, Puranas and the New Antiquarianism," *Indian Economic and Social History Review* 38 (2001), 59. See the translation of *Kādambarī, A Classic Sanskrit Story of Magical Transformations*, by Gwendolyn Layne (New York: Garland Publishing, 1991), and the translator's introduction.
4. See, for example, J. A. B. van Buitenen, *Tales of Ancient India* (Chicago: University of Chicago Press, 1959).
5. Still earlier precursors of the new direction toward interiorized *kāvya* can be seen in Śrīnātha (fourteenth–fifteenth centuries) and the Tamil Pukaḷentippuḷavar (*Naḷavĕṇpā*, thirteenth century). Some of Suranna's contemporaries at the Mughal court in North India, notably Faizi, show similar features in their Persian *masnavis*.
6. See note 8.
7. Allegorical readings of this sort, sustained over a long narrative or dramatic text, are familiar from medieval Sanskrit works such as Krishnamisra's *Prabodha-candrodaya*.
8. See D. Shulman, "First Man, Forest Mother: Telugu Humanism in the Age of Kṛṣṇadevarāya," in D. Shulman (ed.), *Syllables of Sky: Studies in South Indian Civilization in Honour of Velcheru Narayana Rao* (Delhi: Oxford University Press, 1996). See the exhaustive discussion of such themes in Wendy Doniger, *The Bed Trick* (Chicago: University of Chicago Press, 2000).
9. See 4.17, where Kalabhashini tells us she is *krithârtha*, "fulfilled," now that she knows the whole truth.
10. *Bhāgavatapurāṇa* 10. 9.22–23, 10.10.1–43.

11. We wish to thank Kolavennu Malayavasini for discussion of this explanation.
12. Our thanks to Shlomit Cohen for illuminating remarks in this context.
13. *Ṛgveda* 10.72.4. Here, however, desire appears primarily as an analogy: language reveals herself as a woman to her man. See translation at note 16.
14. *Vākyapadīya* 2.433. See discussion in J. E. M. Houben, *Sambandha-samuddeśa (Chapter on Relation) and Bhartṛhari's Philosophy of Language* (Groningen: Egbert Forster, 1995).
15. A. K. Ramanujan, "The Ring of Memory," in Vinay Dharwadker (ed.), *The Collected Essays of A. K. Ramanujan* (New Delhi and New York: Oxford University Press, 1999).
16. *Ṛgveda* 10.71.4.
17. For this cryptic phrase, we follow Sayana, who glosses it (positively) as *jñātârtham: loke yathā jñātârthaṃ puruṣaṃ pītârtham iti vadanti*. Fritz Staal, "*Ṛgveda* 10.71, on the Origin of Language" [in Harold G. Coward and Krishna Sivaraman, ed., *Revelation in Indian Thought. A Festschrift in Honor of Professor T. R. V. Murti* (Emeryville, Calif.: Dharma Publishers, 1977)] translates: "Many, they say, have grown rigid in this friendship."
18. Including, perhaps, Abhinavagupta's *Tantrâloka* and the *pratyabhijñā* texts preserved in Kashmir.
19. Suranna, incidentally, has a fascination with parrots. See, for example, pp. 35–37, 39, 50.
20. Suranna has a name for this process: *bhasviṣyad-artha-vacana*, "the sway of the future," 5.103.
21. Houben, *Sambandha-samuddeśa*, 278.
22. *Vasu-caritramu* 1.19
23. We wish to thank K. V. S. Rama Rao, of Austin, Texas, for pointing out this connection.
24. See Malladi Suryanarayana Sastri, introduction to his 1938 edition of the *Kaḷāpūrṇodayamu*, 17. For the complete text of the verse, see Vedam Venkatarayasastri's introduction to *Āmuktamālyada* of Krishnadevaraya (with *Sañjīvani* commentary) (Madras: Vedam Venkatarayasastri and Brothers, 1927; reprinted 1964), 68.
25. Kattamanci Ramalinga Reddi, *Kavitva tattva vicāramu anu pingaḷi sūranârya-kṛta kaḷāpūrṇodaya-prabhāvatī-pradyumnamula vimarśanamu* (reprinted Visakahapatnam: Andhra University Press, 1980).
26. *Prabandha* is the term modern literary critics use for the genre of courtly poetry, *kāvya*.
27. *Ibid.*, 185–86.
28. *Ibid.*, 128.
29. *Ibid.*, 181.
30. Kaluri Vyasa-murti, *Kavitva tattva vicāra vimarśanamu* (published by the author with the Vavilla Press, Madras, 1940).
31. C. R. Reddy, *Kavitva tattva vicāramu*, 53: In those days poets could not sell

books and live off their income, so they depended on the patronage—and the idiosyncratic taste—of kings.

32. In strictly philosophical terms, this vantage point could be read as what is called Viśiṣṭādvaita, a notion of "qualified nondualism"—a Srivaisnava religious orientation that Suranna associates with his patron, Nandyala Krishna (*pīṭhika*, 96). The individual is here relatively "real," a modus (*prakāra*) of God, who is subject to distinction and qualification. G. V. Krishna Rao, in his *Studies in Kalapurnodayamu* (Tenali: Sahiti kendram, 1956) somewhat too literally interprets the entire text as an allegory along these lines.
33. See note 1.

# APPENDIX

## Guide to Pronunciation and List of Characters

Long vowels are double the length of short vowels and are marked with a macron. The Sanskrit diphthongs *e*, *o*, *ai*, and *au*, are always long and are unmarked; we mark the short Dravidian vowels *ĕ* and *ŏ*. Sanskrit names ending in a long vowel, appearing in Telugu texts, are consistently shortened, in keeping with Telugu practice.

*ṭ*, *ḍ*, *ṭh*, *ḍh*, *ṇ*, and *ḷ* are retroflex, pronounced by turning the tip of the tongue back toward the palate. *ñ* is a palatal nasal, and *ṅ* is a velar nasal.

*c* is pronounced like English *ch* (or, in Telugu words, before *a/ā*, *u/ū*, *ŏ/o*, like English *ts*).

Telugu and Sanskrit have three sibilants:

*ś* is palatal, close to the English *sh* but with the tongue touching the palate.

*sh/ṣ* is retroflex, pronounced with a retraction of the tongue.

*s* is dental, like the English *s*.

Āgamas One through Four—sons of Yajñaśarma/Alaghuvrata, advisors to King Madāśaya.

Abhinavakaumudi—an *apsaras* from heaven, courted by Śalyâsura, married to Kaḷāpūrṇa.

Alaghuvrata, "Determined in his Vow"—Malayali Brahmin who acquires the *maṇihāra* necklace at the temple of the Lion-Rider. Previously he was Yajñaśarma, a Brahmin from the Pandya country committed to feeding Brahmins.

Brahmā—god of creation, with four heads, married to Sarasvati.

Dattātreya—a sage and master, guru to Svabhāva.

Jāmbavati—wife of Krishṇa.

Kalabhāshiṇi, "Sweet-spoken"—courtesan and musician of Dvaraka. In her previous life, she was a parrot in Sarasvati's palace in heaven. She is reborn as Madhuralālasa.

Kaḷāpūrṇa, "Full Moon"—king in Aṅgadeśa. Son of Sumukhâsatti and Maṇistambha. Maṇikandhara reborn. Married to Abhinavakaumudi and Madhuralālasa.

Krishṇa—god (Vishṇu) ruling in Dvārakā on the western coast of India.

Lakṣmi—wife of Vishṇu, the supreme god.

Madāśaya "My Heart"—king of Dharmapuri in the Godavari Delta. Devotee of Dattātreya. Promised by Svabhāva at Srisailam that he would conquer all kings except Kaḷāpūrṇa.

Madhuralālasa, "Craving for Sweetness"—Kalabhāshiṇi reborn. Child narrator of the master narrative. Wife of Kaḷāpūrṇa.

Maṇigrīva—son of Kubera, brother of Nalakūbara, cursed by Nārada to become a tree for failing to cover his nakedness.

Maṇikandhara, "Jewel Around his Neck"—gandharva student of Nārada. Master musician and poet, author of the *daṇḍaka* to Krishṇa and the *lakshmī-vishṇu-saṃvāda*. Wears the *maṇihāra* necklace on his neck. Reborn as Kaḷāpūrṇa.

Maṇistambha, "Jeweled Pillar"—magician (Siddha) who brings Kalabhāshiṇi to the Lion-Rider's temple. Previously Śālīna, a shy man married to Sugātri. "Mother" of Kaḷāpūrṇa.

Nalakūbara—son of Kubera. Most handsome male in the universe. Lover of Rambha.

Nārada—sage who travels between heaven and earth, feeding off quarrels.

Rambha—courtesan of the gods, most beautiful woman in the world.

Rukmiṇi—wife of Krishṇa.

Rūpânubhūti, "Love of Beauty"—wife to Madāśaya. Mother of Madhuralālasa.

Sarasvati—Brahmā's single-faced wife. Goddess of speech and poetry.

Satyabhāma—wife of Krishṇa.

Satvadātma, "Close to Yourself"—minister of Kaḷāpūrṇa. Previously, Sugraha, king of Maharastra. Falls in love with Maṇistambha in the form of Sumukhâsatti.

Śālīna, "Shy"—husband of Sugātri. Later, Maṇistambha.

Śalyâsura, "Porcupine Demon"—cousin of Mahishāsura, the buffalo demon. Falls in love with Abhinavakaumudi. Killed by Maṇikandhara. Also known as Crowbar.

Sugātri, "Beautiful Body"—wife of Śālīna. Devotee of the goddess Śārada/Sarasvati. Later, Sumukhâsatti.

Sugraha, "Good Planets"—king of Maharastra, cursed with amnesia. Later, Satvadātma.

Sumukhâsatti, "Proximity of Beautiful Face"—old woman at the shrine of the Lion-Riding Goddess. Sugātri in her previous life. Wife to Maṇistambha and "father" of Kaḷāpūrṇa.

Svabhāva, "One's Own Nature"—submarine guru, father of Sugātri. Brings bow, arrows, and gem to Kaḷāpūrṇa at the latter's birth.

Tumburu—famous musician of the gods. Rival to Nārada.

Vishṇu—god.

Yajñaśarma—Brahmin from the Pandya land. Sells his four wives into slavery to pay for feeding Brahmins. Later known as Alaghuvrata.

# Index of Names and Technical Terms

## Other Works in the Columbia Asian Studies Series

### Translations from the Asian Classics

*Major Plays of Chikamatsu*, tr. Donald Keene 1961

*Four Major Plays of Chikamatsu*, tr. Donald Keene. Paperback ed. only. 1961; rev. ed. 1997

*Records of the Grand Historian of China, translated from the Shih chi of Ssu-ma Ch'ien*, tr. Burton Watson, 2 vols. 1961

*Instructions for Practical Living and Other Neo-Confucian Writings by Wang Yang-ming*, tr. Wing-tsit Chan 1963

*Hsün Tzu: Basic Writings*, tr. Burton Watson, paperback ed. only. 1963; rev. ed. 1996

*Chuang Tzu: Basic Writings*, tr. Burton Watson, paperback ed. only. 1964; rev. ed. 1996

*The Mahābhārata*, tr. Chakravarthi V. Narasimhan. Also in paperback ed. 1965; rev. ed. 1997

*The Manyōshū*, Nippon Gakujutsu Shinkōkai edition 1965

*Su Tung-p'o: Selections from a Sung Dynasty Poet*, tr. Burton Watson. Also in paperback ed. 1965

*Bhartrihari: Poems*, tr. Barbara Stoler Miller. Also in paperback ed. 1967

*Basic Writings of Mo Tzu, Hsün Tzu, and Han Fei Tzu*, tr. Burton Watson. Also in separate paperback eds. 1967

*The Awakening of Faith, Attributed to Aśvaghosha*, tr. Yoshito S. Hakeda. Also in paperback ed. 1967

*Reflections on Things at Hand: The Neo-Confucian Anthology*, comp. Chu Hsi and Lü Tsu-ch'ien, tr. Wing-tsit Chan 1967

*The Platform Sutra of the Sixth Patriarch*, tr. Philip B. Yampolsky. Also in paperback ed. 1967

*Essays in Idleness: The Tsurezuregusa of Kenkō*, tr. Donald Keene. Also in paperback ed. 1967

*The Pillow Book of Sei Shōnagon*, tr. Ivan Morris, 2 vols. 1967

*Two Plays of Ancient India: The Little Clay Cart and the Minister's Seal*, tr. J. A. B. van Buitenen 1968

*The Complete Works of Chuang Tzu*, tr. Burton Watson 1968

*The Romance of the Western Chamber (Hsi Hsiang chi)*, tr. S. I. Hsiung. Also in paperback ed. 1968

*The Manyōshū*, Nippon Gakujutsu Shinkōkai edition. Paperback ed. only. 1969

*Records of the Historian: Chapters from the Shih chi of Ssu-ma Ch'ien*, tr. Burton Watson. Paperback ed. only. 1969

*Cold Mountain: 100 Poems by the T'ang Poet Han-shan*, tr. Burton Watson. Also in paperback ed. 1970

*Twenty Plays of the Nō Theatre*, ed. Donald Keene. Also in paperback ed. 1970

*Chūshingura: The Treasury of Loyal Retainers*, tr. Donald Keene. Also in paperback ed. 1971; rev. ed. 1997

*The Zen Master Hakuin: Selected Writings*, tr. Philip B. Yampolsky 1971

*Chinese Rhyme-Prose: Poems in the Fu Form from the Han and Six Dynasties Periods*, tr. Burton Watson. Also in paperback ed. 1971

*Kūkai: Major Works*, tr. Yoshito S. Hakeda. Also in paperback ed. 1972

*The Old Man Who Does as He Pleases: Selections from the Poetry and Prose of Lu Yu*, tr. Burton Watson 1973

*The Lion's Roar of Queen Śrīmālā*, tr. Alex and Hideko Wayman 1974

*Courtier and Commoner in Ancient China: Selections from the History of the Former Han by Pan Ku*, tr. Burton Watson. Also in paperback ed. 1974

*Japanese Literature in Chinese*, vol. 1: *Poetry and Prose in Chinese by Japanese Writers of the Early Period*, tr. Burton Watson 1975

*Japanese Literature in Chinese*, vol. 2: *Poetry and Prose in Chinese by Japanese Writers of the Later Period*, tr. Burton Watson 1976

*Scripture of the Lotus Blossom of the Fine Dharma*, tr. Leon Hurvitz. Also in paperback ed. 1976

*Love Song of the Dark Lord: Jayadeva's Gītagovinda*, tr. Barbara Stoler Miller. Also in paperback ed. Cloth ed. includes critical text of the Sanskrit. 1977; rev. ed. 1997

*Ryōkan: Zen Monk-Poet of Japan*, tr. Burton Watson 1977

*Calming the Mind and Discerning the Real: From the Lam rim chen mo of Tsoṇ-kha-pa*, tr. Alex Wayman 1978

*The Hermit and the Love-Thief: Sanskrit Poems of Bhartrihari and Bilhaṇa*, tr. Barbara Stoler Miller 1978

*The Lute: Kao Ming's P'i-p'a chi*, tr. Jean Mulligan. Also in paperback ed. 1980

*A Chronicle of Gods and Sovereigns: Jinnō Shōtōki of Kitabatake Chikafusa*, tr. H. Paul Varley 1980

*Among the Flowers: The Hua-chien chi*, tr. Lois Fusek 1982

*Grass Hill: Poems and Prose by the Japanese Monk Gensei*, tr. Burton Watson 1983

*Doctors, Diviners, and Magicians of Ancient China: Biographies of Fang-shih*, tr. Kenneth J. DeWoskin. Also in paperback ed. 1983

*Theater of Memory: The Plays of Kālidāsa*, ed. Barbara Stoler Miller. Also in paperback ed. 1984

*The Columbia Book of Chinese Poetry: From Early Times to the Thirteenth Century*, ed. and tr. Burton Watson. Also in paperback ed. 1984

*Poems of Love and War: From the Eight Anthologies and the Ten Long Poems of Classical Tamil*, tr. A. K. Ramanujan. Also in paperback ed. 1985

*The Bhagavad Gita: Krishna's Counsel in Time of War*, tr. Barbara Stoler Miller 1986

*The Columbia Book of Later Chinese Poetry*, ed. and tr. Jonathan Chaves. Also in paperback ed. 1986

*The Tso Chuan: Selections from China's Oldest Narrative History*, tr. Burton Watson 1989

*Waiting for the Wind: Thirty-six Poets of Japan's Late Medieval Age*, tr. Steven Carter 1989

*Selected Writings of Nichiren*, ed. Philip B. Yampolsky 1990

*Saigyō, Poems of a Mountain Home*, tr. Burton Watson 1990

*The Book of Lieh Tzu: A Classic of the Tao*, tr. A. C. Graham. Morningside ed. 1990

*The Tale of an Anklet: An Epic of South India—The Cilappatikāram of Iḷaṅkō Aṭikaḷ*, tr. R. Parthasarathy 1993

*Waiting for the Dawn: A Plan for the Prince*, tr. and introduction by Wm. Theodore de Bary 1993

*Yoshitsune and the Thousand Cherry Trees: A Masterpiece of the Eighteenth-Century Japanese Puppet Theater*, tr., annotated, and with introduction by Stanleigh H. Jones, Jr. 1993

*The Lotus Sutra*, tr. Burton Watson. Also in paperback ed. 1993

*The Classic of Changes: A New Translation of the I Ching as Interpreted by Wang Bi*, tr. Richard John Lynn 1994

*Beyond Spring: Tz'u Poems of the Sung Dynasty*, tr. Julie Landau 1994

*The Columbia Anthology of Traditional Chinese Literature*, ed. Victor H. Mair 1994

*Scenes for Mandarins: The Elite Theater of the Ming*, tr. Cyril Birch 1995

*Letters of Nichiren*, ed. Philip B. Yampolsky; tr. Burton Watson et al. 1996

*Unforgotten Dreams: Poems by the Zen Monk Shōtetsu*, tr. Steven D. Carter 1997

*The Vimalakirti Sutra*, tr. Burton Watson 1997

*Japanese and Chinese Poems to Sing: The* Wakan rōei shū, tr. J. Thomas Rimer and Jonathan Chaves 1997

*A Tower for the Summer Heat*, Li Yu, tr. Patrick Hanan 1998

*Traditional Japanese Theater: An Anthology of Plays*, Karen Brazell 1998

*The Original Analects: Sayings of Confucius and His Successors (0479–0249)*, E. Bruce Brooks and A. Taeko Brooks 1998

*The Classic of the Way and Virtue: A New Translation of the* Tao-te ching *of Laozi as Interpreted by Wang Bi*, tr. Richard John Lynn 1999

*The Four Hundred Songs of War and Wisdom: An Anthology of Poems from Classical Tamil, The* Puranāṉūṟu, eds. and trans. George L. Hart and Hank Heifetz 1999

*Original Tao*: Inward Training (Nei-yeh) *and the Foundations of Taoist Mysticism*, by Harold D. Roth 1999

*Lao Tzu's* Tao Te Ching*: A Translation of the Startling New Documents Found at Guodian*, Robert G. Henricks 2000

*The Shorter Columbia Anthology of Traditional Chinese Literature*, ed. Victor H. Mair 2000

*Mistress and Maid (Jiaohongji)* by Meng Chengshun, tr. Cyril Birch 2001
*Chikamatsu: Five Late Plays*, tr. and ed. C. Andrew Gerstle 2001
*The Essential Lotus: Selections from the* Lotus Sutra, tr. Burton Watson 2002
*Early Modern Japanese Literature: An Anthology, 1600–1900*, ed. Haruo Shirane 2002

## Modern Asian Literature

*Modern Japanese Drama: An Anthology*, ed. and tr. Ted. Takaya. Also in paperback ed. 1979
*Mask and Sword: Two Plays for the Contemporary Japanese Theater*, by Yamazaki Masakazu, tr. J. Thomas Rimer 1980
*Yokomitsu Riichi, Modernist*, Dennis Keene 1980
*Nepali Visions, Nepali Dreams: The Poetry of Laxmiprasad Devkota*, tr. David Rubin 1980
*Literature of the Hundred Flowers*, vol. 1: *Criticism and Polemics*, ed. Hualing Nieh 1981
*Literature of the Hundred Flowers*, vol. 2: *Poetry and Fiction*, ed. Hualing Nieh 1981
*Modern Chinese Stories and Novellas, 1919–1949*, ed. Joseph S. M. Lau, C. T. Hsia, and Leo Ou-fan Lee. Also in paperback ed. 1984
*A View by the Sea*, by Yasuoka Shōtarō, tr. Kären Wigen Lewis 1984
*Other Worlds: Arishima Takeo and the Bounds of Modern Japanese Fiction*, by Paul Anderer 1984
*Selected Poems of Sŏ Chŏngju*, tr. with introduction by David R. McCann 1989
*The Sting of Life: Four Contemporary Japanese Novelists*, by Van C. Gessel 1989
*Stories of Osaka Life*, by Oda Sakunosuke, tr. Burton Watson 1990
*The Bodhisattva, or Samantabhadra*, by Ishikawa Jun, tr. with introduction by William Jefferson Tyler 1990
*The Travels of Lao Ts'an, by Liu T'ieh-yün*, tr. Harold Shadick. Morningside ed. 1990
*Three Plays by Kōbō Abe*, tr. with introduction by Donald Keene 1993
*The Columbia Anthology of Modern Chinese Literature*, ed. Joseph S. M. Lau and Howard Goldblatt 1995
*Modern Japanese Tanka*, ed. and tr. by Makoto Ueda 1996
*Masaoka Shiki: Selected Poems*, ed. and tr. by Burton Watson 1997
*Writing Women in Modern China: An Anthology of Women's Literature from the Early Twentieth Century*, ed. and tr. by Amy D. Dooling and Kristina M. Torgeson 1998
*American Stories*, by Nagai Kafū, tr. Mitsuko Iriye 2000
*The Paper Door and Other Stories*, by Shiga Naoya, tr. Lane Dunlop 2001
*Grass for My Pillow*, by Saiichi Maruya, tr. Dennis Keene 2002

## Studies in Asian Culture

*The Ōnin War: History of Its Origins and Background, with a Selective Translation of the Chronicle of Ōnin*, by H. Paul Varley 1967
*Chinese Government in Ming Times: Seven Studies*, ed. Charles O. Hucker 1969

*The Actors' Analects (Yakusha Rongo)*, ed. and tr. by Charles J. Dunn and Bungō Torigoe 1969

*Self and Society in Ming Thought*, by Wm. Theodore de Bary and the Conference on Ming Thought. Also in paperback ed. 1970

*A History of Islamic Philosophy*, by Majid Fakhry, 2d ed. 1983

*Phantasies of a Love Thief: The Caurapañatcāśikā Attributed to Bilhaṇa*, by Barbara Stoler Miller 1971

*Iqbal: Poet-Philosopher of Pakistan*, ed. Hafeez Malik 1971

*The Golden Tradition: An Anthology of Urdu Poetry*, ed. and tr. Ahmed Ali. Also in paperback ed. 1973

*Conquerors and Confucians: Aspects of Political Change in Late Yüan China*, by John W. Dardess 1973

*The Unfolding of Neo-Confucianism*, by Wm. Theodore de Bary and the Conference on Seventeenth-Century Chinese Thought. Also in paperback ed. 1975

*To Acquire Wisdom: The Way of Wang Yang-ming*, by Julia Ching 1976

*Gods, Priests, and Warriors: The Bhṛgus of the Mahābhārata*, by Robert P. Goldman 1977

*Mei Yao-ch'en and the Development of Early Sung Poetry*, by Jonathan Chaves 1976

*The Legend of Semimaru, Blind Musician of Japan*, by Susan Matisoff 1977

*Sir Sayyid Ahmad Khan and Muslim Modernization in India and Pakistan*, by Hafeez Malik 1980

*The Khilafat Movement: Religious Symbolism and Political Mobilization in India*, by Gail Minault 1982

*The World of K'ung Shang-jen: A Man of Letters in Early Ch'ing China*, by Richard Strassberg 1983

*The Lotus Boat: The Origins of Chinese Tz'u Poetry in T'ang Popular Culture*, by Marsha L. Wagner 1984

*Expressions of Self in Chinese Literature*, ed. Robert E. Hegel and Richard C. Hessney 1985

*Songs for the Bride: Women's Voices and Wedding Rites of Rural India*, by W. G. Archer; eds. Barbara Stoler Miller and Mildred Archer 1986

*The Confucian Kingship in Korea: Yŏngjo and the Politics of Sagacity*, by JaHyun Kim Haboush 1988

## Companions to Asian Studies

*Approaches to the Oriental Classics*, ed. Wm. Theodore de Bary 1959

*Early Chinese Literature*, by Burton Watson. Also in paperback ed. 1962

*Approaches to Asian Civilizations*, eds. Wm. Theodore de Bary and Ainslie T. Embree 1964

*The Classic Chinese Novel: A Critical Introduction*, by C. T. Hsia. Also in paperback ed. 1968

*Chinese Lyricism: Shih Poetry from the Second to the Twelfth Century*, tr. Burton Watson. Also in paperback ed. 1971

*A Syllabus of Indian Civilization*, by Leonard A. Gordon and Barbara Stoler Miller 1971

*Twentieth-Century Chinese Stories*, ed. C. T. Hsia and Joseph S. M. Lau. Also in paperback ed. 1971

*A Syllabus of Chinese Civilization*, by J. Mason Gentzler, 2d ed. 1972

*A Syllabus of Japanese Civilization*, by H. Paul Varley, 2d ed. 1972

*An Introduction to Chinese Civilization*, ed. John Meskill, with the assistance of J. Mason Gentzler 1973

*An Introduction to Japanese Civilization*, ed. Arthur E. Tiedemann 1974

*Ukifune: Love in the Tale of Genji*, ed. Andrew Pekarik 1982

*The Pleasures of Japanese Literature*, by Donald Keene 1988

*A Guide to Oriental Classics*, eds. Wm. Theodore de Bary and Ainslie T. Embree; 3d edition ed. Amy Vladeck Heinrich, 2 vols. 1989

## Introduction to Asian Civilizations

Wm. Theodore de Bary, General Editor

*Sources of Japanese Tradition*, 1958; paperback ed., 2 vols., 1964. 2d ed., vol. 1, 2001, compiled by Wm. Theodore de Bary, Donald Keene, George Tanabe, and Paul Varley

*Sources of Indian Tradition*, 1958; paperback ed., 2 vols., 1964. 2d ed., 2 vols., 1988

*Sources of Chinese Tradition*, 1960, paperback ed., 2 vols., 1964. 2d ed., vol. 1, 1999, compiled by Wm. Theodore de Bary and Irene Bloom; vol. 2, 2000, compiled by Wm. Theodore de Bary and Richard Lufrano

*Sources of Korean Tradition*, 1997; 2 vols., vol. 1, 1997, compiled by Peter H. Lee and Wm. Theodore de Bary; vol. 2, 2001, compiled by Yŏngho Ch'oe, Peter H. Lee, and Wm. Theodore de Bary

## Neo-Confucian Studies

*Instructions for Practical Living and Other Neo-Confucian Writings by Wang Yang-ming*, tr. Wing-tsit Chan 1963

*Reflections on Things at Hand: The Neo-Confucian Anthology*, comp. Chu Hsi and Lü Tsu-ch'ien, tr. Wing-tsit Chan 1967

*Self and Society in Ming Thought*, by Wm. Theodore de Bary and the Conference on Ming Thought. Also in paperback ed. 1970

*The Unfolding of Neo-Confucianism*, by Wm. Theodore de Bary and the Conference on Seventeenth-Century Chinese Thought. Also in paperback ed. 1975

*Principle and Practicality: Essays in Neo-Confucianism and Practical Learning*, eds. Wm. Theodore de Bary and Irene Bloom. Also in paperback ed. 1979

*The Syncretic Religion of Lin Chao-en*, by Judith A. Berling 1980

*The Renewal of Buddhism in China: Chu-hung and the Late Ming Synthesis*, by Chün-fang Yü 1981

*Neo-Confucian Orthodoxy and the Learning of the Mind-and-Heart*, by Wm. Theodore de Bary 1981

*Yüan Thought: Chinese Thought and Religion Under the Mongols*, eds. Hok-lam Chan and Wm. Theodore de Bary 1982

*The Liberal Tradition in China*, by Wm. Theodore de Bary 1983

*The Development and Decline of Chinese Cosmology*, by John B. Henderson 1984

*The Rise of Neo-Confucianism in Korea*, by Wm. Theodore de Bary and JaHyun Kim Haboush 1985

*Chiao Hung and the Restructuring of Neo-Confucianism in Late Ming*, by Edward T. Ch'ien 1985

*Neo-Confucian Terms Explained: Pei-hsi tzu-i*, by Ch'en Ch'un, ed. and trans. Wing-tsit Chan 1986

*Knowledge Painfully Acquired: K'un-chih chi*, by Lo Ch'in-shun, ed. and trans. Irene Bloom 1987

*To Become a Sage: The Ten Diagrams on Sage Learning*, by Yi T'oegye, ed. and trans. Michael C. Kalton 1988

*The Message of the Mind in Neo-Confucian Thought*, by Wm. Theodore de Bary 1989